The Secrets of the

Dark

...the debt of blood is never repaid

I0647288

The Secrets of the Dark

...the debt of blood is never repaid

Arka Chakrabarti

Srishti
PUBLISHERS & DISTRIBUTORS

Srishti Publishers & Distributors
N-16, C. R. Park
New Delhi 110 019
editorial@srishtipublishers.com

First published by
Srishti Publishers & Distributors in 2013

Typeset by EGP at Srishti

Each and every tale starts when another tale ends. I have grown up hearing such tales from my maternal and paternal grandfather; their tales have moved me ever since I was a child.

I would like to dedicate this book to both my grandfathers –
Anup Sarkar and Dhirendra Chandra Chakrabarti.

CONTENTS

ACKNOWLEDGEMENTS

The story in the pages that follow has many dark shades. Yet, I have met many who have shown me the light and for that I have to thank them. These torch-bearers in my life include my parents and my dear friends, Parnali Bhattacharya, Sibasish Banerjee, Aritrya Ganguly, and last but not least, Siladitya Sarkar, who has gone all the way to support me in my own little quest.

I would also like to thank Srishti Publishers for the utmost faith they have shown in my abilities.

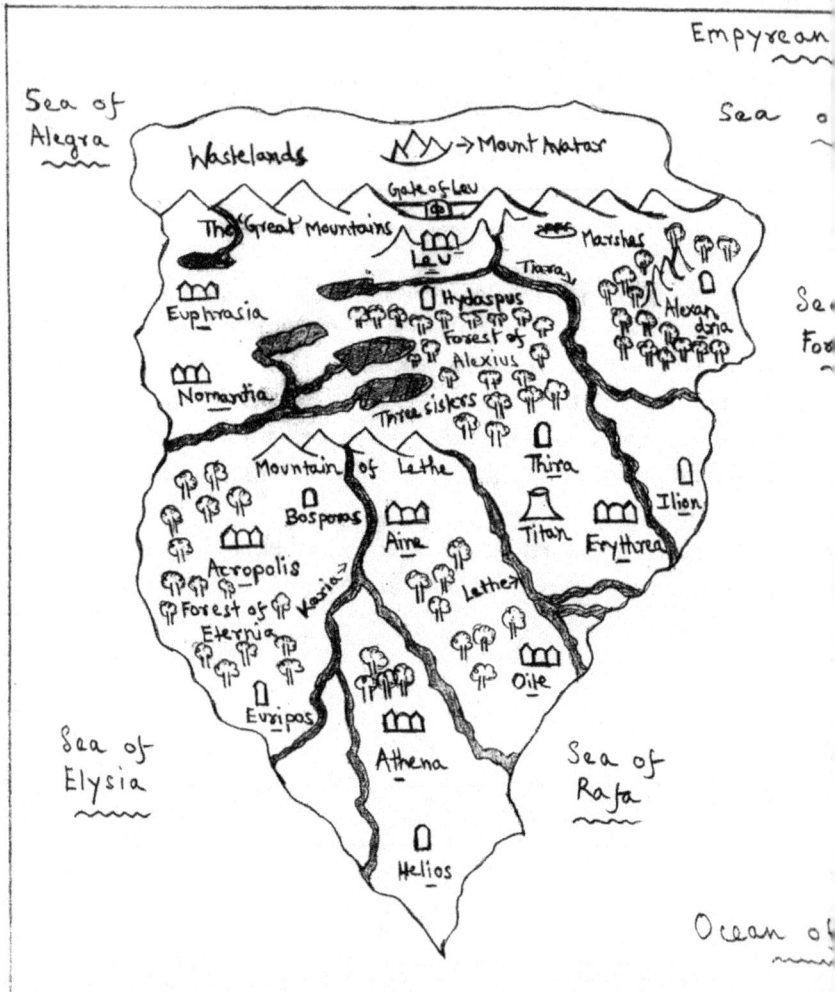

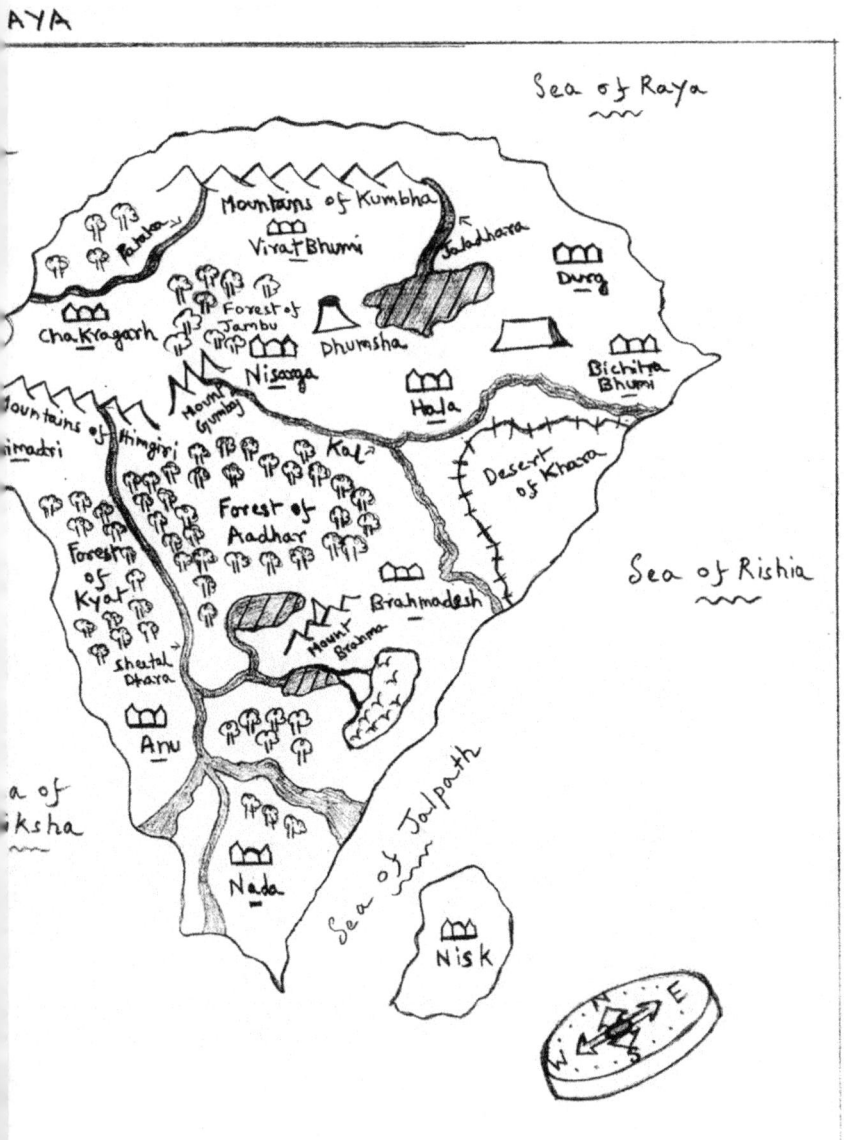

PROLOGUE

The seven ages of Gaya had withered away and there came an eighth, which wasn't supposed to have come at all. It was time for Gaya to merge with the eternal bond of the universe. But a new race of man was born; from the rubbles of the old, the new had come. The seven Sentinels looked over from the sky as the new men started life, all over again, in the magical land of Gaya.

There was war and strife as they bickered over petty things. Then rose a mighty warrior from among the crowd and wielding great power as the king. He fought countless wars and consolidated the vast empire of Gianna. He was known to his people as King Ixus and the strength and unity of men increased under his banner. The great king grew old and passed away, leaving behind an empire so vast that it could not be controlled and men in position who were greedy for more power. The taint of corruption marked the empire and it started to fall apart.

The 'Maker' knew that man would never be able to avert his fate. Finally, moved by the pleas of their own kind, the servant of doom was sent forth. It was said that he will be born from the ashes and to ashes he shall return. The very foundation of mankind shall be shattered by this one being and Gaya shall be freed from the taint of man. The cycle shall repeat itself over and over again until that which is said is fulfilled, or so said the 'Maker', the master of the seven Sentinels who stood between the destroyer and man.

The Maker's wish was prophesied by Darshana, the great sage of the East, 'The light of the Rising Sun':

"Eight shall be the ages of man,

But seven shall be their gods.

The eighth shall be the doom of man,

But seven shall be the odds.

As the end shall come, death will follow,

The kingdom of man shall fall.

For her doom shall be dealt by the hands of their own thrall.

The kings who shall sit the golden throne of the Land of the setting Sun,

Shall always bear the thorn.

From his seed the Servant of the Maker will be born.

The creator can never be the destroyer,

As the well being of the one born from her womb is always a mother's desire.

None shall sway as all is foretold,

For no man shall arise and be so bold to hinder the flow of time and the ways of the old.

THE GLOOM OF THE NIGHT

The royal villa outside Athena was dimly lit. The servants had lit the lanterns and four candles had been placed in front of the Shade, the master of the night who was known by many other names as well. The guards were dozing silently as the pale moon crept up in the midst of thousands of emeralds scattered across the sky, giving a hint of light in the small alleys and roofs. The stable boy was brushing the dust off the King's steed, Marion. King Arkansas had arrived in the dead of the night, wearing a black rugged cloak, alone and unescorted. It took the guard some effort to recognize him in the dark and he was not allowed to enter until he produced his royal face from under the black woolen hood, matted with dust.

It was sometime before the third hour of the moon. The King was already inside and the royal priest had sealed the main door using a holy spell to prevent any darkness from entering the villa.

A scream echoed out of the royal bedchamber, startling the guards. But they eventually went back to sleep and the maids and man-servants moved about as if deaf to the thundering sound.

The queen lay writhing in pain and her hands were held by the two elderly maids, the most trusted by the king.

"How much longer is it going to take Solon?" asked the impatient king peering out of the window from time to time.

"Push child, push harder," said Priest Solon, ignoring the king's question. The Queen groaned and clenched her fists as the servants held on to her tightly.

"I can see the head, push. Just a little longer and the pain will be gone," said Solon.

The queen screamed, her shriek echoed through the halls and then it was filled by the melody of a newborn's cry. The priest held the child in his arms, the smiling face of the king looking over his shoulder.

"It's a boy," he said with a face as expressionless as still water. But the King had a smile on his face. The Queen cried hysterically as the maids caressed her hands. The King walked up to her and sat beside her on the bed. He gently took her hands in his own and smiled, "Don't worry my love, our son shall live, I promise." Tears swelled up in her eyes as she gripped his hand more tightly. "Thank you," she whispered in her shaking voice.

"We should hurry," said the priest Solon. "There isn't much time left, your Highness." Suddenly they heard a commotion near the gate of the villa, which was followed by a loud blast. The King hurried towards the window and saw that the iron gate of the villa lay on the ground, as dark figures started to creep inside the ground under the cover of the night.

"They have come," said the King turning to Solon. The queen and her maids were petrified; their faces were masks of pure horror.

"Quickly, before they breach the main door, my spells won't hold them for long," said Solon to the King. King Arkansas quickly walked up to the shelf on the far end of the room and turned a lever hidden behind one of the books. The shelf started to move, slowly revealing a hidden door behind it. A deafening crash shook the main door. King Arkansas followed Solon into the passage with the child cradled in his arms. He looked back and glanced at his beautiful queen Serene, as tears trickled down her rosy cheeks. The shelf started to move back to its original position and her beautiful face disappeared from his sight.

There was a loud crack outside the door of the royal chamber and splinters flew everywhere. The maids shielded the queen. The door lay ajar and almost a dozen black figures walked inside the room. The man leading the others scanned the entire place. The stench of blood and its stains made his misty eyes shine with a sort of greed. The Queen and the maids hid their faces and shut their eyes, cuddling each other for safety. No mother ever wanted to lay her eyes on the snatchers of the night, or more aptly called 'The Dark Guardians'. There was nothing there for him; his prize had been taken away from his clutches. The man was followed out of the room by the others as he spared one last glance at the women and walked away. Their black horses started to race towards the nearest abandoned harbor, Sonata.

A thousand paces or more ahead of them raced two more steeds through the darkness of the night, Marion and Sage.

"Faster Marion, faster," shouted King Arkansas as the horse cut through the wind, followed by the equally gifted Sage with Solon on top. The child lay cuddled and strapped on the King's chest, its wails fading in the sound of the wind. The horses raced on the brick road, leaving only little clouds of dust in their trail.

"Solon," shouted the King over the wind, "Are you sure all has been set properly? All shall be lost if anything goes awry."

"The man has given his word and you your gold. You chose the man yourself, my king, and seemed promising to me when I met him not so long ago. He shall wait, but not a turn after the fifth hour of the moon, he had said to me. We must hurry," said Solon. The King nodded his head and kicked Marion harder. He knew he had risked everything for his son and would rather die before a dark hand reached up to his son. They had taken away six in the past, but not the seventh. His line shall continue, his blood shall live, whether a king or not, but he shall remain. He thought to himself, his word will be kept. He remembered the day when he had first seen Serene, dressed in the golden cloak and shimmering gown on the day of their holy union. She was the flower of the east, which he had plucked and greedily decided to keep for his own for the rest of his life. Tens of thousands of spectators felt as if on fire as they had kissed in union. The High Priest had predicted before their marriage that she would mother only sons, or so her stars told. So the 'House of God' which was second in power after the 'Abode of the Seven' had been against their marriage and wanted her to be sent back to her homeland in the East. But he had snatched her from their clutches and at the night of their marriage, he had promised her that she would know the joy of being a mother even if she bore only sons. He had told her that he would change her fate and that which was written.

The King was ushered back to reality by a reverberating screech that echoed from the horizons.

"They are nearing us," said Solon in a wary voice. The anxiety on the King's face was reflected as beads of sweat which were swept away by the angry wind.

"At this rate, there won't be enough time left," said King Arkansas.

"Then that which is most obvious should be done," said Solon with a smile on his face. "I hope that I have served you well my King, I can never repay your debts but I can buy you some time." The flicker of a smile was half visible in the pale light as Sage started to slow down.

"No Solon, you must not be the one to do this, you know that very well. We still have time," shouted King Arkansas, but it was too late. "No Solon," King Arkansas called out but Marion had left Solon and Sage behind. King Arkansas looked over his shoulder as Sage disappeared in the darkness behind him. The King's face twisted in agony and uncertainty as the horse raced through the night.

The road was at its end; Marion rushed through the bushes and leapt over the jagged rocks. There was little time left. He knew that even the talented Solon was no match for the Guardians that followed them, yet the loss was too great for him, everything hung in the balance but he had no choice left. "Guide my son great Maker," whispered the King to the wind as Marion kept up the pace. The sound of waves breaking on the rocks floated to his ears, the shore was visible from there. The dust of the road had turned to sand and Marion was slowing down.

"You have served me well, my friend," whispered Arkansas in Marion's ears. Arkansas saw a light emitting from a point on the shore. He rushed towards it. Marion halted in front the man with the lantern, dressed in eastern silks.

"Hurry, we were followed," said the King as he pushed the wailing child into his arms, a stranger he barely knew. For a moment his eyes were stuck on the pretty pink face, a shinning star in the gloom of the night.

"Take care of him," said King Arkansas like a helpless man. The dark skinned man gave a bow and said, "He is a prince and shall be treated like one. I will uphold my part of the bargain at all costs; you have my word." The King caressed the smooth silk-like hair of his son, "Grow up to be a strong man; be happy, my son." His eyes were moist.

The man got into the boat and started to row towards the ship anchored at a distance. It had white sails, the mark of peace in unknown waters and the mark of a merchant. Arkansas saw the boat moving away from the shore with every beat of his heart, with a pain he never knew before, but he endured. Tears trickled down his cheeks and he wiped them away with force. He looked up at the sky and muttered a silent curse to the one above. Many moments passed as he watched them board the ship and then he slowly lowered his gaze. A thin smile spread across his face.

"You are too late," said King Arkansas even without looking. The dark hooded figure was standing behind him. Arkansas turned around and said, "Go and tell your masters that you have failed. My son is safe now."

The hooded man clenched his fists. There was a blinding flash and a heat wave spread across the place. Arkansas felt his feet lift up from the ground and crashed down on the soft sand. His vision started to fade as the gift of life slowly crept out of his body. But his face had a smile on it, a thin one, which meant everything.

The wind was in its sails as the ship sailed towards the eastern lands; there was also the sound of oars in the water for speed was the essence of it all. The dark-skinned man saw the flash and felt the heat like the others on the ship. He slowly shook his head in despair; he had seen the fall of a king that day. He knew that a king never died alone. As he was grieving for the brave king, his eyes fell on the wailing child in his arms. Was one child worth such a great price, he thought to himself. Only the Maker knew, wherever he might be. He knew that the ones he had denied that day were not merciful and they never forgot anything. The man offered a silent prayer to the Eternal one, the Trinetra, as the ship sailed towards the horizon.

THE FESTIVAL OF TRINETRA, THE ETERNAL ONE

It had been twenty years since that dreadful night and Briksha still remembered it as if it was yesterday. He was standing on the deck of his ship named 'Dut', which meant 'the messanger' in the Land of the Rising Sun. It was anchored in the port of Himadri, marking the vessel of a merchant owing to its white sails, swaying with the mild wind. A day didn't go by when the glimpses of that night didn't return to haunt him. The man he had seen that day from afar was . . . of a different make. He had felt his piercing gaze even from that distance after the King had fallen. The horrifying tales of the Guardians were prevalent in the eastern shores also, yet he never knew the horrors of it until that night. No man, not even a King was safe from their clutches and he was just a mere merchant. The Eastern kingdoms had nothing to do with the 'Abode of the Seven' and so the Guardians were never seen to walk the eastern shores. Yet the very thought of them made him shiver. Each night he would close the main door of the Captain's quarters with three different locks. He would pull the curtains and bar the windows. Only then some sleep would creep upon him and he'd hope for a dreamless sleep. The dread had taken its toll on him in the twenty long years and he had grown tired of it. But an oath is an oath, taken before the Eternal one; it was meant to be kept for life. Besides, it was also for the sake of his daughter. He knew that a few nightmares won't bring any harm to him, which seemed more vivid than usual; but he dreaded the day when they would creep out of his dreams; maybe that was the only reason he for his returning to that cursed land after a long period of nineteen years.

"Father," came a feminine voice which startled Briksha. He was so lost in his thoughts that for a moment he didn't even recognize the voice of his own daughter Malini.

"Sorry to have disturbed you father, but have you seen Agni?" she asked.

"The last I knew he was headed for the forest of Seshnag with Prince Yani and your brother," said Briksha with a smile. "Why? Is anything wrong?" he asked.

"No, just that they were supposed to take me to the fair this morning and now they are gone, without bothering to tell me anything." Malini clearly seemed irritated and angry.

"Boys of their age are like that, my child. They tend to be..." he paused, "a little slippery."

"We all are of the same age, father, or have you forgotten that?" she seemed annoyed.

"No, no I haven't," laughed Briksha. "Well, you see, a woman grows faster than a man; so a girl grows faster than a boy."

"You always defend their actions," said Malini grumpily. Briksha only smiled, for it was partly true. His son Vrish was brought up in the palace, while he himself sailed the ten seas. So whenever he came back, he tried his best to show his love for the child. No matter how far he travelled, he always came back to Himadri, as it had grown to be his second home after the sea.

"Will Agni make a good husband father?" asked Malini as she came and stood beside him, leaning over the edge. Briksha was a bit taken aback by the frank question of his daughter but then he made himself remember that she had grown up and would be married soon.

"Well he is a good man and you have chosen him yourself," said Briksha.

"Yes, that I did," she said with a radiant smile on her face.

"You know what will be the most awkward thing after I get married?" she asked. Briksha remained silent. "It will be to stay on land while you sail the ten seas." Briksha felt a strange sadness in his heart. He realized that his daughter was of marriageable age, but never before had spent a single day without seeing her face. At first, he didn't agree with her for many reasons, but then he saw the sadness in his daughter's eyes and slowly nodded his head in agreement. Malini felt the same sadness as she looked into her father's eyes.

"I will miss you a lot," she said and embraced him.

"I will miss you, too," said Briksha. He did his best to prevent himself from crying. He knew that moment would last into eternity as a drop of tear escaped his eye.

At the same moment, somewhere deep in the forest of Seshnag, Agni, Vrish and Prince Yani along with four royal guards walked on the trail of a tiger, the largest carnivore of the forest after the demon cat, the rakshas. Agni and Vrish had grown up with Prince Yani as King Adhirath's ward. Yani was the only son of King Adhirath, the crown prince of Himadri. They were taken in by King Adhirath as his wards and companions of the Prince, his only son, when they were very young. Briksha had accepted readily as Vrish had lost his mother at birth. Thus, they grew up in Himadri while

Briksha sailed the ten seas. The people of Himadri slowly started to look at them as the King's own but it was not so for the king. King Adhirath always firmly believed that he had only one son; it was clear to them from the time they grew old enough to understand. Himadri being a small kingdom, its people always knew what was cooking in the other man's pot. The city housed approximately four thousand souls and had a negligible army. The city stood at the foot of the mountain of Himgiri from which it had derived its name about four hundred years ago. The city was famous for the festival of Trinetra, the Eternal one with a third eye which always sees the truth. It was more of a holy place, an abode of saints and sages. Yet it lay on the easternmost point of the longest east-west trade route, making it the busiest trading port of the east. Himadri had little resources to call its own and it survived solely on the trade from other parts of the east as well as the west. The clever diplomatic ties made by King Adhirath's father, King Yash, was the first step on the long way to the current prosperity of Himadri.

Agni, Vrish and Yani had come a long way into the forest; the Sun was approaching west speedily.

"It's no use for the trail is lost. We better head back; it will be dark soon," said Vrish looking at the horizon.

"Vrish ji is right, sire," said one of the elderly guards. "Rajaji told us to be back by the end of the first hour of the moon."

Yani gave it a thought; he knew his father's anger was not to be tested. He turned to Agni, "What do you say Agni, shall we head back?"

Agni was staring at the bush to their left, "Just another quarter. If we can't catch up with that damned thing by then, we will head back."

"But what use is another quarter, the trail is lost," said one the younger guards Paksha. Agni turned towards him and smiled, "Look at that bush," he said, "the leaves are torn and that too on the top."

"So?" asked Paksha in an irritated voice.

Agni came down from his horse and started for the spot. "So, it means that something heavy with scales and soft feet had passed through there."

"It could be anything, even a wild shell dog, the larger ones have scales too," said Paksha arrogantly. "Maybe," said Agni and knelt down beside the bush.

"Yani, Vrish, come here," he said. They came down from their horses and walked up to him.

"Look," said Agni pointing towards a paw print on the soft mud, underneath the bush.

The unprecedented rain had made it easier for a 'tracker' like Agni. "Six fingers," said Vrish, his eyes wide open. "And what does it mean?" asked Agni with a smile.

"Rakshas, a demon cat," exclaimed Vrish in awe. All of the soldiers, even Paksha had come down from his horse and was peeking over Vrish's shoulders. Yani had a broad grin on his face. "Everyone on your horses," he shouted, "it seems that the prize has become bigger."

೫

King Adhirath was pacing all over the room, his brows were furrowed and he was bubbling with rage. Sir Drake, the famed knight of Erythrea, the strongest kingdom of the Land of the Setting Sun sat on the cushioned mattress. He followed the king with his lazy eyes, suppressing occasional yawns. Finally, he could not bear the hard work for his eyes anymore and said, "Don't worry Adhirathji, they will come back soon."

King Adhirath halted for a moment and said, "With all due respect, Sir Drake, he will be a king one day, yet he clearly lacks the sense of responsibility and manners." Drake leaned back on the cushions and said, "Boys of their age tend to be like that, were we so different?"

"No, but this is not any ordinary day. It's not every day that we have such friends amongst us," said King Adhirath. Sir Drake was pleased, and gave a curt nod.

"Yet, I do not want the young prince to be scolded only because of me. Let him be, Adhirath ji; we can always go to this festival by ourselves and have a good time. Why should we spoil his?"

King Adhirath was about to say something when he heard three knocks on the door, the custom to announce the approach of royalty.

"Enter," said King Adhirath in a gruff voice. The door opened and prince Yani walked in followed by Agni and Vrish.

"Father," said Yani with a courtly bow, Agni and Vrish did the same.

"We have been waiting for you for long. Didn't I tell you that Sir Drake will be coming with us to the festival tonight?" asked the king, his voice thick with anger.

"I am sorry father, but we were delayed," said Yani.

"May I know why?" asked the King, trying hard to control his rage.

This time Yani smiled. "We hunted down a Rakshas," said Yani proudly. But there was no change in the King's expression. The reply came from Sir Drake.

"A demon cat?" he asked and stood up quickly. Yani nodded his head, "I have sent it to a butcher to have it skinned."

"That's quite an achievement. How many of you were there?" asked Sir Drake.

"Me and two of my friends here, Agni and Vrish," said Yani as his chest swelled up with pride.

"Only the three of you? That's . . . that's . . . I am at a loss of words," said Sir Drake. His face had a look of pleasant shock on it. "There were also four guards," put in Agni quickly. Yani gave him an annoyed look. "Still it's a feat worthy of a King," exclaimed Sir Drake. "You should be proud of your son Adhirath ji; it's not every day that one hunts down a demon cat. It's a remarkable achievement." Yani looked at his father, expecting a little praise.

"Go and get yourself ready," said King Adhirath flatly. "And you two as well," he said with his eyes on Agni and Vrish. Both of them gave a curt bow and scurried off to their room. Sir Drake was a bit surprised. Yani was hurt, he gave a curt bow to his father and Sir Drake and left the room without another word. King Adhirath saw his son leave from the corner of his eyes. Sir Drake was shaking his head, not approving of the King's behaviour. Finally he spoke when Yani had left the room. "Adhirath ji, it might not befit a person of my stature to interfere in the ways of a King, but wasn't that a bit harsh?"

"We are a small kingdom, Sir. We need to harden our sons. You won't understand this," said King Adhirath without even looking at him.

ॐ

The King rode on his royal steed, Jhar. Sir Drake rode to his right, Yani to his left, closely followed by Vrish and Agni. Two columns of royal guards marched on either sides. The crowd parted to make way for the royal entourage which also consisted of ten maids and an equal number of man servants.

The King's Prime Minister, Bukka, stood outside the bamboo entrance gate with garlands in his hand. King Adhirath came down from his horse and so did the others. Bukka, along with three beautiful maids, greeted them with garlands and flowers. The maids sprinkled scented incense on them as they passed by.

"Welcome Maharaj, and a thousand greetings to our honored guest, the legend of the West," said Bukka bending as low as his fat belly would allow. Sir Drake nodded and tilted his head towards Yani. "Exaggeration never goes down well in my stomach; unfortunately, it is just a source of gaseous inflammation." He whispered in Yani's ear. Yani restrained himself from laughing out loud but his face twisted in a smile despite all his efforts at controlling it. He was beginning to like that man – smart, yet without any prejudice. Agni heard what Sir Drake had said and it made him smile as well. Vrish stood there, oblivious to it all, ogling at the girls surrounding them.

King Adhirath was being led towards the dais. Agni saw that it had only three chairs; it made him smile. He thought to himself that ward or not, you can always be there for the King, but never with the King. Yani was standing with Sir Drake, deep in a conversation, laughing from time to time. Agni went a little closer to him and said, "I think we better be on our way Prince. Vrish's sister is waiting for us." Yani was suddenly taken aback by the oddity of Agni's approach and he kept staring at him. The word 'Prince' was rare to his ears when it came from his best friend. He quickly gathered himself as Sir Drake was standing beside him and said, "If you may Agni, but I suppose you can join us later, you and Vrish?"

"Certainly," said Agni and gave a curt bow to Yani and Sir Drake, who in turn smiled with a gentle nod.

"Come," said Agni to Vrish who was smiling at a pretty girl standing a few paces away from them. He grabbed him by his elbow and started to walk.

"Where?" asked Vrish, he was a bit startled.

"We promised Malini that we will bring her here, remember," said Agni as they made their way through the crowd. Vrish was a little annoyed. "I don't know why you care for her so much."

As they came out of the gate, they could sense the fair bustling behind them. Singers and dancers gathered in front of the dais. The fire breathers did some flaring and showed off their skills. The magicians pulled off some cheap tricks and the sensuous dancers danced at the centre of the open ground to the beating drums. The ritual of honoring the Eternal God, Trinetra would commence at the turn of the hour. Then there would be complete silence as the *yagna* would start. But for now, the dancers danced to the rhythm of music and the crowd cheered them on.

THE INFERNO AT THE DOCKS

Agni and Vrish started to walk towards the docks, headed for the ship where they knew Malini would be waiting for them. Agni had asked her to wear anything in red; he always liked her in that colour. He was supposed to take her to the fair in the morning and it was already dark; he knew she would be pretty angry with him. So they had taken the shortest route to the place, the brick road through the bamboo forest. The hustle and bustle of the fair slowly started to fade behind them.

"Finally some peace," said Agni and took out two cheroots. He handed one to Vrish and lit his own with the igniter. He threw it to Vrish and he lit his own.

"This is not local, is it?" asked Vrish, examining the small device with flint stones and cotton strands to produce flame temporarily.

"No," said Agni, "Yani gave it to me."

Agni gave out some smoke; the strong flavor made his head spin a little.

"This has been quite a day," said Agni. "First the Rakshas, then this fair." Vrish smoked like a chimney, he put it down from his mouth for a moment and asked, "Are we coming back again?"

"We have to, or else Yani will be angry. And Malini too," replied Agni. But in fact he wasn't eager to come back quickly, if he could sway Malini from her stand in any way possible then he would be glad not to come back again. He knew he could say something to Yani to make him understand. But he knew that would be a tough task. "You don't care for me," she would say when they would be alone and then he would apologize and try to reason. All that aisde, everything seemed to be beautiful when he was with her, even a little hustling. Then he looked at Vrish and saw that it made him happy none the less, the prospect of returning to the fair. He knew that it would increase his friend's chance of a second encounter with that girl in the fair.

"Do we have to bring Malini with us?" asked Vrish.

"We promised," said Agni in a firm voice. Vrish didn't go on, he knew it was the end of the discussion and it was better not to discuss anything else about it. Both of them continued their little break in silence.

"Why were you so anxious to get out of there Agni?" asked Vrish finally. Agni was staring at the tree line. "It is better to leave when you are not wanted," he replied.

"I don't understand," said Vrish.

Agni smiled and put a hand on his shoulder. "You are a good guy, Vrish. There are a few things you still don't understand," he said. Vrish looked more confused than before, "Anyway, I think we should hurry. I want to get back as soon as possible."

"Why?" asked Agni playfully. Vrish had a stupid grin on his face. "It's about that girl you were staring at all the time, right?" asked Agni.

"No, I want to get back at the fair as soon as possible because it happens only once a year," said Vrish quickly. "Right," said Agni with a smile. He turned around and something came out of nowhere and almost knocked him off his feet. Agni stopped a little short of falling. They turned and saw a man speeding towards the fair.

"Be careful you idiot; are you blind or something?" shouted Vrish angrily. The man gave them a quick glance and the pale light of the moon showed a part of his face. Agni's dark blue eyes were shining.

"Stupid bastard," said Vrish angrily. "Are you all right, Agni?" he asked.

"I am fine. But did you see his face?" asked Agni.

"No," said Vrish. "But I should have, that way I could have found him out and taught him some manners."

"No, not that," said Agni in an irritated voice. "His face was completely burned."

Vrish stood there silent. "Oh! I don't know of any such guy in Himadri. Could be fire breather; I have heard that they have burns all over."

Agni didn't say anything but somehow he felt troubled. It was that same feeling he experienced some time before something went wrong.

They had been walking for a while now and the moon was now clear as crystal, lighting their way as they walked slowly down the brick road. The woods had come to a halt suddenly. The ground had turned a bit sandy by then. Vrish was going on and on about his adventures in some smuggler's den, when his eyes fell on the horizon in front of them. For some reason, it had a tinge of yellow light to itself.

"What in the name of the One is that?" asked Vrish pointing at the yellow light.

Agni was also looking at it. "Something's wrong; it's coming from the docks," said Agni quickly. The sense of dread was rising in his heart.

"Come on," he said and sprinted towards that direction, Vrish was already at it.

***

Fumes of black smoke and stench of burning hides, cloths and other things filled the air. The smell was so unusually strong that it made Agni cringe his nose. His first thought was Malini. He rushed towards the water where the ships were anchored. Agni saw that there was complete chaos. His eyes were wide with fear as he stood there, Vrish behind him. 'Dut' was up in flames and three other ships had caught fire as well. The flame licked the wooden body of the ship with its serpentine tongues as it danced over the water. Some of the sailors had taken their boats as close as possible to the burning ships and threw water on the decks from their buckets, but to no avail. The flames were not doused even for a moment and it burned with greater intensity with passing time. Their shock at what they witnessed kept them rooted to the spot for some more time.

"Father, Malini," cried Vrish and ran towards the burning ships. He was about to jump in the water, when 'Dut' erupted in a fresh burst of flames. The sailors on the small boats near it jumped into the water to save themselves from the heat blast. "No, Vrish," said Agni as he caught hold of him firmly before he could jump. "Let me go," shouted Vrish as he struggled to get himself free while 'Dut' continued to burn like a candle.

An old sailor was standing beside them. "No one inside could be alive, son; you will only end up getting yourself killed," he said sympathetically. Vrish was crying, his face had gone red. "I am sure they jumped before this happened; we've got to look for them. They should be here somewhere," said Agni as he prayed his words would be true. Vrish nodded his head and they started looking. Agni and Vrish ran around the dock hysterically, searching for Malini and Briksha among the few survivors who lay there. He was still in shock, it all seemed like a bad dream to him. "Agni, I can't find either of them," shouted Vrish as he wiped his tears. Agni's eyes were moist themselves. "Keep looking, they are bound to be here."

"Maybe, maybe they went to the fair before all this happened. Maybe they weren't here after all," said Agni, his voice trembling.

"I don't know, I don't know," shouted Vrish with his hands over his head. Agni caught hold of a sailor passing by and asked, "Have you seen a girl, tall and fair, with an old man, her father? They were on board this vessel."

"Which ones are you looking for?" asked the young sailor. "Look around, hundreds are dead. I can't find my own brother. He was with that harlot on that ship." He said pointing at the one beside 'Dut'.

"He is tall and dark...." Agni pushed the man away before he could finish. One of the ships started to sink. He felt a searing pain through his head, and when he closed his eyes, all he could see were blinding flashes. He opened them quickly and saw Vrish asking another sailor standing by a heap of goods. He was going through the things which he had managed to salvage in all this hysteria. Agni walked up to them as if in a trance.

"Are there any survivors from that ship?" asked Vrish pointing at 'Dut'.

"Don't know, son," said the elderly man. "But a few were badly hurt in this fire. They have been taken to the Pani inn in the Westside of the docks. The others are doing everything they can for them, not many medicine men around because of the damned festival. You can search there if you like."

A huge explosion threw splinters everywhere. They turned and saw that 'Dut' erupted in a final burst of flames and its remains started to sink in the water.

"There goes another one," said the elderly man shaking his head. He walked up to the group of sailors who had gathered at the edge to see the sight. Vrish fell down on his knees, tears gushing out of his eyes. Agni's cheeks were wet as well. He wiped them off with force and went to his friend. He held Vrish by his shoulders and forced him up on his feet. His small stout frame seemed so fragile then.

"There is nothing left here. They might be alive and I need your help to find them right now. You must not break. We must head for that inn," said Agni, trying to gather his strength. Vrish was staring at him in the eye. He slowly nodded his head.

℘

The stench of burnt flesh reeked the air. Screams and groans of pain greeted them as they entered the inn. It looked like a sea of men and women in the small space. At least a hundred lay there, some were writhing in pain and some seemed dead. The maids and sailors from other ships scurried along carrying fresh bandages and antiseptics.

"Have you...." Vrish was about to ask an old maid but was interrupted in the middle. "Look for yourself," said the maid as she rushed to another corner of the inn with fresh bandages in her hand. Agni understood that asking around won't help; they needed to look for themselves.

"Come on," said Agni as he made his way through the injured and the dead, careful not to step on anyone.

"Move, move," shouted someone from behind them. They cleared the way as four men, probably sailors, carried two others on a wooden plank. Both of them lay there, unconscious and burnt so badly that even their faces could not be recognized. They went from one to the other looking everywhere, but couldn't find anyone they were looking for. Vrish rubbed his forehead. "We can never find them this way, what if...." he stopped short of completing the sentence. Agni knew what he meant. Some of them were burnt so badly that they were barely recognizable. What if the same had happened to Malini? Agni looked around once, twice and then again, but it was of no use. Then he clenched his fists as his gaze dropped to the ground.

"You two looking for someone?" the voice startled him. Agni looked up and saw an elderly man, wiping his hand with fresh, soaked linen. Vrish stood up and answered immediately, "My sister and my father, their names are Malini and Briksha." The man was staring at their costly clothes.

"Names don't matter now," said the man. "How old are they?" he asked.

"Twenty and fifty-four," said Agni before Vrish could answer.

"Did you search for them here?" asked the man. "Yes," replied Agni.

"Hmm," said the man. "There is another room where we have shifted some of the younger women; you may look for your sister there. But I can't say anything about your father," he answered glumly. Agni's face lit up with the slight ray of hope.

"Which way?" he asked. "I am going over there right now, you can follow me," said the man as he started to walk. Agni and Vrish started following him. They went through the main door and came outside, from where they went right and took a small mud road which led to a small cottage beside the main building. They entered a small dingy room, the same smell hanging in the air persistently. Agni saw that there were five beds in there, two of them were empty.

"Malini," shouted Vrish and ran towards the third one. The man who brought them there made himself busy in checking the condition of the other two women. Agni's eyes were wide with shock; the girl who lay on the bed was barely recognizable. Tears streamed out of Agni's eyes as he shut them tight.

"Sister, my sweet sister," cried Vrish holding her hand. He was sobbing hysterically. Malini opened her mouth but words didn't come out; her eyes were fixed on him as tears streamed out from them.

"She is in a critical condition," said the man as he finished his job and stood up. "We pulled her out of the water, and she had this clenched in her fist." He handed a pendant to Agni, covered in blood. Agni kept staring at it as his tears fell on it and washed away some of the stains. Vrish continued to sob. Then he felt a tug on his sleeves. He turned and saw Malini's hand. She opened her mouth again but words never made it out. Her neck was wrapped by a thick coarse cloth.

"Why can't she speak?" shouted Vrish.

"Her throat was slit. I don't know how but it was this way when I took her out of the water," said the man. Agni's eyes became wide with fear.

"What?" shouted Vrish. "How?"

"I don't know how," repeated the man. "I did everything I could," he said and left the room.

Agni knelt down beside her and took her hand in his own. "Who?" he asked simply as his voice quivered. She slowly moved her other hand and started to draw something on the floor with the blood on her fingertips. When she was finished, it looked like a symbol which Agni had never seen before; the faint lines pointed at four directions and the inner edges were joined together like a cone, two vague squares lay inside it. Tears streamed out of her eyes for the effort she made. She gave one final glance at Agni and her mouth twisted in grief. Agni kept staring at her blankly, tears didn't come out. "Don't worry," he said. "Everything will be fine, I promise." Her other hand fell numb on the floor as her eyes became still. Agni kept staring at her blankly; his heart was beating frantically as his eyes were transfixed on her soulless body. Then it slowly became clear to him: the pain in his chest made him tremble, his tears had gone dry.

"No, Malini, no," screamed Vrish and shook her repeatedly. Agni sat there staring at her once beautiful face. The very face which gave him the hope of a new beginning was shrouded with death now. He felt a searing pain in his chest as he continued to stare at her with a blank look on his face. The wind started to howl outside and soon followed the rain.

THE STARTING POINT

Agni lay on the cushioned bed of the royal guest house of Himadri, sleep did not come to him. Vrish was sitting like a stone near the window, his face blank and expressionless. He wiped away his tears from time to time. They had cremated her body the night before and performed the last ritual to show her spirit the path to the other world. They never found Briksha. After the night's search for other survivors, the port officer had declared three hundred and forty souls missing on official count, Briksha was one of them. The missing were assumed to be dead under the circumstances, but they had promised to keep their search on. Yani, Sir Drake and King Adhirath themselves attended the mass cremation. It was said that the fire still raged on after the night and the water was scalding hot, which was unnatural. The royal party had arrived when all was lost but when the King saw everything with his own eyes, he declared that the festival would be stopped from the day forth. The image of the fire burning in the hearth with Malini in the middle was driving him mad. He had felt as if his soul was burning with her and the smoke carried the ashes of his dreams, 'Seven lives together,' he had promised to her, a drop of tear trickled down his cheek; he wiped it away quickly.

Agni looked at Vrish; he knew it was best to leave him with himself for a while. But he was the closest thing to a family that was left to him. The word family brought back the thoughts of that time when everything was so perfect not a night ago, how they had decided to get married at end of that summer. He thought that for the first time in his life he would have a real family, one that was sealed by a bond. He had decided to leave King Adhirath's palace and settle down in the village of Nipun in the foothills of Himgiri. There he would take up some odd job and they would be happy forever. His eyes became moist again; he rubbed them vigorously trying to shove away the thoughts. The strong pain in his heart persisted and it suffocated him. Agni stood up; he wanted to get away.

"Do you want something to eat?" he asked Vrish. "No," came the reply.

"You should be hungry; it's been quite sometime now. We haven't eaten anything since last night," said Agni, desperately wanting to divert his mind to something else.

"You go and eat if that is so important to you right now," said Vrish in an irritated voice. The rage in Agni came bubbling out at the slightest provocation.

"What did you say?" he asked.

"I said, you go and stuff yourself if you want to. Don't bother me," retorted Vrish. Agni walked up to him held him by his collar and forced him up. Vrish grabbed his hand. They were staring at each other.

"I loved them too, you know that," said Agni angrily.

"You loved them but they were my family. What would you know what family means," Vrish poured out his malice on him.

It stung him like a wasp. He kept staring at him, then he let him go. "You are right Vrish," said Agni. "I never knew what the word family truly meant before I fell in love with your sister." Vrish's eyes became wide in rage, "What?' he shouted. Agni continued, "We were supposed to be a family, a real one, as per the law of Himadri." Then he took out that same gold pendant from his pocket. It had his and Malini's name written on it: the token of love, a custom in which one proposed marriage to the other with the gift of gold. "Your father knew about it," continued Agni. Vrish was stunned. "You had your family while mine was destroyed before it started. I don't know what a true family is and Malini had promised that she will show me. I had believed her then, but now she has proved herself to be a liar," said Agni, his eyes fixed on Vrish's.

"We were going to tell you but never thought it would be like this," said Agni and looked away, the pendant dropped on the floor as Vrish stood there with his mouth open in shock.

Vrish slowly picked it up and rolled it over and over again; he couldn't believe his eyes. Fresh tears trickled down his cheeks. Agni was about to go out of the door when Vrish caught him by the shoulder. Agni turned and saw that his friend's cheeks were wet.

"I am sorry," were his only words as his voice broke. Agni turned and Vrish put his arms around him. "I am sorry. I did not know, I did not know," he said as he held him tightly, beginning to sob hysterically, "Everything is lost, everything Agni, everything," he sobbed. Agni put his hand over his friend's head, his face was grim.

"Malini didn't die; she was killed, and so was Briksha. Someone did this, Vrish. Gather your strength, my friend, we have to find those bastards," said Agni, his eyes fixed on the blue horizon beyond the window. He decided to show them what vengeance meant.

ଓଃ

Two days had passed. Agni and Vrish stood outside the Royal Garden of the palace. King Adhirath was showing Sir Drake his pride and joy, the exotic flowers which he had grown himself. No one, not even Prince Yani was allowed to step inside without the King's express permission. Agni waited patiently while Vrish's face became more twisted with every passing moment.

"Adhirathji is coming, stop making those faces," said Agni in a hushed voice. Vrish stood straight. King Adhirath and Sir Drake were walking side by side. The King was explaining to him the technique of growing a rare flowering plant called Kontok. Then his eyes fell on the duo.

"Agni and Vrish, what a pleasant surprise," he said with a sad smile on his face. It looked more like pity to Agni. "Adhirathji," said Agni with a curt bow. Vrish did the same. King Adhirath walked up to them and placed a hand each on their shoulder.

"How have you two been faring?" he asked.

"We will not rest until we find the ones responsible for this," said Agni firmly. "Me too," said Vrish. King Adhirath looked at Agni and then gave a short glance at Sir Drake.

"Please excuse us for a moment Sir Drake, we will continue when I get back," said the King. "Certainly, as the King wishes," he replied with a smile.

"Feel free to look around," said King Adhirath and almost grabbed them by their shoulders and started to walk towards the other end of the yard.

"Agni and Vrish," he said as they walked together. "I have told you two repeatedly that it was an accident for which I truly feel sorry. I have told you before that it was caused by the fire powder in the ships which was brought here for the festival. They make lovely fireworks but if I should have known," King Adhirath shook his head in despair. The false compassion made him cringe but Agni said nothing.

"Anyway, this is the worst thing that could happen to someone, losing near and dear ones. But that doesn't mean that you should speculate murder behind it," his eyes were on him.

Agni felt his anger rising. "With all due respect, Raja ji, throats don't slit themselves," he replied politely. That changed the expression on King Adhirath's face. He turned to him and placed his other hand on his shoulder.

"Look Agni, you are my ward and Yani says that you are a good friend to him. I love you and Vrish like my own sons. But you also know how I deal with speculators and conspirators. Do you have any idea what will happen if the word spreads?"

Agni had known it all along. Trade was the blood of Himadri. If the word got out that the fire was not a mere accident, then the trading activities would decrease considerably, if not wholly. That meant the end of Himadri, her wealth, protection, festivities and everything else.

"Adhirathji, we also love you like our own father." Agni lied. "I promise you that no such word will ever escape our mouth in front of unwanted ears. We love Himadri a lot too; this is our home. We only want to find the truth and we only seek your help to discover it. Not a single man or woman after us shall know of this," said Agni in a solemn voice. King Adhirath was looking at Agni intently; he had always liked the boy for his sharp wits.

"Besides I know that a King with a heart like yours loves his subjects more than himself, so it is only an earnest request for help on my part to uncover the truth," said Agni.

King Adhirath sighed and looked at Agni. "Say if I agree to help you; but you fail even after that, what then?" he asked.

"If I fail, then I promise that this episode and all knowledge of it will be buried with me and not another soul would know," replied Agni.

King Adhirath gave out a deep breath and said, "Very well then. What do you want from me?"

ৎ

Yani was sitting by the window of his room, staring outside at his father's garden. He had a glass of sura in his hand, a locally brewed alcoholic beverage mixed with a few spices. The beautiful flowers of the garden swayed to and fro with the wind. The lush green grass and the colored brick paths crisscrossed each other in the middle. He kept looking out without blinking, it made his mouth twist in anger. He threw the empty glass towards the garden, but it never reached the spot and fell on the pool beside it instead.

"Can I come in, Prince?" the heavy voice made him smile.

"Yes, Sir Drake," said Yani without even looking. The tall and proud knight walked in with grace and seated himself on the cushions opposite Yani The prince turned to him and smiled, "You have an impeccable timing, sir."

"How so?" asked Sir Drake smiling back.

"Never mind," said Yani and stood up. "Remember, I promised you the best of our beverages," he said.

"That you did," replied Sir Drake.

Yani walked up to the small wooden cabinet and took out two golden cups. He came and filled them from the cask from which he had been drinking. "Here you go," said Yani and handed one of the cups to Sir Drake. Sir Drake simply took it from his hand.

"Taste it," said Yani and Sir Drake took a small sip. He coughed a bit and said, "Exquisite, but a little too strong for my taste." Yani laughed, "If you think this is strong then you should taste the ones they serve at the local inns here."

"Maybe someday I will do that too," replied Sir Drake.

"I hope not; that might turn out to be an unpleasant situation for you, good Sir," said Yani. Sir Drake only smiled in response.

Then he looked outside the window and said, "I hope your father doesn't mind me drinking with his young son." He looked at Yani, who looked away. "Don't worry, he has better things to do," he did his best to hide his contempt.

Sir Drake didn't pursue the subject. He leaned back more comfortably on the cushions.

"Where are your friends?" he asked, "Vrish and what was his name again?"

"Agni," replied Yani.

"Yes Agni, I haven't seen much of them lately," said Sir Drake.

"They have...busy," said Yani after a brief pause.

"Rightly so," said Sir Drake. "Any man will need time to get to his usual self after all that; fate have smacked them hard."

"Yes, that's true," said Yani. "But they are strong, especially Agni."

"Yes, I have seen that. He has many qualities inside him, most importantly he always seems to keep his cool," said Sir Drake.

Yani simply nodded his head with a smile. "Don't mind me saying,' said Sir Drake, "the other one, Vrish, he seems as blunt and thick as an iron pellet and I am sure he at least weighs one hundred and eighty of those." Yani started to laugh. Sir Drake was all smiles himself. "I can't believe that they are brothers," added Sir Drake.

"That's because they are not," said Yani with the smile still on his face. "Agni and Vrish are not related by blood; they just grew up together with me." Sir Drake sat up straight.

"Then where are his parents?' he asked more firmly than usual.

Yani hesitated for a moment and then said, "Its no use hiding from you; they all know the story around here. Vrish's father Briksha found him at some port up north in an orphanage when he was still an infant. He brought him here. My father took him in after that and Vrish too."

"Really," said Sir Drake. "Interesting," he muttered more to himself as he leaned back on the cushions again.

"Agni is very smart and a good friend," said Yani with a smile.

"That much I have seen," said Sir Drake smiling back. "Anyway," he said, "Let us not ponder over these things any more and instead let us celebrate our coming hunt in the ancient forest of Kyat. It took a lot persuasion on my part to make your father agree to my proposal."

A grin spread across Yani's face. "A toast to that," said Sir Drake and poured some more sura in their already empty cups.

ॐ

The Sun was up in the sky. The carriage moved slowly through the morning crowd. The vendors were vending their merchandise from door to door, while the shops were buzzing with customers. The city guards were keeping order as they kept the traffic moving. Thousands of pilgrims poured inside the city before the start of the festival a few days back and hundreds more were coming everyday. It was the most profitable time in Himadri. The King had the authority to cancel the festival but not the holy rituals. The inns of the city were overcrowded and the residents gave their spare rooms, cow sheds, stables and even their yards on rent for a fair price. Agni and Vrish had taken the carriage instead of horses. The roads were too crowded for comfort. Agni was staring outside. From time to time he would unfold the cloth and look at the symbol. They had gone to Guru Bhas before, the scholar of the royal court of Himadri and shown him the symbol. He was at a loss. Then after extensive thinking, he came to the conclusion that it was a foreign symbol and there was only one person in Himadri who could possibly posses such knowledge, one of the three great gurus of the east, Mahaguru Sidak. No one had permission to visit him except the King and three of his own disciples who lived with him. Agni got the permission from the King himself, but on the condition that only one of them could visit him. Agni and Vrish both decided that it should be Agni.

"Nervous?" asked Vrish.

"No," Agni lied with a straight face. Then he smiled and said, "A little."

"Ah, don't worry," said Vrish. "I think you are the smartest person around."

"Then one more reason is added to my list of reasons to be nervous," said Agni with a smirk on his face. Vrish didn't get it first. Then he narrowed his eyes and said, "You will pay for that." He grabbed him and started to throttle him playfully. Agni was laughing, so was Vrish. It was after a long time that the sound of laughter brought them a sense of relief.

Three hours of the Sun had passed. The carriage had stopped in front of a small hut near the outskirts of the forest of Seshnag, five hundred paces or more from the eastern gate of the city.

"I will wait here," said Vrish. Agni nodded his head and started to climb down.

"Best of luck," said Vrish as he closed the door behind him. Agni started towards the hut. Three men draped in white came out to greet him. They folded their hands with their palms joined in a formal greeting. Agni did the same.

"Welcome to the humble abode of Mahaguru Sidak. I hope your trip was pleasant?" asked one of the disciples, who seemed to be the oldest of the three.

"Yes, thank you for asking," said Agni politely. "My name is Agni."

"We know Agni, Raja ji had sent us word of your coming. My name is Param and these are my brothers, Pushya and Dhir," he said pointing to the other two in turns. Agni gave them a curt bow.

"Please follow us," he said and they started to walk towards the hut. "It is a rare honor to have the opportunity to meet the Mahaguru himself. You must have done something extraordinary to get the permission from Adhirathji," said Param on their way towards the hut.

Something extraordinary indeed, thought Agni. He had coaxed something out of a man like King Adhirath. But he kept it to himself. "Adhirathji is just a very kind man, I never did anything of such great importance," said Agni instead.

"Modesty is a virtue," said Param with a smile. Agni saw that they had crossed the larger hut and were heading for the smaller one behind it, which he hadn't noticed earlier. He saw that two guards were standing in front of the steps which led to the door of the bigger one as they passed by. They came to a halt in front of the smaller hut. "Please wait here for a moment," said Param and all the three of them went inside. He alone came out after a few moments with a small bowl in his hand.

"Mahaguruji is not to be disturbed except only during his meals. So you will have the honor today," he said as he handed the bowl to Agni. He saw that only a quarter of the bowl was filled by some dark liquid. He looked up at Param, who smiled.

"A man only needs as much as it is required to sustain him in the journey called life," said Param. Agni thought if Vrish would have seen this, he would have fainted right there. Agni felt a little more nervous. Param put a hand on his shoulder and said, "Don't be afraid, Agni. Just set it down in front of Guruji and don't speak if not spoken to first."

Agni slowly nodded his head. "And also remember," said Param, "Two tests and one question in turn of three right answers. So keep your mind clear while you answer Guruji's questions and think twice before asking yours if you pass." Agni was sweating; no one had ever told him that there would be any tests or questions.

"Come, let us not waste any more time," said Param as he led Agni towards the larger hut. Agni breathed slowly and readied himself.

THE GREAT GURU

Agni stepped inside the dimly-lit room and closed the door behind him. It took his eyes some time to adjust to the poor light. The room was simple, small, clean and poorly furnished. Yet the man who sat in the middle of it had a strange radiance to him. He was very much unlike the other sages Agni had seen in Himadri. He didn't have a long beard and unkempt or braided hair; instead, he was clean shaved, bald and not too old. The skin of his face and neck had sagged a little and the whole thing had a sense of mysticism to it. He sat there, still, cross-legged with his eyes closed. Agni saw that there was a chair and a small stool in front of him. Agni went and sat down on the floor in front of the Mahaguru and adjusted himself in a cross legged position. He set down the bowl in front of him. There was a thin smile on the Mahaguru's face which Agni didn't notice. Agni sat there silently and didn't speak a word, as he was told. Moments passed into hours yet the Mahaguru neither spoke, nor touched the bowl in front of him. Agni lost track of time as the Sun could not be seen from the inside of the hut and the only source of light was a single candle set on the shelf to their right, there were no windows; just one ventilator which was also closed from the inside. The strong scent of the incense made him feel drowsy. He felt his feet aching and his legs had gone numb, but he didn't break the silence. Then after a long time, Mahaguru Sidak opened his eyes. Agni felt a sense of relief. Mahaguru took the bowl in his hand and emptied its contents, then he put it down in front of him.

"Agni," a divine voice boomed inside the room. After the long silence it felt like beating drums to him.

"Yes Mahaguruji," complied Agni politely.

"Are you ready for the three questions?" he asked.

There was supposed to be two tests first, thought Agni.

"You have passed them," said Mahaguru Sidak. Agni was a bit startled.

Agni paused for a moment and then said, "I do not understand Mahaguruji."

"A man is known for his humility and excels through his patience. Those were the first two tests," said Mahaguru Sidak.

Then it dawned to him. A guest in the eastern lands was said to be another form of god and he should be treated as such. But when he was asked to be the servant, his acceptance judged his character, his sense of humility. The next was the test of patience; he knew he had passed that, his aching back and numb feet being proof enough.

"Yes, I am ready," replied Agni. Mahaguru Sidak was impressed by the intellect of the young man in front of him, yet he did not show it.

"What is the primary source of greed?" boomed the Mahaguru's voice.

Agni thought carefully, 'wealth' was the first answer that came to his mind, but he didn't say it loud. He thought of it more accurately. Greed is the urge of possession of wealth.

The urge comes from the urge of survival. The primary source of survival is food.

"Food," he replied, his fingers crossed and eyes closed.

"Correct, but what does that mean?" asked the Mahaguru again. "Is this the next question?" he asked. The Mahaguru smiled, "No," he replied. "I want to hear you explain your answer."

Agni tried chalk out his thoughts in the best possible manner. "Well, every man wants to survive and he will do anything for it. He also tries to earn a proper living to lead a decent life. That urge creates greed," said Agni.

"Right, but why does this happen?" he asked again But Agni was at a loss. "I don't know," he said.

"Exactly, no one knows. Every man has greed inside him, whether big or small. One who can control his greed is known to be a good man; one who knows how to satiate his greed without harming others is known as a good man; and ones who cannot do either are called bad men," Mahaguru said with a smile. "So from all this we understand that it is a part of human nature and exists in all." Agni was impressed with his words and realised he had come to the right place.

"Next question," said the Mahaguru. Agni nodded his head.

"When you are facing an enemy, how many are you truly facing and whom do you need to defeat first?" he asked.

Agni closed his eyes, the question seemed very simple, yet he did not understand it properly.

He understood that it was a sort of riddle like the first one. He tried to clear his mind. 'What is the first thing that comes to one's mind when he faces an enemy?' he asked himself, 'vengeance' came the reply from the inside of his heart, but he knew that it was not the right answer to others who were not in a desperate situation like him. He opened his eyes. He was opening and closing his fingers as if trying to grasp the answer out of thin air. The answer seemed to elude him. He felt that he would fail in the very first step of his quest, his quest of revenge. The fear of it made him sweat. Then it struck him - fear. When one faces his enemy, he must first overcome the fear of losing, the fear of death, the fear of failure, the fear in one's own heart.

"The answer is two. A man must face his own fears first in order to face his enemy. If the first is defeated, only then he can defeat the second," said Agni firmly.

"Correct again," said the Mahaguru. He looked pleased.

"Are you ready for the final question, Agni?" he asked. Agni breathed deeply, "Ready," he said.

"If there is a path," he said, "that makes you the master of fate itself, whom will you choose to be, the kind or the just?"

"The just," said Agni promptly without a second doubt. The Mahaguru smiled, "We shall see," he said. Agni did not understand, he felt a bit confused.

"It seems that you have passed all the tests and so now it is your turn, what is it you wish to ask me?" asked the Mahaguru. The sheer enthusiasm in his heart was overwhelming. Agni quickly took out the cloth and unfolded it front of him, revealing the symbol. The Mahaguru sat looking at it intently.

"What do you want to know?" asked the Mahaguru without looking up at Agni. Agni thought of the question carefully, Param had said to him that he would get only one chance. He thought over in his mind and asked, "What is there to know?"

Mahaguru Sidak looked up and responded, "Nothing if you don't want to, after all the emphasis on your urge of knowing is the vital thing."

Agni was stunned; he didn't get it at first. It dawned on him slowly that he had failed to ask the question properly and his urge of knowledge was not emphasized in the question. Instead, he had left it on the Guru to provide the appropriate answer. He clenched his fist and hit the floor hard. Slowly he came to his senses, he had failed.

"I am sorry," apologized Agni for his behavior and stood up slowly. The numbness in his feet made it a little difficult for him. As he was about to leave, Mahaguru Sidak's voice floated to his ears,

"A man can share his thoughts by the simplest of words. What is the most simple question in your mind?" Agni turned around and said, "What does this symbol signify?" Mahaguru Sidak was still smiling, "The theory of Origin, only that much is known, nothing more," he said. "Close the door on your way out," he finished. Agni had a broad grin on his face; he folded his hands and offered his respects. He knew that it would be unwise to ask anything else, as he didn't deserve the answer to the first one to begin with. He left the room and closed the door behind him.

As he made his way out of the door, the only thought on his mind was to find out the meaning of Mahaguru's words. But he could not understand why Malini had drawn him a symbol which pointed to a theory; maybe the meaning would provide new openings. Still, he struggled to find the relation.

"You gave him two chances. Does that mean he is the one or else why would you take such interest in that boy?" was asked to the Mahaguru by a voice which always remained unheard to others.

"I cannot say, as it is not an answer for me to give. Only time can tell," replied the Mahaguru, without moving his lips.

"You don't have to, for your purpose has run its course." The candles in the room went out as a gust of wind left the room. Mahaguru Sidak started to chant slowly.

ೞ

A dark hooded figure was standing on the docks. The black of the night had consumed him completely. The moon was also covered by dark clouds which moved from time to time with the wind making everything partly visible in the lingering light. The wind was strong and the lantern swung to and fro. There was not a single soul on the cursed dock. The sailors had started to believe that the fire was caused by an evil spirit which still roamed the place after the Sun sets. They had seen dark shadows roaming around in the black of the night.

"Have you brought the gold?" came a voice from the darkness.

"Yes," the hooded man replied. An old woman all withered and spotted appeared before him from the darkness. She had a hump and walked with the help of a wooden branch curved into a stick. "Let's see it," she said.

The man tossed the bag full of coins at her. She snatched it from the air and took one out. She bit it hard with a few teeth she had left. She smiled at the taste of it.

"Count it if you want to," said the man with distaste in his voice.

"No need of that," said the old woman as she put it back into the bag.

"I never thought that you people would do such a fine job with those things, those wretches deserved it," she said with a grin on her face. The man gave her a sharp look, his eyes shining in the dark. It made her smile disappear and she lowered her gaze.

"You remember the second part of our agreement?" he asked, his eyes still fixed on her.

"Of course," said the old woman. "My sons leave tonight, the rest has been arranged by the Captain. Then it will be up to you to decide with the Captain himself, as I had agreed to before."

"No one is to know about it, even after I leave, ever,' he said. His words weighed down upon her.

"No one will know. I have taken an oath before the Trinetra and so have my sons; you have my word," she squeaked.

"Good," said the man.

 C3

When Agni came out, it was already dark outside. A strong wind was blowing and it ruffled his black hair. Param was waiting for him outside. On seeing him he got up from the ground and hurried towards him.

"It took longer than usual, everything went well inside?" he asked. Agni nodded his head.

"Did you get what you wanted?" he asked again. "Yes," replied Agni with a smile.

Param looked a bit surprised. Then he smiled back and said, "Then you are the fourth one after us to succeed." Agni was a bit taken aback. "You mean to say..." he stopped.

Param still had his smile on his face. "Yes Agni," he said, "No one except the three of us has ever succeeded in passing through all the tests and questions, except you; that makes you our fourth brother." Agni didn't say anything; he thought if the Mahaguru hadn't given him a second chance, then he wouldn't have been the fourth. But it didn't matter to him, for he had got what he had come for, partly.

Agni gave a curt bow and said, "Thank you, but I still think that I am not worthy enough to be called the fourth brother." Param put a hand on his shoulder and said, "Modesty is a virtue but do not think yourself to be lesser than anyone when you have proved yourself."

"I will certainly keep that in mind," said Agni.

"Come, you must be hungry," said Param as he started for the smaller hut.

His thoughts and the ordeal had made him forget that he had not eaten for very long. But now, a new mystery surrounded him, the Theory of Origin.

"Agni," called Param and he bounced back to reality.

"Paramji," he said, "do you know what the theory of origin is?"

Param looked at him with curiosity in his eyes, then he gave it a thought and said, "Sorry Agni, I don't know of any such theory. Did Guruji tell you that?" he asked.

"Yes, but I don't know what it is," said Agni. Then Agni took the piece of cloth and showed him the symbol. Param was staring at it with utmost curiosity. "When I asked him about this, he only told me that it signified the theory of origin," said Agni.

"What did he say after that?" asked Param.

Agni thought carefully. "Only that much is known, nothing more," said Agni.

Param scratched his head and said, "If Guruji doesn't know anything else about it, then there is little chance that someone else will."

Then Param turned to him and said, "But don't give up hope. Guruji himself taught us that it is impossible for man to know all and everything."

"Right," said Agni. He understood that it was a dead end on this part.

"So let us go and join our brothers for the evening meal," said Param, which made Agni wonder who was hungrier out of the two of them.

"It is a great honor, Paramji, but my friend is waiting for me outside and the prince will be expecting me, too," lied Agni, at least the last part of it. It seemed that Param was a bit let down. "Very well," he said, "Then it shall have to wait for another day I suppose. You will come by again, right . . . now that you are a brother."

"Certainly," said Agni with a curt bow.

"Come, let me walk you to your carriage," he said.

ଔ

The carriage was speeding towards the royal quarters, the streets empty by that late hour. Agni was leaning outside the door of the moving carriage, the wind striking his face making him forget his burden for a while. Vrish had been worrying for Agni as he was gone for a long time, almost the entire day. But when he told him everything, the tests, the questions and the answer, it all left him stunned. Like Agni, he also had no idea what it meant or what it was. The questions were tantalizing and the final answer, even more.

"Who do you think would know about this, Agni? His own disciples don't know anything about it," said Vrish. Agni didn't have an answer to that. Malini had left him a clue which was as difficult as she had been at times. The thought of his times with Malini brought a smile to Agni's face. He remembered how the smallest of mistakes on his part irked her and if he lost his temper once, it meant penance for a thousand years. The best part of it all was the radiant smile he won from her after the quarrel. That used to make his day a little brighter every single time. Suddenly, his eyes were moist; he wiped them quickly before Vrish could see.

"Are you all right?" asked Vrish.

"Something in my eyes," said Agni as he leaned back on his seat and looked away.

Vrish didn't say anything else. He simply looked outside the window and thought that if they find the ones responsible, he would make them pay double for every drop of his family's blood they had shed, and every drop of tear they had.

THE COUNCIL OF THE SEVEN

The biggest chamber of the highest tower of Aine was buzzing with servants. They were cleaning every little thing in the room with such neatness that they shone like silver in the sunlight. The meeting of the Council was to commence soon. The Council comprised of the Seven, the guardians of the 'Abode of the Seven'. They neatly placed the goblets in order and started closing the windows. The discussions that were made inside that room were of the greatest importance and if any word ever leaked, that would mean the death of the one who had heard. The bell tolled seven times, signalling the arrival of the Seven. The servants scurried off, closing the door behind them and locking it from the outside. The Seven were not to be disturbed at any cost. A creaking noise was heard and slowly a door appeared behind the tapestry of the old god of wealth, Opul. The maker was seen in different forms in the land of the setting Sun. Six of them were draped in white, while one in black, from head to toe. They slowly took their places as the door closed behind them. The tallest of them sat on the highest chair at the end of the table. He poured a liquid from the flagon on the table in his goblet and handed it to the one beside him. He did the same and the process continued until all of the goblets were filled. They raised the goblets in the air and started their chant,

"For no man shall arise and be so bold, to hinder the flow of time and the ways of old. The Seven shall always be the odds." They drank deep from the goblets.

"Let the meeting commence," said the one in the high chair.

A man of short stature, two seats to the left of the high chair stood up and started speaking: "This is the day on which I was asked to provide the report of my progress on the task that was given to me by the High Lord himself."

The High Lord gestured him to continue. "My little snake is following his every move. Sir, he doesn't even know that my pet is there, but it seems that he is a little out of my reach for the time being," said the man.

The High Lord shifted in his seat and asked, "You mean to say that your little pet has reached a dead end?"

"No, no. That is not what I meant," said the short man, the tension clear on his face.

"Sometimes a raven is better than a snake," said the one seated opposite the short man.

"The honour was given to me, not you, Raven," snapped the short man.

"Silence," said the High Lord in a stern voice, "I shall not have any bickering amongst the members of this Council.

The eyes of the High Lord fell on the one next to him. "Do you have something to say, Dark?"

A smile spread across the man's face. "Shadows don't need eyes, Light," he said without even looking.

"You know that I don't have that option; I cannot risk an open war with The Protectors when I am not even sure. You know that very well," said the High Lord, the lord of the light.

"They hunt in the dark where no eyes shall see them, you know that very well too," said the man sharply. The High Lord gave it a thought, "We shall see," he said.

"But the honour was given to me," shouted the short man, Snake.

"Sit down, Snake," said Aqua, the lord of the seas.

"No, I will not sit down. I have had enough," he shouted. Dark was looking at him with curiosity in his eyes. The High Lord simply raised his hood a bit and his deep green eyes met his. "Aah,' a scream echoed in the hall. His hand had caught fire.

"You are not immune Snake; maybe to others, but not to me," said the High Lord in a calm voice. Snake jumped out of his seat and tried dousing it with water from the huge jar inside the room, but the flame kept burning his hand.

"I am sorry, High Lord, I am sorry. Forgive me," he started to plead. The fire went out.

"I believe it is understood that voices must not be raised in my presence," reiterated the High Lord.

"Never, I promise," said Snake. He was clutching his hand, now black like charcoal.

"I shall give you more time until the council meets again," said the High Lord. "Make arrangements to prove your worth by then."

"Thank you, High Lord; that's all I need. I will not fail you again," said Snake, his face twisted in agony. Dark had a thin smile on his face, his eyes fixed on the short man.

 beginning

Two days had passed and yet Agni had no clue about the meaning of those words or any theory as such. He sat confused with a heap of books and scrolls lying scattered around him. He had turned the royal library upside down, yet he had found nothing. He had come across a thousand different synonyms of the word 'origin' and a philosophical theory propounded by the great scholar 'Bani'. His theory said that man was made in the image of god, yet it proved to be useless. Agni sat there with his hands over his head.

"Any luck?" asked Vrish. "No," said Agni in an irritated voice. Vrish sat down beside Agni and looked around with wary eyes. "I have been to the docks this morning; they were pulling away the wrecks when they found four of these in all the four ships." Agni looked at him; Vrish was holding something on his palm which seemed to be a metal shell of some spherical object. It was strange, it seemed that the colour of the shell kept changing from time to time and had strange markings on them.

"What is this?" asked Agni as he took it from his hand. It was still warm, as if had been preheated.

"Don't know. The port officer said that they were searing hot when they found these. He said that bubbles were rising from four spots as if something was still burning under water. All the fish were dying near the port side, so they decided to look into it and found these . . . things. Three of his best divers died of burns in trying to dig these out. They had to bury these under the earth for a full day and night and only then it became cool enough to be handled. They are suspecting these to be the reason behind the explosion and fire. They are contemplating that these things were probably brought to Himadri for the festival and the fire show, but they are at a complete loss to figure out what it really is," said Vrish.

"How did you get this?" asked Agni. That thing had an odd stench to it.

"I have my ways," said Vrish with a smile. Agni could feel the frustration slipping away; how could he have forgotten Vrish's greatest talent, making friends! He stood up and started to pace up and down the room.

"If these were actually brought into Himadri from somewhere outside, then there should be a mention of it in the cargo list of the ships," said Agni.

Vrish was shaking his head, "That's the thing! The port officer said that the law of Himadri states clearly that any hazardous material being brought from outside must be mentioned in the cargo list. So much so, that the ship carrying it cannot dock without his permission. There is no mention of these things in the cargo list of any of the four ships and no case of permissions being sought, too."

Vrish leaned back a little and said with a hint of sadness in his voice, "My father was not the one to disobey any laws and I do not remember him mentioning any such thing to me in the past."

"Don't think your father or the others did any such thing. It is a fact for certain that these things were not a part of the cargoes of any of the ships. Don't you think that it is too much of a coincidence that four similar things were brought in four different ships at the same time in the same place?" said Agni angrily.

"The port officer said that it was an extraordinary accident; or that's what he has started to believe lately," said Vrish.

Agni was still pacing. "Extraordinary indeed," said Agni.

"I believe that he is under a little pressure there; he didn't say so, but it seemed like that to me," said Vrish.

"I am certain that it is coming from the golden throne itself," said Agni, the anger in him rising.

Vrish looked around and spoke in a hushed voice, "You mean to say Adhirath…, but why?"

"Don't you get it? Himadri is solely dependent on trade and most of its revenue comes from that. Remember what Adhirathji said? He didn't want a rumour to spread at any cost. That is precisely the reason I was able to coax out that permission from him. Trade is more important to him than his subjects," Agni's voice was booming in anger.

"Lower your voice Agni; someone might hear us," said Vrish and gave a quick glance at the head librarian who seemed too busy in his work to have bothered about what they were saying.

"I understand Agni, but if the King doesn't want them to look into it then the subject is very well closed. We can give it a try but we don't even know where to start looking. It is better to follow the concrete clue that Malini left us," said Vrish. Agni knew what he meant, but he also knew that Malini's clue had led them to a dead end.

"There are two possibilities," said Agni as he came and sat down beside Vrish. "One, they brought the four things into Himadri at once, at the same time; and the second, these were made here and planted on those ships, including 'Dut'." Vrish's eyes became wide and his gaze was fixed on Agni. "You mean to say that someone from Himadri is involved in this?" he asked.

"There is a high probability," said Agni.

Vrish stood up immediately. "I will see what I can find," he said. He was about to leave when he turned and said, "Agni, if what you say is true, then I assure you that I will find them at any cost." Agni nodded his head. He saw Vrish leave the library and closed the book in front of him. He felt the dread of failure draining from his heart; finally there was something to go on after, or at least he hoped.

⟨⟩

Agni was walking towards the royal palace a short distance away from the royal quarters, the servant's quarters was beside the royal quarters but there were two doors between the three compounds which were heavily guarded. Agni and Vrish had the permission to visit the palace anytime they wanted. Agni was in the royal library when a servant had come running to him. He informed him that the Prince had returned from the hunt and wanted to see him immediately. Agni knocked on the door of Prince Yani's bedchamber.

"Come in," came Yani's angry voice. Agni understood that the hunt didn't go well or else Yani wouldn't have returned that early; Yani's voice confirmed his understanding. He opened the door and gave a curt bow.

"How was your hunt, Yani? I was told that you asked for me," said Agni.

"Cut the crap, Agni. It's all because of you," shouted Yani angrily. Sir Drake was also there, seated on a soft mattress while Yani was standing. He was smiling at Agni.

"Sorry, but I don't understand," said an astonished Agni. This time it was Sir Drake who spoke. "Your friend has a firm belief that our hunt failed because of you."

Agni was dumfounded. "I wasn't even there," he said.

"That was the problem, Agni. We didn't have a fine tracker like you this time and the one we took was bloody incompetent. I would have had him beheaded if the holy law had permitted it," grumbled Yani. It made Agni smile.

"I shall try my best to come with you the next time," said Agni.

"No, you will make it certain," said Yani with authority. "Even Sir Drake wants you to come." Agni looked at Sir Drake.

"Yes, Agni," said Sir Drake. "I have heard from the Prince how you tracked down that demon cat. We could certainly use a good tracker like you in our next hunt in the forest of Jambu near Nisarga after our little stay inside the city itself."

"It will be after fifteen days of the Sun and the moon. We will first stay in the city and then if everything goes as planned, we will go for the hunt. Either ways it will be a good experience for you Agni. You have never left Himadri before," finished Yani.

"But it is too soon; I cannot give my word," said Agni, to which Sir Drake raised his brow.

"No Agni, you have to come," said Yani like a child.

"Agni," said Sir Drake, "I will not be here for long. My stay in the land of the Rising Sun is coming to an end. It will certainly make me happy if we can have one last hunt before I leave. And a good one this time! Consider it a request on my behalf." Then he smiled and said, "Besides, it is unlikely for a person like you to let down the Prince of this land. Nisarga is also a good place to be. It is the most beautiful city of the east, the Grand Palace, the woods of Jambu and Adhar, the great canal and the greatest library of the east." Agni was about to say something but he was cut short by Sir Drake again.

"And from the look of things, you need some change," finished Sir Drake, the smile still on his face.

Agni thought for some time. He had gone to Guru Bhas and told him what the Mahaguru had said. Guru Bhas had said that there was a slim chance that he would get anything in the royal library about it if the Mahaguru didn't know himself. Agni had looked still and found that Bhas ji was right. Guru Bhas had also told him that Nisarga had the greatest library of the east and great scholars flocked there to do their research. If anything like the theory of origin existed as per the Mahaguru, then it would be the most suitable place to look. Agni had decided that he would go there soon but then Vrish had come up with the new clue. He needed to be there to help him; but he could also leave it to Vrish and head to Nisarga alone to find the meaning. He was in a dilemma.

"Please Agni, for the sake of our friendship," Yani pleaded like a child. Agni stood there silent; he knew turning down royalty was a great offence in Himadri. The best thing to do in such a situation was to accept the situation and turn it to his own advantage. He would make Vrish understand his true motive.

"So?" asked Sir Drake. Agni slowly nodded his head. "Excellent," shouted Yani in joy, both of them looked pleased.

ॐ

Vrish was seated in a small tavern on the far side of the dock. He had a cup of locally brewed ale in his hand. Droh's tavern was famous, or rather infamous, for its visitors. That place was always teeming with smugglers, brigands, pirates and people of that sort. No respectable citizen ever came to that place. Vrish had a liking for that sort; he firmly believed that their trades might not be legal, but a few of them had good souls. He was waiting for Droh, the owner of that tavern. Droh was the kind of a man who was known all throughout Himadri as the one who should be talked to when you are trying to find something that others could not. In other words, he was the perfect spy for the rich and the poor alike. He became the owner of the tavern at the age of fifteen when his father passed away. He changed the name of that place then. He was much older than Vrish but friendship knew no age. It had been long and Droh was yet to arrive; his sister Bani had sent word the moment Vrish had asked for him. She personally served him the ale, which was good; an occasional smile on her part made it taste better. But still, he was feeling rather impatient. Then he saw the tall, bulky man walk in with grace, his big belly swinging in front of him with the rhythm of his steps as he walked into the tavern.

"Ahh," he shouted in his booming voice, "my long lost friend is here again." Vrish got up and they embraced each other formally.

"I have heard of what happened at the docks. I am truly sorry for you, my friend," he said with compassion. Vrish stood there still, not knowing what to say.

Droh nodded his head as he bore a sad smile on his face and said, "Let us forget these things for the moment, which I know is rather impossible on your part, but no one has the power to go against the will of the Trinetra." His words were clumsy, yet Vrish knew that he didn't mean to offend him.

Vrish smiled and said, "Thank you for your kind words, my friend. But I have come to you for a reason today."

Vrish looked around and said, "Can we talk somewhere else? Safer." Droh nodded his head, "Come," he said and gestured him to follow. They walked out of the main hall through the back door and came to the back of the tavern, the storeroom and the stables were a few paces away from them. There were two empty wooden boxes there. "This is my spot;

we can talk here. I am sure no one will hear us," said Droh as he sat down on a box; Vrish followed suit.

"So what is it that you want to talk to me about?" he asked with a half smile on his face, after they were comfortable.

Vrish took out the metallic shell and held it in front of him.

"What is this thing?" Droh asked as he took it from Vrish's hand. The shell still had its unique look and it made Droh stare at it with curiosity.

"That's what I want to know," said Vrish.

Droh inspected it carefully. "Don't know, Vrish," he said. "Even the markings are strange."

"What I think is that this is some kind of a device. I want to know if there is anyone in Himadri who is capable of making these things," said Vrish as Droh continued to look at it.

"What kind of a device?" he asked as he looked up. Vrish was hesitating and Droh understood that. "Look Vrish," he said, "If you want me to help you then you should tell me everything you know about this thing. I hope you trust me after all these years." Vrish was a bit taken aback.

"Of course, if I didn't trust you, I wouldn't have come to you in the first place," said Vrish.

"Then, spill it," said Droh with a smile. Vrish took in a deep breath and said, "We think, I mean me and my friend Agni, that this is the thing that killed my family back at the docks." Droh was staring at him, "You mean to say that it was no accident?" he asked after a pause.

"That's what we think," said Vrish. "The port officer Kirti gave these to me. He said that he believed that the fire was caused intentionally but now he says that it was an extraordinary accident." Droh smiled and said, "Can't blame him; after all, he needs to save his job." Vrish realised that

Droh had understood what he wished to convey, a man like him was known for his sharp wits.

Then he looked Vrish in the eye and said, "Very well, I will see what I can do. Just one condition, though, and you know it very well."

"That you work alone and I must trust your actions like always," said Vrish smiling. He was not skeptical about it, even a little bit. Droh only smiled back in response.

Vrish put a hand on his shoulder and said, "I thank you friend. I knew I can count on you. But you better be careful this time and don't speak of this to anyone unless you really need to. I want to keep this under wraps. We have no idea where this might lead to."

"No one will come to know of it, I assure you," said Droh.

"Thank you, my friend. You don't know what this means to me," said Vrish, his eyes slightly moist remembering his sister and father. Droh held Vrish's hand resting on his shoulder and said, "You don't have to thank me, old friend. I owe you a lot more for what you did for me."

THE WITCH HUNT

Five days had passed and yet there was no news of Droh. He was supposed to come to them and he had told Vrish not to contact him before he does. Agni had told Vrish about the trip to Nisarga and the real reason for his having agreed to it. Vrish was a little angry at first, for having been left behind along. But Agni made him understand that it was the only way to find the meaning of that symbol and it would be better if they worked on both the fronts, simultaneously. He agreed and decided to search for that man on his own while Agni went to Nisarga. But Agni wanted to hear some good news before he left with Yani. The morning was perfect, the Sun was bright yet the wind was up and it was cool and comfortable. Agni and Vrish were having the first meal of the day, a simple one, some rice which grew in abundance there with milk and honey.

There was a soft knock on the door. Agni and Vrish looked at each other.

"Who could come this early?" asked Vrish.

"Don't know. Go and see," said Agni. Vrish went and opened the door and stepped back. Agni saw a short and cute looking girl walk in. "Bani," exclaimed a surprised Vrish. "Blessed morning," she said, "Blessed morning," greeted both of them.

"What are you doing here this early in the morning Bani? Is something wrong?" asked Vrish.

Bani stood there staring at the ground and biting her lip, the hesitation clear on her face.

"Let her sit first, Vrish," said Agni and cleared away the bowls. The three of them sat together on the mat. "Tell us, what's wrong?" asked Vrish. Bani looked up and said, "My brother asked me not to come to you until he sent me word of his departure, but I was not left with a choice," she said.

"I don't understand," said Vrish, Agni was staring at her intently. She hesitated for a moment and said, "Droh has gone missing for the past three days."

"What?" Vrish was shocked. "But how? What happened?"

"He came to the tavern the night before he left and gave me this," she said and took out a letter from the folding of her cloth and handed it to Vrish.

"Didn't he say anything else?" asked Vrish as he put the letter down on the floor. Agni picked it up and was staring at something on it.

"He said that the royal guards were looking for him. The King had declared him a conspirator and he was accused of conspiring against none other than the King himself. There is also a good price on his head. So he needed to leave Himadri for a few days until it was safe enough for him to return. He said that he would send word to me after he crosses the eastern gate." Her eyes were moist. "I was supposed to come to you after I got word of his departure which was likely to be the morning after that. But three days have passed since and I haven't had any news from him. He said that Dara, the head sentry of the eastern gate and an old friend of his would help him cross over," said Bani.

"Did you go to him, this Dara?" asked Vrish.

"Yes, but he said Droh never came to him. I fear for his life, Vrish. You have been a good friend of ours; and I really don't know who else to turn to," she sobbed. Vrish was at a loss; he didn't know how to console her.

"Don't worry. I will help finding him out, you can count on that," he said. Agni opened the letter and the smile on his face broadened.

Bani was about to say something when Agni interrupted. "Did he ask you to hand this over to us in person?" he asked.

"No, he had said that if I handed this over to the gate keepers, then it would reach you safely," she replied. Agni was now laughing. "Very smart," he said as he stood up. Vrish and Bani were staring at him with their mouth half open.

"Come with me," said Agni as he started for the door.

"Where?" asked Vrish. "I think I know where Droh might be," said Agni as he opened the door. Vrish and Bani looked at each other.

╋

Agni paced towards the servants quarters followed by Vrish and Bani. She gave him anxious looks and he, in turn, gestured her to stay calm for he had much faith on his friend.

"Droh never sent you word because I think he never left the city," said Agni on their way.

"But he said that he would go to Dara and leave the city the next morning," said Bani anxiously.

"Maybe he didn't trust that guy as much as you think," said Agni as they came to a halt in front of the door to the servant's quarters. Two guards stood there, a little away from them. "Open the door," said Agni and they obliged quickly, after all he was the King's ward. But Agni saw that they looking at Bani curiously.

"Blessed morning to you two," said Agni quickly. "Blessed morning, Agni ji," they said to Agni with a half smile on their faces. They made their way through the door.

"Do not shout or do anything that might draw attention," said Agni to both of them. Both of them nodded their heads.

"Good, follow me," said Agni and started to stroll through the passage. The servants were staring at them but none of them had the audacity to say anything to the King's wards.

"What does he look like?" he whispered to Vrish.

"Fat, tall, dark, broad shoulders, hair parted from the middle, black eyes, long hair, a beard and a cut mark on his lower lip," said Vrish after some thought. "But why?" he asked.

"That's all I need to know," said Agni. They walked past several rooms and then they came to the main kitchen. Agni's eyes fell on a large man sitting in the corner by the large clay oven. He was sharpening his knife with a whetstone. He matched Vrish's description, excepting that he had no beard, his hair was cropped short. The cut mark on his lower lip gave him away.

"Is that him?" asked Agni. "Yes," replied Bani before Vrish, she was smiling and had a look of relief on her face.

"Stay here," said Agni and started walking towards him.

Droh picked his gaze and was a bit startled to see the approach of Agni's tall figure. But he quickly recovered himself and got back to what he was doing, the green metal armband signifying him to be a tracker shining brightly on his right hand.

"What is your name, tracker?' asked Agni. "Brahma," he muttered without looking.

"Look at me when I am talking to you," he barked at Droh. "Do you know who I am?" boomed Agni's voice in the kitchen. The other servants looked at them but they quickly got back to what they were doing when Agni gave them a stern look. Droh looked up, still unimpressed.

"My friends wish to learn a few basic techniques of tracking. So you will come with me and tell them what they need to know," said Agni.

Droh looked behind Agni with lazy eyes to see his friends, but when his gaze fell on Vrish and Bani, he stood up immediately.

"I am sorry Agni ji, I didn't recognize you at first. It will certainly be my pleasure to tell your friends what they wish to know," said Droh with a smile.

Agni smiled back, but quickly straightened his face and said, "Good, come with me." Droh followed him outside the kitchen.

ॐ

Agni, Vrish, Droh and Bani walked up to their room in complete silence, with Droh walking behind them as Brahma. Agni had gestured them to stay silent on their way until they were inside their room in the Guest's quarters. Bani gave occasional glances of affection to her brother, but Agni saw that Droh's expression never changed a bit. He didn't even look at his sister on their way back. Vrish opened the door of their room and all of them walked in. As soon as Vrish closed it behind them, Bani threw her hands around her brother and started to sob hysterically.

"I thought I lost you," she cried as her tears made wet patches on his vest.

"There, there, sweet little girl, I am fine and well," he said and lifted her face gently with his hands.

"I had even sent word to mother," she said as she looked up. The expression on Droh's face changed a bit.

"There was no need for that. You must go back and send her word that I am fine and there is no need for her to come," he said. Bani nodded her head like a child. "Good," said Droh. Then he looked at Agni. "So you are Agni. Vrish had told me a lot about you," he said.

"The same here," said Agni with a smile.

Droh sat down on the mat and said, "I presume it was you who thought it out?" asked Droh.

"Right," said Vrish before Agni could.

"Nice work," said Droh, "But how? What gave me away?" he asked with a smile on his face.

"The seal," replied Agni with a smile.

"The seal?" repeated Droh.

"Every letter leaving the royal compound always has the royal seal of the supervisor on it, that which cannot be used by the others," said Agni and showed him the broken wax seal of the great mountain with the river flowing down it's slopes.

"But you knew that already; you used it so that it would reach us unopened. The marker always stays with the supervisor and in order to use it, you needed to be inside the Palace's servant quarters. Moreover, the guards would have never looked inside the palace itself, so you choose it in the first place. You got the opportunity when Yani started recruiting more trackers, your arm band shows that much," said Agni pointing at his armband.

"You couldn't have sent the letter to Bani through someone else or the palace courier because that would have raised the question as to why a personal letter was being sent from the palace to the most infamous tavern of a wanted man. So you snuck out at night in order to deliver the letter yourself. You were to leave the city after that but something happened and you changed your plan and decided to stay and where better than the safety of the palace compound itself.

"But you couldn't sneak out like before for some reason and send word to Bani. Coming to us directly was out of the question as the trackers are not allowed inside the royal guest house or the royal quarters without the permission of the home guard. He, I am sure, would have recognized you at first sight even after you had made the slight changes in your appearance. This is what I think happened, but I cannot understand how you got hold of the seal. It is used only when every letter is officially sent out of the palace compound by a courier," finished Agni.

All of them were stunned. "And you figured this all out in just a few moments after I came in?" asked Bani.

"Pretty much," said Agni with a smile.

Droh was impressed and said, "You are every bit as intelligent as Vrish had told me. And as for the marker, there is nothing that a good amount of *sura* cannot do," said Droh.

"Thank you," said Agni as he nodded his head with a smile.

"You had us worried," said Vrish, as he came and sat down beside Droh. "What happened?" he asked.

"Yes, what happened brother? You said you were going to leave Himadri?" asked Bani too.

Droh leaned back on the cushions and said, "Do you have something to drink and I don't mean water?" Vrish got up and took out a cup and a flagon. He poured him some locally brewed *sura* and handed him the cup. He took a sip and relaxed, "Fine stuff. Let us get to business then."

Then he started to narrate the whole set of events, "The day Vrish came and told me everything, I started asking around. I met a man called Sashi; he acquires and passes on information for a price and we've known each other for quite some time. So I went to him and showed him the shell that Vrish had given to me. At first he didn't want to say anything, but after a little coaxing and some gold, he spilled it out. He said that there is only one person in Himadri who can make such things, an old woman named Krumi. I have written it down in the letter," he said pointing at it in Agni's hand. Agni nodded his head in approval and Droh continued his tale, "After a lot of asking around the next day, I came to know that the old witch lives someplace inside the forest of Seshnag and rarely comes inside the city. She has three sons and all of them work on ships and the port as hired hands." Then he shifted uncomfortable in his seat.

"I went back home and everything changed from the next day onwards. The next morning I went to the tavern and heard that the royal guards had come looking for me and there was also a reward on my head. I understood that Sashi or someone else had given away the secret. I understood what Vrish had said before about the King not wanting anyone to look into it. So obviously I had to leave." Agni understood that King Adhirath had come to know of this through some leakage in the chain. After all, the king had his spies everywhere, but Agni also knew that there was a slim chance that he and Vrish could be tracked down from this after Droh had pulled off that fine disappearing act.

"But, why the palace?" asked Bani.

Droh smiled and responded, "Remember what I always used to say to you sister? Always hide in plain sight."

"What about Dara? Why didn't you go to him?" she asked. Droh's smile was gone. "That bastard was trying to sell me out even after everything I did for him," said Droh.

"What?' she was shocked. "But Dara would never do that; he is an old friend of yours."

"Friend or foe, a hundred mudras of gold can change everything. I was going to send you word through him after I had left, but he was already there waiting with his friends. When I asked he said that for a hundred mudras he could sell his own wife, that bastard," said Droh as he spat on the floor in disgust.

"Then?" asked Bani.

"Then what? I escaped because of my amazing skills," said Droh with a smile. "Yeah right," she said and both of them started to laugh at once. That brought a smile on Agni's face, but Vrish wasn't smiling.

"I am sorry Droh. It's my fault. I should have never dragged you into this entire mess," said Vrish as he placed a hand on his shoulder. Droh stopped laughing and pushed it away from his shoulder instantly.

"And where was this bloody sense of modesty when you risked your neck for me and my sister? You could have turned back or refused to help after she was carried away by that scum. But you didn't, did you? And now you are saying all this when there is a chance for me to help you. Or do you think that you are better than me?" asked Droh angrily. Vrish seemed aghast by the sudden outburst.

"I didn't mean to...." Vrish began saying, but was interrupted by Droh before he finished.

He held him firmly by his shoulders and said, "That's what friends do. There is no place for gratitude or remorse. You have better things to worry about right now." Then he turned to Agni and said, "Agni, you are very smart for your age, but I must tell you one thing. This is a lot bigger than you or I can even imagine. So you two better be careful." Then he stood up and said, "But one thing I can promise, you two are not alone. I swear in the name of Trinetra that I will help you two, whatever it costs."

"It seems so," acknowledged Agni with a smile. Then he stood up and said, "And also I thank you for all that you've done till now." Vrish stood up and embraced his friend. Bani was also smiling to have been rid of her worries for her brother. It was a bit too dramatic, but Agni felt a sense of relief for now he knew for sure, they were not alone.

ॐ

Agni, Droh and Vrish walked towards the dock. After two days of constant search and using some of Droh's reliable contacts, they had come to know that Krumi's eldest son was named Bali. He worked on the ship called 'Ryau' which had docked a few days ago. Droh had drawn his hood for no one would ask anything as long as Agni and Vrish were with him. But still, he was not the one to take chances and rightly so. The docks were always bustling with different sorts of people in the morning. Travellers, porters and fishermen with their morning catch didn't leave much room for them to walk. They slowly made their way towards Ryau, anchored in the eastern end of the docks. The salty sea breeze was soothing even in the heat. An elderly man, broad of shoulders and short in frame stood guard over the wooden plank which seemed to be the only way in and out of the ship. They came to halt in front of him.

"What do you want?" he asked in his husky voice.

"We are looking for Bali," said Vrish.

"Which one? The tall one or the short one?" he asked again. Vrish was scratching his head and the man was eyeing him suspiciously. "The one with two brothers," said Agni quickly. The man looked at him. "Then it's the tall one you want," he said. "Bali," shouted the elderly man, "Someone is here to see you."

A few moments passed by as they waited for the man to show up. The one who walked down the plank startled Agni by his sheer size. He was a hand or two taller than Agni and double the size of Droh; his muscles were pumped and his bare chest heaved with every breath he took.

"The tall one? He ought to have asked the short one or the giant one," whispered Vrish to Agni as the man came down and stood in front of them.

"I will take it from here," said Bali to the elderly man who seemed like a child in front of him.

"All right," said the elderly man and went away muttering something under his breath. Agni understood that the man in front of them was the biggest and worst dog around there and it would be hell of a job to get something out of him.

"Were you looking for me?" he asked staring straight at them.

"Yes," said Vrish. "Your name is Bali, right?" It surprised Agni to see that Vrish never flinched for a moment.

"Yes, it is," said Bali as he eyed the trio suspiciously. "Why?" he asked.

"I have an offer for you," replied Vrish.

"What kind?" he asked. Vrish took out the metal shell and showed it to him. Bali's eyes lingered on it for a moment, but he forced them away.

"Not interested," he said plainly and started up the plank. "Hey wait," called out Vrish.

"Not interested," he barked as he made his way up the plank.

"Not even for this," said Vrish and took the pouch full of coins and jiggled it in the air. Bali stopped. He threw it at Bali who caught it in mid air. He opened the pouch and looked inside; the gold coins were reflected as a spark of greed in his eyes. He smiled at the look of it.

"There's plenty more from where that came from," added Vrish.

"What do you want it for?" he asked as he lifted his gaze.

"Not your concern," said Agni before Vrish could answer. The smile disappeared from Bali's face, he was staring at Agni. Agni understood that he was not used to being talked back like that, but he didn't care. The smile reappeared again.

"Wait here," he said and disappeared inside the ship. He came back with two other men, slightly shorter than him but looking menacing none the less.

"His brothers," whispered Droh in Agni's ears. Agni did not like it one bit; he was engrossed in thinking if it came to something violent between the two parties, then it would be pretty tough to get out. The three men stood in front of the trio. Bali was the first to speak, "Walk behind us and do not speak to anyone. We will settle the payment once we are inside the forest."

Agni became sure that Droh's information was correct. Vrish nodded his head. "Good, follow us," said Bali and the three brothers started to walk, closely followed by Agni, Vrish and Droh.

The Sun was high up in the sky, but they knew that there would be little light inside the forest, where their next step lay.

AN UNEXPECTED TURN OF EVENTS

It was already over two hours of the Sun and they were yet to see any cottage or hut or anything remotely close to a dwelling place. The sky was barely visible from under the canopy of leaves; they were deep inside the forest. Agni had guessed that they were at least two thousand or more paces away from the 'small gate'. Even the mud road had ended abruptly some time back and they were making their way through thick bushes and shrubs. The high humidity inside the forest was making them sweat profusely and Droh had taken off his hood.

"How much longer is it going to take?" Vrish finally asked.

Bali came to a halt. "You are right; this is far enough," he said and turned around. All the three brothers were smiling. Agni knew that something was wrong from the instant the mud road had ended.

"First tell us who sent you three jokers?" asked Bali. Agni's hand went instantly for the hilt of his sword. Bali noticed that and smiled to his brothers.

"The taller one is bringing out his sword. From the look of the hilt, I think it's not a cheap blade. I hate cheap things." said what seemed to be the youngest of the three. The other two started to laugh. Agni frowned at them.

"Look, he is frowning. Doesn't he look a lot like our old aunt?" smirked the youngest and the other two roared in laughter.

"Enough fun for one day," said Bali finally.

"Tell us who sent you?" Bali asked again, and this time with a deafening roar.

"You have your gold. Give us what we want and that'd be the end of the deal," said Vrish.

The three were still smiling. "That won't work now Vrish," said Agni, his eyes fixed on them. "He is not only the tallest of the three dwarves, but also the smartest," said the younger brother with an intimidating smile on his face.

"Now that you understand the situation, let me make this simpler. You tell us what we want to know and we give you three nice, clean deaths. It will certainly be less painful," said Bali.

Agni had a cruel smile on his face, "Do you even know what those things did?" he asked.

"It killed a few sea rats and whores, that's all. No big deal," said Bali plainly and the other two started to chuckle.

"No big deal," snorted the youngest of the brothers.

Agni's eyes were dark; Malini's scarred face floating in front of his eyes. "I was right about the three of you," he said and slowly took out his sword. The little light in the forest was dancing on the blade.

"Nice sword! Good of you to have taken it out for us," said the youngest one as he took a few steps towards Agni. Agni was as still as stone. Vrish was looking at his friend, his body seemed frozen but a flame lingered in his eyes. He had never felt such rage emanating from him before, even Droh seemed to have taken a step back. The air around him had turned hotter; there was something unusual about him. The man mocked Agni as he took small steps towards him, "Oh look, he is angry! Soon he will go on swinging that pretty sword of his." Then he came a little closer to him.

"Look," he said turning to his brothers, "His eyes are moist." Then he turned to Agni, "Are you going to cry, little boy? Did we kill someone you knew?" he asked with sneer on his face.

Bali was looking at Agni intently when he saw the fire in his eyes; he did not like it. He called out to his brother, "Shorty, enough! Come back here." But his brother paid no heed. "I am so afraid," the youngest one continued his act.

"Shorty," he shouted again. He danced closer to Agni, tilted his head sideways a little and then spoke in a very low voice, "Or did we kill some bitch you loved?"

Everything that happened after that took nothing more than a flash; the short man was engulfed in a black flame which came out of nowhere. He screamed and started to roll on the ground. Vrish was dumbfounded.

"Shorty," shouted Bali and ran towards his brother, quickly followed by the other one too. They tried to douse the fire with dirt and anything they could lay their hands on, but its intensity kept increasing. The man continued to scream the most horrible of screams Vrish had ever heard before, as he stared at him in utter disbelief. Agni didn't flinch for a moment; he seemed to have frozen stiff. Bali stomped on his brother, tried to cover him, did everything that he could but the fire kept raging.

Finally, he collapsed in front of Agni and started to cry. "Please," he sobbed. "Please, let my brother live; I will do anything you want," he pleaded but the fire did not stop.

"Please, we did not know what they were going to do with it, please," he begged and grabbed Agni's feet. His tears trickled down Agni's boots. Vrish was shocked to see the turn of events. He had set out to make everyone who had anything to do with the fire at the docks to suffer, but not like this.

"Agni, please snap out of it," Vrish said firmly. But Agni stood there, with Bali still at his feet. "Malini would have never wanted this," he said finally. His last words did something. The darkness in his eyes started to disappear. The fire started to subside slowly. The man had stopped moving by the time the fire had gone out. Bali ran to his brother and took him up in his arms. He was still breathing, barely. Droh stood at a distance.

"Help," pleaded Bali weakly. Droh started to walk towards them and Vrish followed. They helped him heave him up from the ground and on his shoulder. But Agni stood there, the fiery hatred in his heart had subsided after the turn of events. He slowly came to himself as tears came to his aid. His eyes were transfixed on the burnt figure. For some reason he felt so ashamed; his thoughts pondered over Malini and what she would have thought about him if she had seen him doing this to someone. Was he so different from them?

ဆ

Bali carried his youngest brother on his shoulder and almost ran towards the small hut inside the forest, barely a hundred paces away from where they were. Droh and Vrish walked beside them as Agni followed them from a distance. He walked in a trance, his eyes seeing only the forest floor covered with leaves.

"Mother, open the door," shouted Bali as he banged on it with his fist. An old woman, withered and thin, opened the door of the hut. Bali rushed inside, almost pushing the old witch away. She gave out a shriek at the sight of her youngest son.

"Who did this?" she asked Bali as she started to sob.

"Where is the salve?" he asked as he placed his brother's unconscious body on the floor. She pointed at a small almirah. Bali took out a small bowl from the inside with a white paste inside it. He opened his brother's mouth put some of it inside and started to apply the rest on his burnt body. "How did this happen? Who hurt your brother?" she asked as tears streamed out of her old eyes.

"It's all because of you," said Bali in a rage as he continued to do his work. "I told you repeatedly not to have anything to do with any of this. But your greed, your lust for gold," he said with gritted teeth.

"Who did this? Who?" she asked time and again, oblivious to all else around her, tears streaming down her old wrinkled cheeks. Vrish and Droh stood there at the door as mere spectators.

"He is outside," shouted Bali as he stood up. "He has the power of the dark fire," he screamed as he grabbed her by her shoulders. He shook her, "Don't you remember what you used to say, don't you?" He shouted. The woman looked stunned. Her tears had stopped.

"Where is he?" she asked again as if in a trance. Vrish and Droh were staring at each other; they didn't have a hint about what they were speaking. They only understood that it had something to do with Agni, yet for some unknown reason he felt a sense of dread which seemed to have overwhelmed him.

Agni was standing outside, the wind a little stronger in the open ground. His heart was heavy, yet his body was burning from the inside. The mere thought of what he had just done to that man made him uncomfortable. And more so because he didn't know how.

"Are you the one who did this to my son?" came a small voice from behind him. Agni turned and his eyes fell on the small frame of an old woman.

"How is he?" he asked. The woman was staring at him with odd mismatched eyes, her face gaunt and tired. Agni did not know if it was hatred or something else.

"What's your name?" she asked.

He hesitated for a moment and then steadied his voice to say, "Agni".

A faint smile spread across her face. "Suits you," she said. Agni stared at her blankly, not realising what she meant. "You seem troubled?" she asked tilting her head a little. Agni knew that he didn't know the old woman and yet in his heart he felt a strange urge to ask her the very question that was troubling him. She was smiling and staring at him, a cruel smile.

He wanted to restrain himself from asking but couldn't, "How?" he asked finally.

"How?" she repeated the word and started to cackle. The noise was harsh to his ears. She slowly started to circle Agni, "It's not how but when," she said. Agni followed her with his eyes. "You have no father, no mother, no brother, no sister and no one to love you, isn't it?" she asked. Agni remained silent. "You were born for a reason; a reason much greater than any earthly bonds. Your coming was foretold long ago." Agni could feel the sense of dread rising in his heart.

She continued, "The price we paid for foretelling your coming is too much to bear, yet we did, we did. But now you will pay us back with blood of the ones we hate, the blood of everyone, you will release us from our pathetic existence."

"I don't understand," said Agni.

She walked up to him slowly and placed a hand on his chest. "You are the one," she had a half smile on her face. "You will turn this world to ashes. I never stopped believing. And you will understand this with time." The smile on her face persisted; a few teeth she had left glistened in the Sun. Agni took a step back.

"I will do no such thing," he shouted.

She started to laugh. "It is destined,' she cried out aloud and her laughter continued. The cacophony echoed out in the woods.

ભ

Vrish, Droh and Agni trekked out of the forest. There was complete silence. Vrish and Droh had come to know from Bali that the old witch never saw the face of the man who asked it to be made or took the device from them. Her mother was asked to do it because such ancient arts were only known to a few. The device when activated by application of a lot of heat causes a raging inferno which chars everything around it until only ashes remain. The heat blast from one device activates the others. They wanted his mother to make four of them. The materials required to make those things was supplied to their mother by the captain of Ryau, the ship on which they worked. The money was also paid to their mother by a stranger, or that is what she said.

Their part was to make and supply the device and to help a man get on to Ryau unnoticed by the others on the ship, except the captain. Bali also said that they helped the man get on board after the fire at the docks. His face was completely wrapped and covered. But he swore that he didn't know when or where he got off; the ship never docked and came back after two days of waiting in the sea of Rishia near the desert of Khara. He said that the captain knew the rest and he was staying at the Pani Inn near the docks. He swore in the name of his brothers and the Trinetra that he knew only that much. Bali asked them not to bring his name up in all this as it would mean the loss of his life and the entire family. He said that he would make all arrangements to leave Himadri within two days and go to the Pari village in Anu, his mother's native place. The old witch had disappeared into the forest after her little encounter with Agni. But Vrish decided to keep it a secret from him. They had decided on visiting the captain of Ryau but the biggest problem remained, Agni.

Vrish and Droh gave each other occasional glances but not one of them spoke a single word. Whatever happened back there seemed like a bad dream to them. Vrish would look at Agni from time to time but he remained the same. Droh left them near the royal guest house and himself headed back towards the servant's quarters. Agni walked inside their room without a word and went to sleep, or so it seemed. Vrish blew out the candles. Agni lay under the blanket with his face covered, but his eyes were wide open. The old woman's last words echoed in his ears, "It is destined."

೮

Vrish woke up the next morning and found Agni's bed empty. He looked around and couldn't find him anywhere inside. He got up quickly and changed into a fresh set of cloths. He went out in the yard and started looking for Agni. He saw Agni sitting on a wooden bench on the eastern side of the yard. The sun still hadn't come out fully from the eastern horizon but its pale light partly illuminated the night sky. He went and sat beside Agni.

"What are you doing out here so early in the morning?" asked Vrish.

"Nothing," he replied sharply.

"Did you sleep last night?" he asked.

"A little," replied Agni. He looked sick and tired.

"What happened back there?" asked Vrish finally. Agni remained silent. Vrish waited for a reply, but none came. At last he stood up.

"If you feel like talking then you know where to find me," said Vrish and started for the room.

"I don't know," floated Agni's voice to his ears. "The old witch said," he paused for a moment and took a deep breath before adding, "She said that I will be responsible for the deaths of many." Those were not her exact words but Agni could not bring himself to tell the entire truth.

Vrish smiled a little. "And you believe what she said?" he asked.

"You saw what I did to that man," snapped Agni. Vrish had seen it with his own eyes, the man was charred like a piece of wood in a wild forest fire. He didn't say it but even he was stunned and scared. But all of it aside, he had ample faith in his friend and knew that the secret was buried in Agni's past life. His father had never told him or the others about Agni or where he had found him. Vrish had learned to ignore it back then. The incident in the forest had triggered the questions afresh. He knew his friend needed his trust and he was going to do it for him.

Vrish gathered his thoughts and replied to Agni's questioning eyes, "I did. But did you like what you did back there?"

"Don't be stupid," said Agni angrily.

"That's exactly what I mean," said Vrish.

"I don't understand,' said Agni.

"You never liked it and you never will. Hurting people is just not your thing. I have grown up with you, Agni, and I know what I am saying," said Vrish.

"But what if she is right and I do the same thing I did today, without even realising?" Agni finally said the question aloud to Vrish after having thought about it for the entire past night.

"Look, I am not so good up here like you," he said pointing to his head. "But I know one thing for sure – there is always a choice."

"Why do I have this, this thing, this power?" asked Agni.

"Now you want me to tell you the answers to everything," he said with a smile. It made Agni smile too. "Well, I think it's good," said Vrish. "I wish I also had some strange powers. Who knows maybe your real parents were the servants of the Light or something. I have heard they have such powers."

"What if it happens again? I mean it gets out of control?" asked Agni.

"Then you should learn to control it or carry some salve for others," said Vrish with a grin on his face. "Or you should make it sure that you lose your temper bedside a pond or a stream or something like that," bantered Vrish. That made Agni laugh.

"Jokes apart, Vrish. It's a fact that I don't feel the same anymore," said Agni as his face grew serious again. His smile was fading again.

"You can sit here and sulk all you want," Vrish said as he stood up. "But I know one thing," he said with a smile, "My sister never chose poorly. She judged people through her heart, not her eyes."

THE PRINCESS OF LEU

The kingdom of Leu was the third largest kingdom in its geographical area in the 'Alliance of the Setting Sun' after Athena and Erythrea. It was the neighbouring kingdom of Erythrea separated by the forest of Alexius and was the farthest in the north. Its walls extended to the foot of the Snowy Mountains and beyond its north gate lay the wastelands, land of the demons. The north gate had remained closed for five hundred years as the Knights of Leu guarded it with their life. The capital of Leu, the city, was the first city between the realm of men and the demons of the wastelands. The knights were called the keepers of the gate and defenders of the realm. It was said that in older days, scores and scores of demons came from the north and the Knights of Leu were the only ones to have stood between them and the other kingdoms. The gate was raised then to protect the realm of man.

King Crixus, the fourteenth king of Leu, chosen independently by the Great Council of Leu from the royal bloodline, had no sons like the other kings of the West but had a daughter, Lysandra. She was barely in her twenties and yet she was justly called the warrior maiden of Leu. The people of Leu looked up to her as their true queen, but the king knew in his heart that the Seven would never let a woman sit on a throne. He was growing older and frailer with every passing day. Soon the time would come for choosing a new king and he worried what would happen to his daughter then. It was not that he never had sons, but he lost them all to the Dark Guardians because of some damned prophecy made five hundred years ago. His mind told him that the Council would choose his brother's eldest son Demetrius as the next king. He favoured the younger one, Damianus who was also lovingly called 'Damian' by the King, not for the reason that he was his ward, but because he was the complete opposite of his elder brother.

The Kingdom of Leu had prospered under his rule, a pleasant place for him and the others to live, but he knew everything would change soon.

King Crixus sat on his throne lost in his thoughts. His once strong charismatic form was subdued by the weight of old age and he was only a frail image of what he once was. Illness had taken its toll and was continuing to do so every day. The court had been moved to the Senate where the chosen members of the council also sat. It was done so after the king fell ill due to an unknown disease and was deemed to be unfit to take care of the day- to -day needs of the kingdom. Only the royal sceptre remained in his hand, alongside a powerless chair once called the throne. He got up from his seat and headed for the balcony of his personal chamber; it looked over the city, or at least a part of it. He sat there in the open and the cold mountain wind made him feel light.

There was a soft knock on the door. "Come in, child," said King Crixus without even looking. Lysandra walked in. She had always wondered how her father always knew that it was her and whenever she would ask he would only smile and say, "A father always knows when his child is at his door." She had stopped asking a little while back.

"Father, I wish to speak to you if you are feeling well. It's a bit urgent" she said politely.

King Crixus stood up with difficulty. "Let us go inside," said the king as he walked back inside his room followed by Lysandra. She helped him to sit by the edge of his bed. He had not only grown old with time but equally frail as if he was withering away. It always saddened her to see him in this condition. He looked up at her daughter's beautiful face, the streaks of brown locks swaying gently with the morning wind.

"You seem troubled, my child," he said concerned.

She hesitated for a moment and said in a low voice, "I know you are not well, father, and I should be the last person to disturb you but…." She paused. King Crixus smiled and held her face between his palms.

"You are that one person whose presence shall never disturb me," said the king. A thin smile spread across her face. "Now tell me, what's bothering you?" he asked.

"Demetrius wants us to abolish the duty of the eastern ports. He says that the Abode has been our ally and friend for a long time and we should refrain ourselves from imposing taxes on the trade routes of the holy city as they are our most valuable ally," said Lysandra.

"This is sudden," were the only words that escaped the king's mouth.

"But that would mean that the kingdom's revenue going down by a fifth," said Lysandra. King Crixus' brows were furrowed.

"What does the Senate have to say in this?" asked the King, he had not been to the place for over a year.

"You know what they have to say, over fifty of them are with Demetrius," she replied in an irritated voice.

"Then there is little choice," said the King finally. Lysandra was a bit taken aback.

"But father, this is not right. The cost of maintaining the Gate has gone up from last winter and another will come soon," she protested.

"You can do nothing here Lysandra. No one can go against the decision of the Senate," said King Crixus.

"But you can father, can't you? The people of Leu will suffer for this. Pass a royal decree and I will go and pin it on Demetrius' head," Lysandra said angrily.

King Crixus knew that his house was already in troubled waters and if he did what Lysandra was asking of him, then the council might ask him to step down sooner than expected. Then his daughter would be left alone amidst all those schemers with a few by her side. King Crixus placed a compassionate hand on her shoulder and said, "Lysandra! You are as brave and strong as any man who will be chosen by the council to sit the throne after me, but you must understand that it will not be you. Let things take their own course. Let the people have the Senate."

"The Senate is corrupt, father, and you know that very well. And it will stay that way until the likes of Demetrius are ousted from it," said Lysandra.

"And you know that will never happen. Then a new king shall come," said King Crixus.

"Yes, that will be after a long time and we still have the time we need," said Lysandra. King Crixus didn't want to tell her daughter that it might be sooner than she expected.

"Maybe or maybe not," said the King. "But what I truly want for you is to have a good life. Let everything take its own course, do not try to force it. Do not walk this path Lys, you will only find thorns on it."

Lysandra looked into her father's eyes, "I will never let anyone unworthy to sit on your throne, father. That I swear," she said and left the room abruptly.

King Crixus saw her daughter walk out of the room, the pain in his chest was back. But the pain of uncertainty was the only thing that made him sweat that morning.

⚃

The debate on the abolition of duty on the eastern ports, Alexandria and the small ones alike, raged on. Princess Lysandra had gathered the heads of the trade unions and the labour lords in favour of keeping the taxes. The morning session was a heated one. The heads of the unions and labour lords had threatened to halt all kind of trading activities all through Leu if the proposal was passed by the Senate. The abolition of duty meant higher taxes on their earnings as well the earnings of the common people of the kingdom. Lysandra walked out of the Senate hall after the session had ended for that day with Damian at her side.

"The way things are going, we might soon get the upper hand Lys," said Damian with a smile.

"There is no question of might. We certainly will," Lysandra said with a broad grin on her face.

Damian was about to say something but stopped abruptly. They had come face to face with Demetrius, who was also coming out of the Senate hall through the next door. He was surrounded by his aides.

"Ah, Lysandra and my brother! How have the two of you been?" he asked in a jovial voice. The buzzing around them stopped instantly.

"You are in our way," said Lysandra coldly.

"Am I? Do you mean literally or…?" He smiled. Lysandra didn't say anything.

"Anyway, I am hurt sister. We might be rivals inside the Senate, but definitely not outside. We still share the same blood and a bond, remember?" said Demetrius with his persistent smile.

"I share no bonds with the likes of you," said Lysandra angrily.

"Tisk, tisk! If we were on the same terms, it would have been so much easier for you and me," said Demetrius. His men stared at each others' faces.

Lysandra smiled out of sheer curiosity, "If you want to be on the same terms with me, then all you have to do is change your terms," she said. Damian smiled. A few of Demetrius' bootlickers smiled too and it did not escape the corner of his eye.

Demetrius took a step forward, "If only you were a man, I would have given you a proper answer but alas, that you can never be, irrespective of how much you pray for it," he said with reproach.

"Hold your tongue Demetrius, our sister is the Princess of Leu and she is not less than any man, forget the likes of you," said Damian angrily.

"That we can't know unless we pull that shabby garb of her," said Demetrius and the lick spits behind them started to cackle. Damian's hand instantly went for the hilt of his sword but Lysandra put a firm hand on it.

"You be careful with that brother; it's not a toy anymore, you know," said Demetrius eyeing his brother's sheathed sword with half a smile on his face.

"Her name is Eugene and you must remember that. Someday she might have your tongue," said Damianus angrily. Lysandra's people were pouring out of the hall through the gates.

"Is there something wrong, Princess?" asked Torman from a distance as he got out. He was the General of the Army of Leu.

"No, we were just having a little brother-sister talk. We were just leaving," replied Demetrius in her stead. He gave a formal bow to the Princess and started walking, but on his way he whispered in Damian's ears, "You are a fool and father knew it, too." Damian turned around, his rage pouring out of his eyes. In the meantime, Demetrius gave a wink and turned the corner.

Lysandra heard that and swore to herself as his shadow vanished round the corner, "I will never let you sit on the throne, Demetrius. I promise."

ଔ

The next two days saw chaos in the Senate as many debates raged therein. What could have been a simple discussion was turned into a show of strength from both sides. Lysandra's cause was more potent than the other.

Lysandra and Damian stood outside the door of the Senate hall with Demetrius on the other side of the corridor. The matter was finally put up for vote. She stood still and occasionally glanced at Demetrius. He stood there firm and confident. He would give occasional glances at Lysandra and would smile whenever their eyes met. That made her blood curl. She offered silent prayers to the maker of all for she had no faith in the Seven. There was a sudden uproar from the inside of the hall from the other side of the door. All the members and commoners except the parties directly involved were allowed inside during the vote and the count. The doors flew open and Torman walked out with a broad grin on his face.

"The count is seventy-six to seventy-four. You have won by a margin of two," said Torman. Lysandra almost leapt in joy and hugged Damian. Her supporters were already pouring out and congratulating her. Lysandra looked sideways where she could see Demetrius, his face grim as his band of bootlickers came out with their heads lowered. His confidence had evaporated into thin air. He walked up to her slowly as was the custom to offer his congratulations.

"Well done sister, it seems that you have won," he said with a fake smile on his face. The crowd had gone silent.

"Thank you . . . brother," she said after a pause. "See, it doesn't always depend on whether you are a man or a woman, it depends on how much of a man you are," she said with a pinch.

Demetrius' smile disappeared. "This does not end here," he hissed and started to walk.

"And brother," called out Lysandra. "I have heard that you are good with your tongue in other things. The next time, learn to use it more inside the Senate hall." The crowd burst into laughter. Demetrius clenched his fists as he walked away.

"Well, it is time then to celebrate this victory," shouted Damian. The crowd echoed his words.

"Beer and sausage," shouted one of them.

"Dancing with pretty maids," shouted another.

"Let us bring our wives too," said one of them, the shouting stopped abruptly. "Someone throw him out," said the one beside him and the others started to laugh.

Lysandra was smiling. She had not felt this good in a long time. She knew that it was a small victory, but a victory nonetheless. She was not alone. There was still some justice left in Leu and the Senate had not been corrupted entirely. There was still hope.

"Thank you," she whispered softly to the Maker. But among all the joy and the happiness, little did she notice that every step she took was being watched by a figure lurking in the shadows. The more steps she took, the closer it came.

THE END OF THE TRAIL

Two days had passed since the episode in the forest. Agni had returned to his old self, again after much persuasion from Vrish and Droh. He had finally decided to forget the incident as a whole. But now he felt a strange sensation that he was more alive, his senses were keener than usual. There was one thing which had started troubling him more than it ever had – his past. He always knew that his real parents were not from Himadri and Briksha had found him in some small port up north near Chakragarh but he never said anything about his parents. What Vrish said about his parents possibly being the servants of the Light seemed far-fetched if he was actually found where Briksha had said. Briksha, Vrish and Malini were a lot closer to him as friends. Althought he was King Adhirath's ward, he was not treated by him the way Briksha did – like a sort of equal, despite the difference of their age.

He had never known any place except Himadri. He recalled how Malini would come back from her trips and would tell him of the marvels of the outside world. He always wanted to head out to those places but Adhirath ji would never give him permission to travel. With Yani's hunting party, he was supposed to step outside Himadri for the very first time. He remembered how once he had told Malini about his desire to go to the outside world in search of his real parents. Malini had promised him that they would do so as soon as they got married and he gets out of the shadow of the King. But that could never happen. That very thought brought back the strange pain in his heart. It was so intense that it made him feel like screaming. He wished to find his parents and tell them all about Malini, who she was and how she loved him. But first, he needed to finish what had been started by the cycle of fate. First, he needed to avenge her death.

The gust of wind brought him back to reality. They were heading for the inn Bali had mentioned. Agni had been so pre-occupied with himself for the past two days that he never asked the name. He knew Vrish knew the place so it didn't matter much. They had to wait for the last two days as Droh had informed them that the captain had left the inn for some reason. But since Ryau was still at the docks, they knew he'd be back. Droh had informed them last night that the captain had returned to the inn.

They had missed their first chance to meet the captain the day after they came back from the woods. The captain had left the evening after. But nothing was lost and they were sure to find what they were looking for. Droh could not come as he was sent for some official tracker duty which he had to do to avoid drawing attention. Agni wondered how Droh was faring as a tracker. From what he knew, Droh knew very little of tracking wild animals. But he also knew that he had an uncanny ability to handle a situation.

"We are nearly there," said Vrish. Agni didn't respond.

"Are you all right?" asked Vrish. Agni hated being asked the same question over and over again for the last two days, especially when Droh and Bani were around. Bani had come to see him after she heard about the whole thing from Droh. Agni was annoyed with Droh to have shared that episode with Bani. The carriage was moving at a fair speed, heading towards the docks.

"Where is this inn?" asked Agni. Vrish remained silent.

"It is that same inn," replied Vrish. Agni was stunned for a moment. He had decided that he would never go to that cursed place again, least of all at that moment. The carriage screeched to a halt in front of that same dreaded place. A small board hung by the window with 'Pani' written on it in blue and orange. Agni's eyes instantly went to the narrow mud road that went to the other side of the inn to that same cottage. The very place where Malini had taken her last breath a few days back. For a moment he wanted to turn around and run away. But instead, he forced his eyes away.

"Let us go inside," said Vrish, his face grim. They opened the door and entered the main hall. The place was just as shabby and still had an odd stench to it. It almost made him puke.

"What can I do for you?" asked the keeper as he scurried towards his prospective guests, his only guests.

"We are looking for the captain of the Ryau," said Vrish as he covered his nose with the back of his sleeves. The expression on the old keeper's face changed immediately.

"The captain has asked me not to disturb him; he has some important guests upstairs," said the old man. Vrish smiled.

"Thank you and don't worry old man, we will do all the disturbing ourself," said Vrish as pushed him away gently and started for the stairs.

"It won't take long," said Agni quickly and followed Vrish.

"Hey stop, it's not right. The Captain told me, please," pleaded the old man as they climbed the stairs.

The stench was a little less up there. There were three large windows facing the sea opposite to the three doors. Two of the doors lay ajar expecting guests while the third by the corner was closed. Vrish and Agni went for the third one.

"Should we barge in?" asked Vrish whispering softly.

"The keeper said that he has guests with him; we don't know how many," said Agni.

"We should knock first," said Vrish and gave gentle tap on the wood. There was no reply.

"Do it again," said Agni. This time Vrish knocked on it a lot harder and kept at it for some time, still there was no reply. He knocked for the third time and still it did not open.

"Maybe he is sleeping, or he is in the washroom or something," said Vrish turning to Agni.

"The old man said that he has guests. Something is wrong," said Agni.

"Could be that kind of guests," said Vrish, smiling.

Agni's face was humourless, "From what the old man said, it doesn't seem like that. On the count of three," said Agni. Vrish nodded his head and they positioned themselves with their shoulder facing the door.

"One, two, three and push," said Agni and both of them threw their weight on the door together. It clanked open from the hinges and fell flat on the floor. A gust of wind met them. The window was open. The Captain lay on the bed, his eyes wide open and the white bed sheet smeared red with blood.

Vrish went near him and placed a finger near his nose without touching him. "We are too late," he said as removed his hand.

The keeper had come running up the stairs, "What's going on?" he shouted but when he saw the captain, he screamed.

"Shut up, old man! No one will hear you out here," barked Vrish. The caretaker was about to flee, but Vrish caught him by the shoulders. He tried to set himself free but Vrish was too strong for him. Agni stood there, his fists clenched. The final piece had been removed and it was all because of him. If he had not wasted valuable time that morning, they could have been here before it all happened. The symbol had been of no use. The track was lost for good - Bali had left the city and the captain lay dead.

"The trail ends where it all started," thought Agni to himself. He started to laugh, the hysteria too much for him to bear.

∞

Agni and Vrish were sitting by the window, their eyes glued to the gates of the royal compound. Agni had ordered the gate keepers to let Droh visit them whenever he wanted to. They were waiting for his arrival. Droh had gone in search of Bali after they had told him everything that had happened inside the inn that morning. Bali and his brothers were the only persons who could tell them if anyone had come to them after they were gone and was he the one who had informed them that Agni, Vrish and Droh were looking for the captain. Agni and Vrish wanted to go with him, but he had wanted to work alone, as he always did.

"There are a few places in Himadri where the Raja's wards are known," he had said to Agni when he had insisted on going with him. He was thinking of how they had found the captain in a pool of blood and their escape from there in time. They had to pay the inn-keeper a considerable sum to keep his mouth shut and to get rid of the body after they left. It was their good fortune that he did not recognize them as the King's ward. They had sworn in the name of Trinetra that they did not do it but from the look on his face, Agni knew that he never believed them. Still he took the gold and promised to do all that was asked of him. The sum of five hundred mudras was his five years' worth profit and he knew that a captain of a small ship would not be missed much. The old man, while taking the gold from Agni had said, "I do not know if you two are telling the truth; nor do I wish to know. All I know is that this will be put to good use in my daughter's wedding." He had smile on his face. That was all the conviction Agni needed.

"I am getting worried; he should have been here by now," said Vrish. Agni had been thinking of the same thing. Vrish stood up and stretched his arms and legs.

"Droh can take care of himself," said Agni.

"I know that," said Vrish. "But with all these things happening around us, it makes me worry more these days." Agni couldn't agree more. He knew that Bali's hut was inside the forest but a few bell hours journey would have been enough to cover it. He will not be able forgive himself if something happened to Droh.

The sudden knock on the door made him jump. Vrish looked at Agni. "Could it be him?" he asked. "I didn't see him coming," replied Agni and there was a second knock.

"Who is it?" asked Agni.

"It's me, Drake," came the voice from outside. Vrish opened the door and Sir Drake walked in with a smile on his face.

"I hope I am not disturbing you two?" he asked with an open air of courtesy.

'No, of course not. Please have a seat," replied Agni.

"No, no. I have come here for a reason. Prince Yani wanted to see you two. He couldn't find any servants at this hour so I offered myself in his service. He is waiting for us in his room," said Sir Drake. Agni thought that for a man of his stature, he seemed to be a much simpler man and devoid of ego and over-estimation of oneself. Agni looked at Vrish, who seemed much annoyed by the unexpected summon at that hour, especially when they were waiting for Droh to return.

"Surely, let us go then," said Agni as he stood up and they walked out of their room. Vrish followed them reluctantly.

"So, what does he want from us now?" asked Vrish. Sir Drake seemed mildly surprised by Vrish's question.

"He meant that it is unusual for him to call us at this hour," said Agni and gave Vrish a stern look.

"I understand," said Sir Drake with a meaningful smile. "It is truly unusual to call on someone at this hour but you know Yani much better than me. He wanted the three of us to see a painting he has made, his first work of art. But first he will show it to his father and then our turn shall come."

"Great," said Agni but he wasn't half as excited as he showed. Vrish wasn't pleased at all. They turned the corner and heard raised voices.

"Stop wasting your time in all this, you will be a Raja one day not a painter," came King Adhirath's angry voice from Yani's room.

"But you can at least see what I have made for you," said Yani angrily.

"Yani, don't you know why I am sending you to Nisarga? The time is ripe. If you can impress the daughter of the High Senator then can you imagine what will happen. The bond between our small kingdom and the might of Nisarga will raise Himadri to new heights. Yet you waste such precious time in trivial things as this," said the King. Yani was silent. "For once, make me proud," he finished. There was a brief pause.

"What do you want me to do father?" asked Yani, his voice an armour of icy courtesy.

"We better come back later," said Sir Drake.

"Right," said Agni, he felt pity for his friend. The trio headed down the stairs.

"It is not my place to say this, but I must. This is no way to treat one's son," said Sir Drake with a hint of anger in his voice. Then he turned to Agni and asked, "Has it always been like this?" Agni had never seen King Adhirath embrace his son, after he was nine or less. That also happened when Yani tamed a wild horse that the stable hands couldn't.

"More or less," said Agni. Sir Drake was shaking his head slowly.

"So much pressure can leave deep wounds," he said with reproach.

"What about you Agni? What do you think of the King? You are his ward and Vrish too," said Sir Drake. Agni had no proper opinion. King Adhirath was always generous with his gold but not with love or care.

"He is a good king," said Agni.

That made Sir Drake smile. "I see," he said.

"Let us go and sit in the garden for a moment, then we shall head back to Yani's," said Sir Drake. Agni hesitated for a moment, he himself wanted to head back and see if Droh had returned. It meant a lot more to him than making Yani happy.

"Don't worry, it won't be long. I have been here for over three weeks now and the most the King stays in his son's room is less than half a bell hour," said Sir Drake. Agni had no choice, he nodded his head.

"I think I should head back, I am not feeling well," said Vrish promptly.

"Why? What's wrong?" asked Sir Drake.

"It's my head. It's hurting bad," said Vrish as he touched his head, trying to put up a little show.

"Shall I call the royal practitioner?" asked Sir Drake.

"No, no. I will be fine. I just need some rest," he said as rubbed his forehead. "I will take my leave."

"Certainly, take care of yourself. I will let the prince know when we get back," said Sir Drake in a concerned voice. Agni refrained himself from laughing.

"Thank you," said Vrish and started to walk.

"Well, he is the smarter one, isn't he?" asked Sir Drake, smiling behind Vrish's back. Agni couldn't stop himself from laughing any longer. He was beginning to understand why Yani had come to like that man so much in such a short time.

 egg

It was already the middle of the night when Agni came out of Prince Yani's bed chamber. He had been itching to get out of there. He wanted to head back and see if Droh had returned, whether he was successful in finding Bali or his brothers. He still had the symbol and what proved ineffective here may be of great worth in Nisarga, that is what he had been telling himself all day after they got back. A timekeeper roamed about in the night announcing the arrival of the seventh hour of the moon in a hushed voice for the few who were still awake. Prince Yani had announced to him that they would leave for Nisarga the next morning, which made him panic a little. If it all went well then he would have to leave Vrish behind and go to Nisarga by himself. The Prince didn't show them any painting and never spoke of any hunt. Agni knocked on the door of their room and to his great relief, Droh was the one who opened it. He was now known as Brahma, a close friend of the King's wards, so the guards were not a problem anymore.

"You got us worried," said Agni as he placed a hand on his shoulder.

Droh's brows were furrowed yet he had a smile on his face, "Do you think I cannot take care of myself?" he asked.

Agni smiled back, "I have ample faith in that," he said and both of them walked inside after closing the door behind them.

"Took you long enough," said Vrish, in a bad mood for some reason. Agni spared him a glance.

"We have to leave tomorrow and as a tracker, you have to come along, Droh," said Agni.

"That's just great, nothing happens as planned," said Vrish angrily.

"Well, its better this way," said Droh. "There is nothing left here."

"You didn't find Bali, did you?" asked Agni.

"No," replied Droh. "I went to his hut and it was empty. So I went to the south gate and I described Bali to the head sentry and asked whether a man as such had passed by. At first, he didn't want to tell. But a little token of gratitude made him speak. It proved to be bloody useless. He said that no such man had passed the gate since the last seven days and he was even willing to show me the records. Then I went to the docks to give one last try. I met a few sailors on Ryau and asked them if they knew anything about the reason of the ship not docking and if it carried any cargo or not or anything they knew of that voyage that might prove useful to us. Most of them repeated what Bali had said that the ship came back from mid sea. But one sailor said that another ship with white sails and no name came by in the middle of the night two days after they left, and some of the cargo was transferred to that ship by the captain. But he insisted that the ship was a pirate vessel and that is why it had no name on it," finished Droh.

He sat down on the cushions and said, "I am afraid to say this but the trail ends here."

"It has been ended," said Agni angrily as he slammed his fist on the wall.

"Don't give up hope; we still have that symbol, the one Vrish said we are going to search for in Nisarga," said Droh. Agni knew that Droh was correct. They had told Droh about the symbol, but not the connection to theory of origin. Droh knew how to read and write, but that was it. Vrish seriously doubted that he had ever read a single book in his entire life. So that part was mostly overlooked and it was on Agni to search for it.

Agni nodded his head, for he knew they still had the main clue. A tough one, but he would go to any lengths to solve the riddle. Agni was about to ask Vrish whether he wanted to go to Nisarga or not as there was nothing left there.

But before he could say anything, Vrish stood up. "Then we better start packing. There is no use for me to stay here anymore," he said and walked towards the small almirah. Agni had a thin smile on his face.

"Next time we will be extra careful," said Droh.

"There might not be a next time, my friend," said Agni turning to his new friend, as uncertainty lingered in his heart.

THE JOURNEY BEGINS

The next morning, the whole castle was abuzz with activity. The servants ran around preparing all the wagons for departure. The departure was fixed with such suddenness that the servants had started their work from the middle of the night. The sun was shining brightly now, but they were still at the preparations. Even a few days back, Agni would have found this arrangement surprising. Forty servants, almost fifty drivers for the wagons and carriages, one hundred and fifty men at arms, ten of the King's guards, twenty trackers and scouts, five medicine men and two royal practitioners. Agni, Vrish, Prince Yani and Sir Drake formed the hunt party, but it could easily be called an army. The wagons were loaded with herbs, spices, incense, exotic silks, costly jewels, chests of gold, different types of dresses from different lands and other essentials for the journey, i.e. meat, ghee, vegetables, fruits and rice. Agni and Vrish stood there as the head servant checked all the items that were to be sent with the Prince. The caravan seemed ready. King Adhirath stood by the large window overlooking the castle grounds.

"Everything is in place Agamji. We are ready to leave," said the head servant to Agam, the captain of the royal guards.

"Good," replied Agam.

"Agamji, how many days will it take for us to reach Nisarga?" asked Agni.

"Seven days of the Sun and seven of the moon, not more I guess," said Agam. He had known Agni and Vrish ever since they were children. He was also their first tutor in the practice field. He was the one who taught them how to hold a sword.

"Wow, that's a pretty long journey," said Vrish.

"It would have taken us not more than two or three days if there were only horses. But with this many wagons, we will be slowed down considerably," said Agam.

"Then we should start for its already the third hour," said Agni looking at the Sun dial.

"We should have started a long time back," said the elderly man, clearly annoyed. "But you know..." he stopped. "Here he comes," he said as they turned to see the approach of the Prince alongside Sir Drake. Yani was dressed in white silks with golden flowers embroidered on his vest, the slacks and the cloaks were also made of silk with matching white high boots. Sir Drake was dressed in the colours of his house, satin green vest with white pants and thick leather boots. For the first time Agni saw his sword, the kind of which was not used in Himadri, a long sword with a blade twice as long and twice as broad as a normal blade, even the hilt was much longer and broader. It was strapped around his back.

Prince Yani carefully made his way towards his horse, his unusually long robe making it difficult for him to walk. But he made it without tripping over. Paksha was following them from a distance.

"Are we ready?" he asked cheerfully.

"That we are, Prince," said Agam with a bow.

"Agni, Vrish and Sir Drake! Let us begin this wonderful journey," he said enthusiastically. All the three of them smiled and nodded their head in unison. Prince Yani walked towards his horse. "Where is Droh?" asked Agni in a hushed voice to Vrish.

"He is with the other trackers at the head of the column, he said that he will find us once we reach Nisarga," replied Vrish in a whisper.

Prince Yani placed his foot on the stirrup and was about to put the other round the horse when he slipped. Paksha was holding the reins and he quickly placed his palm under Yani's slipping foot to give him support and break the fall. There was a cracking noise as he did that, as if something broke.

"Are you all right, Paksha?" asked Yani upon hearing the sound. Then his eyes fell on Paksha's hand. Paksha was holding the wrist of his right hand as the little finger of the same hand had turned ninety degrees to the wrong side due to the sudden pressure of Yani's boot.

"Someone call a medicine man," shouted Yani in anxiety.

"I am all right, Prince; no need of that," said Paksha and twisted his broken finger in the right place. "See," he said to Yani's utter shock.

"How did you do that?" he asked still staring at his hand. Paksha started to laugh, "It's a trick," he said.

"A bloody good one," said Vrish.

"Truly," said Sir Drake. "I have seen people mend dislocated joints that way but never a broken finger before. I heard it break clearly, someday you got to show me how you did that."

"Someday," said Paksha with an air full of pride. Agni was much impressed himself. Paksha gave him a sly look as he went past him. Agni had learnt long back that Paksha didn't like him much, but he never paid much heed to it. He knew some people have issues, and Paksha was surely one of them.

Drums were beaten as the caravan started rolling. Agni, Vrish, Yani and Sir Drake took their positions at the head of the column for the people of Himadri to see. Droh, meanwhile, followed them on his horse along with the other trackers. Yani looked back at his father as they left and waved at him. King Adhirath only raised his hand in a kingly gesture. Thus the journey started.

ca

The Palace of Leu was built atop Mount Atlas under the supervision of King Crixus in his youth. He always used to say that a king must be able to keep watch over all his subjects; that's why he sat in the tallest chair. Princess Lysandra sat by the flowers of the palace garden. The wall around the garden was low and on the other side of it was a sharp drop. The whole city could be seen from that point. She used to sit there with her father and Damian when she was a little girl, and her mother was a part of it till she lived. It was her place of memory, joy and remembrance.

"Lys, I have brought you some tea," said Damian with a smile. Damian was her paternal cousin, but as against his elder brother Demetrius, he was chosen as the King's ward when he was an infant. King Crixus had always treated him like a son and she had, like her brother. He had always walked behind her from a very tender age.

"Thank you, brother. Have you been to father's chamber this morning?" she asked. Damian nodded his head. "How is he?" she asked.

Damian shook his head and reported, "Not good, his body is becoming weaker every day."

Sadness crept up on her face. King Crixus had taken ill a few years back but it had turned more serious now. His condition had continued to deteriorate drastically from then as hundreds of practitioners from all over the west had come and gone. The royal practitioner only gave him milk of poppy to soothe his pain as nothing else could be done anymore.

"Don't worry, Lys. We will certainly find someone who can cure father," said Damian as he placed a reassuring hand on her shoulder. He sat down beside her.

"I will not rest until father is well. I am going to Nomantia after a few days. I have heard of a great healer there who can cure any kind of diseases," said Damian.

She just smiled, "You are a good man, Damian, a good son and a good brother. I will find you someone equally good, I promise," said Lysandra without thinking.

The smile disappeared from his face. "Some things are not meant for some people, Lys, and you know that," he said. Lysandra was silent; she didn't mean to hurt him.

"I better go and see what Torman wants from me. I heard from the servants on my way that he was looking for me," said Damian and stood up.

"All right," said Lysandra. He gave a curt bow and left. She knew that Torman was not looking for him but her brother went looking for something else, solace.

慓

The caravan was making fair progress. Within two, days they had crossed the river Sheetaldhara and had entered the forest of Aadhar which was two days' journey from Brahmadesh.

The farewell from Himadri was grand and hundreds had gathered to watch them leave, most of them wondering why a simple hunting party comprised over two hundred men and fifty wagons. For those who knew, it was an instance of Adhirathji's wish to keep things under wraps to spare Yani the humiliation if he failed. Agni was still unsure why he was being dragged along; he never complained as it served his purpose well.

The journey after that had been quite mundane as Agam had forced them to march till nightfall for the past two days. On the third one, Yani refused to take his meal inside his wagon. He had ordered the servants to roast fresh lamb with herbs, spices and honey and make rice pudding with cinnamons for everyone.

Agni, Vrish, Sir Drake and Yani were lying on a cushioned mattress in the middle of the forest. The soldiers were also resting. Some of them had taken their armor off, a few took a dip in the nearby pond while some of them played dice, betting the little gold or silver they carried with them. Agni saw a few young men of his age flirting with the maids. Everyone was enjoying themselves in some way or another.

"Now, this is what a journey should be like," said Yani. "Good food, beauty of the forest and the sound of laughter."

Vrish heard him but he was enamoured by the roasting meat and its tantalising fragrance. "Can I go and see if it is ready or not?" he whispered in Agni's ear.

"You better go and bring Droh here. This is a good time to acquaint him to the others so that he can ride with us," Agni whispered back. "And also, let me do the talking," he added.

"Right," said Vrish, a bit let down.

"Yani and Sir Drake, I would like you to meet our good friend Brahma," said Agni to both of them.

"Certainly," said Sir Drake.

"Is he with us, I mean right now?" asked Yani stupidly.

"Yes, he is. He is a tracker and a good one at that. I had recruited him myself before the start of this journey," said Agni.

Yani sat up straight, "And you didn't tell me this before. Your friend is my friend Agni. Send for him right away," he said.

Agni gestured Vrish to go. He was about to stand up when Agni said, "Oh and also, Vrish would like to go and see if the meat is ready or not. I hope you don't mind Yani?"

Yani gave him a glance. He seemed to be annoyed with him for the last two days for some reason. "All right, if you want him to," added Yani. Sir Drake was smiling. Vrish didn't mind the icy look, he seemed very happy with it.

"Thank you," he said to Yani and left in a hurry, but Yani didn't respond.

"You should have told me earlier, Agni," he said after Vrish left. "The poor man had to travel at the top of the column for the last two days, when he could have travelled with us inside the wagon if he wanted. He must have saddle sores by now."

"Quite a few," added Sir Drake. Agni smiled, he always liked Yani for his sensitivity and yet he sometimes disliked him for the very same reason. Yani leaned back again, "The feast is a good idea, but there should be something more," he said more to himself as he gazed at the open blue sky above.

"Ah, there comes your friend, Agni," said Sir Drake. Agni turned and saw Vrish coming towards them, followed by Droh. "He is quite a big guy for these parts," said Sir Drake, who himself hailed from Erythrea.

"I agree," said Yani as Droh came and stood in front of them. "I will be right back," said Vrish even before Agni could say something. He almost rushed towards the temporary kitchen.

"Prince," said Droh giving a curt bow as Agni had taught before the start of the journey.

"He is the friend I was talking about. Brahma," said Agni and then he turned to Droh and said, "Brahma! Everyone knows Prince Yani. The brave knight to our left is the famed Sir Drake of Erythrea."

"Sir," said Droh and gave another curt bow. For a man of his background he was much graceful.

"Enough with the courtesies already," said Sir Drake with a smile.

"Please sit with us, Brahma," said Prince Yani. "I have told Agni that you have my permission to travel in the wagons from time to time. You are my best friend's friend after all," said the Prince showing his generosity at the first chance.

"Thank you very much, Prince Yani," said Droh, pleasantly surprised.

"Why are you still standing? Sit," said Yani.

"God bless your honeyed tongue," Droh whispered to Agni as he sat down beside him.

"Brahma, you seem to be an intelligent man," said Yani. Droh didn't know how to react; he had been called many things in the past, but never intelligent.

"Tell us, how we can find some entertainment around here?" he asked. Agni looked at Droh; he knew this was his best chance to seal his place. He scratched his head a little and said, "Fighting and drinking are the best things from where I come from."

Yani sat up, "That's a very good idea. Why don't we hold a few fights among the men? That way we can have some fun and the winners get five mudras each. One can challenge anyone he wishes to," said Yani enthusiastically.

"But with the blunt practice swords, the ones we have brought with us for our practice. Bruises are better than blood," said Sir Drake aptly.

"Right," said Yani and then turned to Droh. "Good thinking, you will make a fine companion," said Yani with a smile. Droh had a broad grin on his face.

"Agam," he shouted and the old man came with swift steps.

"Yes, Prince?" he asked after a formal bow.

"Tell everyone to get ready. We will hold a few fights before the meal. Anyone can challenge anyone and the winner gets five mudras," said Yani.

"Yes, Prince! But is that a good idea; things could get out of hand," he said politely.

"That's an order, Agam," snapped the Prince.

"As the Prince wishes," said Agam and walked away displeased. Yani didn't bother to give him a second look.

"Finally something exciting," said Yani as he stretched his arms.

☙

The Sun was high up in the sky, barely visible as dark clouds gathered around it, making it partially dark. Three ships were sailing towards Alexandria, the second largest city of the Kingdom of Leu and the largest port of the west. The sails caught the wind and it seemed like a storm was heading that way. A stout man draped in white and hooded stood on the deck. The sigil of a grey beast on the sails rippled with the wind, the same symbol was engraved on his breast plate and stitched on his cape.

"We are nearing Alexandria. Shall we dock when the time comes, my lord?" asked the Captain of the ship.

"No, we are to wait between the sea of Fortuna and Aeotolia. Do not cross their border until the word is sent to us," said the man.

"As the Lord wishes," said the captain and stepped back, his head bowed in respect.

'If all goes well, we shall have the door to us without lifting a finger,' he thought to himself. 'If not...' a faint smile marked his face.

PRINCE YANI'S TOURNAMENT

Apart of the open space inside the forest was cleared of weeds and shrubs. A ring was made by wooden pikes marking the borders. The idea of earning five mudras made them rise with enthusiasm. An entire hour of the Sun had passed by the time all the preparations were done. The ground was levelled and a cushioned mattress was placed a little away from the ring for the Prince and his friends to sit on. Agam was to oversee the fights and judge the winner along with the Prince and his friends. The maids and the others had already started gathering. Prince Yani came and sat down on the mattress with Sir Drake beside him. Agni, Vrish and Droh were standing near the Prince. Agam was already inside the ring.

"The rules are simple," anounced Agam, "There will be friendly fights and they will be fought with practice swords and nothing else. No one is to carry any other weapons with them, no low cuts or skull bash and if the opponent surrenders the other is to step back immediately."

Then he turned to the men and said, "The one who breaks the rules will have to deal with me." Agni was impressed by the old man's self-confidence even at that age. Agni knew that Agam was nicknamed as 'the artist' as he was said to fight with such grace that it was a sight to look at. Agni had been witness to one such tournament in Himadri, and he couldn't have agreed more.

"So who shall come first?" asked Agam.

"I," shouted a large man, strongly built and darker of skin than others. He walked inside the ring with great confidence. The small crowd cheered for him.

"What is your name?" asked Yani.

"My name is Kalki, Prince Yani," said the man.

"And whom will you like to challenge?" asked Yani.

"Jarwa," he said pointing to a man on the other side of the ring, tall and lean.

"Do you accept the challenge, Jarwa?" asked Yani.

"I do, Prince," said the man and walked inside the ring. The crowd went up in an uproar.

"Very well, pick your swords," said Yani pointing at the practice swords piled in a heap beside the ring. Both of them picked up one sword each, they were all of the same size and width.

Agam walked between the fighters and said, "You two know the rules; fight strong and fair." Both of them nodded their heads but their eyes were fixed on each other. Agam looked at Yani.

"Let the battle begin," he shouted and walked back. Both of them started to circle each other slowly. Agni watched them carefully. He had also entered in a few tournaments, big and small, in Himadri and had won only one. But he also knew that people and competitors considered him to be a good swordsman for his age.

The first attack came from Jarwa. He rushed towards Kalki and made a vertical swing, but Kalki took a single step back and let the blade miss him by inches.

"Nice foot movement," said Sir Drake more to himself, totally engrossed. Agni agreed, for a man of his size moving faster than a leaner opponent was much difficult, so precision in movement was the key. Jarwa quickly spun around and went for his right flank but this time the blow was deflected by Kalki's blade. Jarwa continued to push on but Kalki only parried his attacks.

"The broader one is a much better swordsman; he has a much cooler head than the leaner one," said Sir Drake to Yani.

As time passed, Jarwa's speed was slowing down due to the exhaustive rush attacks. Jarwa stepped in for a piercing blow but Kalki spun around quickly and grabbed his sword hand with his left and then he dashed the hilt of the sword on his cheeks. Jarwa spurted out blood and reeled back a few steps. If Kalki had chosen to use the flat of the blade, the match would have ended then and there. But it seemed he wanted it to continue. Sir Drake could not control his excitement. He stood up and started to clap. The crowd cheered for Kalki, as he stood there smiling. Jarwa rubbed his swollen cheek violently and spat out more blood.

"They are taking this rather seriously," said Vrish.

"They are after the same girl," said Droh. "See, that one," he said pointing at a fair maid standing on the other side of the ring.

"Women are always the cause of strife," said Sir Drake sighing.

Yani smiled and asked, "Is this the reason why you never married, Sir?"

"I have had my share of good luck and that was enough for me," said Sir Drake, smiling back.

Agni didn't agree with Sir Drake but it was not his place to say so.

Meanwhile, the battle raged on inside the ring. Kalki had started his barrage of blows on the visibly weakened Jarwa. Kalki had landed some very heavy blows by then and Jarwa was getting weaker by the second. Kalki charged in and gave him strong body bash, Jarwa was on his knees. Kalki swung the blade in a loop in his hand and walked up to him to end it. "Do you give up?" he asked first.

"No," said Jarwa with a smile. Kalki lifted his blade in the air and was about to land the final blow when Jarwa threw a handful of dust in his eyes. Kalki was blinded for a moment when Jarwa swung his sword with all his strength and landed a devastating blow on his left ribs, the spot turned blue instantly as Kalki gave out a scream. Everyone stared in disbelief as Kalki fell down on his knees.

"That's cheating," shouted Vrish.

"No, Vrish," said Sir Drake coldly, "It is not against the rules to use your surroundings to your advantage. But you can say that it's not an honourable way to fight."

Jarwa was looming over Kalki who managed to block most of his blows with his right hand, but Jarwa never gave him a chance to stand up. He gave a strong kick on his jaws and he rolled over. Kalki was lying face down on the mud. "Stand up," whispered Agni to himself but Kalki did not move. Jarwa threw his hands up in the air but the crowd had gone silent. It was all over, thought Agni. But he was astounded to see the bleeding and bruised Kalki push himself up with the help of his blade. His groans became louder as he straightened up. The crowd roared in joy at the spectacular sight. Even Jarwa looked at him in disbelief and admiration. Agni saw that the girl was smiling and offered a silent prayer with folded hands. Agni understood that they were on the same side.

"Truly amazing, never seen such a spirited man before," said Sir Drake. Agni thought of telling him that it was something else but he didn't as he knew that he would never have understood.

"Kalki, Kalki, Kalki," the crowd started to chant as Kalki covered his bruise with his left hand. Jarwa started to circle him. Agni saw Kalki gripping his sword firmly, realising that the next blow would decide the victor. Jarwa rushed towards Kalki's injured side as he knew that he would be a lot slower that way, he swung his sword again. Kalki did not move, and to Agni's surprise, he took the full blow on his left forearm. In turn, he smashed the flat of the blade right across Jarwa's right cheek. The blow was so strong that the blade cracked as it sent Jarwa flying away. He crashed on the ground with a thud and blood oozed out of his mouth and ears as he lay there unconscious. Kalki didn't use the blunt edge of the blade as the sheer force of the blow would have cut through his opponent's face and it would have meant Jarwa's death. He could have done that easily and yet he didn't, even after being cheated. That spirit made Agni clap, a true warrior's sprit. Agam went closer to Jarwa and knelt down beside him, he was still breathing.

"We have a winner," said Agam as he pointed towards Kalki. There was a huge uproar and several poured inside the ring to greet the victor.

"Truly amazing, truly," said Sir Drake as he continued to clap. Prince Yani stood up and the crowd fell silent. Kalki stood with his friends in the middle of the ring as Jarwa was being carried out by the medicine men.

"Well done, Kalki. If all the warriors of Himadri were like you, ten would have been enough to defeat an army of thousands," he said, and the crowd greeted his words with applause. "There is no one more worthy here to have earned this," he said and threw him a pouch.

"There are ten mudras in there, the extra for your bravery," said Yani and Kalki bowed down to show his appreciation for the Prince's gift. Agni saw that Kalki walked towards that girl with his mouth twisted in pain, she threw her hands around him. He thanked the Maker in his heart that it ended well for them. Agam walked inside the ring again after sometime.

"We have witnessed a great exhibition of strength and endurance a few moments ago, but one good deed must follow the other. Who shall be next?" he shouted and the crowd roared in anticipation. Agni was already feeling tired of this, but he knew that it was going to be a long day.

og

Princess Lysandra was standing outside the door of her father's chamber. King Crixus had a visitor, a hooded man draped in white, bearing the mark of the Seven. Damian was also with her.

"It's been too long since that man went inside," said Lysandra in an agitated voice.

"Shall we go in then?" asked Damian.

"Sometimes I think I have the same brother I had ten years back. Of course not, it's against the custom of hospitality and we are royal blood," said Lysandra.

The door banged open and the hooded figure walked out and passed by without sparing them a glance. Lysandra didn't care. She went inside immediately with Damian on her heels. King Crixus was sitting on his bed, the pale rays of the Sun glistened on the edges of his shadowy figure. He looked distraught.

"Are you all right, father?" she asked.

King Crixus tried to smile, "I am fine, Lys. Come, both of you, sit by me," said the King. They sat on the edge of the bed on either side.

"What did the man want?" she asked.

"Not much. Nothing for you to worry about," said her father. Lysandra was a bit surprised. It was the first time in her life that her father was willing to keep her in the dark about something she had asked.

"As you say, father," said Lysandra as her gaze dropped. He lifted her face with his trembling hands, "Don't misunderstand me, Lys. Some things are better left unknown, but I assure you I will tell you later. It is not that important though."

"Right," said Lysandra trying to smile. King Crixus was staring at her daughter's face, "It was a blessed day when I saw your beautiful face for the first time, my child," he said. Then he turned to Damian and said, "And you are the son I always wanted to have of my own blood and yet you have proved yourself to be nothing less. I know that you are truly worthy of my crown and you love your sister very much. I know that Leu would have enjoyed it's lasting peace for more years to come if you sat the throne, but believe me son, it is not in my power to give you that." Damian was pleasantly surprised. He had always seen King Crixus to be the man who would love unconditionally. Though he had proved so with his deeds, this was the first instance of expression in words.

"Don't say so, father. I know someone as worthy as you will sit the throne of Leu after a long, long time, for now it belongs to the worthiest king of all and will continue to do so for many more years to come," said Damian.

"I doubt that Damian," said the King. "Maybe that is why you should have been the perfect choice."

King Crixus looked outside the window. "After Alicia left us, you two have been my treasures," he said. "Now I am old and frail and can do nothing to shield you two or give what you truly deserve," said the King with a sad smile on his face. There was a drop of tear in his old eyes. Lysandra quickly wiped the tear away, her eyes moist too. She had never seen her father cry.

"What is wrong father? Why are you saying such things?" she asked hugging his thin frame which once was the envy of all the men of Leu.

"Nothing, nothing," he said trying his best to smile. "It's a beautiful day outside, isn't it?" he asked.

"It is, father," replied Lysandra still staring at her father's face. King Crixus tried to stand up by himself, his condition deteriorating with every passing day. Damian helped him up.

The king took in the mountain air. "I wish to go outside," he said. Lysandra and Damian were shocked. He turned to them, "Why don't we go to Old Riley's like we used to?" he asked with a smile. They looked at each other's faces with broad smiles. The moment of sadness had vanished like the wind.

"I will let Torman know immediately," said Damian and rushed out of the room. Lysandra offered a silent prayer to the one above for it'd been over a year since her father had wanted to step out of the palace.

"Help me choose an attire worthy of a king," said her father. Lysandra nodded her head, trying her best to hold back the tears of joy.

ଔ

The fifth fight was on in the forest of Aadhar, but none of rest as good as the first one between Kalki and Jarwa. The fire seemed absent. It turned to be more of a practice session rather than a real tournament. Yani was starting to get bored and Agni hoped that he would end it soon.

"And we have a winner," shouted Agam. The victor came up to Yani and he tossed him the pouch without even looking. The man gave a curt bow and left.

"Maybe we should have our meal now Yani?" asked Agni.

Yani gave it a thought and said, "Yes, you are right Agni. This has lost its charms." Agni was about to get up.

"Wait," said Yani and sat up straight. Agni looked and saw that Paksha had walked inside the ring. He had championed the last two tournaments in Himadri and three others in the cities of Nada and Anu. Agam was staring at him and then he walked up to him and asked, "What are you doing Paksha? Don't you remember what I said?"

"I do but I thought that some harmless fighting was a good way to work up ones appetite," he said smiling at his commanding officer. Then he turned to Yani and said, "I am sure that the Prince wouldn't mind."

"Of course not," said Yani, mildly excited again. None of the Royal Guards had participated in those fights before him and now as he had, it was bound to be a good one. Agam stood there, glaring at Paksha, but he didn't dare speak against the Prince.

"And whom do you want to challenge, Paksha?" asked Yani.

"Him," he said, his fingers pointing straight at them. Yani was a bit confused, "Who?" he asked again.

"Agni," said Paksha with a smile on his face. Agni was smiling himself. He had known it the moment Paksha had stepped inside the ring.

"You are joking, right?" asked Yani, his voice hinting anger.

"No, Prince. I mean it. You said so yourself that anyone can challenge anyone he wanted to," said Paksha to Yani, but his eyes were fixed on Agni.

"Paksha, know your limits. You cannot challenge Rajaji's own ward," said Agam in a threatening tone.

"Hm, if he doesn't have the stomach for it, then I will challenge someone else," said Paksha, "while he watches and learns." He added with a smile.

"Paksha," shouted Agam angrily. There was complete silence.

"No," said Agni as he stood up, "I will fight him," he said. A broad grin spread across Paksha's face.

Yani quickly pulled him by his sleeves, "You don't have to do this. Agam will deal with him," he said anxiously.

"Yani is right, Agni," said Vrish.

"Let him fight if he wants to, it's not a duel to the death," said Sir Drake. Yani gave him a sharp look, for the first it seemed that Yani was offended by Sir Drake' comment.

"I will be all right, Yani. And Sir Drake is right; it's not a duel to the death, so don't worry," said Agni as he slowly took out his sleeve from Yani's grip.

Vrish looked on, discomfort clear on his face. The crowd started to cheer as Agni walked towards the ring, more for Paksha than for Agni.

"He is weak on his left," said Agam in a hushed voice as Agni was passing by. That made him smile, Agni halted for a moment beside him.

"Thanks, but isn't that unfair?" he asked, the smile still playing on his face.

"Just come out of there in one piece," said Agam without even looking at him, his eyes on Paksha. On the other hand, Paksha was grinning at the old man. Agni understood that he wanted to avoid a disaster at all costs for he was given the charge by King Adhirath to lead that caravan safely to the city of Nisarga.

"Right," replied Agni and walked inside the ring followed by Agam. Vrish and Droh were standing beside Yani and Sir Drake with tensed faces.

Paksha cracked his knuckles, "I have waited a long time for this," he said with that same persistent smile on his face. Agni never understood why Paksha hated him so much. They stood there in the middle facing each other. Agam brought him a blunt blade while Paksha had already picked his before he entered the ring.

"Agni, are you ready?" asked Agam.

"Yes," replied Agni, knowing it was going to be a hard fight as Paksha was famously called 'the clinical finisher'.

"Paksha, no cheap tricks," said Agam turning to him but the latter didn't bother to reply.

"You two know the rules. Now begin," said Agam and stepped back, but did not leave the ring.

"I am going to enjoy this," said Paksha as he took his stance.

Agni took one step back and gave a gentle blow to his right, which was deflected with ease. Paksha didn't attack. He was so deeply basked in his self-confidence that he was grinning and standing still. This time Agni moved to his left. Paksha made another swing and missed, but it seemed that Paksha moved a lot slower than before. Agni understood that

Agam was right. He moved in to his left and then rushed in with full force but Paksha swung around and aimed a low cut to make him trip. Agni leapt over it and dodged it, barely.

"No low cuts," shouted Agam but Paksha paid no heed and aimed another blow on his ribs in a sequential three-sixty-degree move. Agni dodged it too by a sort of half vault; the crowd cheered.

"Good move, Agni," shouted Sir Drake, his eyes shining. Agni landed on his feet but Paksha was too fast for him. He followed his move and rushed in, the hilt of the sword was dashed in his guts even before Agni could get his footing. That made him lose his balance and the crowd gasped in horror seeing Agni was falling on one of the wooden pikes that marked the border of the ring. He tried to shift his body weight on the other side to dodge the pike, but wasn't able to do so completely. The sharp thing slid close to his left shoulder, piercing his flesh and turned that portion of his vest red immediately.

"Agni," shouted Vrish. Then he turned to Yani and said, "Please stop this match, Yani, Agni is hurt."

"No," roared Sir Drake, "It is against the pride of a warrior. It will shame him for his whole life."

Yani was staring at him, but Sir Drake' eyes were fixed on Agni. Agam looked at Yani, it seemed from his look that he also wanted to stop the match but Yani remained silent and then he raised his hand. Paksha was about to charge Agni when he heard Agam's voice, "The match is over. Paksha, stop!"

Paksha stopped abruptly, his smile vanished and his face got twisted in rage. His eyes pinned Yani for having stopped the duel in between.

"No," shouted Agni as he stood up. "This isn't over yet, and I shall fight it to the end," his gaze was fixed on Paksha, the same rage rising in him slowly. The smile reappeared on Paksha's face. Agni's shoulder was bleeding and the crowd erupted in a roar of applause at his words, "Fight, fight, fight," they started to chant.

"No, Agni," said Agam strictly, "You cannot go against the decision of the Prince." "Yani," shouted Agni, "Give us the permission to continue." The crowd was still chanting. Yani looked helplessly at Agni. Then he gestured them to continue and the crowd's cheering resumed.

"Good, it seems that you are not a coward after all," sneered Paksha. "I thought you would give up."

"In your dreams," replied Agni angrily.

Agni took his stance and this time Paksha began circling him. 'Control your anger, don't let it cloud your thoughts,' he repeated to himself as he followed Paksha's step from the corner of his eyes. He knew one other blow like the previous would end the match. Paksha rushed in suddenly, surprising Agni for not having aimed at his bleeding shoulder, but for his ribs instead. Paksha was almost on him but Agni did not move, 'wait for it, wait for it,' he could hear Agam's voice from the practice sessions. And there it was, the right moment. Agni swung around, ducking his head a bit like a dance move and let the blow pass over his head. He used his own blade and placed it aptly between Paksha's moving legs, making him lose his balance. He thanked Agam in his heart for having taught him the trick. Paksha slipped and fell on the ground, face first. He lost his grip on the hilt and the sword fell a few paces away from him. He rolled over and was about to grab his sword but Agni was quick to put the blunt edge of the blade on the apple of his throat by then. The crowd was stunned, so were Vrish and Yani. But Sir Drake was smiling.

"That's enough, Paksha," said Agni, his breathing heavy but the blade still held firmly against his opponent's throat.

"We have a winner," shouted Agam instantly, without even looking at the Prince. Paksha gritted his teeth and gave a piercing glance to the old man. The crowd had come out of the trance by then.

"Agni," shouted one of them and the others roared for the unexpected winner.

Paksha stood up slowly, staring at Agni with disgust in his eyes. "This does not end here," he said and walked away. Agni started to walk, Agam rushed to him and grabbed him by his shoulder allowing him to lean on him; the support was welcome. "Someone call the practitioners," shouted Yani.

Agni was losing a lot of blood, his vision was getting blurred and his breathing was heavy. After that, all he could remember was Vrish's panic-stricken face looming over him and Yani's voice, "Where are those bloody practitioners?" Yani was shouting at the top of his voice.

THE KING'S FINAL REQUEST

The Lord of the Light sat on the decorated chair of his solar. His hood was not drawn. He gently stroked the armrest of the chair, the soft fur passing through his fingers. The man had a gaunt face and all his hairs had gone grey, yet there was a fire in those purple eyes. There was a gentle knock on the door.

"Come in," said the man as he pulled down his hood. A man walked inside the room and gave a curt bow.

"My Lord, Raven has sent us a message," said the fourth of the Lords, Aqua.

"What does it say? Has King Crixus agreed to our terms?" he asked. Aqua hesitated for a moment, "No my Lord, he hasn't. It is just like you had said."

"Then it's time," said the Lord of the Light. "Tell your puppet to do his part and if all fails, send word to the Beast, he knows what has to be done."

"As the Lord commands," said Aqua and started for the door.

"Remember, Aqua," said the Lord and the figure stopped abruptly, "The third option is our last, our last resort if all else fails. We still have some time."

"Yes, I understand," said the man with a smile on his face. Whatever the others might say, this was the very reason he still had respect for the Lord of the Light. He was different from the other Guardians.

"You may go now," said the Lord. Aqua gave another bow and left the room, closing the door behind him.

The Lord of the Light was staring at the shattered pieces of a shield that lay encased on his table in a box made of glass. He closed his eyes. The torment would end soon, he thought, and finally that, for which he had waited for so long, would be his.

෧

The Sun was high up in the sky by the time they were nearing 'Riley's corner'. It was famous for its exotic treats and mulled red wine. The King had insisted on riding by himself instead of taking the carriage. They had him straddled on Lightning, his faithful courser. The beast knew the touch of its master and had appreciated it by licking the King's hand. The royal entourage riding out of the palace after a year or so was a rare and great sight.

"Open the gates," Damian had called out as they started their march followed by the ten crimson guards and knights of the house like olden times. The sigil of the lone warrior standing guard with his spear in his hand was flying high in the sky as the wind acknowledged its presence.

"It's an honour," said old Andre as he had pushed open the gate with the help of his son. The servants had gathered at a distance to watch their beloved King march after such a long time. King Crixus had a faint smile on his face but there was also a hint of grief which escaped Lysandra.

The mighty horn was sounded and the pedestrians on the King's Road stood stunned. They saw the column appear out of the bend of the Great Rock, led by the three. They parted to make way as their eyes fell on Lightning trotting down the undulating path with the King on its back. The shopkeepers came out leaving their wares behind. King Crixus with Lysandra and Damian on both sides walked the memory lane again.

"How are you, Eddy?" asked King Crixus to an old shopkeeper, standing to their left.

"Wonderful my king, it's a, it's a...." his words were choked in his throat as his eyes got moist. He quickly threw his fist in the air and shouted, "Long live the King."

"Long live the King," shouted another. "Long live the King," slowly the chant was taken up by all and it vibrated to the very core of Leu.

The Sun was nearing the end of its journey west by the time they had walked inside Riley's Corner. Old Riley was ecstatic to see the King again after such a long time. He knelt down to show his respect and eternal gratitude, for everyone in Leu knew that Riley would have died of hunger if the King hadn't come forth on his royal steed and asked his men to take him to the royal healing house. The King had even given him some gold to set up his little 'corner'. The King and the other two took the same place in the small garden on the edge of the steep fall looking over the river Tiara. The name of the river had been taken up by the locals for the nature of her course; the river came down from Mount Agnes forming a half loop near the top like a tiara.

King Crixus was staring at the open space beyond the fall, the mountains, the plains and the extended city on either side of Tiara with the high walls guarding it from the outside world.

"She is such a beauty, isn't she?" asked the King, his gaze transfixed on the city below. The table in front of them had three glass bowls on it filled with sweetened yogurt mixed with nuts and crushed apples, their favourite.

"Yes father, she is," said Lysandra with a smile.

Damian also had a smile on his face. "It's been such a long time since we have been here together," he said.

"Yes, it's been a long time and soon it will turn into another beautiful memory," said the King as he shifted uncomfortably in his seat.

"Is it the pain again?" asked Lysandra.

"I don't know which one, there are so many," said King Crixus smiling. Lys' smile was gone because she couldn't bear to see her father in such a condition.

"But there is one joy in growing old," said King Crixus, "It is to see that he is leaving behind such wonderful things like you two to remember him by and memories which will last forever."

"It will be after a long time, we still have many memories to make," said Damian quickly.

The King smiled and then he took their hands in his own, "I know you two love me a lot," he said. "But it is an undeniable fact that I am growing older and the last day may come sooner than expected." Lysandra was about to say something but the King continued, "So that when I am gone you can tell your children and the love of your life how we were here together and how much we loved each other."

Lysandra and Damian were both stunned. "Father, don't worry so much. You will be with us for a long time to come, and you can tell our children yourself," said Lysandra trying to put on a smile.

"No, Lysandra," said the King sternly. "The truth is that my days are numbered." He looked her into the eye and said, "I want to see you happy and settled before I leave."

Lysandra was silent. Then he turned to Damian and said, "And you Damian, you are my son and I have loved you like my own. I want the same for you. It is unwise for a man to linger in his past." Damian dropped his gaze.

Then he gave out a deep breath, "Soon a new king shall sit the golden throne and then there shall be…difficulties," he finished.

"I am not ready yet father, neither is Leu," said Lysandra helplessly.

"Leu will find a new defender like she had done before, and for you, always remember that marriage doesn't shackle you like you think," said King Crixus. "I married your mother when I was your age and she was much younger than you, and we had our share of difficulties and happiness alike. We used to lean on each other for support, and that is what marriage is." Lysandra was incessantly scratching the wood of the table with her nails.

"My last wish is to see you two married and settled in life," he said finally. There was a brief pause.

Lysandra gave out a deep breath and said, "Father, I have not yet found a man who can understand me and share my life; but if this is your wish then I will oblige." Her voice trembled a bit as she finished.

"Me too," said Damian, his face was grim.

"Good, you two have made me happy, like always," said the King as he leaned back on his chair.

They had barely touched their food, Lysandra and Damian. She knew that even the sweetness of the yogurt couldn't keep away the bitter taste in their mouth. She knew that she wasn't ready yet and it would be too late before Leu finds a new defender.

CB

The throbbing pain in his shoulder woke Agni up. At first he couldn't see anything, his vision was blurred. Then slowly it all became clear. The flame of the candle flickered inside the tent. He tried to get up from his bed but the searing pain made him flinch and he slumped back again. His left hand was numb and the bandage had turned red from the effort. Then he saw someone approaching. It was that same maid he had seen around the fighting area cheering Kalki. She saw Agni with his eyes open, drenched in sweat.

"You are awake, how are you feeling?" she asked in an ecstatic voice.

"What time is it?" asked Agni, his own voice sounded peculiar to him.

"It's already night, but that you can see. Can't tell you the exact hour for there are no bells here," she said it so fast that Agni couldn't catch the last bit.

"Water," he said hoarsely, his throat was parched.

She poured some water in the goblet beside him and helped him sit up a bit. She poured it down his mouth but it spilled all over him, yet a little that made its way down his throat made him feel good. His thirst was quenched for the moment.

"You lie down. I will go and call the others," she said as she helped him lie down, her smile was never gone.

"What's your name?" asked Agni.

"Abani," she replied.

"Thank you for the water Abani," said Agni. She was a bit taken aback.

"You are most welcome, Agniji," she said as a broad grin spread across her face. She seemed to be much younger than

Agni and very high in sprit. She spared him a second glance as she left.

Agni lay there, gazing at the roof of the tent in the dim light. The pain in his shoulder was subsiding but it still throbbed a little. A few moments passed and the head practitioner Aamod entered tent, closely followed by Yani and Vrish.

"How are you feeling now?" asked Aamod as he started unwrapping the bandage.

"You got us all scared for a moment there," said Yani in a concerned voice. Vrish stood behind them staring at his friend. He had a look of relief on his face.

"No need to worry, it's just a small wound," said Agni with a smile.

"I beg to differ, Agni ji. The wound may look small, but it isn't. Your shoulder was partly dislocated but we have fixed that. There was considerable blood loss too. It surprises me to think that you stood your ground after this happened, or so I heard," said Aamod. "I didn't see it myself, but I must say that it was both foolish and impressive," finished the elderly practitioner with a smile.

"Much more impressive than foolish, I must say," said Sir Drake as he walked inside the tent. "It is the way of the warrior and I would have expected nothing else from the man of whom the Prince speaks so highly." Sir Drake placed a tender hand on his shoulder, "I hope you are feeling well now," he asked smiling.

"Better," said Agni.

"Good," said Sir Drake, "I am sure you will be up and at it in no time."

"No Sir, I think otherwise. It will take some time to heal fully," said Aamod as he finished changing the bandage.

Vrish was still standing there. "He needs a lot of rest," said Aamod as he stood up straight.

"Then we better let him have it," said Yani before anyone could say anything else.

"Right, get well," said Sir Drake and turned to leave with Yani and Aamod with his side.

"Everyone out now," said Yani. Agni knew that his words were for Vrish, but Vrish was still standing there.

"Yani," said Agni, "I would like Vrish to stay back for some time."

Yani looked back. "All right, he can stay," said Yani coldly and left the tent followed by the others.

Vrish came and sat by the edge of the bed, "The maker only knows what his problem is," he said in an irritated voice. "Anyway," he said and turned to Agni, "How are you feeling now?"

"For the third time, good, better," said Agni. Vrish was staring at him. "It was a stupid thing to do," he said finally. "Paksha has always been like that and I can bet all my gold that he will stay that way. But you should have let it pass," said Vrish. Agni didn't reply.

"Where is Droh?" he asked.

"He was waiting for you to come around but then he was sent for the first watch," replied Vrish.

"Anyway, Paksha is being sent to Nisarga before us as Yani's messenger to the Senate. I thought you should know," said Vrish.

"And whose idea was it?" asked Agni.

"Yani's, of course," replied Vrish. "He said that he will speak to his father about Paksha when we return to Himadri."

It won't matter much, thought Agni. Paksha was always the King's creature. He was always in his favour, no matter what. But it didn't matter to Agni as he was used to those things by then and he was sure to beat Paksha every single time he tried something again. He remembered his face after he fell down, that made him smile.

"What are you smiling for?" asked Vrish.

"Nothing," said Agni. "I was just wondering why he hates me so much. I can't remember doing anything wrong to him."

Vrish rolled his eyes and said, "Next you will be asking why King Adhirath's face is always grim."

"You should not waste time in petty things," Vrish said it like the king and it made Agni chuckle. Vrish was smiling himself.

"Some things have no reason behind them, it's simple," he said. Agni never believed that, there is always a reason behind everything, he thought.

"Anyway, you should get some sleep now. It's getting late," said Vrish as he stood up and stretched his arms and legs. Then he yawned and said, "I better get something to drink, or else these darn bugs won't let me sleep all night."

"You do that," said Agni. For a moment he thought that a gulp would have soothed his pain also, but he didn't say it out loud.

"Sleep tight, brother," said Vrish with a smile.

"You too," replied Agni. Vrish left the tent and he himself felt much tired even after all that sleeping. The dull ache was never fully gone. He closed his eyes and unlike Vrish, drifted slowly to the oblivion of the dream world.

 G3

"This is bullshit," shouted Torman as he banged his fist on the desk. The council had gathered there in the Senate hall that morning along with other members of the Senate after the news of a holy law being passed in Aine by the Abode of the Seven. The law stated that henceforth the Abode would decide on the right of ascension to the throne of Leu. The alliance had also supported their action.

"The right to choose their king belongs to its people, not some old bags of bones sitting on the high chair at Aine," shouted Torman. Lysandra had never seen him so angry, but her own anger was raging in her heart. "This means war," said Torman hotly.

"Be careful of what you say, General. It's the Seven holy Lords you speak of," warned Demetrius.

"To hell with your lords boy, they are threatening us with war if we do not oblige. My scouts report three of their battle ships in our waters. They will strike as soon as we send back the word that we have not accepted their terms," retorted Torman.

"First, they take our Prince and now they want the throne. I say, enough is enough. We won't stand by and let them do whatever they please," he shouted.

"Hear, hear," said almost all the members except the ones who stood by Demetrius. Lysandra was staring at her father's empty chair in the centre of the hall. King Crixus hadn't occupied it for over a year and his condition had greatly deteriorated after their little trip to Riley's.

Demetrius stood up. "My fellow members of the council and the Senate alike, I understand your sentiments. But do know this, if we defy the will of The Seven, Leu will not face one enemy but many. The combined strength of the West will be against us. Do we have the strength to stand against all of them?" he asked. The crowd became silent. Lysandra knew what Demetrius was saying was true. The oldest of the council members as well as of the Senate, Agapito, stood up slowly.

"I understand what you say is correct, Lord Demetrius. But to give up our right is to give up our freedom. The Abode is our ally, not our master. We cannot stand by and let them do whatever they wish. Moreover, the most surprising fact is that they have not given us a proper reason for their actions," said Agapito.

"Then what do you propose?" asked Demetrius with a smile. "Do we take up arms against such an overwhelming force and let our kingdom burn instead of bending our stiff knee? It seems wisdom does not come with age," mocked Demetrius.

Agapito's brows were furrowed, "You never knew how to hold your tongue like your insolent father, but we will not bear it anymore," he said angrily.

"So you wish for war, is it?" shouted Demetrius letting the slight pass.

"I never said that. War is our last option," said Agapito.

"But if it is inevitable, then there is little choice," added Torman.

Demetrius started laughing, "Do you all hear what our old and wise friends have to say? They want us to go to war with the Seven. The Seven, the strongest force on Gaya." He said turning to the other members of the council. The crowd started to murmur again.

"That's exactly what we want," came Lysandra's voice at last. The crowd became silent. She walked up to the centre and stood there facing the others.

"Revered members of the Senate and council alike, let me ask you one thing. What does the council and the Senate of Leu stand for?" she asked. They remained silent.

"Freedom," she said. "Freedom of its people. Leu was built from scratch. Her people survived on the rugged land, tilled the soil and laid it brick by brick." She turned to Demetrius and said, "We didn't have the lush green fields of Erythrea or the open ocean like Athena, yet we grew into one of the greater kingdoms of the west." She turned to the others and said, "Finally, we are the guardians of the gate. The gate that protects the realm of men, the gate to Mount Avatar. We will prevail in face of any danger like we had before. No force has yet crossed our gates and none ever shall. Leu will stand forever," she said, her nostrils flaring. Her fervour had rendered all listeners speechless, even Demetrius stood there silent. Agapito stood up slowly and started to clap. Torman joined in, so did everyone else, except Demetrius and his men. Slowly the whole hall was filled by the sound of applause. Demetrius stood up and started to walk out, followed by his supporters.

"You have sealed your fate, sister," said Demetrius as he walked past her. She saw him disappear out of the hall followed by his band of bootlickers. She stood there at the centre as the others clapped on.

She dropped her gaze and closed her eyes. She slowly whispered to herself in the middle of it all, "I am sorry father, but Leu needs me."

THE STRANGER FROM BEFORE

The caravan was on the grand marble road to Nisarga. Two more days had passed and they were already nearing the city. Agni had insisted on leaving the very next day and they had moved with haste after that because they were to reach the city within a specified time for the occasion to start. They had arrived two days sooner than expected, despite the various delays, only because of Agam's forced march. He had refused to halt in any of the villages on their way and they had stopped only at Fort Krumi to change the horses. The city of Nisarga was a grand sight to look at even from the distance. Vrish and Agni had never seen anything like it before. The great marble path led straight to the gate of Nisarga, which seemed to be three times higher than the tallest West Gate of Himadri. The wall around the city wound in a circle with thick pillars supporting it. The pillars were shaped as gigantic human beings to the give impression to the onlooker that a thousand giants were holding the wall in place, the pavement above the wall was supported by their hands and shoulders. Several towers with golden domes on their heads towered over the white wall. Agni presumed the Grand Palace of Nisarga to be built over a mound or hillock as it was visible above the wall even from that distance. The giant towers of the Palace pierced the sky like three lances and glimmered in the sun as if made of pure gold. Agni and Vrish had their mouth open in awe and wonder.

"Nisarga is famous for its marble pits and gold mines. It is the richest and grandest city of the land of the Rising Sun," said Agam when he saw the expression on their faces. Agni remembered that he had read that somewhere but even in his dreams he had never imagined something like this, now right in front of his eyes.

"They have the tallest towers in the east. Do you see that one, the one with the giant eagle on top?" he said pointing at one of the taller towers. Agni nodded his head.

"It is the ancient library of Darshana, the greatest library of the east. The eagle was the sigil of his father, the overseer of the southern villages of Prasati," said Agam. For once Agni was impressed by Agam's knowledge also, along with his skills.

"Who is Darshana?" asked Vrish.

"The founder of Nisarga," replied Agni.

"And he is also the one who wrote the two great prophecies," joined in Sir Drake.

"With all due respect, Sir Drake," said Agam, "It is only a myth, there is no proof that those prophecies were written by Darshana himself and everyone around here knows that."

It seemed to Agni that Agam was offended. But Agni had no clue about the subject of their conversation. Vrish's expression made Agni feel the same for his friend as well.

"We, the people of the west, do not agree with you," said Sir Drake with a pleasant smile.

"What prophecies?" asked Agni. He knew very little of Darshana and Nisarga, he only remembered a few things taught to him by Guru Bhas when he was still a child and that was very negligible.

"Good of you to ask, Agni," said Sir Drake as he moved his horse a little closer to Agni.

"There are two of them, together they are called 'the truth'," he said as he spared a glance at Agam.

"The first one is called the will of the Maker; it speaks of a destroyer being born of a King's seed by the will of the Maker in the land of the setting Sun. He shall be royal blood and will become a man of many talents. The second is known as steps to destiny. There it is said that the destroyer will come of age and he shall learn of the evils of man and how it is incurable. Then he shall open the gate of eternity in the land of the demons and the age of man shall come to an end. Then only Gaya can merge with the eternal flow and the seven gods shall leave this dying world as their oaths to the Maker shall be fulfilled. But the Seven are not devoid of pity, they have stood firm against the will of the Maker for their love for mankind. That is why the Abode of the Seven was built to worship the seven odds," finished Sir Drake with a smile.

Agni felt a little uneasy because the whole thing sounded similar to what the old witch had told him inside the forest.

"It's a myth and nothing else. There is no land of demons and no such gate," said Agam abruptly.

"It seems so," concluded Agni.

"What is a myth?" came Yani's voice as he joined them from behind.

"Nothing, Prince. I was just telling Agni about the old prophecies of Darshana," said Sir Drake.

"My father says it's a myth," said Yani.

"And what do you think?" asked Sir Drake.

"I don't know; it could be true," said Yani after giving it some thought.

"Good," said Sir Drake. "Wonder is the path that leads to knowledge and in turn to wisdom," he said smiling at him.

Yani was pleased by the praise. "Thank you," he replied with a broad grin on his face.

"A pleasure," said Sir Drake tilting his head a little towards him. Then he turned to Agni and said, "Even if you believe it's a myth as your old friend says, only remember this that they sometimes tend to have more truth in them than you think." He winked at him and fell beside Yani. Agni only stared at Sir Drake, with a strange discomfort in his heart.

ఇ

The great bell at the bell tower tolled thrice. The people on the streets looked up at it in utter confusion. There hadn't been an attack on Alexandria for over a century after the captain of the last pirate fleet, Albatross, was slain by Princess Alexandra the third. There was smoke rising from the eastern docks. A great roar shook them up and brought them out of their trance. The animals, domestic and stray alike, started to act violently. The horses threw their legs and started to chew on their leashes. The stray dogs jumped on any passerby and sunk their teeth deep into their flesh. Then suddenly, out of nowhere, a huge iron ball smashed into the bell tower and it started to collapse. The huge bell broke loose from its hinges and fell on the streets, throwing people into panic. People started to scream and run and a mass stampeded started.

The eastern dock was under attack. A fire raged in the port officer's office and the nearby store houses. Scores and scores of men bearing the mark of the seven swords of the Abode of the Seven and the preying vulture, the sigil of the house of King Hermes of Erythrea, jumped on the docks from the ships every passing moment. A few barracks on the eastern side were set on fire with the soldiers still inside them. A few guards who stood their ground were soon overrun by the regulars of the enemy's ranks. The hooded man stood on the deck looking at the chaos unfolding in front of his eyes, a large shadow cat moved behind him lurking in the shadows. A man wearing the commander's arm band ran up to him. He was panting from the effort.

"My lord we have the docks; shall we push inside the city?" he asked. His eyes fell on the cat and he stepped back a little.

"Yes, tell your men to march inside the city. Tell them to leave none standing. They shall know the meaning of war and the consequences of defying the will of the Seven," said the Lord.

"As the Lord commands," said the commander and left the deck with haste.

"Come rage," said the hooded man. "It's time for us to hunt."

ॐ

They were trotting down the Palace road of Nisarga on their horses. Agni, Vrish, Yani, Sir Drake and Agam were at the head of the column. Droh had to fall back with the other trackers as they entered the city. They had passed underneath the massive gate and had fallen on an equally great road. It was much wider than Himadri's palace road. It was so wide that ten or more wagons could have moved side by side without any problem. The city was nothing like Himadri, it was more organized in all aspects. The streets were broad, made of Marble and granite. The tall trees on either side provided some relief from the sun to the travellers on the road. The drains ran alongside the road and were covered with large marble slabs which were in plenty in Nisarga. All the houses were taller and larger than the normal houses of Himadri and they were made of different coloured bricks, most of them red. There were pavements made of marble which led to the front door and there were small gardens in front of every house they passed. The important buildings were marked by golden domes and there were sundials in front of every house. When they came to the first four point crossing Agni saw that the whole layout of the city had been curved on a huge granite block for the visitors' convenience. He saw that the city was divided into three tiers, the first one seemed to have common houses. The second one had slightly bigger ones like mansions and small villas. The third one accommodated the council members, administrators and important structures like the great library, great baths, administrative buildings and, most importantly, the Grand Royal Palace. Agni saw that the road they were on led straight to the royal palace. Agni looked at Yani from time to time, finding it hard to believe that his friend would get married soon if fortune favoured him. Yani had come up to Agni and Vrish on their way to the palace sometime ago and told Agni about the 'swyamvar,' the ceremony where the bride chooses a suitable groom from a bunch of suitors. He had been all smiles then and Agni liked the little change in him. Agni had given his best wishes to Yani and appreciated that he and Vrish were told by him first hand. He had congratulated his friend in earnest and had promised that he would do all in his power to help him. Yani had promised that they would go for a grand hunt if his quest succeeded and would name it after Agni. Yani had also admitted that he had brought Agni with him not only because of the hunt, he had also wanted to surprise him with the good news once they entered the city. Further, he said it was Sir Drake' idea. Agni didn't tell Yani that he had known the reason for his visit from Himadri itself, he just smiled. Yani had been in a jovial mood after that. Agni felt a strange sadness in his heart; he thought how happy he would have been to tell Yani about Malini if she were alive. He tried to force the thought out of his mind and then his eyes fell on Agam.

"Agamji, can I ask you something?" asked Agni.

"What is it?" he answered Agni's question with his.

"I have been thinking that if as it is said Nisarga is a republic then how come it also has a palace?" he asked.

"Good question," said Agam. Then he scratched his head a little and said, "Well as I know it, the palace also functions as the Senate."

"Sorry, but I did not understand," said Agni apologetically. Yani was riding on Agam's other side.

"Agamji, if you don't mind, shall I answer Agni's question for you?" he asked.

"Certainly, that's very kind of you, my Prince," said Agam and almost gave out a sigh of relief. Vrsih noticed him and smirked a little. Agam's face turned red when he saw Vrish, and Agni understood that politics was not his strong point.

"I better check the rear of the column, I think we are slowing down," he said and fell back a little. Agni couldn't help but smile, it was never his intention to put him in such an odd situation, he was acting as his guide till then so he thought it was better to ask him. He turned his head a bit and saw Agam riding back and then his eyes fell on Sir Drake who was dozing silently on the horse as it moved behind them.

"Yes Agni, as you were saying,' said Yani after Agam had disappeared behind the carriages and the wagons.

"Nisarga was founded by the great scholar Darshana but then it was only a seat of learning and there were only a few small villages here. It was raided and conquered by General Cabasa, the great of Hala, after Darshana's death. Hala was the strongest nation of that time. General Cabasa was given the honour to rule over Nisarga. The city of Nisarga was built over a period of hundred years and ruled by the sons and grandsons of Cabasa after him. They ensured their freedom through the payment of tribute while it continued to be the great seat of learning and progress. But as time passed, the strength of Hala diminished and Nisarga rose to great heights after the discovery of the gold mines and marble pits close to the already prospering city. It was Cabhan, the fifth of Cabasa's line, who demanded that Nisarga be turned into a republic and a free city. Indraudh, the high senator of Hala refused to accept his demands and sent the army of Hala to take back the city from the hands of Cabhan. The army of Hala was beaten back by the sheer military genius of Cabhan and then he marched to the gates of Hala with his remaining forces. Indraudh had no choice but to accept his terms. Then Cabhan declared the independence of Nisarga and built the marble palace as the symbol of his victory. He said that his sons and the generations to come will reside in the palace and rule the marble city with others of equal power. Thus, the Marble Palace became the seat of power of a virtual king; it symbolizes the perfect mix of the Republic propaganda with the concept of monarchy," finished Yani with a smile.

"That's deep," said Vrish, who had been oblivious to what the Prince said, his eyes on someone else.

"I never knew you were so good in history," said Agni, genuinely impressed. He was sure Yani had explained it as best as Guru Bhas himself would have.

"I was busy studying under Guru Bhas when you were out hunting," replied Yani.

"True," said Agni. "But I was never good with names." Then both of them started laughing.

The crowd by the side of the road was getting thinner as they neared the small gate of the third tier of the city. Agni saw many leaving as the show was about to end and it seemed that they were the last party to arrive before the welcoming ceremony started. They passed by random faces but then his eyes fell on a strange man, hooded in black and a part of his burnt face clearly visible under the sun even from a distance. Agni looked away at first but then he turned his head quickly for a second look; the man was gone.

"Vrish, Vrish," Agni pulled him by his sleeve as he was riding beside him; he was looking the other side.

"What?" he asked in an irritated voice. For the last few hours, Vrish had set his eyes on the most beautiful faces he had ever seen.

"It's the same man," said Agni.

"Which one?" asked Vrish. "We have never been here before."

"No, the same man from Himadri, the one who bumped into me that night, the one with the burnt face. Remember?" said Agni.

"You mean the one from the forest road," asked Vrish and gave a look at the crowd on Agni's side. Agni was looking intently too.

"He is gone," said Agni.

"So what about it?" asked Vrish casually.

"Don't you find it odd?" asked Agni.

"What's so odd about it? Maybe he is visiting the city like us. I told you before that he seemed like a fire breather to me and there is supposed to be a festival here in a few days," said Vrish.

"Still it seemed that he was staring at me all the time," said Agni.

Vrish's face grew serious, "You mean to say that a man with a burnt face is stalking you?" His mouth got twisted and he burst into laughter.

"Stop it, Vrish! I am serious," said Agni angrily. Yani and the others were riding a few paces ahead of them.

"All right, all right. I was just kidding," he said, the smirk still on his face. Then he placed his hand on his shoulder and spoke in a voice more serious than before. "Look," he said. "All that we have found about that night doesn't even hint towards the presence of an outsider. Moreover, we ran into that man near the festival grounds. If he would have been involved in it in any way, how could he have covered that long distance in such short period? We heard that the fire started an hour or so before we got there, no man can run that fast and that too, for such a long period. Don't you think I thought of it too when we started looking for the clues. I think you are making a mistake," said Vrish decisively.

"I know what you saying is true, Vrish, that is the exact reason that I didn't give it a second thought myself. It is impossible for the fastest runners to run near that speed, covering three thousand paces in an hour is nearly impossible. But now seeing this same man here creates a lot of doubts,' said Agni.

"But why would an outsider be a part of this?" asked Vrish.

"Think of it this way, Vrish. The cat may be from Himadri itself but the cat's paw is not. The persons who are behind all this had planned it very carefully and executed it to perfection. They even removed the final piece of the puzzle, the captain, before we got to him. Hiring someone from outside to do the job would be the safest bet," said Agni.

"But how can you be sure that this is that same man?" asked Vrish.

"Remember what Bali said to you? He had said that he helped a man get on board but didn't know where he was dropped off," said Agni.

"But the ship never got close to Nisarga, and Droh said that the cargo was transferred to another ship," said Vrish.

"Exactly," said Agni, "He could have hidden in one of the crates easily and then he could have been dropped off anywhere. It could as well have been near Nisarga," said Agni. Vrish was silent and lost in thought. "And now a chance encounter with the same strange man from the same night! If he could have covered the distance between the docks and the festival ground somehow then my theory fits in perfectly. But I could be wrong too," Agni paused.

"We need to be sure," said Vrish. "For that we need to find him," he added.

"And that we will," said Agni.

THE ROYAL PALACE OF NISARGA

The Palace of Nisarga was even more beautiful up close. It was the grandest edifice that the men of the east had ever built. The towers had three segments each and a golden ring separated one from the other. The central structure was a curved block of solid granite with a huge marble dome covering its head. The dome was engraved with several figures of Trinetra. The pillars stood erect with several climbers winding upwards. The most remarkable feature of the Palace was that it seemed to be suspended in mid air as water gushed out from beneath it and filled a man made pool around it. There were four arched pavements which led to the four doors on the four sides. The central palace was surrounded by an extended garden of exotic plants and there was a large yard to the east of it. The massive structure and the exquisite and detailed design made any visitor stare and wonder as they stepped into a heaven made by man.

They walked up the archway as the others were led to the camping ground by Agam where Paksha would be waiting for them. Agni, Vrish, Yani and Sir Drake were led by an attendant up the archway to the door of a large hall. A man in golden brown clothes and tight pants stood at the entrance of the main hall with other attendants. All of them had their hair dyed in different colours.

"May you be so kind to give us your name, sarkar?" asked the man to Yani who seemed to be the head of them.

"Prince Yani and his friends from Himadri," replied the Prince with an air full of confidence.

"Thank you, Rajkumar. It is our great honour to welcome you to Nisarga," said the man humbly. Yani only nodded his head in a kingly gesture.

"Rajkumar Yani and his party grace us now with their presence," shouted out one of them announcing the arrival of what seemed to the last of the High Senator's guests.

A few in the crowd of men and women turned to see while the others remained oblivious to their arrival. As they entered the hall, five women dressed in single cloths provocatively draped around their body held a large silver bowl in front of each of them to wash their hands and faces. Agni followed what Yani and Sir Drake did. Then they gave them fresh dry linen to wipe their faces, neck and hands. Following that, they were showered with local perfumes and scented flowers. Each of them including Vrish and Agni were presented a red rose by the women as they made their way inside the hall.

"Now this is more like a royal welcome," said Vrish as he looked back and gave a second look at the women. Yani chose a place in the corner of the hall. Agni saw that he seemed much tensed after entering the hall and would wipe his forehead from time to time as they went and stood in the corner. Himadri was a small kingdom and its Prince was also small in the eyes of some of the guests. But Sir Drake seemed relaxed and it seemed to Agni that he was used to all these things. The servants were serving twenty different types of beverages ranging from sura to imported honeyed wine. The appetizers included local fish on stick, roasted pork feet, oysters with garlic dip, baked strips of boneless fish, raw pickled shrimps, heavily spiced boiled lentils, liver of duck dipped in tarter sauce and many other exotic things.

"Yani, I don't mean to be rude or anything, but can Vrish and I leave?" asked Agni after a bit of hesitation.

"No, Agni," said Yani frowning. "You can't, I know that you don't like gatherings like this one, but this one is not a simple occasion. This could change my life forever and I need you to stay," he said it more strongly than he used to. "Even father had asked me to keep you by my side," finished Yani.

Agni was a bit surprised by that, he never thought that King Adhirath cared for him that much.

"But the camp," his thoughts immediately went to Droh. They needed to be outside rather than enjoying the luxuries of the palace.

"You are worried about Brahma right?" asked Yani. "Don't worry about that, all his needs will be taken care of," said Yani even before Agni could reply. "Besides, I need you by my side; this place is as new to me as it is to you," Yani smiled at Agni. Agni didn't know what to say, he never thought that Yani would ask him to stay with him.

"Yani is right, Agni. It is better if we stay here," said Vrish. Agni gave him a look.

"For once you have said the right thing, Vrish," said Yani with a smile.

"Why live in a camp when you have the grandest palace of the east to stay in?" mocked Sir Drake. Some people have that talent of saying the exact wrong thing in the wrong place and Vrish was one of them, thought Agni grudgingly.

"Good, then it's settled. You two will be staying with us inside the palace," said Yani, like they had any other choice, thought Agni.

"Now let us make some friends, come," he said and started to walk towards a small group of men and women a little away from them. Sir Drake followed them.

Agni was staring at Vrish as they followed Yani in a sluggish pace. "What?" asked Vrish in a hushed voice.

"Do you always have to talk?" whispered Agni angrily.

"Why?" asked Vrish with a puzzled look on his face.

"Why?" retorted Agni but in a hushed voice. "If we had stayed at the camp then it would have been easier for us to look for that man. Now every time we leave the palace, we shall have to seek Yani's permission first," said Agni trying to control his voice, his temper rising fast.

Vrish scratched his head a little and said, "I thought if we stay here, it will be easier for us to get access to the library."

Agni was a bit taken aback, "Why? I thought anyone could visit it," said Agni.

"Droh had said to me earlier that the library had three sections and only the first one was open to visitors and citizens. One needed the permission of a Senate member to visit the other two. I thought that if we keep Yani happy, then he might make this easier for us," said Vrish.

"And how does Droh know all this?" asked Agni, pleasantly surprised.

"He has been here a couple of times before. He said that he knows the city well," said Vrish.

Agni was impressed. He couldn't help but smile at his friend. "For once you have thought before you acted, I take back my words and I must say that I am very impressed," said Agni with a cheerful slap on the back of his friend.

"I am not as dumb as you think I am," said Vrish with an annoyed look on his face.

"That I can be certain of now," said Agni smiling. "Come let us make some friends," Agni said it like Yani and it made Vrish smile.

ೞ

Princess Lysandra was stroking the back of her steed Storm with a gentle hand. The white destrier was barded in white metal plates. The light plates of steel glimmered in the sun and the sunrays danced on her as if she was wrapped in silver. Storm outshone the other five hundred that stood behind her. The rest of the five hundred of Torman's men were to meet them on the banks of Tiara comprising mostly of heavy infantry and archers. The Senate had declared war on the Abode when the news of the fall of Alexandria reached the Capital. The Abode had struck even before they had sent back a formal word of refusal in accepting the new law to Aine. Somehow the word had reached their ears right after the Senate's decision. The Senate had earlier decided to ask for a committee to be set up with the senate members of Leu along with the Seven to deal with the issue at hand peacefully but all had changed after the dreaded news had reached their ears. The army of Leu was being sent to take back the fallen city from the invaders and Lysandra had asked the members to give her the permission to lead the forces of Leu by herself along with Torman. The Senate had obliged against her father's wishes.

"We are ready, Princess. We await your orders," said Torman. Princess Lysandra looked up at the high window of her father's chamber. He wasn't there. King Crixus was strictly against her decision of going to battle, yet in her heart she had hoped that her father would stand there and bid her farewell. Her gaze dropped and she placed her foot on the stirrup.

"Let us march and meet our foe," she shouted but her voice did not echo in her soul. Her eyes incessantly went for the window of the King's chamber. She tore away her gaze and held the reins more firmly. Damian was on her side, armoured and helmed. He put down his visor as they started to trot out of the palace grounds. Drums were beaten and flags bearing the sigil of King Crixus' house were hoisted up in the sky. The knights started to bang their lances against their shields. Every stroke echoed in the strings of eternity. The servants stood in awe at the sight of it all. The palace gate was in front of her and yet she looked back again, there was still no one there. She looked to her front as old Andre and his son held the gates open for them.

"Alexandria was liberated from the pirate lord by Princess Alexandria herself. Now marches her mirror image to her rescue again. Hail the victorious," shouted old Andre as he stood straight, his chest jutting out with pride. She smiled at him, yet her face bore a sadness which the old man couldn't help but notice. She looked back again for the final time. The window would disappear out of her sight once they take the first turn down the hill. But this time, she saw a shadow emerge behind the window. She could not understand whether it was a figment of her imagination or not, but when the Sun came out of the veil of clouds, her father's face shone in the morning light. It was clear as crystal to her even from that distance.

She clenched her fists and held back her tears of joy; she did not look back again. She had what she wanted. This time she shouted, "Let us take back what is ours; let us take back

Alexandria," her war cry came from her heart and echoed to the horizons as half a thousand lions roared as they marched.

Agni, along with the others, stood in the middle of the hall in anticipation of meeting their host who was yet to arrive. The few who stood beside them were Prince Yani's new friends, Prince Sudrak of Durg and his sister Princess Abharana. The one who was standing to Agni's left was Aadi, the son of the high senator of Hala and nothing less than a prince. The other honoured guests included Prince Abalendu of Nada; Zama, the overlord of the tribes of Khara; Prince Shakti of Anu, Prince Vajra of Viratbhumi; King Akakios of Euphrasia of the land of the setting Sun; Lord Augus of Athena; Sir Dion of the small kingdom of Erasmus; and many others from the small kingdoms of the east and west alike.

The musicians began playing on flutes and harps. They were accompanied by more local instruments in complete harmony. It was a mix of the east and the west, much like the guests present inside the hall. The short attendant from the door walked towards the other end of the hall and gave a curt bow to the guests. Then he started to speak, "The honoured Rajkumars, Rajkumaris, Kings, Knights and senators from lands near and far, it my greatest pleasure to present to you your host for this evening, the high senator, the kind and the noble lord himself, Lord Kubha and his greatness's beautiful daughter Aadrika ji."

The door behind the short man opened as he scurried off to the other side. The host walked in with the hand of his daughter lightly held in his fingers with a sceptre in his other hand, the hostess was nowhere to be seen. They were greeted by a round of applause.

"Thank you, my friends. You all honour me with your presence," he took in a deep breath and smiled with a lordly gesture of bending his back a little, flaunting his good charms even at that age.

"The day for which you have come is both feared and dreamt of by a girl's father," he said smiling at his daughter. Then he stood up straight and spoke again, "A father always dreams that his daughter finds a match worthy of her and yet fears that her choice may not suit her in the long run. I hope that one of you will prove me both right and wrong."

His words were greeted by a loud cheer from the guests. Agni was beginning to understand why that man was loved by all.

"My beautiful daughter is like the wind, she will comfort you in your days of ill luck but may blow you away in the next moment if you are not careful with her," he said and some of the guests laughed. Agni noticed that the High Senator's daughter's face was expressionless, even after the little jest from her father's part.

"And men are like the storm god, they know how the wind blows," said someone from the crowd.

"And I certainly hope that this storm god may present himself in flesh at the end of this affair," said Kubha and the crowd laughed.

"For that sole purpose, I shall hold a tournament which may help my daughter decide. She is quite fond of battles," said Kubha with a smile. The crowd had gone silent. Yani seemed to be the most tensed of them all.

"Relax, I never said that the winner gets the bride. I firmly believe that it is not so important how well you can use the sword but how well you can use the ones who wield it best," he said with a wink.

"I just want a good tournament. Any contender can send a champion of choice and the winner gets this," said Kubha as tossed it in the air and caught it like a performer.

"Yes, my friends, The rumours have proved themselves to be true for the first time it seems, the grand jewelled sceptre of my great ancestor, Cabhan, the heirloom of my house, is the prize," he said.

Then he glanced at it and said, "This is said to be one of the greatest treasures of the east, yet I would willingly trade it for the happiness of my daughter." Then he looked up and said, "But I certainly wish that it remains in the hands of my future son-in-law." Kubha had a broad grin on his face.

The party had ended and the guests were led being by an attendant each to the guest rooms. The palace had one hundred and eight rooms for the guests alone, so it was not much of a difficulty to arrange the accommodations.

"I want that sceptre," said Yani as they were being led to their rooms. The attendant walked a little ahead of them. Agni knew that he wanted it more for King Adhirath than for himself.

"The one who wins the sceptre has a better chance at this," added Yani.

"I agree," said Sir Drake. "High Senator Kubha won't give away his ancestral heirloom without a proper reason; he wishes to influence her decision of marriage indirectly."

"Now that one can choose a champion it has become a lot easier. I can always ask Agam. He will be honoured by this opportunity," said Yani ecstatically. Sir Drake didn't share his enthusiasm.

"Agam is a good sword, Prince, but his style is orthodox. I have seen that much in the practice yard. Moreover, Agam is an old man; it will be quite a challenge for a man of his age to face stronger and younger opponents. Some of the young knights of the west will fight themselves despite what High Senator Kubha said. Say, take Sir Dion, he will certainly fight himself and if Agam faces him in battle, his scimitar will be of no match against his long sword," said Sir Drake.

"You need someone with an unconventional style, someone with a few tricks up his sleeves, who doesn't think twice before striking the final blow. I mean someone for whom winning is more important than pride," he finished with a smile.

"Paksha?" asked Yani, the smile on his face was gone. Agni felt the dull pain in his shoulder come back to him.

"I think he is the best choice, yet you must be the judge of it," said Sir Drake earnestly. Yani thought for a moment.

"What you say is true Sir, but…" he gave a glance at Agni and their eyes met.

Agni smiled and said, "Anything for the greatness of Himadri."

Yani smiled back. "Right," he said, "then Paksha it is."

THE WHITE DREAM AND THE BLACK

There was a mist everywhere and everything was cold. Agni was walking on a road he didn't know and could not see. Suddenly he felt some heat and his eyes fell on a light in front of him, glowing at a distance. He walked towards it. It grew brighter as he came nearer to it and the mist began clearing. As he got close enough, he saw several faceless shadows circling the fire as it burnt in the hearth of the unknown place. They were chanting something in a language he did not know. A little away from the men stood a man chained and strapped to the wall. His dark mane came down to his shoulders, his cheeks covered with an unkempt beard. His eyes were closed. A little away from him stood another man enclosed in what seemed like a vortex of energy. A shadow crept up towards the chained prisoner with a sharp steel weapon shining in his hand.

"There is another way; there is another way," shouted the man trapped inside the vortex.

"It is for the good of mankind," said the shadow and pulled the chained head up by his hair. The man opened his eyes and his eyes met Agni's. He had the same blue eyes like him. He kept staring at Agni as the man took the blade to his throat. Then there was a scream that seemed to bleed his ears, he felt the air sucked out of his throat. A dark fire came swirling out of nowhere and engulfed him. Agni opened his eyes, at first it took him some time to recognize the place he was in. He was sweating profusely, the bed sheet was wet with it. He sat up on his bed.

"Are you all right?" came Vrish's concerned voice. Agni wiped his brow and said, "Nothing, only a bad dream."

"Guessed that much. The way you were twisting and turning in your sleep, must have been real bad I guess. I tried waking you, but it seemed that you were in some other world," said Vrish.

"Did I wake you up?" asked Agni apologetically.

"No, it's all right. I was already awake. You know I can't sleep in a new place for the first night and it is already dawn," said Vrish pointing at the window.

"So what was this dream about?" asked Vrish. It was the strangest dream Agni had ever had. He remembered every single bit of it and it seemed so vivid.

"Nothing, just some weird dream. I was walking down a dark road and I saw a few men doing some ritual of sorts and another guy in chains. One of those men killed him in cold blood," said Agni, he could still hear the scream in his ears.

"You were saying something over and over again in your sleep," said Vrish.

"What?" asked Agni.

"I don't know, didn't understand a word of it," replied Vrish. "Anyway," he continued as he got up from his bed and stood by the window, "It seems that we are going to have a nice day ahead of us. Everything outside looks great. It is going to be one of those perfect mornings," he said.

"Do you remember how we used to spend a day like this one back at Himadri before ..." Vrish stopped abruptly, his face became dark. Agni didn't say anything either, those memories brought happiness and pain alike. Then he got up from his bed and walked up to his friend.

"I remember our little outings when Malini came back with Briksha. I remember those more than anything else," said Agni placing a hand on his shoulder.

"Sometimes it feels so unreal, Agni. Even now when I wake up sometimes, I forget that we don't have anything left back there or anywhere. If only…." His voice trembled as he spoke.

"She loved you a lot, Vrish, you were the little brother to her. Your father loved you too, he never showed it but I could always tell," said Agni.

"I loved them a lot, but I was always angry with them. Father was always on his ship and Malini was always with him, I envied her for that. So I always tried to avoid them whenever they came back from their journeys," said Vrish, his eyes were moist. "I only wish I had been good to them when I had the chance. Now they are gone, forever." A drop of tear trickled down his cheek.

Agni knew the pain, strange, heartless and searing. It charred him every time like the fire that destroyed his only family.

"They loved you more than you could ever imagine and I know they also knew how much you loved them. Let us only remember them in our happiness and not in our grief. Let them stay as beautiful in our memories as they were in the real life," Agni managed to say, but in his heart he knew he needed vengeance to wash that taint away.

Vrish looked at him, his eyes red, "And have you been able to do that, my friend?" he asked. Agni was silent.

"Then we should help each other," he said trying to smile. "Let us forget our troubles and spend this day like we used to when she was with us," said Agni. Vrish smiled.

"Agreed," he said. "The two of us."

"The two of us," repeated Agni.

The Sun dial showed three hours and a half past sunrise. It was a fine morning indeed. Agni and Vrish were on their horses out in the city streets. The city of Nisarga seemed a little different from the way it looked for the first time they had set their eyes on it. It was a bustling city, well kept but still with a mild touch of anarchy to it. The morning bazaar had opened some time back and the regular buyers stormed the place. Unlike Himadri, Nisarga had several morning markets where the vendors from all over the city would flock in one place for the convenience of the buyers. Their merchandise had no fixed prices and varied with the nature of the buyer. Agni and Vrish trotted down the crowded street, watching the men and women totally engrossed in the process of bargaining, none of them were bothered about the onlookers.

"Isn't she a beauty?" asked Vrish, he was staring at a short and cute girl with curly hair, standing by a vegetable stand.

"Which one?" asked Agni.

"That one," replied Vrish pointing incessantly at the girl.

"All right, all right, I see her," said Agni quickly. Then he smiled and asked, "She looks a lot like Bani, doesn't she?"

Vrish was astounded, "How did you..." but he stopped a little short of finishing the sentence. Agni scratched his chin and said, "I can always guess but it seems that I have placed my finger on the right spot," the smile still playing on his face.

Vrish's face had gone red. "I just...she just," he fumbled with his words.

"Have you told her yet?" asked Agni plainly.

"Soon, after we get back. I met her before we left," said Vrish.

"And what did you say to her?" he asked.

"Nothing much, just a simple goodbye," said Vrish. Agni gave out a sigh, he didn't say anything else.

"She asked me to bring back something for her," he said quickly. Agni looked at him.

"That's good," he said. "Then you should buy something for her." He wished he could do the same, but then they wouldn't have been here if Malini was still alive.

"Here we are, the inn, the stable boy told us about," said Vrish. Agni looked up and read the wooden board that hung from the ledge above the door, 'Anandbhavan - we serve the best food and the best beverages.'

"Well, this is the place, let's go inside and have a good time," said Agni.

"A very good time," said Vrish and Agni nodded his head with a smile.

As they came down from their horses, a short and stout man outside the door came running to them.

"Blessed morning good sirs, welcome," he said with a broad grin on his face. From the look of things and his words, it seemed they had had many visitors before them who had come for the swayamvar.

"And how do you know we were heading for your inn?" asked Agni.

"You just said so yourself, which means you are going in right now," said the man as he took the reins from their hands. Both of them smiled at the man' words.

Agni tossed the man a 'gini'. He caught it and gave another bow as he held the door open for them.

The place was crowded even at that hour of the morning and from the look of it, they were not there for the morning meal. It was a raging party. Agni saw that most of the guests seemed to be outsiders as their tongue was different and so was their accent. Agni only knew the language of 'Dailect' which was more predominant in the western parts of the Land of the Rising Sun and mostly everywhere in the Land of the Setting Sun. It was more of a common language in all parts. Agni also knew a bit of 'Vakya' and 'Kal' which were more predominant in the eastern parts. It seemed like a very costly place to be. The whole floor was covered by a fur carpet stretching from one corner to the other and the chiffon curtains separated one low table from the other. There were feathered cushions lying around for the guests to use. The food and beverages were being served by sultry maids in scanty outfits as they treaded the floor barefoot. The whole place was a bit dark and the rays of the sun barely penetrated the closed windows.

"Let us find another inn," said Agni. This was not what he had in mind when he said that they were going to have a good time. He wanted to find a serene place to sit down and have a good meal with a little sura or honeyed wine.

"No, this one looks good to me. I like this place," said Vrish with a broad grin on his face. Agni only thought of the stable boy and how much he was making from this.

A gorgeous woman, barely in her mid-twenties, dressed in what seemed like a little more than provocative single piece draping walked up to them. "Shall I show you to your place?" she asked with a smile.

"My name is Vrish," said Vrish with a silly smile on his face. The girl couldn't help but giggle.

"Please follow me, Vrish ji," said the woman and led them inside. Vrish followed her as if in a trance. Agni took in a deep breath and followed him. They were shown to a low table for two by a window which had its curtains drawn.

"What can I bring for Vrish ji and his friend?" she asked in her musical tune.

"Anything you like," said Vrish, that stupid smile still on his face.

"I will have some rice pudding," said Agni quickly.

"Relax," said Vrish. Then he smiled at her and said, "You bring something good for my friend too."

"Certainly," she said and left with a huge smile on her face. Agni quickly checked his coins. The woman came back with a tray with two huge goblets set on it and platter full of different types of game meat roasted and spiced.

"I shall come back when these are finished," she said to Vrish.

"What's your name?" he asked.

"Aasha," she replied as she struck a pose.

"You have a beautiful name, Aasha," said Vrish looking at her pretty face. They kept looking at each other with smiles on their faces.

"Well, Aasha," said Agni at last. "It seems you have brought enough for the two of us."

She bent down a little in front of Agni, smiled one of her intoxicating smiles and said, "Once you have drank from our goblets, you can never have enough."

"Well, that I can certainly see," said Agni with a sharp smile. By then Vrish was gaping at her.

"We shall ask for you once we are done," said Agni politely.

"Right," she said and stood up straight. "I will be near that corner," she said pointing to the turn by the wall ahead of them. "All you need to do is shout," she said and left. She waved at Vrish on her way and Vrish waved back.

"You can close your mouth now, she is gone," said Agni as he picked up a strip of roasted pork from the plate and put it into his mouth. He couldn't deny the fact that it tasted really good.

"She is a beauty," said Vrish with a gullible smile on his face.

"To you they all are," replied Agni casually.

"A toast for our good health?" asked Agni quickly.

"Yes, a toast," said Vrish happily. Both of them knocked their goblets against each other's, spilling a little of whatever it had inside and drank deep from it.

ඥ

Princess Lysandra came down from her horse Storm. They were standing in the middle of the village of Old Gate, or what was left of it. The enemy had sent several raiders along the old road and they went unchecked burning and pillaging at will. They had already come across three such bands at Seven Streams and the marshes. The news was that one such infamous band had gone south. They were led by a psychotic killer known as the Collector. The Capital had dispatched some of the best knights of Leu to stop them, the rest were commissioned to take back the city of Alexandria.

"How can a holy man let this happen?" asked Lysandra, she was astounded by the havoc that had been wreaked there, killing innocent souls. The village was in a state of complete ruin and most of the major structures had been gutted by the recent fire. Only smoke rose from the rubbles. The most astounding fact was that they had not come across any survivors of Old Gate and the records of inhabitants of other places coming to the Capital didn't mention anyone from Old Gate either. So they had decided to stop by the village on their way.

"War is raged by men Princess, whether they are holy or not doesn't matter," said Torman.

"But all of this happened so fast, we should have done something to prevent this," said Lysandra.

"They didn't even wait for a proper reply, they choose to act first and talk later. But I promise in the name of the Maker that we will have their heads," said Torman angrily.

They continued to head farther inside the village. They had sent Damian and a few others to look for survivors, which seemed to be a slim chance.

"If we didn't even send a proper reply, then how could they have known what was going to be our answer?" asked Lysandra.

"They knew Princess, they knew very well from the start. They had approached His Majesty himself at first. It was only when he refused that they sent their word to the Council," said Torman.

Lysandra was shocked, "But father never told me," she said and then the memory of that day before they went to Riley's came back to her. The hooded man bearing the mark of the Seven. That was why her father seemed so distraught that day. But at least he could have shared his burden with her, thought Lysandra. She looked hurt.

Torman smiled, "A father only wants his children to be happy," said Torman. "That holds true even for a king," added Torman. Still, Lysandra felt sad, she was not a child anymore.

"But," said Torman, "you have proved yourself the Warrior Princess of Leu yet again, despite what his highness thinks and wishes. In my heart I know that he will be very happy with you once we return victorious." That brought the smile back on her face, she wished Torman's words to be true. She brought herself back to the situation at hand.

"So tell me Torman, how should we lead the attack?" she asked.

"Well Princess, for first, we know that Alexandria has high walls and for the next part we will think of something else when we get there," said Torman with a smile. That made her laugh. The same old Torman she thought, always not much up for planning and always known for his valour.

They came to a halt in front of a barn which seemed to be in a much better condition than the other buildings. Damian's destrier along with the other horses stood outside with their riders out of sight.

"Did you find anything in there?" shouted Torman. There was a moment of silence. Damian came out alone, his face was grim.

"What's wrong?" asked Lysandra.

"We have a survivor," said Damian.

"Where is he?" asked Lysandra. "Bring him out then, his tale may prove itself to be useful for us," said Torman.

"First of all, it's a girl, a little one," said Damian. "And she is hiding in a store room inside the barn. She had refused to come out even after out repeated efforts." Lysandra was surprised.

"Have you told her who we are?" she asked.

"Yes, but…" he paused. "It seems she is afraid of us, she attacked one of my men when he tried to force her out," said Damian.

"Why?" asked Torman, he had a puzzled look on his face.

"I will go and see," said Lysandra. She was led inside the barn by her brother. The mere stench of the place made her crinkle her nose, there was little light in there and it took her eyes some time to adjust. Then her eyes became wide. There were stains of blood everywhere, as brutally hacked bodies and mutilated parts lay scattered everywhere. She could taste bile at the back of her mouth, but she held herself together. She had seen the brutalities of battles before but what lay in front of her was completely different, it was a massacre.

"These are the villagers, Lys, this is why we couldn't find any one of them. It seems they were gathered here before they were..." Damian stopped, falling short of words.

Lysandra's face was dark. "Where is the girl?" she asked.

"There, behind that door," said Damian pointing at the door a little away to their left.

"Wait here," she said and walked up to it. She opened the door and had to duck to make her way through the small opening. It was a small store room with gunny bags neatly stacked everywhere. She didn't see anything at first. Then her eyes fell on a shadowy figure in a corner. She got a little closer to it and saw a little girl sitting there with her head between her knees, she looked frail.

"Child," called out Lysandra in a compassionate voice. The girl looked up at her. "Stay away," she shouted.

"I am here to help," she said in her soft voice.

"No, get out. I don't need your help, leave me alone," she shouted at her and picked up a knife which Lysandra hadn't noticed at first.

Lysandra stopped, "Please throw that away, I will never harm you," she said. There was poor light in there but Lysandra saw that the girl was staring at her sheathed sword strapped to her waist. She slowly unbuckled her sword belt and threw it away. Then she took off her gauntlets and her winged barbute. Her cascading brown locks came down to her waist.

"See," she said. "Now I don't have anything that might harm you." The girl was staring at her blankly and then she slowly lowered her knife.

"What's your name?" asked Lysandra.

"Melissa," replied the girl, her voice quivering. The girl was on the verge of crying.

"Melissa is a beautiful name. My name is Lysandra, but you can call me Lys," she said with a smile. Her father and brother used to call her that.

"Princess Lysandra?" she asked.

"Yes, dear," she replied. The girl kept staring at her, streams of tears started to trickle down her cheeks. "Why didn't you come earlier?" she asked as Lysandra stood there silent.

Then she knelt down in front her and said, "I am sorry, Melissa. I did not know," she said with an unbearable sadness in her heart.

"They burned her," she said as drops of tears made wet patches on her tunic. The girl dropped the knife and ran into her arms. "They burned her," she started to cry hysterically. Lysandra held her in her bosom as tightly as she could. The little girl cried her grief away and her tears washed away her pain a bit. Lysandra only kept on staring at the darkness in front of her.

THE PURSUIT

Two men treaded the soft forest floor barefoot; the forest of Aadhar was a dangerous place to be after Sun sets. They were clad in white clothes, their heads shaved clean and only one of them carried a sword. There was a rustling sound from the bush in front of them.

"Guruji there is something up there," said the man with the sword.

"Could be a wild animal. If we leave it alone, it won't harm us," replied the older man, seeming unfazed.

"But what if it's a wild cat or the ones we do not speak of at night?" asked the other, clearly scared.

"Then we have a problem," said the elderly man with a visible smile.

"We better go round this place," said the younger man.

"You are my guide, Param. Do as you think best," replied the elderly man.

Param was about to turn around when a faint groan floated to their ears, stopping them abruptly. Then it was heard more clearly, a faint cry for help.

"I think it's a man, Guruji," said Param as he stood there.

"Quickly go and see, it's the first duty of a human being to help a fellow man in need," said the old man.

Param nodded his head and ran up to the place. He saw a hand sticking out of the bush. He chopped off the thorny branches and pulled the man out. There were several wounds on his bare chest and his body was covered with dried blood. Some of the wounds were still leaking pus and blood.

"Water, water," groaned the man. Param immediately took out his water skin and poured some of it on his dried, cracked lips. He opened his mouth and let it trickle down his parched throat. He coughed up some blood. Param took out a vial and opened it.

"What's your name, stranger, and who did this to you?" asked Param as he poured a drop on each of his wounds. The man was huge and heavily muscled.

"They killed everyone," said the man in his faint voice as fresh tears trickled down his cheeks. "My brothers, my wife, everyone. I didn't even see their faces when they killed them one by one." The old man had walked up to them by then.

"His wounds are deep, Guruji," said Param turning to his master.

"I am being punished for my sins," he sobbed. "I let them burn those men at the docks; some of them were my friends." He spat out more blood as he tried to speak. Param looked at his master.

"Do you mean the incident at Himadri?" asked the old man.

"Yes, I was the one who took him to my mother. I helped him do it and then escape," said the man in his shaking voice.

"Were they the same, the ones who killed your family and the ones you helped?" asked the old man again.

"No," the man's eyes became wide with fear. "They were different. They chased us and then they placed a hand over each one's head. Just a touch and everyone I knew began shivering and screaming. They were dead before I could do anything. When I tried to stop them, they flung me away. When they were done with the others, their eyes fell on me. I ran, ran and ran," said the man, his breath getting heavier with every word.

"I do not understand a word he is saying, Guruji," said Param turning to his master.

"We better hurry," said the old man as he looked around with wary eyes. The man lying on the forest floor was gasping for air by then.

"What about him, Guruji?" asked Param.

"He has reached his last moments," said the old man and knelt down beside him. His words were true for the man was having much difficulty breathing.

The old man slowly knelt down beside him and took the man's hand in his own. "The eternal one, the Trinetra, the Maker of all, show your son the path to your abode, show mercy to this tormented soul for you are the Maker of man and God alike," spoke the old man in a solemn voice.

"You have shared your burden with us and have already started on the path of atonement," said the older man as Param looked on with sadness in his eyes. Tears came out of the man's eyes as he listened to the older man speak for his atonement. He was on the verge of losing the battle with life and surrender to death.

"What is your name, son?" asked the older man.

"Bali," he said and slowly closed his eyes.

"Embrace the gift of death and forget your past life, rest in peace now Bali." His breathing had already stopped by the time the old man had finished saying his words. He closed his half open eyes for him and folded his hands.

ଔ

"We are the kings of the land, kings of the sea and the kings of the sky,

But we have no more gold and no more silver and our cups have gone dry,"

Sang Vrish at the top of his voice as Agni held him by his shoulders. He was barely able to stand straight, let alone walk. Vrish's song was so harsh on his ears that Agni thought it could have cracked open any thick glass. To his relief, the roads were deserted at that hour of the night. Agni remained sober as he had refused to drink another round of that foul stuff and Vrish had taken it up from there. They had to leave their horses behind as they had nothing left to pay the stable boy with. So they had to walk to the palace on foot. Agni had to pay an outrageous sum of ten mudras, seventeen ginis and twelve tamas for their little binge. Vrish handsomely tipped the waitress with two mudras before Agni could act and then they were left with nothing.

"Agni," said Vrish, his eyes red and his breath reeking of sura and other foul things mixed in that goblet.

"I am glad you are still with me. You are the only one left in this whole world now whom I can call my own," said Vrish.

Agni smiled, "Me too," he said.

"You would have made a fine husband for my sister. She would have been the happiest woman on Gaya. And I know for sure, you would have been the best brother-in-law," said Vrish, his eyes moist.

"I would have been the luckiest man on earth," thought Agni to himself.

"Damn these stupid tears," shouted Vrish as he wiped them away forcefully.

"I never thought that any man can love my sister so much. You never gave up," said Vrish, his mind was intoxicated but his heart was not.

"And I never will until I find them," said Agni with a smile.

"Then what will we do?" he asked. "Doesn't it feel like our lives will end when we find them?"

Agni was silent, he didn't know what he would do after all this was over. His dreams and the very bane of his existence were destroyed that night.

"Do you know why I didn't say anything to Bani before I came here?" asked Vrish.

Agni shook his head in reply.

"Because I don't know if we will return or not. People who can kill that easily could kill us as well," said Vrish as he fumbled with his steps.

"It will take a lot of effort to kill someone like you when five goblets of that foul stuff couldn't," smiled Agni.

Vrish chuckled and a little spit flew out of his mouth. He rubbed his mouth with the back of his sleeves. His face grew serious again.

"Jokes apart, my friend, the truth is that I am afraid; not for my life, mind you, but something else. I don't know what, but it is there," he said, his eyes pouring into his and the dread was clear in them. Agni had felt the same dread in his heart from the very day they got there, the nightmare, the stranger with the burnt face and unknown things working behind them. In his heart he always felt that they were in the middle of things which were much different than it seemed.

They were nearing the gate of the second tier; Vrish had gone silent by then. He looked sick. He fumbled with his steps here and there as Agni almost dragged him along. Then he stopped abruptly. There was a sound coming from the intersection of the road ahead of them. If it was someone else then it might have escaped them but Agni had the ears of a tracker. He listened more intently; it was the sound of iron sole falling on the brick road.

Maybe it was someone like them returning from an inn or a party or maybe it was a guard on night patrol, thought Agni, but he wanted to be sure.

"You wait here for me," said Agni as he made Vrish sit on the steps of a nearby shop. "I will be right back," he said.

"Hmm," said Vrish, already dozing off.

Agni started walking in the direction of the sound, his feet falling lightly on the ground. The sound became sharper. He increased his pace. The intersection was near him, it became more prominent than ever. Agni almost ran as lightly as he could. Then he slid behind a pillar to see who it was. The sound stopped. Agni could hear his heart beat but not another sound. As if the source had vanished into thin air. Agni leaned a little out of the shadow of the pillar to see if anyone was there, but there was no one. Agni screened the place properly and then he came out. He stood there at the four point crossing, confused, looking all around. He was sure he had heard it correctly. He rolled his eyes all over the place and then it got stuck to a corner to his left. The shadow, it moved a bit. Agni started to walk towards it, his senses keener than usual. Then something happened, a shadow jumped out of the corner and whirled past him with amazing speed. He was almost thrown off balance but he turned quickly and broke his fall. He saw the tail of the black cloak as it vanished round the corner to his right. He quickly sprinted behind it. He turned the corner and saw that the road was deserted. He looked up at the roofs and saw the shadow sprinting on the rooftops towards the east. Agni quickly climbed up on the roofs and chased the man. He was at least fifty steps behind him. Agni was a reputed runner, but the man's speed seemed unmatchable. It was as if he was flying with the wind. He chased him none the less. Agni ran as fast as he could, his legs were on fire. He jumped from one roof to the other with ease and pushed himself as hard as he could. His legs were burning by then, and he didn't know how long he could keep that up. For a moment it seemed that he was gaining on the man. Then his foot fell on a loose tile and he slipped. He caught hold of the ledge before he fell and climbed up with some difficulty. By the time he stood up again, the shadow had disappeared. He looked around a bit and there was no one in sight.

"Ahh," shouted Agni out of his frustration and slammed his fist on the loose tile breaking it to pieces. His scream of agony echoed in the night sky, he was certain that it was that same man.

"I will catch you, I promise, even if it is the last thing I do," Agni whispered to the wind as beads of his sweat fell on the broken pieces.

ભ

The next morning Vrish woke up with a serious headache. He opened his beady eyes with some difficulty and saw Agni sitting by the window, staring outside with a cheroot burning in his hand.

"My head is splitting," said Vrish as he sat up on his bed.

Agni turned to him and smiled. "I have kept some lime water in that flagon," he said pointing at the flagon on the small stand beside Vrish's bed. "Drink it, you will feel better and oh, blessed morning," said Agni with a smile. Vrish took up the flagon in his hand.

"Some blessed morning it is," said Vrish and drank deep. "Foul stuff," he said with disgust as he spitted out some of the seeds.

"What happened last night?" he asked as he got out of his bed.

"The usual," said Agni. "You drank too much and passed out."

"Well that thing was pretty strong, didn't think only five goblets could knock me out like that," he said with a yawn. Agni wasn't listening; he was staring outside the window as the cheroot burned in his hand. Vrish noticed that.

"There is something more, isn't there? You never smoke in the mornings,' said Vrish.

"I ran into that man again," said Agni.

Vrish leaned forward, "And?" he asked.

"He ran when he saw me. I chased him but couldn't catch up. Then I lost his trail," said Agni as he gave out some smoke which formed a mist around him.

"You weren't able to catch him?" repeated Vrish, he was more shocked than surprised. Agni was the best runner of Himadri, even the likes of Paksha couldn't match him at that.

"Hmm, he had the same kind of speed that would have been necessary to cover the distance between the festival ground and the docks in that short period and, most importantly, he ran when he saw me," said Agni as took another puff.

"So, you are saying your guess was correct?" asked Vrish. Agni nodded his head.

"Or else, why would a man run, Vrish, if he didn't have something to hide?" said Agni.

"But if what you say is true, then how did the captain of Ryau die? Bali said that the man had left Himadri right after the festival, much before the captain was murdered. We saw it with our own eyes; the corpse was fresh when we got there. There wasn't the slightest sign of decay," said Vrish.

"It means only one thing," said Agni as he looked at Vrish. "Someone was helping him back at Himadri, the ones who are behind it all." Vrish was silent.

"But that is not what is troubling me," said Agni. Vrish was still staring at him.

"I am confused as to why someone would hatch such an elaborate plan just to kill a bunch of sailors? Were they after someone specific?" said Agni as he put out the butt of the cheroot and threw it outside the window.

"I don't understand," said Vrish.

"The way I see it, this game was planned from long before. I don't think that they were after a bunch of sailors; they were after someone specific. They chose the time of the festival to make it look like an accident caused by the fire powders when the fact is that they used those devices. Someone killed Malini Vrish and you said that Bali told you that activating one of the devices would activate the others, so whoever did that went abroad Dut that night," said Agni. Vrish was shocked,

"You mean to say that they were after someone on Dut?" he asked.

"That's what I think," said Agni.

"But still, Agni, it all seems a little far-fetched. We still don't have any proof that this is our guy," said Vrish.

"Weren't you listening?" said Agni in an irritated voice. "That is why we need to find him. I firmly believe that even if he is not our guy, he knows something. That is why he ran when he saw me." Vrish remained silent.

"I will go and speak to Droh. He has been here before, he must know someone who can help us," said Vrish as he stood up straight.

"Vrish, be careful. Ask Droh to be as discreet as possible. We still don't know all the pawns in this game," said Agni in a wary voice.

"Right," said Vrish and left the room.

Agni sat there staring outside the window, the plot had deepened. The mystery was getting thicker and thicker. The answer to the biggest question still eluded him, 'Why was she murdered? What did she see?'

os

The Seven were seated in the grand hall of the tallest tower of Aine. The city of Aine was a small one, yet it was called the heart of the west. The Abode of the Seven had their seat of power at Aine. It was ruled by the Seven and guarded by the holy warriors, or more aptly called the army of the Seven.

"So Snake, it seems that you have kept your word," said the Lord of Light.

Snake stood up and said, "I have better news, my lord; the boy has been found."

"What? Are you certain?" asked the Lord as he sat up straight, pleasantly surprised.

Snake gave a sideways glance to Raven and smiled, "Yes, my lord. He is at Nisarga right now."

A visible smile spread across the Lord's face. "You have done well, Snake. Much better than I expected of you. When the time comes, you shall be rewarded," said the Lord.

"It is my pleasure that I am able to serve you, my Lord," said Snake with humility.

"You have served us all, Snake, including yourself. The day shall come soon when all shall be settled and the cycle of fate will be sealed. But, for now, we must wait," said the Lord.

"All of you," he spoke out loudly. "Leave us now. I have something to discuss with Dark." Snake was a little annoyed but he had seen before the outcome of protesting against the will of the Lord of the Seven.

Raven was the first to leave; Snake was smiling as he saw him almost rush out of the door.

"You have proved yourself worthy, Snake," said Aqua. "The Lord will now hold you in high esteem like the others."

They walked out of the door behind the portcullis. Lord of the Light waited for the marble slab to adjust itself over the opening after they left.

"Dark, this is where you come in. It is time for us to act. The Protectors have broken their oath, now I am sure of it," said The Lord.

Dark smiled and said, "I knew that brother, the news reached my ears first and I have acted already."

Light was a bit shocked and then rage came to his aid. "Did Snake give you that information before he laid it down before the Council?" he asked.

Dark was simply smiling and there came no reply. "I shall find out the truth but that comes later. First I must deal with your insolence," said Light.

Dark slammed his fist on the table and it shook. "I do not take orders from you, brother. You are their Lord, not mine," he retorted.

"I am the Lord of the Seven and that means me myself as well. Even my actions are not free from the rules laid down at birth," he said calmly.

"You are so naïve. Do you really think I do not know what you are up to behind the veil of those rules of yours?" said Dark.

Light didn't flinch. Light was staring at Dark with a hint of coldness in his eyes. "Do you wish to replace me, brother?" he asked as Dark made his way towards the door.

"It is from that day you forgot who we truly are, brother. That time may come sooner than you expect," he said and left.

THE GREAT LIBRARY OF NISARGA

"Welcome to the great library of Nisarga, the pinnacle of knowledge, the high seat of learning, the pride of the east, founded by the great Darshana himself and now under my care," said the man called Dobra with a smile on his face to Agni and Vrish as they stood at the main entrance.

"I will be your host today and each day you visit the library. Let us start our little tour of the place. Come, Agni ji and Vrish ji," said the man as he led them inside.

"He talks more like a showman than a head librarian," whispered Vrish in Agni's ear. Agni smiled and nodded his head.

The Great Library was not so great from the inside; it seemed like any other library. The only difference was that it was ten to twenty times greater in size than any library they had ever seen before. The winding wooden stairs reached up to the sky. Vrish's mouth fell open.

"You expect to find the meaning of that symbol and Sidak's words in this heap of books and scrolls? Good luck with that," said Vrish. Agni had feared the same for the library of Himadri was much smaller in size, yet it had taken him ages to go through half of the books it had.

"Leave the books to me. Did you speak with Droh?" asked Agni.

"What do you think I have been doing since yesterday? That is why I didn't come back, I went with Droh," said Vrish rolling his eyes.

"Did he take you with him?" asked a surprised Agni.

"Yes…more or less. I made him do it, but he said that he won't be able to take me with him the next time because…"

"Some places are not safe for a king's wards to visit," Agni finished the sentence for him. Vrish smiled.

Dobra went on telling them about the history of the great library but both of them paid little heed to that.

"I spoke with Agam ji yesterday," spoke Agni in hushed voice.

"About what?" asked Vrish.

"About that man," replied Agni. "What?" said Vrish a little loudly.

Dobra turned around, "Did you say something Vrish ji?" he asked.

"No, no I was just saying that the decorations are exquisite," said Vrish. Dobra looked pleased.

"These are very old, each piece of art was chosen by Cabhan, the sixth himself," said Dobra.

"That is why it looks so grand," said Vrish.

Dobra gave a radiant smile and said, "As I was saying, the sixth scroll was discovered from the Grand Temple of Trinetra in the forest of Jambu…" Dobra continued to walk ahead of them.

"Why did you speak with Agam ji?" asked Vrish, aghast.

"Relax," said Agni. "I have sense enough to not tell him the truth. I said that my purse was stolen by a man with a burnt face the night before yesterday; he escaped before I could catch him. It had a gift for Yani in it, so if he came by such a man he must apprehend him and bring him to me," said Agni.

Vrish was staring at him, "That was some smart thinking," he said. His face had a smile on it again. They had come to a halt in front of the winding stairs which seemed to lead to other tiers of the Library.

"The letter from the High Senator says that you want to visit the upper tiers?" asked Dobra.

"Yes," replied Agni.

The tall, lean man in his shabby clothes scratched his cheeks, and said with a smirk on his face, "Pulled a lot of strings, have we? I am tempted to ask you two don't seem to be either scholars or gurus, yet you have interest in the old books as you want to go to the upper tiers. The biggest question is, what are you two looking for?"

He was staring at them intently, a questioning smile on his face.

Agni and Vrish looked at each other, "Please excuse us for a moment," said Vrish and almost dragged Agni away. "Show it to him, it may save us a lot of time," whispered Vrish.

"No," Agni whispered back angrily. "What if he is also a part of this?"

"For the sake of Trinetra, Agni, he is only a librarian," said Vrish.

"It's too much of a risk," said Agni.

"Look Agni, we have only one day and this is not Himadri. What if we do not get a second permit again? Do you think you can go through all these books or a tenth of it in one single day. It's impossible. We have to take the risk," whispered Vrish. "Trust me," he said.

Agni was staring at Vrish, a part of him knew Vrish was right. It was impossible to find anything there in just a day, especially when it is abstract in nature and they might not get a second chance too.

Agni slowly walked up to Dobra who had a broad grin on his face by then. "So?" he asked with a smile.

"You are right. We are looking for something specific," said Agni with a little hesitation.

"Yes, I was right," said Dobra enthusiastically. "What is it? Tell me," he said, his eyes shining with a sort of greed.

"A symbol," said Agni, he didn't mention the part of 'the theory of origin' that the Mahaguru had said to him before.

"What symbol? Show it to me," said Dobra, his extended hand was shaking with excitement.

Agni slowly brought out a piece of cloth on which the symbol was drawn. Dobra almost snatched it from his hand. He unfolded the cloth and looked at it. He kept staring, turned it sideways and looked at it from all angles possible. His brows were furrowed.

"I don't understand," he said. "I have come across a thousand symbols or more but never a single one like this." He was scratching his clean shaved cheeks.

"So?" asked Agni. Dobra looked up, the man seemed clearly troubled.

"Come with me," he said and almost sprinted up the stairs.

"Hey wait," shouted Vrish and both of them ran after him.

The man ran up the flights with remarkable speed which only came with practice, Agni and Vrish were right on his tail. They had reached the uppermost tier of the library.

"Guruji, Guruji," shouted Dobra and came to a halt in front of an elderly man seated alone on the floor in the middle of the room, almost a hundred books and scrolls lay scattered before him. Agni came to a halt behind him; Vrish climbed the final steps gasping for air.

"What is it, Dobra? How many times have I told you not to disturb me at this hour?" said the man angrily and then his eyes fell on Agni and a visibly panting Vrish.

"And who are they?" he asked in an irritated voice.

"Thief, thief," said Vrish, his words barely made it out between his heavy breathing.

"Be quiet Vrish," said Agni.

"Who are you two?" asked the man, his white beard glistening in the light.

"They are my friends, Guruji," said Dobra before Agni could reply. "They wanted to know what this is," said Dobra as he unfolded the cloth and showed him the symbol. The elderly man took it from Dobra's hand and looked at it, the furrow on his brow deepened.

"And where did you get this from?" asked the man looking straight at Agni.

"A friend," replied Agni without a flinch. The man kept staring at him and then a smile marked his face.

"Right," he said. "Come a little closer." Agni went a little closer to him.

"What is your name?" asked the man.

"My name is Agni and this is my friend Vrish," said Agni curtly.

"Agni is a good name. Do you know what it means?" asked the man.

"Fire," replied Agni promptly.

"Not just fire, it means the eternal fire. 'Agni' was a god of the ancient days. His name meant 'the fire that will burn through all the ages of man'," said the man with a smile.

"What is your name, Guruji?" asked Vrish. Dobra gave him a glance.

"Satadru, Guru Satadru," said the man. "Come sit," he said.

Agni sat down and gestured Vrish to do the same. Dobra also sat down without a word.

"Now let us come to the symbol," he said without delaying the matter. "The meaning of the symbol that you seek has no proper name or meaning at all, or more aptly its purpose was never discovered. It is only known as the symbol of balance, the perfect mix of spirituality and human existence. This was taken up as the sigil of the house of Darshana himself in his earlier days."

Then he turned to Dobra and said, "Bring that scroll, Dobra, the one with the seal of the eagle," said Guru Satadru pointing at the rack behind Dobra. Dobra got up immediately to fetch it.

Guru Satadru turned to Agni and said, "As I was saying, this symbol is more of a mystery and has become an urban legend. Some have come to believe that Darshana was trying to acquire some divine knowledge and this is the key, but none has come forth to prove it yet." Dobra came back with the scroll and handed it to Guru Satadru. He unrolled it and laid it down on the floor, it was written in some language that Agni did not understand.

"What language is this?" asked Agni.

"This is 'Chhanda', the ancient language of the first era. It is also called the 'rhyming language' in the west. This language is based on rhymes and riddles. Guruji is teaching me how to read 'Chhanda'," said Dobra happily.

"Silence, Dobra," said Guru Satadru angrily. Dobra fell silent immediately, not a single word escaped his mouth for the next few moments as it took Guru Satadru some time to go through the phrases and rhymes. "Here," he said putting a finger on a line. Agni, Vrish and Dobra leaned forward to get a better look, but it seemed that all of them were at a loss. It seemed even Dobra couldn't manage to understand a bit of it.

"It speaks of the ancient symbol of Darshana. The symbol has four hands joined with each other, extending partly in four directions which are neither east or west nor north or south. The same symbol was the sigil of the house of Emperor Ixus, the first emperor of Gaianna, the first empire of man," he said as he closed the scroll. "This is the most I have ever found."

"As I told you many had come to believe in different tales but they are not at all true. Maybe Darshana was truly searching for something but there is no proof. Many have come to Nisarga before you and they all have failed in their quest," he finished.

"This is the most that I can help you with as there is nothing else," said Guru Satadru. Agni knew that was his cue to leave. He stood up followed by Vrish. They folded their hands and joined their palms; Agni was the one to speak. "We thank you for your help, Guruji. I hope we can repay you somehow," asked Agni.

Guru Satadru smiled, "There is no need of that. I only hope that I have pointed you to the right direction and I think you are smart enough to understand what I mean. You two are much too young, don't waste your life in a fool's quest," he said.

"We understand," said Agni curtly.

"Good then, you have my leave. Dobra, show them out and don't come back for another hour or so. I don't want to be interrupted again," said Guru Satadru to Dobra.

"As you wish, Guruji," said Dobra and stood up.

"Our thanks again," said Agni and started down the stairs followed by Vrish and Dobra.

The trio reached the front door after a long descent. Dobra wanted to show them around a bit more, but Agni had refused politely. The library was bustling with people by then, young scholars and bibliophiles.

"Guru Satadru is one of the five great sages of Jambu. He may seem a little rough, but he always loves the seekers of knowledge," said Dobra.

"I saw that today. He is a good man. Moreover, I must thank you as it was because of you we found out about the symbol," said Agni.

"I had hoped that there would be more to it," said Dobra, he seemed a bit let down, so was Vrish from the look on his face.

Agni never mentioned what Sidak had said to him and from the way of things it wouldn't have mattered much. It looked as if only Guru Sidak knew what he meant when he spoke of that theory to Agni. One way or the other he would find that man and once he had done that he wouldn't need that symbol anymore. But what troubled him was how Malini came by that symbol and what was its relation to that man.

"I will continue my own search on this but I hope you will let me know once you find something new about this, this symbol I mean?" asked Dobra like a child.

"Certainly," lied Agni.

"We better be on our way," said Agni with a smile.

"See you later, my friends. May fortune favour you," said Dobra and waved his hand as they walked out of the premises. The roads were crowded and sun was hot outside.

They didn't bring their horses as the Library was a short distance from the palace.

"Well, that was a waste of time," said Vrish finally as they started to walk towards the Palace.

"Not completely, my friend. Now I am completely sure that we are in the right place," said Agni with smile.

Vrish looked a bit confused. "How so?" he asked.

"Where did we come across that man?" asked Agni.

"Here in Nisarga, if your guess is correct," replied Vrish. Agni ignored the second part.

"Who was the founder of Nisarga?" asked Agni again.

"Darshana," replied Vrish.

"Who took up this symbol as the sigil of his house?" asked Agni, his eyes pouring into his.

This time Vrish smiled himself, "Darshana," he replied.

"Exactly," said Agni as the grin on his face became broader.

☙

Sir Drake was sitting beside Yani in the royal garden of Nisarga. They were waiting for Agam. Yani wanted to speak to him first about his decision to make Paksha his champion. He didn't want to offend the old man as he had served his family for more than forty years, from the time when King Adhirath was a child. Moreover, Agam had been Yani's first teacher in the practice fields. Yani always believed that loyalty should be paid by kindness, unlike his father.

"Sir Drake, I always wanted to ask you something. It's just out of curiosity though," said Yani.

"Shoot," he said with his easy smile. Yani hesitated for a moment and Sir Drake assured him, "Prince, I assure you whatever you ask shall remain between us. I think you already know that very well," said Sir Drake. Yani smiled back.

"I just want to know how the kingdoms or the nations of the west are ruled. I mean based on which principle? Take Himadri for instance, it is ruled by a king, my father and I shall rule after him, Nisarga has a Senate and its principle is a mix between monarchy and republic," said Yani.

"A good question, like always," said Sir Drake with a hint of appreciation. "It's like this Prince, the kingdoms of the west is much like Nisarga, yet a little different."

"I don't understand," said Yani apologetically.

"No fear, I shall explain," said Sir Drake. He took a deep breath and started, "The Abode believes that kings were sent to Gaya by the Seven guardians or Sentinels to rule other men as they were more worthy than the others. But the Maker had spoken that the destroyer of all mankind shall be born from the seeds of a King of the west. So the Abode, which is based on the principle of the Seven that man has the right to exist, tried to chalk out a perfect system. 'The truth' speaks that a woman can never be the destroyer. Yet they wanted the blood of the kings to flow through the veins of man in the coming age and also they wanted to prevent the rise of the destroyer. So they made the Law of Ascension," said Sir Drake.

"What did the Law say?" asked Yani.

"That a king can never be chosen by the right of succession. The people of his kingdom will choose one among the ones in his blood line as the king. That is why a King in our lands cannot have a son," said Drake with a sad smile on his face.

"What if a son is born?" Then what happens?" asked Yani.

Sir Drake face became grimmer. "Well, that is the cruelest law of our land; the Prince is taken at birth by the Dark guardians, the snatchers."

"I thought they were only a myth," said Yani, astounded.

"Oh no, Prince, they are very much real. They do not walk the land of the rising Sun so they are considered to be a myth only here. But they are very real from where I come from," said Sir Drake.

"Have you ever seen them?" asked Yani, the curiosity in him rising fast. Sir Drake hesitated for a moment.

"Yes," finally he replied. "It's a dreadful sight Prince Yani, a new born child snatched away from a mother's bosom as those charred fingers coil around the beautiful pink flesh. You will feel that they are tightening around your own neck while you are helpless and can't do anything to stop them." There was a moment of silence, Yani was shocked and the very terror of the image made his smile disappear.

"I am sorry, Sir Drake, I didn't mean to bring back any bad memories," he said apologetically.

Sir Drake looked at him, his easy smile returning to his face. "It's all right," he said. "I always liked your curious nature."

"Maybe there is something more to it. The way I see it the law is tainted," said Yani abruptly.

Sir Drake remained silent, for some reason the smile on his face was gone.

"Ahh, there comes Agam. We will speak of this later, all right good Sir," said Yani. Sir Drake slowly nodded his head, but Yani didn't notice those piercing eyes.

ଔ

"How many men do they have in there?" asked Torman. The war council included Princess Lysandra, Damian, Torman and three of his lieutenant-captains Agnes, Kosmas and Old Theodore. They had set camp in the festival grounds of Small

Woods famous for the Pelagos festival in the summer. Pelagos were type of fish with two tails which came to lay their eggs near the shallow waters during the summer and they would hatch by the rainy season. The fishermen would collect the small fish and bring them to the festival grounds. 'Pelagos' was said to be the tastiest fish when cooked with garlic.

"My scouts on the hill-top report at least three large base camps inside the walls, maybe three thousand or more attackers," said Kosmas.

"A direct assault will be suicide," said Agnes.

"I agree," said Damian. "We are outnumbered three to one and they also have the higher ground."

"What is your opinion in this, Princess?" asked Torman. Lysandra was scraping off some wood from the edge of the table with her dagger. The others were staring at her. She was deep in thought about the little girl, Melissa. She was running a fever by the time she found her and her condition worsened. She was sent back to the Capital with a medicine man and a knight named Sir Halus. She had asked them to send word of their arrival.

"Lys?" called Damian, she looked up to him startled. "Building siege machines is out of the question as we do not have enough men. What of the sea? Is there a way through there?" she asked quickly.

"They have three war ships waiting for us there and they took out our entire fleet one by one on their way to Alexandria in the sea of Fortuna. It was all preplanned; the birds reached the Capital last night. They sent us word this morning," said Old Theodore.

Everyone sat there staring at her, in complete silence. Damian was the one to speak first, "The way I see it, a thousand rats would have served us better now than a thousand men.". Torman gave him a stern look. "Sorry," he said, but with a smile.

"What did you say, Damian?" asked Lysandra.

"If we had a thousands rats?" asked Damian, he was a bit surprised.

"Thousand rats," she repeated, everyone was staring at her with surprised looks on their faces.

"You are brilliant, brother," she said with a broad grin on her face. Torman and his captains looked at each other's faces.

"Sorry Princess, but what's so brilliant about it?" asked Torman.

"Why did the pirates always raid Alexandria from the time of Alexandria the first?" asked Lysandra.

"Because it was the richest port of the west," replied Torman.

"Why?" she asked again. Torman was staring at her blankly.

"Because of her gold mines," replied Agnes instead.

"Right," said Lysandra.

"Father once told me that there was a mine inside the city. It was much nearer to the shallow waters than the others. The workers accidentally made a hole in the wall and it made the sea to flow in, so the mine had to be sealed. That mine was the only one in a working condition even till a few years back. If we can find the exact position of the mine, we can make it inside the city unnoticed," said Lysandra with a smile.

"But finding a hole in an entire coastline is like finding a needle in a hay stack. This is absurd," said Agnes.

"Shut up, Agnes. Do not forget that you speaking to the Princess of Leu," said Torman angrily, the woman fell silent immediately.

"That is why we need to find an old map of Alexandria, at least ten to twenty years old. The imprint of the city will show the exact location of the mine inside the city. That way it will be much easier," she said with the same enthusiasm as before.

"I think it's worth a try, if someone doesn't have any better plans," said Damian.

"But how can we find such a map, I doubt that even the royal library of Leu or the records department will have a twenty-year-old map. All we have are the new ones and they don't show the old mines," said Kosmas.

"There is another problem," said Old Theodore. "How can we break through a solid brick wall if we remain underwater and the Maker only knows how long it will take us to reach it."

"We enter the caves when the tides are low. That way the water shall recede from the upper part of the caves," said Damian.

"And the map?" asked Agnes in a low voice.

"I think there is one place where we can find such a map," said Torman. All the others looked at him.

"Where?" asked Lysandra. Torman hesitated for a moment.

"Inside the archives of library of Alexandria itself," said Torman finally. "But the risk shall be too great and there shall be a single chance and no room for error," said Torman. The council fell silent.

"I will go," said Lysandra immediately.

Torman was drinking some water from a flagon, "No,' he shouted and almost choked. Agnes patted his back and he spurted out some water. He wiped his moustache and said, "You cannot go."

"Why?" she asked.

"I said you cannot go, Lysandra," he said it in a way that brook no argument, but she was never the one to listen. "I am sorry, but we will find someone else," said Torman without giving further explanations.

"I am not a child anymore, Torman," said Lysandra angrily. Torman remained unmoved.

"I am going," she said.

"No, you do not have my leave girl," shouted Torman at last. The others were a little taken aback by his outburst, so was Lysandra herself.

She calmed down a bit and said, "Look, I know you care for me, but you need good climbers. You know me and Damian were trained by Sir Egio himself in the seven arts for these days, Torman. Father himself sent us to him so that we can serve Leu in any situation. You know well that I was never raised to be a Princess." Both of them were staring at each other. "And I doubt either you or any of your captains have ever scaled a fifty hand wall," said Lysandra turning to his captains. "We need someone who is trained for this and from the look of things I am the only one," she finished.

"We have other climbers," said Torman.

"Yes, we have," said Lysandra. "I bet that they can climb but can they keep their mouth shut if they are caught?" she asked. Then she walked up to him and placed a tender hand on his shoulder, "This will be the key to our attempt in taking back Leu, you have seen what they did at Old Gate. God knows what they have been doing inside the city. There is no one else, Torman," said Lysandra.

"You are not going," said Torman right on her face. She felt her anger rise in her because of his mindless arrogance, yet he had been like a second father to her and her teacher.

"There is no one else," she repeated helplessly.

"Well, there is someone," said Damian with a yawn as he stretched his arms.

Everyone looked at him at once. "Who?" asked Kosmas.

Damian smiled, "Me, of course. She wasn't the only one who was trained by Sir Egio," he said.

"No, Damian," she said in a wary voice.

"We cannot count on just anyone to do this job, you said so yourself. You are needed here to lead the attack and Torman and his captains are unskilled, no offence," he said quickly turning to Torman.

"None taken," he replied.

"So that leaves only me," he said smartly.

"Then I shall come too," said Lysandra.

"Lys, you know very well that in this kind of a situation, one is better than two," said Damian.

"I don't want your suggestion, brother. This is an order," she said angrily.

"I am sorry, Lys, but scouting comes under my jurisdiction and this is almost like scouting," said Damian. Lysandra was taken aback by her brother's words. He got up and went to her, "Don't mind my words, sweet sister, just think of it this way. Maker forbid, if I get caught, then who will take care of father. Think of him first," said Damian in a low voice so that the others couldn't listen.

"And don't worry. I won't give away the plan if I get caught," he said loudly with a smile.

"This is not a game," said Lysandra angrily.

"I know, Lys. You can count on me, I won't fail and I promise that I will be all right," he assured her. Torman was silent and so were the others, to her surprise they did not object to his suggestion.

"So, do I have your leave?" he asked.

"No," she said flatly and walked out of the tent.

THE TOURNAMENT

A great arena was erected out of bamboo and wood in a matter of days beside the broad canal of Nisarga. A huge tent was raised to house the warriors and the stands were set for the common people to watch the games. A dais was raised on the other side, close to the tent for the guests and important members of the Senate to be seated. Yani was sitting there beside Sir Drake along with Agni and Vrish. The spectator count was much higher than expected and the common stands were too crowded for comfort. The floor of the ring was being flattened and made ready for the fights, which were to commence soon.

"He isn't back yet? Is he?" asked Agni.

"No," said Vrish. His face was dark. Agni knew that Droh would first come to Vrish after he returns.

Droh was gone for the past three days. He went looking for that man with the burnt face and Agni knew it was hell of a job to find one man, whose name they didn't know among a hundred thousand commoners in Nisarga. But still it was unlikely that Droh wouldn't turn up at nights to give the news of his latest findings. Agni and Vrish were also doing their part and they were going round the markets and the slums in the lower tier for the past two days looking for the man and Droh alike, but still they didn't have any luck either way. Agni knew that Droh was a very smart man and had a habit of pulling off very good disappearing acts when the time demanded. But that meant that he was in some sort of danger. Agni had, thus, decided on speaking with Agam about Droh being missing if he didn't turn up by the time the sun set that day.

Agni was about to say something to Vrish but his words were drowned by the words of the announcer with a cone shaped mouth piece in his hand. The man was dressed in all the colors known to man with a kettle hat, worn probably to protect himself from the misdirected shots of the contenders.

"The day for which we have waited so long has come forth," shouted the man in his mouthpiece. "Rajkumars of lands near and far, mighty lords of great republics and tribes, and Kings and Kinghts of the west have come to our great city for the hand of the lovely Aadrika ji, the daughter of the man we all love and respect, the High Senator himself." There was a round of applause and the short man gave a curt bow to the High Senator.

"This tournament will bring forth a victor whose master the beautiful Aadrika ji may consider appropriate to be her match. We wait to see the man who wields his blade like Asi, the god of war himself to bring together his master and our emerald of the east," shouted the man, his words were greeted with another round of applause.

The short man turned towards the tent and said, "Now coming out are the sixteen champions who will take the leap of faith as they contest against each other for the glory of their house and the gift."

"There are also a few who don't believe in depending on others to do their job and have taken up the blade in their own hands to claim the prize." The short man took out a piece of paper. "I bring to you Sir Dion of Erasmus," shouted the man. The crowd cheered as the huge knight with a long sword strapped around his back came out of the tent.

"Lord Zama of Khara," he shouted again and Lord Zama walked out with his scythe in his hand.

"Sir Justim of Athena representing the house of Lord Augus," he shouted.

"Kara, the famed warrior of the south representing the Prince Abalendu of Nada."

Then he paused for a moment as he peered into the piece of paper in his hand. "Now here is something interesting," he said as he looked up. "This warrior calls himself 'The Stranger' and he is representing the house of King Akakios of Euphrasia."

A man equipped with a dark metal plate armor walked out of the tent. He didn't wear any helm; there was a hood instead. Yet it couldn't hide the burns completely.

"Give your hands for 'the stranger'," shouted the man and the crowd cheered again.

Agni stood up and so did Vrish. "It's him," whispered Agni.

"Are you sure?" asked Vrish.

"Certain," replied Agni as he pinned the man with his gaze.

"What in the name of Trinetra is he doing here?" asked Vrish. Agni remained silent.

"What now?" he asked again. Yani noticed his friends standing.

"Is everything all right, Agni?" he asked. Agni was biting his lips out of frustration.

"Yani, I want to represent our house. Ask Paksha to take his name out of the tournament," said Agni quickly.

"What?" asked Yani. "Have you gone mad, Agni? This is not some small tournament in Himadri. Every one there is a seasoned fighter and what of your shoulder. It hasn't healed fully yet," he said angrily.

"My shoulder's fine," said Agni, still looking at that man. Then he turned to Yani and said, "We better hurry. If they call out his name, then it's over."

"But, why do you want...." Yani was interrupted in the middle by Agni.

"Please Yani, you've got to trust me. Once, this time only. I will be all right, I promise." Sir Drake had a grim look on his face as he continued to stare at Agni, but he ignored it. Yani let out a deep breath.

"But I don't understand why?" asked Yani with a pensive look on his face.

"I want it to be me Yani and I will explain everything later, but now please do as I say?" pleaded Agni.

"I cannot do that Agni, you have to understand that," said Yani sternly.

Agni went closer to him and held him by his shoulders, "There are a few things that I need to do and honestly I can't explain right now. It will be for the good of all, Yani. I won't let you down, I swear. I know this tournament means a lot to you," he replied, his honesty was completely disarming. Yani thought it was true that his friend had never let him down in the past and yet this was different. He took in a deep breath and asked, "Tell me just one thing Agni, what will I say to father if something happens to you?"

"Anything for the greatness of Himadri," said Agni with a smile as he started to make his way through them. But Sir Drake grabbed him by his wrist when he tried to pass him.

"Don't do this, Agni. Whatever might be your purpose, it can be taken care of later on," said Sir Drake.

Agni wrenched his hand free from his clutches and said, "I will be fine.". Agni came down from the dais followed by Vrish.

"This is madness, Agni. We can catch that guy later. Don't do this," he said as they started towards the tent.

Agni turned to him sharply, "We have been after this guy from the day we came here and we didn't succeed in finding even his tail. And now Droh has gone missing. All the answers to our questions are with him and I am not taking any chances anymore," he said and continued walking.

"What if we have the wrong guy?" asked Vrish.

"Then we will know soon," said Agni as he increased his pace.

∞

Damian slipped on the black leather gloves and strapped the metal plate round his back in case he fell down from a good height.

"Don't you need to dress more lightly?" asked Torman, Damian smiled back. They stood inside the tent of the war council. Lysandra wasn't there and she didn't speak a word to him after he decided to go on with the plan.

"When the sun sets, I will send my best archers to the western gate of the city. That will create a distraction for you to slip through their defences," said Torman.

"Right. Where is Lys?" asked Damian. Torman remained silent for a moment.

"She has gone to the small temple of the faceless one in the middle of the forest," said Torman. The same old Lys, he thought. She would always run to the gods whenever something didn't go her way. That brought a smile to his face.

"I will go and see her," said Damian. He was about to walk out of the tent when he felt Torman's hand on his shoulder, he turned around.

"Be careful out there, boy. I don't want to be one to bring any ill news to the King at this hour of his life," he said. Damian smiled at him one of his easy smiles. It was the only thing common between him and his elder brother. He knew that it was Torman's way of saying that he cared.

"Don't worry, I will be fine," he said.

"All right then, go to her and see that you calm her down a bit," said Torman. Damian gave a curt nod and left the tent.

Princess Lysandra was on her knees, her arms on her bosom and her head bowed in front of the demigod, who was said to be made from the essence of the Maker himself.

"You pray to the one who doesn't even show his face?" came Damian's voice from behind her.

"I pray to him because he has many faces," she replied without looking at him.

"Why have you come?" she asked in a rigid tone.

"You pray for me and yet when I show up, I get this," sighed Damian.

Lysandra looked at him, he was smiling like always. That made her heart melt and she couldn't keep up the walls between them. She walked up to him and grasped his hand.

"Don't do this brother, please," her rigidity had melted into pure agony.

"Sweet sister," he said as he placed a tender hand on her cheek. "I am doing this because I must. I can never let you go in there while I am still around. Yet think of the lives that will be lost if we do not take back Alexandria. The very existence of Leu depends on us," said Damian looking into her eyes.

"Then take me with you. I am as good a climber as you," she said quickly.

Damian was still smiling at her. "Then if we get caught together what will happen to Leu? What will happen to our father?" he asked. Lysandra was silent, her gaze had dropped to the ground.

He forced her face up towards him tenderly. "You are the Princess of Leu, people have looked up to you and they always will. If you take a risk, that would not only mean that risking your own life, but of thousands of others as well."

"We can make a direct assault and if it fails, then we can certainly hold them off at the gates," she said, her desperation clear on her face.

"If we march back empty handed, even without trying, the spirit of Leu will be shattered. Didn't you say so yourself that Leu is a thought, a dream which should be kept alive," said Damian. Lysandra felt helpless.

"I don't want to lose you. I cannot make the same mistake that I made earlier," said Lysandra. A drop of tear trickled down her cheek.

"The warrior Princess of Leu never cries," said Damian as he wiped away her teardrop.

"I will come back, I promise." His easy smile brought little hope to her.

೦೩

Agni stood alongside the other fifteen warriors in the middle of the arena. His eyes transfixed on the dark figure that stood a few paces away from him. Agni knew that this was the only way to come face to face with him or else he wouldn't have been there then. He swore that he would make him talk even if it meant pulling out each word with his blade. He thought of how he had walked inside the tent with Agam and Vrish a few moments ago. When Agam had told Paksha that Agni would be replacing him, he had only looked at Agni with malice in his eyes. He threw away his sword and then left the tent without a word. The next thing, Agni was standing there, all dressed up for the event. He wore a leaf armored vest and a spiked leather cap over his head. He had a short sword in his hand which suited his style. Agni looked up at the dais and his eyes looked for the man called Akakios, but there were so many unknown faces that he couldn't even guess. Agni knew that he would soon find out, as soon as the 'Stranger' wins a battle. It was a custom to give a formal salute to one's master after a battle was won. His eyes got stuck on the tensed faces of Yani and Vrish, even Sir Drake had a grim look on his face.

The short man with the mouth piece came and stood in front of Agni with his back turned towards him.

"Here stand the sixteen warriors who will go through hell for the glory of their house. The rules are simple," he said and started to pace. Agni's ears were already ringing.

"There will be three rounds. The eight who shall be victorious in the first will move on to the second. Then they will face each other in the third and then there shall be the final battle," he shouted out aloud. "There shall be no room for errors," shouted the man and the crowd cheered, it rose like a storm and fell. The announcer had raised his hand in the air to silence them. "Their names shall be drawn at random from the box. So are we ready for the tournament to begin?" he asked, the crowd roared in reply. The announcer came up to them and spoke in a soft voice which Agni never thought the man to be capable of.

"Please make your way to the tents, you will be called when your turn comes," he said politely.

"Whom shall I be facing first?" asked Sir Dion, he was the scariest of them all, huge to be precise.

"It will be decided soon, Sir Knight," said the man curtly.

"Make sure I am the one to fight the first battle. I dislike waiting," said the veteran knight with a heavy accent.

"I will try my best," replied the man meekly.

"Good," said Sir Dion and started to walk towards the tent. The others followed his lead. Agni fell in with the others in the line as his eyes remained glued to the man who walked a few paces ahead of him.

ॐ

The first battle started after a few moments and every man inside the tent fell silent. Not a single one of them spoke a word as their eyes were glued to the two men in the centre of the ring. The announcer had kept his word. The first battle was between Sir Dion and a man with equally menacing looks, named Asi after the old god of war himself. Asi wielded two scythes in his both hands but he wasn't even getting close enough to land a blow as Sir Dion wielded the heavy piece of metal as if it was made of wood. Asi was quick enough to avoid his crushing counter blows. The crowd cheered them on. Sir Dion made a horizontal swing but Asi dodged it, seeing an opening he charged in towards his legs. But Sir Dion shifted his sword's weight in one hand and dashed his fist into the man's face, Asi reeled back a few paces. His nose was broken and a few of his teeth shattered.

"Your tricks won't work on me, little man," shouted Sir Dion, the crowd cheered for the huge man's self belief and raw masculine strength. Asi grinned, a few of his front teeth were missing. He spat out some blood and brought out three balls made of glass, out of his sleeves.

"You haven't seen any of my tricks yet," he said and threw the balls on the ground. They broke open and some liquid spilled out on the ground. Sir Dion's eyes were fixed on Asi, but his small frame slowly disappeared in a mist that shrouded the place within moments. Sir Dion's huge frame was only partly visible. There was a sound of steel scraping on steel. "Coward," came Sir Dion's roaring voice from the middle of the mist. Agni did his best to look through it but the mist got more opaque with every passing moment. There was another sound of steel searing through flesh and steel plate alike and then was a scream. The crowd held their breath, so did Agni. It all started to clear slowly. When the mist had disappeared Sir Dion lay on the ground writhing in pain and a pool of blood. There were stains on the chain mail near his armpits, behind his knee and loose hinges of his breastplate. Sir Dion was clutching the right side of his chest. Asi stood there with a sneer on his face. Sir Dion gritted his teeth as he tried to stand up but collapsed on the ground from the effort. Agni's mouth was wide open, he never thought that a knight of Sir Dion's stature could be beaten so easily and within such less time, he swallowed some air.

"We have a winner," shouted the short man in his mouthpiece. "The famed master of the mist, Asi of the southern island of Nisk." Asi waved his hand in the air and the crowd clapped for the winner. He gave a curt bow to his master and walked out of the ring with his head held high. Sir Dion was picked up in a stretcher. Agni thought that if that was the level of the competition, then maybe Yani was right.

"Scared, boy?" came an unknown voice to Agni's ears. He turned and saw a man standing to his left, dressed in a pale blue leather vest.

"You will be facing me, the famed Gora," he said with an air full of pride. The others were looking at them. Gora took out his sword and Agni's hand instantly went on the hilt of his own. The Stranger looked on with curious eyes.

"Relax boy, I won't kill you here. What fun it would be? I want to give them a show, stay down when I say and maybe I will let you live," he laughed and walked out of the tent.

"Don't worry, losers always talk big," said the young man with blonde hair sitting beside Agni. He had a smile on his face, a young knight called Sir Justim. Agni smiled and nodded his head. He took in a deep breath as his hand went for the pendant in his pocket, the one with Malini's name written on it. He rolled it between his fingers; the announcer was already calling out his name. He started to walk towards the ring.

"When you are facing one enemy, how many are you facing and whom do you need to defeat first?" the voice was ringing in his ears.

"Two, and firstly I must defeat the fear in my heart," whispered Agni to himself and there was a smile on his face.

"Here comes the opponent, Agni of Himadri," shouted the short man as Agni jogged out in the middle. The whole thing looked so different from the stands, he thought. His eyes went for Yani and the others, and he saw even Agam standing beside them.

"The fear in my heart," he repeated to himself and started to shake his legs to warm up a bit.

"Well, he seems to be in high sprits. Good luck to both the fighters. Begin!" shouted the short man and almost sprinted out of the ring.

"Don't forget what I said, boy," said Gora and took out his sword. Agni hadn't noticed it in the first time, but his blade looked different than the others. It was a thin blade, rather many many sharp blades joined together by a central beam to form one.

"Ready or not, here I come," shouted Gora and charged in. His speed surprised Agni and he had to do some quick back steps to block his attack. The crowd cheered as the fight commenced.

"Good, nice feet you have there," said Gora as he continued to press on, his blows were directed to the same spot over and over again. It seemed like that he was only toying with him. Agni made a quick three sixty degree swing and tried to jab his sword in his left shoulder but Gora deflected it with ease. Agni bounced back with consecutive horizontal swings but Gora simply leaned back and avoided them craftily. Agni leapt towards him right at that moment giving a full body bash which made Gora fall down on the ground, but he quickly rolled over and stood up. The crowd cheered for Agni.

"Very good, nice," Gora said with a cruel smile on his face as he brushed of the dust of his cloths.

"My turn," he said and charged in. Gora swung his sword horizontally, Agni quickly lifted his sword in time to block his attack but Gora's sword turned into a sort of whip and danced round his blade in mid air. It made a deep gash on the same shoulder, the wound reopened and Agni let out a scream. He grasped his shoulder and stepped back a little. Drops of sweat trickled down his neck and forehead as the pain came back again. His friends stood up. Yani grasped the ledge and squeezed it. Agni was looking at the sword.

"So do you like my sword, her name is Lata," said Gora with the persistent smile on his face.

"Nice," said Agni with gritted teeth.

Gora chuckled, "You are something," he said. "We will put on quite a show together."

Then Gora charged in, he cracked his whip-like-sword in mid air and made a curve, dodging Agni's sword again. Agni let out another scream as it chiseled out some flesh from the same shoulder. Then another blow scraped some flesh from the back of his thigh. Agni came down to his knees, the pain too strong for him to bear.

"Stop it, Agam, before he gets himself killed," said Yani with reproach. Sir Drake and Vrish were staring at him but both of them chose to remain silent. Agam nodded his head and started to walk towards the announcer standing at the edge of the ring. Yani was in two minds: if he stopped the fight then that was the end of it. He would be so ashamed that he won't able to look at his father in the eye. But if he let it continue, then it could mean the death of his beloved friend. Yani looked at Agni, he was sitting ducks. But then, he slowly stood up again.

"Agam," shouted Yani. Agam turned around and Yani gestured him to come back and let the fight continue.

Gora rendered blow after blow on Agni as he barely kept himself on his feet. In between each blow, Gora would coil the blade around his gauntlets like a whip and undo it again to strike the next blow. His steel gauntlets had pointy things protruding out of it like jagged spikes. He had a broad grin on his face as he enjoyed the sight of Agni bleeding all over.

The crowd had gone silent. They looked on as if it was more of a slaughter than a fight.

"Scream boy, the crowd isn't enjoying this mundane show," shouted Gora like a madman as his blade slashed through the wound on his bleeding shoulder once again. Agni screamed and he could feel his vision getting blurred like before. Some of the women in the crowd had their hands covering their mouths.

'I cannot lose,' he whispered to himself and stood up with the help of his blade.

"Good, good. Stand up now, slowly," he said with that same smile. Agni looked at him. He saw that Gora's blade was wound around his gauntlets as he made himself ready for the next blow. Gora's gauntlet was custom made and had three protruding spikes like a grappling hook, only much smaller. Agni looked at his own gauntlets and they were almost the same but a little different. If only he could make the damn thing hit where he wanted, then he could catch it and do the same like Gora. Agni spat out some blood as he stood up with a smile on his face.

Gora was a bit surprised. "What are you smiling at boy?" he asked.

"No, I was only thinking. You have landed say some ten blows by now and yet I am standing and you call yourself the famed Gora," sighed Agni. A few in the crowd laughed and Gora's face turned red with anger and humiliation.

"Well the way I see it, it is going to be a long day before you are done. I hope they have come with theirs meals packed and ready," said Agni pointing at the crowd. This time all of them laughed at Gora.

"What in the seven hells is he doing?" shouted Yani angrily. "Why is he taunting him?"

"Maybe he has a plan," said Vrish. Yani gave him a look and didn't believe what Vrish said.

Gora was fuming by then. "I thought that I was going to spare your life but it seems that you wish to die real bad," said Gora as he twisted the hilt of his sword or whip or what ever it was.

Agni made himself ready, knowing it was his final chance.

"Die," raged Gora and swung his sword in the air with all his strength. The thing came flying towards Agni. It was so fierce that it made a whirling sound as it came right towards his neck. The crowd looked on, air seemed to have got stuck in their throats. All of them were out of their seats. Then there was a sound like a clank. The crowd didn't understand at first. Agni had caught the blade and quickly rolled it around his forearm. Gora was shocked out of his wits, he gave it a pull but it didn't come lose.

"I knew you would aim there. Your sword is only good for slashing attacks, not for piercing. So I knew that you needed to take off my head to kill me with one strike," said Agni with a smile, the crowd roared in delight to see the turn of events.

Gora pulled it harder, but the more he pulled, the tighter it got coiled around Agni's forearm.

"Why isn't it coming loose?" shouted Gora out of frustration as he continued to pull.

"Come here, I will tell you," said Agni and gave a hard pull with all his strength. Gora was shocked to see the power of it as he almost came flying towards Agni. Agni curled his right fingers into a fist and dashed the steel of the gauntlet hard into his face. There was a sickening crunch. Gora fell down on the ground, his lips broken, his teeth shattered and blood gushed out of his nose. Agni laid the bare steel on the apple of his throat and said, "Our gauntlets are almost the same." The crowd broke into a roar of an applause.

THE 'UNBURNT'

The shadow of the night had swallowed the forest as a whole. The city of Alexandria became more prominent as the fires raged inside the city in many places. It looked like a thousand pyres had been lit at once. The top of the walls were dotted by hundreds of flickering lights as the guards patrolled them. It seemed like the very pits of hell from high up there.

"Great Maker of man and gods alike, guide me to my goal so that I may return with my prize successfully," he whispered to the one above with his eyes closed and his palm on his black chest guard. He was dressed much lightly than normal, a black chest guard and a back plate, no helm or helmets, leather gloves, light leather greaves and leather knee caps. The light bastard sword was strapped round his back and a dagger dangled from his belt. A grappling hook with a long rope was coiled around his waist.

Suddenly there was a hue and cry, the flickering lights started to rush towards the western gate. That was his cue, Torman's archers had come. He jumped off the edge, skidded through the wet soil of the slope and came to a halt on the edge of the marshes. From there he made his way down the woods, he had decided to climb the southern wall as it seemed to be shorter in height and much more rougher on the outer surface when he went scouting near it in the dead of the night before that one. The sound of battle became more and more distant as he crept up to the base of the wall. Damian looked from one side to the other. Then he took off the grappling hook and uncoiled the rope. He tied the rope with the hook and checked the knot. He made a few practice swings at first, loosening his arm a bit. Then he started to swing it in a larger loop.

"One, two and three," he said and threw it up but it fell down. "One, two and three," he counted and threw it again, but it fell down again. His frustration was rising; Torman's men would retreat any moment. Time was running out. He took a deep breath and started to swing it again, only harder this time.

"One, two and three," he almost shouted and threw it up with all his strength. This time it didn't fall. He pulled the rope twice to check it and to his relief, it didn't come loose. He balanced himself by winding his legs around the rope in a leg lock and began climbing. The surface was rough and it helped him to place his feet on the edges from time to time; it became easier for him. He was almost midway when he heard raised voices. He stopped then and there. He was hanging in the middle when he heard them getting closer. There were at least two of them. He looked down, it was a long fall. He held his breath as they came nearer, dots of sweat appeared on his forehead.

"Hurry up, we don't have time. The western gate is under attack,' said one of them.

"How many?" asked the other.

"Can't say. Those bastards are shooting from the cover of the woods. I was sent to get the others," the man replied.

'So why only the two of us?" asked the other man.

"I have sent Anton to the base camp, they need archers first," said the man as they rushed past him. The voices grew fainter. Damain hung on. His hands were starting to hurt. To his relief, the voices were gone completely. He gave out a low whistle and started to climb. He offered thanks to the Maker for it had been a close call. They had missed the grappling hook in their rush. He continued to climb and after a few moments he was standing on the top of the wall, the cool breath of wind ruffling his hair.

He gathered the rope and coiling it into a loop, hung the hook from his belt. He moved along the wall as lightly as possible and found a stair leading to the level ground. He came down beside a granary. He quickly went around it into the shadows and took out a hand drawn map given to him by Torman. He laid it open on the ground in the little light of the moon. He peered into it and strained his eyes to make out the exact markings. It seemed that he had come down a little away from where he had actually intended. The Library was a fair fifteen hundred paces from where he stood. He folded it and pushed it back inside his pocket.

He stepped out of the dark and went straight into the alleys. The moon lit his path as he made his way through the deserted narrow lanes. He noticed from the corners that there were several fires raging on the streets and there was an unavoidable stench in the air. The most horrible of thoughts came to his mind but he pushed them away. He ran as lightly as he could and reached the backyard of a small house. He saw that there was an inn on the other side of the road and a fire raged in front of it. He was about to take out the map again but he was startled by the scream of a woman. He peeked out and saw that a man came walking towards the inn with four soldiers and a woman behind him. She was barely in her thirties. They were dragging her along as they followed the man. Damian looked closely and saw that he bore the mark of the Seven. He was a priest of the Abode.

"No, please no. I haven't done anything wrong. Please don't do this," she pleaded with them as they dragged her along by her hands. The soldiers made her stand straight in front of the priest.

"Please," she begged with folded hands. "I will do anything, anything you want," she sobbed. Her face was clear to Damian as she faced him and the priest's back was turned towards him.

"Kneel, child, so that I may atone you for your sins," said the Priest. She knelt down on her knees and her face disappeared out of his sight, but her sobs were clear.

"Do you accept your sins?" asked the priest in a solemn voice.

"What sins?" she asked sobbing.

"The sin of selling your flesh and defiling your body for petty gold in exchange," said the Priest.

"I had no choice, please. I have a son. I only did it for him, for us to survive," she sobbed hysterically.

"This is the voice of your corrupt soul and as the great beast has said, it is only fire that can cleanse the soul of the living," said the Priest. The soldiers quickly grabbed her by her arms before she could move.

"No, no. Not that. Please," she pleaded as the soldiers dragged her towards the raging inferno. Damian wanted to go out and save the girl but if an alarm was raised then that would be the end of their plans to liberate the city. It was five against one. He heard her pleading and every nerve of his body was straining itself to go out and save her. But then he thought of the others, maybe there were thousands like that girl in there and they could be saved from a dreadful fate if their plan went well. He slumped back in his spot and looked away, feeling completely helpless. He closed his eyes and would have closed his ears if he could. Her pleading was burning his heart. He took out his dagger and held the sharp blame against his palm. Then came the most piercing shriek that he had ever heard. He gripped the sharp edge firmly. Blood dripped from his hand as her screeches filled the night sky.

೮

Agni sat inside the guest room of the palace. A practitioner applied a healing salve on his wounds. The first day of the tournament had ended sometime after he was rushed back to the palace. He missed the chance to see the Stranger fight. Unlike the others, he was facilitated in his own room as requested by Yani rather than going to a healing house. They had their own head practitioner Aamod, but it was a rule that only the charted Practitioners of Nisarga could treat the injured and certify them fit enough for the next match. So the practitioners from Himadri were not allowed inside the palace, they were to stay at the camp until the tournament got over. It was mostly because of the reason that some medicinal herbs could be misused in the process but that wasn't a problem that some mudras couldn't solve.

"How bad is it?" asked Yani. The practitioner looked up. "I will not lie to you Rajkumar, it looks bad. I will certainly advise you not to let him fight tomorrow," he replied. "His left shoulder is in poor condition."

"Will it be good enough to move a little?" asked Agni.

"I think so because no bones were broken. But there is a huge chance of an infection if the wound reopens again," said the practitioner.

"I will fight tomorrow," said Agni flatly. Yani was surprised by his vigour.

"Well, think again Agni! You have won the first round and if the charted practitioner says then we have the option of replacing you with Paksha," said Yani. Agni looked at the practitioner and said, "Can you give me something to kill the pain during the fights?" asked Agni.

"I can...but," he paused.

"But?" asked Vrish. The practitioner remained silent.

"You don't have anything to worry about. Whatever you say here will remain between us," assured Yani. The man gave a sideways glance at Sir Drake. "He is a trusted friend," said Yani quickly.

He took in a deep breath and said, "Well I have a better option," then he paused. "There is herb called 'Uddeg'. It will not only kill the pain but it also augments one's skills greatly for a short period, say five to six hours of the sun or the moon. After which when the effects wear off, it weakens a person to a great extent. He may pass out in the middle of things. But I must warn you," he said. "It is not legal."

"We have guessed that much already," said Yani with a smile.

"Five hours is all I need," said Agni. He was least worried about breaking some rules then.

"What if you pass out in the middle of a fight?" asked Vrish and then turned to Yani. "You said you could replace him," said Vrish.

"No," Agni flared up.

"He could be replaced if the charted practitioner says so, but there might be a few problems," came Sir Drake' voice. They turned towards him. "Well, see, there are a few common rules of a tournament. One has to be dead or bed-ridden to be replaced. Now our good friend here may be kind to us," he said looking at the practitioner. "But I doubt the others will be when they come to check on Agni," "That is why I asked him not to enter the tournament in the first place," finished Sir Drake looking straight at Agni.

"I did not know that," said Yani scratching his head.

"But this is insane, how can he fight in this condition," said Vrish helplessly.

"Stop this Vrish. I will be fine," said Agni in an irritated voice.

"Then there is little choice, it's a risk we have to take," said Yani at last. Vrish gave him a look.

"It's a risk *he* has to take," he wanted to say.

"Then it's settled. You will bring that herb tomorrow," said Agni firmly.

"I am warning you once again: the effect of this herb is not fully known yet. It can cause more harm than good," warned the practitioner.

"I have decided," said Agni.

The man looked at Yani and then said, "Very well, I will see to it."

"I will show our friend out," said Sir Drake and led him outside the room. Yani came and sat beside Agni.

He smiled and said, "I know you will win, I have faith in you my friend."

"I will not let you down," replied Agni. But in his heart he knew that he was not doing this either for Yani or for Himadri. The tournament was his only chance to come face to face with the stranger if he was as capable as he believed. Yani didn't have to know the truth. Agni's hand went into his pocket again for the pendant.

"I shall leave you to rest. You have a big day tomorrow," said Yani and stood up. Agni gave a curt nod.

"Come, Vrish," said Yani as he walked towards the door. Vrish didn't want to leave. "Come now, Agni needs his rest," called out Yani. Agni gestured him to leave but he got closer to him and whispered, "Don't do this. This is plain stupid."

"Come," came Yani's voice floating to him again, he was standing outside.

"I will be all right, now do as he says. We will talk later," said Agni strongly. Vrish left without another word. He didn't even spare him a second glance. Agni knew that his friend was angry with him, but he also knew that he would come around soon. There were bigger problems to be solved and there were questions which remained unanswered. He rolled the pendant between his fingers again.

"Bring me luck, Malini," he whispered to himself.

ය

The fire still raged on, but the screams couldn't be heard anymore. Damian stood up, his bleeding hand still shaking from the horror that he had witnessed a few moments ago.

"They will pay," he muttered to himself under his breath. He tore a part of his sleeve and tied it around his self-inflicted wound. The drops of blood could attract unwanted attention in the wrong places. He slowly stood up and started to make his way through the dark lanes. The road ahead of him was long. He stuck to the corners in the dark shadows. In some places he heard raised voices but then he didn't stop to look. He tried to keep his mind clear, but the vision kept coming back to him like a bad dream. At one point, he saw a group of men going through the wares of a blacksmith's shop. The blacksmith himself was nowhere to be seen. He thought that the blacksmith must be one of those many faces he had seen in the long queue of men, women, children, carts and horses who had left their home behind and were heading for Leu everyday or that's what he hoped. It was a fate much better than what he had witnessed that night.

He sneaked past them unnoticed, as they continued finding a new suit of armor for their friend. After an exhausting sprint through the darkness of the alleys, Damian finally saw the front gate of the Library's compound, but for some reason there were four guards standing outside it. There was no way that he could have sneaked past them unnoticed. He turned the corner and went round to the back of the compound. He came to a halt in front of the high wall, there were no back gates. He could have easily climbed the wall with his hook, but jumping down on the other side would have proved to be much difficult and it would have spelt disaster if he had broken his ankle or any joint somehow in the attempt. But there was little choice on his part. He threw the hook up and climbed up the wall. He coiled the rope around his waist and hung the hook from his belt. He leaned forward a bit and saw the drop. It was a fair fall. He looked around to see if anyone was coming and then positioned himself on the edge of the wall. He jumped and fell on the ground on his feet and then rolled over. To his luck, he didn't suffer any injury from the fall. He stood up and looked around for a back door. He turned the corner and saw a door made of black wood. He gave the door a gentle push to avoid making any sound but it seemed locked from the inside. He gave a stronger push the next time and it made a creaking noise.

"When all of this will be over, I will become as rich as a saffron trader," came a voice.

"Yes, me too," said the other voice happily. "I have found a chest full of old coins. I bet they will fetch me a good sum back at Erythrea."

Damian started to sweat. The guards had started their patrol and they were heading his way. He looked around for a place to hide but couldn't find any. There were small bushes which would hardly conceal a grown man. He started to push frantically, the light from their torches could be seen from round the corner. He gave it one hard push with all his strength and the door creaked open. He rolled inside just in time and closed the door. His back was resting against it as he took in a deep breath.

"I think I heard something," said one of them as the light from their torches illuminated the edges of the door.

"I didn't hear anything," said the other.

"But I did. I heard someone closing this door," said the man firmly.

"That's plain stupid. The walls are too high to jump over and we all were standing at the gates for the last hour of the moon or so," said his friend.

"No, I am sure that I heard it," he insisted. "Help me," said the man and Damian started to panic, the tension rising in him steadily.

"On the count of three," said one of them and Damian held the ledges to prevent it from opening.

"One, two and three," shouted the man and pushed. The sheer force almost threw him backwards but he held on.

"Another," shouted the man and gave another push, both of them together. Damian held his place barely.

"See, it's locked," said the one from before as he panted from the effort.

"I am not going anywhere before I take a look inside. I want to be sure" said the man arrogantly.

"All right, then. If you have to look, then let us get our back on it," said his friend as they positioned in front of the door again, Damian held his breath. "One, two and three," they counted again and they threw their weight against it. The door almost came loose from its hinges and dust flew everywhere. The guards walked inside the room. It made the other one cough; he put his hand over his nose. The man who was desperate to get inside raised the torch high above his head. He rolled his eyes all over the place. He stood there still.

"See, there is no one in here. Please let us get out of here before I choke to death," said his friend. He rolled his eyes all over the place and gave a nudge to a few things that lay scattered here and there.

"It seems you were right. Maybe I heard it wrong," said the man as they walked out of the room.

"I am always right," said the other. They adjusted the partly broken door in its place.

Damian slowly opened the lid of a huge chest to the right of the door. He had crept inside it just in time. He had taken off the piece of cloth from his wounded palm and tied it around his nose to prevent himself from sneezing. The scent of his own blood filled his nostrils as he crept out of the old trunk. He looked around in the little light and saw that it was sort of a store room for old books and useless old scrolls, which had been copied into new books. He stood there trying to get himself together, too much excitement for one day. Getting in was the first part; but finding what he wanted was an entirely different thing. That's what he realised when he came out of the little store room and found himself staring at the winding wooden stairs climbing at least four floors. There would certainly be a hundred rooms and a few halls, but he needed to find the archives first and then look in other places if Torman's words proved wrong. Still it was going to be a long night; there'd be at least a thousand scrolls in there, he thought to himself.

 og

"How is your friend now?" asked Sir Drake as Yani walked inside the room.

"He seems all right. Good enough to fight," said Yani as he closed the door behind him.

"That was quite a fight he put on there," said Sir Drake. Yani sat down on his bed.

"Right," he mumbled unmindfully.

"You seem troubled," asked Sir Drake. Yani remained silent. "It is all right if you don't want to speak about it, Prince. We can always talk about something else," said Sir Drake as he poured some more honeyed wine in his glass.

"I somehow feel that he is not doing this for me or Himadri," Yani blurted out.

"Why do you feel like that?" he asked with a smile on his face.

"Doesn't it seem obvious, Sir? If it was the other way around he would have come to me before the tournament started," replied Yani. Sir Drake choose to remain silent. "Everything happened so fast, I am so confused," said Yani more to himself than Sir Drake.

"Maybe you are right," said Sir Drake, Yani looked up at him. "Did you force him or insist upon him telling you the exact reason for his decision to enter his tournament?" he asked.

Yani shook his head. "Why?" he asked again.

"I don't know, it didn't seem so important, just odd and most importantly, I have faith in his abilities and I can also trust him with my life," he replied.

Sir Drake leaned a bit closer to him. "Look, you are a Prince. One day you will rule a kingdom. It doesn't matter why he is doing this. The only thing that matters is the result, and you know that very well. That is why you didn't ask; because he won the match." Yani was staring at him. He leaned back a little and said, "If he would have lost, then I presume it would have been a completely different matter."

Then he leaned closer to him again and put his hand on his shoulder, "Remember, Prince, all you need is the result. Not the means, not the reasons, only the result. Or else your father will be very angry with you and you said that you trust your friend." Yani had a bemused look on his face.

"And how do you know that my father will be very angry with me if I fail?" he asked with a smile on his face. Sir Drake seemed unfazed.

"I overheard everything the night your father came to your room and Agni and Vrish were with me too," he replied flatly. "I also know that you made the painting for him and you wanted him to be the first one to look. But I was a bit hurt when you didn't even show it to me after he refused," complained Sir Drake.

Yani laughed out aloud. "Good Sir, you have been the best of friends to me lately and I apologize for not showing it to you. But I must tell you that I have decided to do something else with it," said Yani, smiling.

"What?" asked Sir Drake.

"I have decided to give it to my champion. Win or lose, he will be the first one to see it," said Yani. Sir Drake leaned back on the cushions.

"Then I will not take his prize way. Whatever might be his reason, I must say that he is giving it his all," said Sir Drake.

"True," said Yani. Sir Drake stood up.

"Let us not ponder over the details, instead let us celebrate your first victory," said Sir Drake as he poured some of the honeyed wine in another glass and handed it to Yani.

"To your champion Agni. May he be victorious" he said as he raised his glass in the air.

"To Agni," repeated Yani, tapping each other's glass lightly. Both of them drank deep.

ଊ

Damian had gone through the entire floor and had found nothing. There was no sign of the Archives. Torman had said to him that it was most likely that the old maps would be kept in there. There were no signboards anywhere as most of them had been toppled over by the visitors in the rush to leave the place during the time of the invasion or by the invaders themselves, and most of the wooden stands lay in ruin.

Damian climbed the wooden stairs as lightly as he could. He made his way towards the passage of the second floor. He was about to open the door of a small room when his eyes fell on the corridor beside him. A room to his left had its doors open and light was coming out of it. He slowly started to make his way towards the place to see if anyone was in there. He heard the sound of turning of pages as he got closer. He halted near the edge of the door and peeked inside.

A huge man, massive in his shoulders sat on a chair in front of a small desk. He was going through some of the old books which lay scattered around him. A glimmering white robe strapped to his shoulders shimmered in the light.

There was a symbol on it and he noticed that it wasn't the mark of the Seven, the seven swords pointing in seven directions enclosed by a circle. It was a single mark and as Damian looked closely, his mouth fell open. It was the symbol of the Chimera of the Beast, the third guardian. 'That is why the place was guarded and the guard wanted to be sure that no one had entered the building,' thought Damian to himself. It was said that the Seven Lords weilded such powers that it was beyond the thought of a common man. They wielded magic. Damian stepped back immediately and he was about to turn around when the screams of that woman echoed in his ears. He stood there still. He turned around and looked at that man. 'It was all because of him,' he thought. If he could take him out right there, all of it would come to an end and Alexandria could be taken back with one stroke. But what if he got caught? Lysandra's face came floating in front of eyes, 'I will come back,' he had promised to his sister.

Then he shook his head; he needed to be strong. This was the same reason for which he lost Irene. If only he would have stood up to his brother then, she would have been alive. The wretch had pushed her over the edge of the balcony and had blamed her drinking habits which she had taken up sometime after her marriage to his brother. Her maid told him that it was better that way for no woman could bear the unspeakable horror that was inflicted on the love of his life,

Irene. He had cried then and cried some more, yet there was no end to it. But his tears couldn't bring her back as she was gone forever.

Damian clenched his fists. There were a few things that should be done then and there, when there is still chance. That was the lesson he had learnt. Damian took out his dagger and walked up to the edge of the door again. The man sat with his back turned towards him. He knew he would have only one chance with this, one, and he could not fail. He needed to be swift and lethal like lightning. Damian took in a deep breath and positioned himself to move in for the kill. 'Lightning,' he whispered to himself and the candle beside the door flickered as he rushed past it with amazing speed. His dagger went for the back of the man's neck. The next thing he remembered was flying back a few paces and crashing into the shelf. The man had turned around with an impossible speed and his elbow had struck him right across his face. The mere touch had sent him flying back. The candle stand fell beside him as the shelf cracked into two from the impact. If it wouldn't have been for his back plate his spine would have been shattered. He tried to get up but felt a strong pain in his back and slumped back on the ground. His sword was stuck somewhere in his back plate and he saw blood, but strangely he didn't feel any pain. The lower part of his body had gone numb. The Beast slowly stood up.

"It is not a worthy thing to do for a Lord, attacking a holy man from behind," he said. Damian had a look of surprise on his face.

"The ring on the index finger of your right hand," said the man. Damian looked at his ring. Every royal house had a different coloured stone as the mark of their family, King Crixus' was red.

Damian had a look of disgust on his face. "You call yourself a holy man and yet you burn innocent citizens alive," he said. "You are nothing but a monster," he completed in a voice full of anger and disgust.

The Beast smiled. "I do not expect you to understand, you are still young, much young. But it is the truth that it is only fire that can cleanse the soul of the living. Dread is the greatest weapon to prevent a man from making mistakes," said the Great Beast.

Damian was talking to the man with his eyes locked to his, but his fingers searched for something that could be used as a weapon. He saw from the corner of his eyes that his dagger lay a few paces away from him and he couldn't bring out his sword. The Beast got a little closer to him.

"You have that fire in your eyes, boy," said the Beast. "But I can sense that you hold secrets, a secret that makes you weak. Like others your heart needs to be cleansed to make you whole." Damian found the hilt of the candle stand and noticed it still burning from the corner of his eyes. The Beast was approaching him.

"I will not burn you like the others but there is something that I can do for you," he said.

Damian smiled in response, "It looks like you need all the cleansing you can get," he said and tossed the burning candle towards him. The Beast had not been able to guess his intentions and as the candle went flying towards him, it fell on the lower part of his robe.

His silk robe caught fire quickly, engulfing him in flames within a short time. But to Damian's surprise, the man stood there, unmoved. Not a single scream escaped his mouth, instead a grin was visible on his face as the flames charred his clothes. Damian was shocked out of his wits as he looked on.

"As I said, it is only fire that can cleanse the soul of the living," said the Beast. He began laughing as Damian watched on in horror. His eyes were wide with fear. He tried to get up but his body had gone cold. He was petrified as he kept looking at 'the unburnt'. His piercing laughter echoed in the empty halls of the Library as the inferno raged on.

THE SEARING BLADE

The next morning, drums were beaten as the spectators poured in for the next round to begin. Agni was sitting inside the tent, every muscle of his body aching. He gave occasional glances in the direction of the entrance into the tent, but there was no sign of the practitioner and his magical herb. He also didn't see the Stranger there.

"So how are your wounds?" asked Justim as he came and sat down beside Agni.

"Could have been worse," said Agni with a smile. Justim seemed to be the only decent fellow among the contenders.

"That was a hell of a fight. I never thought you would win," said Justim straight away, he seemed pleased.

Agni smiled, "Well, thank you for your vote of confidence," he said and Justim laughed.

"No, no. I didn't mean to say it that way," he said as he stopped laughing. "I only wanted to say that you did very well out there."

"Well, I was a bit lucky, too," said Agni.

"Luck had nothing to do with it, you outwitted the fool fair and square," said Justim. Then he smiled and said, "I hope we come to face each other in one these matches. It will be a good fight." Agni was a bit taken aback.

"Now that's a scary thought. You outweigh me by at least thirty iron pellets and you are a good deal taller than me, too," said Agni.

"Size doesn't matter, Agni, you have seen that already. Or else Sir Dion would have been a certain winner," said Justim. Agni knew that his new friend was right, for the battles inside the ring were won with wits and skills alone.

"Did you see the Stranger fight yesterday?" asked Agni.

"You mean that guy in the hood?" asked back Justim. Agni nodded his head.

"Yes, I did, and he is hell of a fighter. King Akakios is lucky to have a hand like that," said Justim. Then he pointed towards the ring, "Do you see that small crater?" he asked. Agni looked at where he was pointing and saw a moderately big crater in the middle of the ring. He couldn't remember it being there when he had fought.

"This Stranger is so strong that he dashed a man called Kata on the ground so hard that the impact made the shallow crater. The man called Kata is still said to be in a critical condition and he did that with his bare hands. He never took out his sword for once," said Justim. Agni was looking at him in the eyes. Then he removed his gaze and let out a low whistle. Agni had asked Yani about King Akakios that morning and he had learnt that he was a complete introvert like his champion and barely talked to the other guests. He had brought very few men with him and most of them seemed like mercenaries. That was the one thing that seemed odd to Agni. It was common knowledge that a king never travelled without a large party to escort him. But after hearing Justim, it seemed to him that the Stranger was the only escort that would have sufficed and Akakios seemed to know that pretty well. Agni gave anxious looks towards the opening of the tent; he needed that herb. There was no way that he could fight a man like that in his present condition.

Agni was lost in his thoughts when Justim said, "Agni, there is someone by the opening of the tent and I think he is looking for you."

Agni looked up and saw the practitioner standing there. He almost jumped up at the sight of him. Agni saw Justim staring at him and quickly added, "He is an old friend of mine," said Agni out of impulse. "Please excuse me," he said.

"Certainly," said Justim but he followed him with his eyes as he walked out of the tent. The practitioner started before Agni but he caught up.

Both of them started to walk towards the desolate field at the back of the tent near the outskirts of the dwarf forest. "I thought you would never show up," said Agni as they reached the field where no one was expected to hear them.

"It takes a lot of time to prepare. I have crushed it into a paste and rolled it into a pellet," he said as he handed over a pouch to Agni.

"Take it before your first fight, not before that. I can't guarantee how long the effects will last," said the practitioner.

"What are its immediate effects after I eat it?" asked Agni.

"I can't say for sure. This is the first time I am giving this to someone, but I think it won't bring you any harm," said the man with some hesitation.

"Thanks," said Agni with a smile, he felt a lot safer already. "Well," he continued, "You have been a great help in the times of need and let us now come to your fee," he said.

"Don't worry about that, your Prince has taken care of it already," said the man with a broad grin on his face. It seemed to Agni that it was more than taken care off.

"I wish you luck, farewell," said the man and left in a hurry. Agni watched the man walk out of the field. He shook his head as he saw the man scurry off.

Agni was about to head back when he sensed someone behind his back. He turned around on impulse and his eyes became wide as he saw the Stranger standing at a distance. Agni hadn't felt his presence till then. His hand instantly went for the hilt of his sword.

"Restrain," floated the Stranger's deep voice to his ears and a glow of light surrounded him. Agni could not move. It was as if he was bound by a thousand invisible shackles. He couldn't even flex his muscles a little.

The man in the black plate armor walked up to him. Agni could do nothing but look on helplessly, the rage building inside him. He came and stood right in front of him. He could feel his breath on his face, a part of his burnt ugly face visible from under the hood and his eyes shining from beneath the thin cloth. Agni looked into those bloodshot eyes with reproach and unbound hatred. He tried to move again, but couldn't.

"Take your name out the tournament; you don't know what you are getting yourself into, boy. Do as I say if you value your life and your friends," said the Stranger in his deep voice. His menacing eyes were fixed on him. Agni wanted to scream out, he wanted to say that he would kill him, even if that was the last thing he did. But his words were stuck in his throat. Agni couldn't do anything as the Stranger walked past him, and farther away.

"Release," he shouted and the bondage was gone. Agni quickly turned and sprinted behind him, but he was already inside the tent.

ଓ

Lysandra was pacing in the open ground in front of her tent. It was morning already and there was no sign of Damian yet. He was supposed to return by the first hour of the morning and it was already the fourth. She saw Torman approaching and almost ran up to him.

"Any news?" she asked trying to keep her face straight, but the panic was clear from her voice.

"No Princess, my scouts haven't found anything," said Torman, his face was dark. Her gaze dropped to the ground, it was as she feared. They do not even know if he got in or not. Maybe he was captured before he set foot inside the city or maybe, she shut her eyes.

"I told him not to go," she said, her eyes moist. "I begged him but he wouldn't listen."

She looked up at Torman, her face bore the same helplessness that it did on the day they took away her infant brother from her mother's bosom.

"It was his choice, you couldn't have done anything," said Torman flatly.

"Yes, I could have and I should have, like the day they took my brother. I should have run away with him to the eastern shores," she said with scorn.

Torman gazed at her; the anger in him was rising fast. "And then, then what?" he asked. "What would have happened to Leu and to your father?" Lysandra remained silent.

Torman placed a tender hand on her shoulders. "Stop blaming yourself for everything that happens around you, girl. It is sometimes more important to forgive oneself before being forgiven by others," said Torman.

"Did my mother forgive me before she died?" she asked. Torman was still staring at her, her pain clear in her eyes. He slowly smiled and said, "You are the daughter every man and wife wish to have. I am only your teacher and servant, yet I love you like my own, the daughter I never had. So do the people of Leu. We are all proud of you."

He put his hand over her head and said, "We will find a way, I am sure. And I know that Damian is alive, too." Lysandra only wished that his words were true.

Lysandra nodded her head. "Good, I will call the others so that we can plan our next step. We will get Damian back," he promised and left.

Lysandra stood there, looking up at the sky. She knew Torman would never give up, yet she knew they needed help. She closed her eyes and prayed to the Maker to lend them a hand; anything , something that will show her the way.

"Felix returns, she returns from the sea," Lysandra was startled. "She returns home safely," shouted one of Torman's scouts as he climbed down from his horse and ran into the crowded camp. He halted in front of the Princess, "She returns Princess, the Pearl of the sea returns," he shouted in joy. "I have seen it with my own eyes. She makes her way towards the Gulf of Thasos."

Lysandra smiled at the man. "Go and tell the General. Send someone to signal Felix, let them know where we are, let them know that Leu marches," she said. The man gave a curt nod and ran off towards the tent of the war council. She saw the soldiers stand up as the spark returned to their eyes. The man was followed by the others towards the tent. The news spread like wild fire. The lions were up on their feet. She looked up and saw the sky clearing up, rays of the sun danced around her. "Thank you," whispered Lysandra. Then her gaze fell on Roxane, her diamond edged sword and she felt the strength returning to her arms.

ෆ

Agni was sitting there inside the tent, his thoughts concentrating on the Stranger. Agni had chased him inside the tent after that incident but couldn't catch up to him as he was already inside the ring. It was his turn to fight. So Agni couldn't do much. After the fight was over, the Stranger didn't return to the tent. He had made his way straight for the empty grounds behind the tent as soon as the match had ended and he had been declared the victor. Agni had gone after him but the man had disappeared completely. The man had a talent of escape, thought Agni frustrated as he sat there inside the tent waiting for his turn. But the thought of facing him soon made him feel relaxed. All he needed to do was to win his fights and from what he had seen that day, it was most likely that the Stranger would win without much difficulty. But he didn't know what he will do when he faced him.

The third fight was over and the last fight of the second round was between Agni and a man called Pasha from Viratbhumi in the north. Justim walked in, he had won his fight but had several bruises on his face, neck and hands.

"Well done," said Agni to his friend with a smile.

"It was easy enough," said Justim with an air full of pride.

"Right," said Agni. The announcer was calling out his name.

"I wish you luck, may you be victorious," said Justim as Agni stood up.

"We will speak when I get back," said Agni. "Right, that's more like it, now I feel a more positive vibe from you," said Justim with a smile. Agni grinned back in return.

He was about to go out of the tent when he gave a sideways glance at Pasha. He seemed to be a huge man, broad of shoulders with strong arms but not nearly as big as Sir Dion. The man also stood up, his huge war hammer lay on the ground mostly visible from the other side. Agni started walking towards the ring. He took out the pellet and put it into his mouth before he came out into the open. It tasted like mud mixed with stale potatoes. It made his mouth twist and he almost puked, but ended up swallowing it with all the determination he had.

It took effect immediately, he felt light headed and the pain in his shoulder was gone instantly. Everything slowed down as Agni went and stood in front of the crowd.

"Here stands the man who came back from the jaws of death, Agni," shouted the short man into his mouth piece. The crowd cheered and clapped for him more than they usually did for the other contenders; he had become a sort of favourite after that show last day.

"He is not a man, he is a boy and a cute one, too," shouted one of the younger women from the crowd and the others guffawed.

"Indeed," said the short man, "and a talented one," he shouted and the crowd cheered.

"Agni, Agni," someone started to chant and it was taken up by the others but it died down quickly.

"And now comes the crusher of the north, the mighty Pasha," shouted the short man and crowd cheered for him. But it was nothing like they did for Agni. Pasha walked in with the same war hammer in his hand. Agni thought the thing must have weighed at least a hundred iron pellets. He stood in front of Agni and swung his war hammer in a loop with one hand, the crowd cheered.

"Warriors, get ready," shouted the short man.

"Let them cheer for you till I crush that pretty face of yours," said Pasha with a contemptuous sneer on his face. Agni had a stupid grin on his face instead, the effects of that herb was much stronger than he expected.

"Begin," shouted the short man and ran off in a hurry. Pasha didn't waste a moment, 'Argh', he shouted and swung the massive thing with just his left hand. Agni saw it coming slowly towards him. He took a step back and let it miss him by a hair. The crowd gasped but Agni was still smiling.

"I will knock that stupid grin off your face," shouted Pasha angrily and charged on him. Agni dodged his attacks as if they were nothing. Agni danced around his blows with ease. Pasha couldn't match his speed. He went for his legs but Agni vaulted over him like an acrobat and landed on his feet.

"Excellent technique," shouted the announcer as the crowd cheered for their favourite.

"Woooow," gasped Yani. "That thing really works. It was good of you to suggest it to the practitioner," said Yani to Sir Drake with a smile on his face.

"Not so loud Prince, someone might hear us," said Sir Drake in a hushed voice.

"Right," said Yani and looked around with wary eyes. Inside the ring, the battle was going completely in Agni's favor. Pasha had been unable to land a single blow on his opponent by then. It seemed as if Agni was toying with him. Pasha started to circle Agni trying to find an opening while Agni stood still. Pasha made a swing but missed; Agni took the opportunity and rushed in.

He came straight at him. "Wrong move," shouted Pasha and shortened his grip for a slam but Agni swung around like a dancer and dodged it. Pasha quickly made a short swing but Agni stood there still as the heavy piece of metal head came straight towards him, everyone was on the edge of their seats. Agni made a chop and the sharp edge of his sword met the wooden handle near the base of the metal head instead of the metal head itself. The hammerhead went flying away as Pasha stood there, shocked, with only the wooden handle in his hand. Agni realised that the herb had also made him a good deal stronger. Everyone stood there stunned. Pasha once looked at the handle then at Agni, his mouth wide open in awe. Agni pointed the tip of his blade at him, "Do you give up?" he asked with a smile on his face.

Pasha's gaze dropped to the ground as he threw away the handle, "Yes," he replied. That led to an uproar, the crowd went berserk and Yani almost jumped up onto Agam's lap.

"We have a winner, the mesmerizing Agni," shouted the announcer. The chant started again and Yani was beaming at Sir Drake.

ଓ

"This is suicide," shouted Torman. His captains stood silent.

"This is the only way," said Lysandra in a calm voice. "No Princess, you may have command, but I am still the general of Leu. I can't let you go in there alone," said Torman angrily.

"I won't be alone. I will have thirty others with me. Felix will take us near the abandoned dock and from there we will swim. Once we are inside we will open the southern gates," said Lysandra.

"No," said Torman in a stern voice. "The same plan won't work twice and even if you make it inside we don't even know how many you will be facing on the streets on your way to the gate. The chance of making it will be much slim and I can't let you take that risk," said Torman.

"But..." Lysandra retorted, but was interrupted by Kosmas.

"Princess, pardon me the insolence, but I think that the General is correct. You will be outnumbered one to hundred in there if they raise an alarm," said Kosmas.

"That is why I have chosen the cover of the night. Felix will make it sure that their attention stays glued to her if something goes ill. Damian did it alone, we have an army," argued Lysandra.

"There is a difference between one and thirty one when it comes to sneaking inside a guarded city," said Torman.

"Princess, we know that you love your brother very much but there is little chance that he will be alive in there," said Old Theodore.

Lysandra turned to him, "Good Sir, this is not about Damian. This is about Leu," there was a hint of anger in her voice. "It is true that I wish to find Damian at all costs but I will go looking for him after I open the gate," she added. Theodore fell silent. She walked up to Torman and held his hands, "You said that we will find a way; *this is* the way. Even the Maker favours us. Felix arrived out of nowhere just in time. Without her, this plan wouldn't have been possible," said Lysandra.

"I never meant it like this, I only meant..."

"I know what you meant," interrupted Lysandra.

"But this is my decision and it is final," she said firmly. Both of them were staring at each other.

"You do not have my permission, yet if you want to go you have the authority to overrule my decision," said Torman and looked away. Lysandra was a bit taken aback.

The others looked on as mute spectators.

"Can I say something?" asked Agnes finally, with a little hesitation in her voice.

"What?" asked Torman angrily. Lysandra was silent.

"There is one way to clear the streets for the Princess while she makes her way to the southern gates," said Agnes. Lysandra turned towards her.

"How?" she asked.

"If only you surrender, General," she said looking at Torman.

"What in the name of the Maker are you saying,? Have you gone mad?" shouted Kosmas at her.

"I know exactly what I am talking about," said Agnes. She had a smile on her face.

෪

Agni was drinking some lime water as Yani and the others sat beside him.

"You did very well out there, Agni," said Sir Drake.

"Thank you," Agni replied and gulped down the rest of it from the flagon. Justim was in another corner of the tent with a few of his own people surrounding him too. There was a beautiful woman with them who once looked at Agni and their eyes met. Agni had looked away out of decency as it was not right to stare like that, but he had to admit that she was really beautiful and much elegant. Agni looked around and couldn't see either the Stranger in there or the other contender except the two of them, him and Justim.

"Well, we must leave now. The third round will begin soon. I know you will win and then we go up to the finals," said Yani with full confidence. "I wish you luck," he added as he stood up.

Agni gave a curt nod. Sir Drake gave them a smile and the duo left with Agam escorting them out of the tent. Vrish stayed back and this time Yani didn't ask him to leave with them.

"How's your shoulder?" asked Vrish.

Agni flexed the muscles of his left hand and said, "Can't feel a thing. That thing worked like magic," he had a broad grin on his face.

"It did, if only you could have seen yourself fight that guy. It was stunning," said Vrish, smiling.

"I can feel it myself, it all happened so instinctively. When I was fighting I felt as if I had no body weight at all. It has also increased my strength considerably," said Agni opening and closing the fingers of his sword hand.

"Then it's a good thing," said Vrish. Then he hesitated for a moment, "What if you don't face the Stranger in this round and he doesn't make it to the next? Then what?" he asked.

Agni had a grim look on his face. "You don't know this guy, I am sure he will win. Even if I do not come to face him in this round I will certainly face him in the final match," said Agni and he also told Vrish what had happened outside the tent before the start of the last round.

Vrish's mouth fell open, he looked flabbergasted. "But that is sorcery. Who in the seven hells is this guy?"

"That's what I intend to find out," said Agni. The announcer had started his small talk as the third round was about to commence.

"You better go, the third round will start any moment," said Agni to Vrish.

Vrish leaned closer instead, "Are you sure you want to face this guy Agni?" he asked.

Agni smiled and put a hand on his friend's shoulder, "We have come a long way from home Vrish, only to find the truth and now I cannot let it go when it is so close, within my reach. Whatever might be the consequences,"

At that point, Agam walked in. "Vrish," he called. "Prince Yani has asked for you."

"There he goes again," said Vrish in an irritated tone. Agni was sure that Agam had heard it, but not a single word escaped from his mouth.

"Go," said Agni. Vrish stood up. "Be careful, Agni," were his only words in front of Agam.

"Right," said Agni as Vrish left with Agam.

Agni knew what Vrish wanted to say was true. The Stranger was the strongest foe he would ever face, be that in a tournament back at Himadri or real life. He needed the herb's qualities and also a straight mind to beat a man like that. But the herb still clouded his head a little. He rubbed his forehead a bit.

"Getting sick, are we?" asked Justim in his usual jovial way. He was on the other side of the tent and had walked over after Vrish had left. Agni didn't notice him approaching. His friends had left before Agni could have looked up.

"No, just a little headache," lied Agni.

"Get yourself together. The final match will be between us, the unbreakable Justim versus the mesmerizing Agni," he said smiling.

"The name feels more like a stage act," said Agni and Justim laughed.

"You have a bloody good sense of humour," he said. The announcer called out Justim's name. "Sit tight, I will be right back. I will make short work of this Stranger," said Justim with full confidence.

"You are facing the Stranger?" asked Agni.

"Yes, didn't you know?" he asked back. Agni remained silent. He had hoped that he would come to face the man in that round.

"No," said Agni at last. In his heart, he wanted Stranger to win, but he also didn't want Justim to get hurt.

"When all this will be over, we will sit over a cup of good ale, or sura or whatever you call it here," said Justim with a smile. Agni nodded and smiled back. Justim was ready to go out, "Luck?" he asked.

"Luck," said Agni. Justim left the tent in high spirits and the crowd cheered. Agni went and stood near the edge of the ring.

The announcer called out the name of the Stranger, a moment passed but no one came.

"The Stranger," shouted the man again but still there was no sight of him. Agni gave anxious looks everywhere, his eyes looking for that the man in the black armor. 'He can't quit now,' he said to himself. He looked at the dais and saw that King Akakios was still there.

"For the final time, 'The Stranger,'" shouted the man in his mouthpiece at the top of his voice. The same shadowy figure emerged from behind the stands. He wasn't wearing any helm or barbute; his face was covered in the same travelling hood when Agni had first seen him. Agni was relieved. The crowd cheered for the fighters as Stranger made his way to the centre of the ring and stood in front of Justim.

"Finally," shouted the short man. "Now stands before us the unbreakable Sir Justim and an equally fearsome man, the dark horse of the tournament, The Stranger. I will not delay this epic battle any longer, warriors get ready."

Justim took out his sword but the Stranger stood there still.

"Begin," shouted the short man and scurried off.

Justim went after him without a single word, an uppercut, a lower cut and a jab. But the Stranger danced around all the blows with ease. Justim followed his steps and again made a horizontal swing. The latter dodged it too, his sword still remained sheathed. Justim continued to push on, he quickly moved to his left and made a jab but Stranger was quick to do a side-step. He grabbed his hand and landed his fist on his right cheek. Justim stepped back, the pointed edges of Stranger's gauntlets had left a deep gash on his cheeks.

"Take your sword out," shouted Justim angrily, but didn't get a reply. "Then I will not hold back anymore," said Justim and charged in. The Stranger moved to his left as Justim's blade came rushing towards his right ribs but missed. Justim quickly grabbed the hilt of his sword with both hands and split his sword into two swords. He aimed the other one for his neck in a simultaneous swing.

"Repel," shouted Stranger and Justim flew back many paces even without a touch from him. Agni looked at the crowd and saw that they were dumbstruck; they didn't have a clue of what had just happened. Agni turned his gaze to the High Lords on the dais and saw that their faces had turned serious. Justim stood up slowly, he had the look of utter confusion on his face.

"Sorcery! But how could that be?" were his only words. That next time, he did not rush in. He slowly started to circle Stranger. "Who are you?" he asked, but got no response. Justim was almost on his blind side as Stranger stood there. Then everything happened in a flash. Justim had rushed in from behind and then there was a sudden discharge of heat which Agni felt even from that distance. Stranger had arched back a little and swung around rapidly. The crowd looked on in bewilderment as Justim opened his mouth, and blood gushed out of it instead of words. He looked down at his breastplate. It had been cracked open and the broken edges were glowing red. Blood started to pour out after sometime from the deep wound beneath it. Stranger had a jade black sword in his hand and blood was dripping from its pointed tip. Justim collapsed on the ground and a woman screamed. Agni's eyes were wide with fear. Stranger started to walk out of the ring as he wiped the blood on his sword on his dark robe and sheathed it. The short man ran inside the ring and rolled Sir Justim over, putting a finger near his nostrils. Then he removed the broken steel plate and put his ears to his chest. He slowly stood up, all bloodied, his face gaunt. He looked up and said,

"High lords and citizens of Nisarga, and lords, kings, Princes and Rajkumars of lands near and far, I fear that Sir Justim is dead."

THE FINAL SHOWDOWN

Agni sat inside the tent, waiting for the final battle between him and Stranger to commence. This happened because of the sudden demise of his opponent, whom he was supposed to face in the third round. It was said that he had succumbed to his injuries, which seemed to be very negligible at first. He was declared the winner by default and had moved on to the final match.

There were whispers going around after that incident took place inside the ring. Some were saying that King Akakios had hired a dark sorcerer from the cursed city of Basporas in the west to win the tournament. While some said that the man was an escaped convict charged with genocide by the Abode. Agni didn't care.

"There is no way that you can beat this guy, Agni, let alone make him say what you feel the truth is," said Vrish when they were alone inside the tent. Vrish was doing his best to persuade him to give up the match, but Agni remained adamant.

"I have come too far to give up now," said Agni without turning away. The effect of the herb was starting to wear off and the dull pain in his shoulder had returned.

"Agni I loved my sister too, but this is suicide," said Vrish again.

"Do you think he will wait for us to find him after this is over?" asked Agni angrily. "Even if this is suicide, as you say, I have to see for myself. If this guy gets away and we don't find him again, then I will never be able to forgive myself, Vrish," said Agni aloud.

"How can you be so bloody sure that this is the guy? Do you have any proof," shouted Vrish, his voice was rising with each word.

"He is a cold-blooded murderer. Didn't you just see it yourself?" Agni almost spat his words in anger.

"That still doesn't prove your theory," said Vrish.

"I just know," said Agni arrogantly.

"What if you are wrong, damn it? What if he is not the one? You are no defender of Justice, Agni. I know he killed your friend in cold blood, but do not go so far to prove the old witch wrong," shouted back Vrish.

Agni was stunned for a moment. He was staring at his friend. He never thought that Vrish would bring that up, his words stung him.

"Get out, Vrish," said Agni in a calm voice.

"But Agni, I..."

"Get out, now," shouted Agni.

Vrish clenched his fists and said as he rushed out of the tent, "Fine! Throw away your life." He almost collided with Yani and Sir Drake on his way out, but he didn't stop to apologize.

"Are you all right, Agni?" asked Yani as he glanced back at the opening of the tent.

"Yes, I am fine," his tone hinted anger but he controlled it.

"Listen, Agni, I know that this tournament means a lot for Himadri but you can withdraw if you want. Even Kubha ji doesn't want this fight to happen and he will cancel it if you withdraw. He said that you will be declared the winner after some time," said Yani. Agni sat there silent. Yani continued, "Besides, Sir Drake thinks this is the same man that had escaped from the prison of Aine a year back."

"Yes, Agni," said Sir Drake pressing on the point. "I believe that he is the dark sorcerer the army of the Seven is looking for. He was charged with genocide by the Seven. I have spoken with Lord Kubha and we came to the conclusion that Yani mentioned before. I have already sent back word to Aine and I will apprehend him after all this is over," finished Sir Drake.

"Not till I am done with him," said Agni as he stood up. "I have come a long way to turn back now," repeated Agni more to himself than the others. He picked up his sword and started to walk towards the ring. Yani and Sir Drake could only look at him as he walked out of the range of their vision.

The only thought that lingered in his mind was the question that Vrish had asked before he left, 'What if you are wrong?'

Agni walked out of the tent and stood outside in the open air. The stands were full but silence prevailed as everyone was standing to pay their final respect to the two warriors who had passed away. Agni eye's fell on that same woman with blonde hair standing near Lord Augus, her head bowed in mourning as she occasionally wiped away her tears. Agni looked to his right and saw The Stranger standing out of the other's view in the corner by the stands.

The moment passed away and the announcer lifted his gaze.

"Now I call forth the two warriors who will face each other in this final combat on this fateful day," said the man, the excitement in his voice had faded away. Agni walked in followed by Stranger. The crowd jeered at the sight of him but he remained unmoved. The short man looked at High Senator Kubha and started his short speech.

"The final match is about to begin, but it brings us no joy," he said and paused a bit. "Unnecessary blood shed was never appreciated in Nisarga and is still not, yet we have witnessed one death and heard of the other. So the Lords of Nisarga have insisted that the participants show mercy to one another if the other falls," Agni knew that his words were meant for Stranger.

"Do I have your words on it?" asked the man looking more at Stranger than Agni. Stranger merely nodded his head and so did Agni. The short man looked up at the dais and Agni saw Senator Kubha nod his head.

"Good, get ready then," said the short man turning to both of them.

"Fight a fair match and with honour," said the short man. "Good luck," he whispered to Agni on his way out as the crowd started to cheer for Agni.

"I told you to stay away," said Stranger as he took out his sword at the start of the match for the first time in the entire tournament. Agni felt the same heat from it like before.

"I will make this quick," he said and took his stance.

"What is your name?" asked Agni as he took out his own sword. His eyes were always on him.

"Begin," shouted the short man from outside the ring. Agni got no reply to his question. Instead, for the first time in the entire tournament, Stranger rushed in first. His searing blade came right towards his forearm but Agni blocked it in time with his sword. He retaliated with a fierce uppercut but Stranger jumped back. Agni saw that the edge of his blade was partly ruined just from one small blow. He needed to dodge his attacks rather than block them and finish the fight as fast as he could before the effects of the herb completely wore off, thought Agni to himself.

In the meantime, Stranger rushed in again with a low attack aiming for his thighs. Agni did a back-flip and landed on his feet as the crowd cheered for him. Agni had been able to dodge the attack, but he felt himself getting slower every moment, his hands were starting to strain. Realising that he does not have much time, Agni charged the hooded man. He made two repeated jabs followed by a left swing and a right but the opponent jumped back. Agni was on him within moments.

"Restrain," shouted Stranger but Agni dived to his left in a hurry and nothing happened. Agni stood up smiling, "So this is a one way attack," he said. Agni lifted his sword for another strike when he felt a sharp pain on his neck and the same shoulder. He tried to land the blow but it missed its mark by miles, while Stranger had already jumped back a few steps. Agni knew that he was getting tired, the effect of the herb was wearing off and he won't be able to keep it up for long. He started to circle him slowly, trying to hide his weakness.

"Who are you Stranger?" he asked again, his eyes fixed on the man. "Who sent you?" asked Agni, but still there was no reply. The man stood there like a statue.

Then Agni held his breath and finally asked, "Are you responsible for the fire at the docks of Himadri?"

This time Stranger looked at him and their eyes met. Agni rushed in with ferocity and made a violent slice in the air. Stranger was astounded by his speed but he managed to dodge Agni's sudden ferocious stroke, though not completely.

The thin chain mail and the tunic underneath were torn from the middle as a thin line of blood appeared on his burnt skin. Something was hanging round his neck; Agni looked closely and saw that it was a pendant that hung from a gold chain. It had an odd shape and was made of a strange white metal, it had a blinding white glimmer unlike anything he had ever seen and then his eyes became wide. It was shaped exactly like the symbol Malini had drawn that night with her own blood, the meaning of the symbol they had come looking for in Nisarga. It dawned on him now how Malini knew of the symbol. There was no secret, no mystery. The truth was that she saw that unique pendant that hung by the chain round his neck that night and that was why she drew it for Agni so that he could find her killer. Finally his search was over. He didn't need any assurances anymore.

His fingers tightened around the hilt of his sword, "You did that to her, you bastard," roared Agni and sprinted towards him like the wind, all his pain was forgotten as a cindering rage filled his heart, his mind was bent on one thing and one thing only, Stranger's blood.

"Restrain," shouted Stranger quickly and Agni was caught in the vortex like before. He felt the same shackles around him. He screamed and pushed himself forward despite the overwhelming force that tried to bind him, his eyes fixed on the man who destroyed his life.

"Reminiscence," shouted Stranger, looking straight into his eyes. Agni saw a flicker of a light.

The whole arena dissolved in front of him and he found himself standing in the middle of a fair. Agni looked around confused; he was back at Himadri again. "Come on," came Malini's voice and Agni turned around. She had the same beautiful face, the one he remembered, "Don't just stand there, we will miss the show," came Vrish's voice as he tapped him on his way. Both of them were running towards a cluster of people ahead of them.

"Come Agni, hurry," shouted out Malini and Agni started running. But the more he ran, the further they got away and he fell back steadily.

"Wait," Agni wanted to shout but it didn't come out. Then everything started to go dark again. Agni came to a halt.

The cool breeze made him look back. The sun was nearing the end of its journey to the western horizon. The breeze was up and the sky was cloudy. The waves came in more frequently and crashed into the rocks. The spray of salt water drenched him and her, Malini, standing very close to him. She was wearing that same red chiffon gown which Agni had bought for her from a ship which came from the west when it docked at Himadri. Agni was speechless and only looked on.

"It's a beautiful evening, isn't it?" asked Malini. Agni nodded, he wanted to cry but he felt so happy.

"This is a beautiful dress," she said and looked down. Then she got very close to him and whispered, "Will you love me like this forever?" Agni nodded his head.

"Ever and ever," were the words that came out of his mouth. The sun cast its last drop of orange nectar on them as they kissed for the first time. Then it started to rain. Agni closed his eyes.

Then it all disappeared again and there was this horrible stench; it made him want to puke. Then he saw Vrish sobbing hysterically as Malini lay burned and scarred on the floor of that inn. She drew the symbol and then her hand dropped on the floor. The tears stopped as her eyes lay still, her gaze fixed on him. The pain, the pain made him squirm, made him scream as tears gushed out.

"Come back, come back please," he shouted and his voice was cracking as it all started to fade. Then there was this cool breeze again and sound of oars in the water, he couldn't see anything. He felt so helpless. Then he felt heat and heard a crackling sound in the air. It felt as if his heart was torn in a thousand pieces.

A violent scream escaped his mouth and then there was fire. He felt its warmth engulf him, but it didn't hurt. It was spreading through his veins, through the very core of his heart. The arena started to appear again in front of his eyes, but there was a pulsating energy around him. Stranger appeared in front of him again and the rage started to burn in his heart. The dark fire started to swirl around him.

"Restrain, restrain," shouted Stranger at the top of his voice but the shackles started to strain and vibrate.

"You will burn," spoke another voice. The fire danced around him as Stranger folded his hands and began a lucid chant: "Great immortal overseer of Gaya, the one with the three eyes, I call on your strength of protection. I call forth the 'holy shield'. Hear my…"

The swirling flame burst into pulsating energy before he could finish the incantation and the shockwave sent Stranger flying away. Agni collapsed on the ground.

CB

"Look, he is coming around," floated a voice to Agni's ears. Everything was hazy as he opened his eyes. Agni blinked quite a few times and then it all started to get clear.

"How are you feeling?" asked Yani.

"Where is 'Stranger'?" asked Agni and sat up abruptly.

"Relax, Agni! You have won. We have won," said Yani smiling at him.

"He escaped, Agni, right after that. There was so much chaos everywhere and he used it to his advantage," said Sir Drake.

"No," shouted Agni and banged his fist on the soft bed. Yani was a bit taken aback.

"What happened in there Agni?" he asked. The events started to come back to him, the visions, the darkness, the last time he saw Malini alive and finally the sound of oars and the heat. Then there was only pain and redemption.

"It was some dark sorcery and we are glad that it backfired," said Sir Drake quickly before Agni could say a word.

"The man called Akakios, where is he?" asked Agni.

"We will catch him. I have asked Yani to send Agam after him so that we can turn him over to the Abode for using and aiding an escaped convict. He might arrive any moment," said Sir Drake. Agni's face lit up a bit.

"Excellent," said Agni in delight. "Vrish, get my cloths please," said Agni as he tried to stand up.

"Agni, you are still weak," protested Yani.

"I am fine," replied Agni as Vrish brought him his cloths. Agni slipped on a loose cotton shirt. The pain in his shoulder made him flinch for a moment as he lifted his hand in the attempt.

"Here, have this," said Sir Drake as he handed him a small vial. Agni looked at him.

"It's a rejuvenating potion; it will help," said Sir Drake in an assuring tone.

"Thank you," replied Agni and took it from his hand. He opened the cork, and after some hesitation, emptied the contents into his mouth It was bitter and tasted very bad like any other medicine. A few moments passed and Agni felt a bit of his strength returning to him. They heard a hue and cry outside the tent and Agni turned his head.

"I haven't done anything, please let me go," Akakios was being dragged inside by two men followed by Agam.

"Please," shouted the man at the sight of the others.

"Shut up or else I will rip out your tongue," spat back Agam and the man fell silent immediately. But he started to sob silently and Agni saw that he seemed nothing like a king.

"Prince, here is the man you asked for. We couldn't catch the mercenaries with him; they escaped as soon as they were cornered by my men," said Agam.

"Thank you, Agam. We will handle it from here," said Yani politely. Agam nodded his head and left with his men behind him. The man lay on the floor sobbing like a child. Agni slowly walked up to him. The man's eyes became wide as he saw Agni approach.

"I didn't do anything, I swear. Please don't kill me," blurted out the man. Agni knelt down in front of him.

"Listen," said Agni. "We don't have anything against you. Tell us everything we want to know and we will let you go." The man was staring at him stupidly. "Trust me," said Agni. The man dropped his gaze and nodded.

"Good," said Agni. "Who are you?" asked Agni. "And I don't want to hear any lies," he added.

The man remained silent for a moment. "My name is Doris," he said. "I am a travelling performer from Athos in the west. I came to the east to earn some gold and then I met him."

"The Stranger?" asked Agni.

"Yes, Stranger. He said that he had an offer for me. He said that I would have to impersonate King Akakios and go to Nisarga with him. There he will enter the tournament under my house, sorry King Akakios' house," he apologized quickly.

"You impersonated a King. This is outrageous," shouted Sir Drake.

"I am sorry," pleaded the man. "I did it for my family. He offered me five hundred mudras at first and said he that he would give me five hundred more at the end of the tournament," he said and started to sob.

"Hey, hey, look at me," said Agni. The man looked up. "Why did he want to enter the tournament?" he asked.

The man gave it a thought and said, "I don't know for sure, but he wanted that thing, the prize," he said.

"The scepter?" asked Vrish.

"Yes, the scepter," said the man quickly. "He said once I collect it from Senator Kubha and bring it to him, I will get the rest of the gold," said the man, his voice breaking under the pressure.

"He wants the scepter," said Agni with a smile as he stood up straight.

"I don't know anything else. I swear it on my children. Please let me go," pleaded the man.

"You can go," said Agni flatly. The others were surprised.

"Are you sure, Agni? He might come looking for him," said Sir Drake.

"I am sure. He has no need of him now. His plan has failed," said Agni decisively.

"Thank you, thank you good sirs. May God bless you all," said the man as he stood up quickly.

"I will never do anything like this again, I swear on my children," he said as he made his way out of the tent and gave at least ten bows on his way out. Then he turned and made a run for it.

Agni turned to Yani and said, "Come Yani, let us go and fetch your prize."

ങ

A stage was erected in the centre of the ring for the closing ceremony. High Senator Kubha stood along with the other Senators beside him. Aadrika was also there, standing beside her mother, a little behind the others. Yani walked out of the tent followed by Sir Drake, Agni and Agam. Vrish had decided to stay back, which Yani didn't mind. Agni had taken Vrish out of the tent before the ending ceremony started and told him all about the pendant. Vrish stood there, silent.

Agni was about to head back when he had caught hold of him by his shoulder and said, "I am sorry Agni, I should never have doubted you." Agni had forgiven his friend then and there and they had embraced each other to remove the bitter thoughts from their minds.

The crowd erupted in applause when Agni stepped on the stage.

"Wave at them," said Yani and Agni waved his hand.

"And here is our champion, the mesmerizing Agni," shouted the short man and the crowd cheered some more.

Senator Kubha was pleased as he gazed on the prospective groom for her daughter. They all seemed to have ignored the small details of the set of events that had unfolded that day in that same ring. Yani pulled Agni by his side as he stood in front of Senator Kubha. He patted Yani's back and said, "That's quite a champion you have there, son." He looked at Agni and said, "Well done." Agni gave a courtly bow in return.

"He is like a brother to me; we grew up together," said Yani with a smile.

"Then he is a good brother to have," said Kubha proudly.

Then he turned to Agni and said, "Agni, this damned stick is for your brother. But you have certainly earned a prize worthy of your efforts. Name it and it shall be yours."

"I have the trust of my Prince and my brother, that's all I need," said Agni with a smile and Yani beamed at him with pride and affection.

"Ah, a modest man," said Kubha. "A good man. But there must certainly be a way by which we can honour your efforts?" he asked.

"For the first, he can certainly dine with us tonight," said Aadrika, her gaze of appreciation lingered on Agni. Her mother gave her a nudge but she ignored it completely.

"It's a gift worthy of a king," said Agni after some thought.

"But I have something else on my mind," he replied with another bow. She seemed a bit let down.

"Certainly, speak of it and it shall be yours," said the High Senator Kubha with confidence.

Agni paused a little, "I wish to know Aadrika ji's decision on marrying Yani. I don't want to see my efforts go in vain," said Agni looking at her. Kubha was a bit taken aback and so was Yani. He was staring at Agni with a puzzled look on his face. Kubha turned to his daughter. Aadrika was smiling.

"If that is the prize you seek, brave Agni, then the answer is yes," she said with a coy smile on her face.

"Yes?" asked Kubha, astounded. "Yes," he shouted. "Yes, she said yes," said Kubha turning to his wife, elated.

Yani looked at Agni and embraced him. "I hope that solves your problems a little?" whispered Agni in his ears.

"Thank you," was the only reply that came from Yani as he held on to his friend firmly.

"Tell the citizens of Nisarga that I present the heirloom of my house to my future son-in-law," said Kubha with joy to the short man with the mouth piece.

The man immediately turned towards the crowd and announced, "The days of festivities have come. His Greatness has found a new son." The crowd erupted in joy.

"Take this, my son," said Kubha as he handed the scepter to Yani. Yani gave it to Agam who took off his gloves to receive it as per the custom of the east. Kubha embraced his soon to be son-in-law and then he embraced Agni.

"I shall be forever in your debt," he said as he held him firmly by the shoulders.

THE INCURSION

Thirty-one souls swam through the dark waters in the cover of the night. The moon was hidden behind the clouds and there was complete darkness. The three large ships were looming over them. They were to come out in the old abandoned southern docks of Alexandria beside the new docks. Felix had dropped them near the coastline and stayed back in the darkness waiting for their signal. They swam in small groups to prevent any unwanted attention.

"Look," said Kosmas pointing at the torches that flickered near the shore.

"There are guards in there. What should we do, Princess?" asked Agnes.

Lysandra looked on. She was wearing tight slacks and a black light vest. She wore no armor and her sword was strapped round her back with a knife on her waist. "Wait here," she said and started to swim before the others could say anything.

She got closer and watched closely. She came back and said, "There are five to six of them, I guess. Choose three of your best men, send them ahead and ask the others to stay behind," she said.

"Right," said Kosmas and pointed to three of his men and they swam up to them. He gestured the others to stay back.

Lysandra started to swim towards the shore followed by the five. They came to a halt behind a jagged rock protruding out of the water and she spoke in a very hushed voice.

"There are six of us and probably six of them. Each one of us will go after one of them but remember it should be done at one stroke. If they raise an alarm then we will not even get a chance to escape, so we need to be very careful." Then she turned to Kosmas and said, "You are the best archer we have, so if any of them escapes and one of us fails, it falls on you to deal with him."

"Right," replied Kosmas with a nod.

Then she turned to the other three and said, "It all depends on precision. If one of us fails the other should improvise."

"As you command, Princess," said the three of them together in hushed voices.

"Agnes, you will stay with me," she said and Agnes gave a curt nod.

"Leu is as much yours as it is mine," she said to all of them. "Lightning," she said. "Lightning," repeated the others. They swam out of the cover of the rocks and started swimming towards the shore with gentle strokes. One of the guards was standing at the edge of wooden dock staring at the open ocean. She raised her hand and the other five came to a halt. Then there was a huge uproar, the hue and cry echoed throughout the city as the horn blasted twice. The guard immediately ran up to the others, their backs turned towards the water.

"Perfect timing," she whispered to herself with a smile and signalled the others to follow her. She crept out of the water followed by Agnes, Kosmas and the other three. They sprinted towards the guards and jumped on them even before they could turn around. Lysandra caught hold of the man in front of her and ran her knife through his throat. Agnes and Kosmas pinned down their targets and did the same. One of the three that remained freed himself from one of Kosmas' men and made a run for it. But another jumped on him and put his knife through his throat even before he could shout. Kosmas lowered his bow which he had brought out in a flash.

"Good work, all of you," she said as she wiped the blood on her knife on her slacks. Then her eyes fell on something unusual. A huge metal cylinder with one side open and the whole thing placed on a set of wheels.

"So this is what they were guarding," said Agnes as she brushed her fingertips over the smooth metal body. "What is this thing?" she asked looking at the Princess. Lysandra had no idea. She was looking at the iron balls near the wheels, neatly stacked together.

"I think this is some kind of a weapon," said Kosmas. "We can use this thing to our advantage," he said turning to the Princess.

"We don't even know what this is, Kosmas. How can we us it even if we don't know what it does?" said Agnes. Kosmas kept staring at it, as if fascinated.

"What's that smell?" asked Lysandra.

Agnes breathed in some air and said, "You are right, there is an odd smell in the air."

Kosmas started to look around and found a sack behind that thing. He ripped it open and its dust like content of yellowish color spread out all over his hand. He lifted his hand to his nose and said, "Fire powder." "Now I am sure that this is a weapon," said Kosmas as he stood up. He went near the water and washed his hands. Lysandra understood that it was that very thing they tried to sneak into Leu through Damian before the attack began. She realised that all of this was planned from the very beginning. Her hatred for Damian surged through her body. Kosmas came back wiping his hand on his already dry vest. The wind was up.

"We should not waste time," said Agnes.

"If we can figure out how to use this thing, then maybe it will give us the edge we need," argued Kosmas.

"Agnes is right," said Lysandra before Agnes could say something in reply. "We can learn of its uses and take it back to the Capital but now is not the time. Signal the men to come up and put out the torches after you are done, we need to open the gate," said Lysandra in a tone that brooks no argument.

"As you say, Princess," said Kosmas displeased and picked up the torch that lay on the ground in front of him. He seemed a bit upset. He went near the water and waved the torch thrice in the air. The splashing sounds started. Lysandra was staring at the battle ships, the ships were a fair distance away from them yet one small mistake could give them away. Kosmas was about to put out the torch when Lysandra said, "Let them burn, all the six of them." Kosmas looked at her.

"The ones on board those ships cannot see the men, just the torches. If we let them burn, then they will think that the guards are still here," explained Lysandra.

"Very smart thinking, Princess," said Kosmas appreciatively and handed one torch to each of them.

"Bring out the map, Agnes, we need to plan our next step," said Lysandra.

Lysandra slipped into the armor of one of the slain guard and so did the other five. The armor of the guards would help them walk the streets without the possibility of being detected. They were to cover their faces with one full helm of the captain and five helmets with visors but keep their own swords.

"Kosmas and Agnes, tell the others to climb the ships as we make our way towards the gate. They are anchored and will be lightly guarded. Our enemy will never think that their precious ships will come under attack right at the docks," said Lysandra as she strapped the leather bands of her gauntlets.

"But twenty-five men won't even be enough to sail one ship, let alone three," said Kosmas.

"I do not want them to sail the ships. I only want them to attack them and hold them until our main force arrives. Tell them to signal Felix, as planned, after half an hour of the moon before they begin their attack. We will reach the gates by then," said Lysandra.

"Is it wise to separate our forces?" asked Agnes.

"It is for a little while, Agnes. Felix has mostly three hundred sailors and these ships together may have over five hundred even if they are lightly guarded, they will appreciate all the help they can get. Besides, it will be better for us if we move in small packs, it will draw much less attention," said Lysandra.

"As you say, Princess," replied Agnes.

"And Kosmas, tell your men to burn the ships if Felix doesn't reach in time," said Lysandra to Kosmas.

"Right, I will go and explain it to them," said Kosmas and left followed by Agnes.

Lysandra tied her hair in a loose bun and put on the full helm, it was a bit tight for her, yet there was little choice. She was checking all the straps of her breastplate when Kosmas and Agnes came back. The mark of the seven swords looked unusual on her.

"I have explained everything to them, Princess. They will begin after half an hour of the moon after we leave," said Kosmas.

"Time is the greatest weapon we have, Kosmas. Do they have a good timekeeper with them?" asked Lysandra.

Kosmas smiled and said, "Don't worry, Princess, some of my men are the best time keepers in all of Leu. They have spent countless years out of cities and villages; they have learnt to keep time themselves."

"Good," said Lysandra. "We will follow the street that goes parallel to the base of the wall until we find the stairs as I said before. We must stay together and we must not engage in any conversation with the other soldiers. But everyone should greet them in return if we are greeted on the way, not more than that. Everyone understands what I said?" asked Lysandra. The five of them nodded. "Good," said Lysandra. "Put on your helmets then and follow me." The five followed her orders and put on the helmets. They put down their visors and started to walk behind Lysandra towards the southern wall.

As they came to the streets, they saw the devastation first hand. The pyres still burned at places and the stench was unavoidable.

"Monsters. Maker only knows what they have been doing in here," said Agnes with disgust as she crinkled her nose. Lysandra looked around, the once bustling streets of Alexandria were empty and the city itself had been turned into a ruin. The stench became stronger with the rise of the wind and it was unbearable. 'They burned her' the voice echoed in her ears. She shook her head and tried to focus.

They came to a halt in front of a pyre, its fire had gone out. They saw something glitter in the ashes as the light from their torch fell on it which made them halt in the first place. Agnes moved closer out of her curiosity and started moving the pieces of the charred wood with the tip of her blade. Lysandra didn't stop her. For some reason she wanted to see herself. Then a human skull came tumbling down. All of them were stunned. It lay on the ground and had turned black with soot. Lysandra noticed a large diamond nose ring in the ashes which might have belonged to the woman whose charred skull lay in front of them.

"They couldn't have," said Agnes as she cringed in horror. Her eyes were wide and she started to sweat.

"They will pay," said Kosmas with gritted teeth.

"With blood and iron." Lysandra was shocked out of her wits. Her faith in the Abode had been destroyed the very day they had taken her brother away, but she never thought that they were capable of such atrocities.

"The time for retribution will be soon at hand," she said, her anger vexed her soul.

"I will kill each and every one of them," said Kosmas. He banged his fist on the skull and shattered it in a fit of rage. Three guards were walking by when they saw the six of them standing there.

"There is nothing in there," shouted one of them. "Try the shops." Kosmas looked up; his eyes were red with rage. Then he smiled.

"I think I saw something in there, I think it's a diamond ring," shouted Kosmas at them.

"Really?" asked one of them and the trio started to walk towards the six.

"What are you doing, Kosmas?" asked Lysandra, Agnes was equally surprised. But the guards were already near them.

"Where?" asked one of the guards leaning over the pile of ashes.

"There," said Kosmas pointing towards the shattered skull as he slowly took out his dagger. In the next moment he simply put it through the back of the man's neck. He fell face down on the pile of ashes with his mouth wide open in shock. The other two were about to take out their swords but Kosmas' men took care of them. Lysandra and Agnes stood there silent as they saw the guards being murdered in cold blood. Kosmas wrenched the dagger free from the lifeless body of the guard.

"There was no need for that, Kosmas," said Lysandra in a calm voice trying to control her anger.

"I beg to differ, Princess," Kosmas answered in anger.

"We are not like them," said Lysandra.

"They were going to die anyway and besides there is no rule of war. Even if there is, they were the ones to break it in the first place," said Kosmas as he wiped the blood away. Then he turned to his men and said, "Take care of the bodies."

The General of Leu stood in front of the 'West gate' with twenty others. They were first made to wait for quite some time as the commander got ready for the big event, the surrender of Leu's forces. They were being led towards the commander with their hands up in the air. The symbol of the sentinel with the spear glistened on the robe worn by the General in the light from the torches. The commander was standing at the base of the wall with his men around him. He had come out from the safety of the walls dressed in satin black clothes. Twenty unarmed men along with the General came and stood in front of him.

"You can put your hands down, General," said the commander with a broad grin on his face.

The General did as the man said. The commander was looking at him with a smile on his face.

"A general," he said. "And yet look at you. You come to us with your hands up in the air like a chicken. The chicken-hearted General," shouted the man to his men and the soldiers guffawed.

"Why don't you flap them a little for me," said the commander smiling. His men cackled.

Then he started to circle him. "Frankly speaking, I never thought of Leu to surrender this easily, but it seems that finally you fools have learnt your lesson," said the man.

"So, where is your Princess? I have heard that she was riding at the front?" asked the man.

"The Princess is not here," said the General in a calm voice.

"She ran away? Did she?" asked the man with a contemptuous sneer on his face. Then he turned to his men and shouted, "The warrior Princess of Leu has run away to her little city with high walls."

Then he turned to the General and said, "She might have run away for now but the time will soon come when she will bend her pretty little knees in front of us. That day we will see how beautiful she really is."

The General clenched his fists and it did not escape the commander.

"Angry, are we?" he asked with a smile.

"If this angers you then I wait to see you on the day when your precious little city is taken and your old king bends his stiff knees in front of the Seven to kiss their feet," he said with scorn.

There was a sudden uproar. "The South Gate is opening," shouted one of the few guards who remained on the walls.

"What?" shouted the commander and then turned to the General.

"Leu will never be taken by the likes of you and our old king will never bend his stiff knees in front of your Seven bastards. And yes, you can kiss your ass goodbye," said the General and lifted his full helm. Old Theodore had a broad grin on his face as he threw the helm on the ground.

"Archers," he shouted and ducked, so did his men. A hundred arrows came whirling from the cover of the forest. The commander with many of his men fell on the ground.

"Swords," shouted Old Theodore and his men took out small swords barely larger in size than standard daggers, hidden underneath their faulds.

"Charge," he shouted and the remaining knights of Leu rushed out of the woods and went straight for their utterly confused enemy.

ᘓ

Torman was sitting on the back of his black courser at the edge of the southern forest, his eyes shining with anticipation and worry. Three hundreds of his best knights were behind him. His thoughts were bent on Lysandra. He never wanted her to go in there and he waited for the first chance to see her alive and well. There was a hue and cry near the portcullis of the southern gate. Then a flaming torch was seen swinging from side to side in the air over the gate.

"Men to battle," he shouted and started the race down the slope towards the gate. "Leave none standing," his cry echoed in the night sky and was greeted with a roar from the lions of Leu.

They came down like a wave crashing on the rocks and their war cry rose like a storm. Torman could see the gate in front of him. He raced past it and entered the city. Kosmas and Agnes were waiting at the other side. They were in their vests again by then, with the torch burning in Kosmas' hands. Torman halted in front of them.

"Where is the Princess?" he asked, the other knights raced past him and poured into the city.

"She was heading towards the new docks by the time we opened the gates," said Agnes. "Why? I asked her to wait for me," shouted Torman angrily.

"She was with us when we took the gate, but then we caught one of the guards alive. She asked her about Damian and the guard told her that he is alive and he is being held captive in one of the three ships," said Kosmas.

"And you two jokers let her go?" roared Torman in rage.

"But..." Kosmas was about to say something but Torman didn't wait to listen. He kicked the belly of the beast furiously and raced towards the southern docks.

"Faster Angel, faster," he shouted as he kicked the horse over and over and again.

"Maker protect her," he whispered to the wind. It was rumoured that the enemy was being led by one man. And he was rumoured to be one of the Seven holy Lords. One of the ships bore his mark and Torman prayed to God that this lord be in anyplace else other than the docks. "Maker protect her," he whispered to the wind again as it picked up.

CB

Lysandra ran as fast as her legs could carry her, the new docks were in her sight. She saw that the fighting had already started and one of the ships was set ablaze. Felix was right beside the other two as Kosmas' men and sailors of Felix fought the enemy on the decks of the other two enemy ships. She ran closer to where the ships lay anchored. Then she heard a scream as one of Kosmas men came flying off the deck of the ship in front of her. He crashed on the wooden planks of the dock, the sheer impact had killed him then and there. A man jumped out after him and landed on his feet like a cat a little away from where Lysandra stood. He wore a shimmering white cloak and the hood was drawn which only revealed a part of his face. The symbol of the great beast, the Diger (a cross of a demon cat and a tiger), was engraved on his breastplate. Lysandra already had her sword out, her eyes fixed on the emblem.

"Ah, we finally meet. My nose is never wrong, especially when it comes to women. It is an honour to finally meet the famed warrior Princess of Leu, Lady Lysandra herself," said the man with a courtly bow. Then he looked up and said, "You have grown more beautiful with every passing day. I remember you from when you were barely thirteen." Lysandra couldn't recall. The Beast was smiling.

"So you are the one they call the Beast?" she asked.

"Yes, it is me. Forgive me, Princess, I should have introduced myself to you first but it seems you are good with not just swords, but certain other things too," said the man politely. Lysandra did not know what he meant, she just kept still.

The Beast started to pace, "It seems that your fame is well-deserved, Princess. You have outwitted me completely. You have planned a three point incursion, that's much impressive. For that, I commend you," said the Beast with another bow.

"I do not need your praise," she said coldly.

"Then what do you need? I am at your service," he said with a wink.

"Where is my brother?" she asked.

"Your brother?" asked the Beast in an inquisitive tone, a bemused look on his face. "Oh, you mean that young man who sneaked inside the city last night and tried to stab me from behind? I knew that he is royalty, so I have treated him as such. He is our honoured guest," said the Beast smiling.

"But I must admit that I did not know that he is your brother, Princess, or else I should have treated him better," he continued.

"Where is he? Tell me or else...," shouted Lysandra.

Beast ignored her threats and continued, "It breaks my heart to see this day come forth when we fight amongst ourselves. This is such a shame. If only your father had listened. He is old and to see his kingdom ravaged by war must be such an unpleasant sight at this age. We told him that if he does as we say then we will let you keep your place, after all we need great warriors like you to guard our realm."

Lysandra pointed the tip of her sword at him, "I will ask you one last time. Where is my brother?"

Beast laughed and said, "All right, all right. If you are so anxious then I will tell you." He pointed his finger to the ship in the middle and said, "Your brother is on that ship. You can go to him if you wish, but there is a catch," he smiled. "If you can go past me or even touch the ship once, I will let you go and see your brother."

"Agreed?" he asked.

"I will go through you," said Lysandra in a calm voice.

"Excellent, let us begin then," he said and to her surprise he threw away his broad sword in the water. "I think this will level the playing field a bit," he said smiling.

Lysandra was smiling herself. "Your over-confidence shall be the reason of your demise," she said.

"No, Princess," said Beast. "I am a humble man; rather it depends on your definition of a man." Lysandra did not understand his words.

"Let us begin then. I am not so famous for my patience," said he, cracking his knuckles. She must not underestimate that man, she thought, for he was one of the Seven who are said to wield power far greater than any other man. She needed to plan her attack carefully. She slowly moved around with the sword held high, the tip pointing towards him, looking for an opening. Beast remained unmoved. She started her assault. She went for his neck straight away but he dodged her attack and jumped to her right. She made a lower cut and Beast vaulted over her head. She turned around quickly, her sword swung with the same motion as her slender body. All Beast did was to take one step back and let it pass. Lysandra realised that for a man of his size, he had unbelievable speed. This was the first time that Lysandra was facing someone whose speed was greater than hers. Lysandra rushed in and rendered one blow after the other; Beast dodged them with ease or blocked them with his gauntlets. She continued to push on and he continued to step backwards. She made a vertical swing and Beast took one step back. Only that this time, he almost toppled over the body of the dead soldier which he had slain moments ago. Lysandra took the opportunity and made a vertical slice, the sword made contact. The diamond edged sword ripped through the breastplate and tunic alike.

But nothing happened. She didn't see any blood come out or any reaction.

Beast ripped off his ruined breastplate and threw it away. Lysandra was shocked out of her wits because there wasn't even a scratch on his skin. No metal was strong enough to withstand her diamond edge sword, yet it did not even leave a single scratch on his bare chest.

"Very sharp sword, what have you named her?" he asked. Lysandra was too shocked to notice his words.

"Never mind that. I have stopped naming swords after the many I have used over the years," said Beast.

"How?" she asked, the words were stuck in his throat for sometime. The grin on his face became wider.

"Don't waste your precious sword on me, Princess. Why don't you try fulfilling the other condition instead," said he.

Lysandra knew that she had to kill him for he could not be trusted. The question was how. She went for his neck again and made a furious swing, but to her surprise Beast didn't even move. The sword made full contact and there was a scraping sound. She took back a few steps.

Beast started to laugh, the harsh sound echoed in the night sky.

"You can try all you want, Princess, but your efforts will prove to be fruitless. Now that I come to think of it, it is unfair that I should be your opponent. So let me bring forth my next proposal. Why don't you fight my friend instead? And like I said, if you reach the ship, you win," said the man called Beast.

"Let me introduce him to you," he said. "Rage," he called out and within a few moments a huge shadow cat leapt out of the deck of the ship and landed softly beside Beast. Its teeth were glistening with blood in the light.

"Meet my friend, Rage," said Beast. The shadow cat purred in pleasure as its master scratched the back of its ear. "Rage is a good friend and he listens to me always. It will be his pleasure to play with you a bit," said he. Lysandra had a petrified look on her face. She had never laid her eyes on a creature as big as the one that stood before her. She had seen 'tuskers' before and they were larger but they were peace-loving creatures. But nothing like the huge cat that stood in front of her. It was nearly ten hands in height, a giant cat. She took a few steps back as her eyes were fixed on the great cat, her eyes wide with fear.

"Go,' said Beast and gave a slap on its back.

The giant cat rushed towards her. Lysandra started to run but the cat proved faster than she thought. The thing pounced on her and its claws tore away the soldier's armor as if it was made of silk. She hadn't taken it off for that precise reason yet her farsightedness proved to be useless. She never thought of facing a shadow cat in the enemy ranks. Its fangs pierced her left pauldron and sunk deep into the flesh. She screamed as blood spurted out of the wound. She spat out some blood as the thing pinned her down on the ground.

"Rage," shouted Beast. "Don't be so rough with her. We need the Princess to be with us. After all she hasn't enjoyed our hospitality yet." The cat let go of her and leapt back a step or two. Lysandra tried to stand up but fell down on her knees instead. She was clutching her shoulder.

"I am sorry, Princess, Rage tends to get a little violent sometimes. But rest assured, he won't kill you. We need you alive," Beast said, his eyes beaming in the dark night. Then he moved a little closer and said, "The Lord Light says that you are the key to winning this war even without fighting it. He knows how King Crixus loves his little daughter and how can I harm such a beauty." Then he clapped and said, "But I must admit that I personally love these games a lot."

An arrow came whirling through the air and went deep into the cat's right eye. It howled in pain and went reeling back. "Me too," came a voice, Torman was standing at a distance, his bow ready at hand for a second shot. He shot a second, a third and a fourth within moments. The creature howled in agony and tried to rush towards him. But Lysandra grasped the hilt of her sword and jumped on it. Torman shot another bolt through its leg and Lysandra put her sword right through its neck. The blade went searing into the flesh. The creature gave one last howl and collapsed on the ground. Lysandra wrenched her sword free from the flesh of the creature and then went down to her knees again.

"No," shouted Beast as he stood there watching. Strangely, he did not move; nor did he come to the rescue of his pet. Torman rushed towards her and helped her stand up.

"You shouldn't have interfered. I wanted this to be a fair fight. He wouldn't have killed you, Princess, so you shouldn't have done that," said Beast, his voice had changed.

"You call this a fair fight, you monster," shouted Torman.

"You leave me no choice," he replied and unclasped his cloak and threw it away. For the first time Lysandra saw his face. His hair was the color of silver but his skin was that of the wood. There was a bunch of coarse hair on either of his cheeks. One of his eyes was green and the other yellow. He even had fangs like a beast which Lysandra hadn't noticed earlier.

"I will not kill you, Princess, but I will certainly kill your friend and then you shall be mine," he said with malice. "And once this night is over, you will regret what you have done."

"Never can you touch her while I draw breath," shouted Torman in rage.

"That can be changed," said Beast and rushed towards them like the wind without a warning. Torman pushed Lysandra out of the way. Beast was on him even before he could take out his sword. Torman was flung away like a child. Lysandra jumped on him from behind, her sword in her hand. But he caught hold of the sword with bare hands and pulled her off his back along with it and held her up in the air. She never let go of the hilt. A wooden beam crashed on his chest, the sheer impact made him let go of her sword and take back a few steps as the splinters flew everywhere. Torman threw away the rest of it and took out his sword. He charged in and rendered blow after blow but Beast blocked them with his bare hands.

"Run away, Lysandra," shouted Torman.

"No, I won't leave you," she said and charged in. Beast gave her a gentle push and she went flying back a few steps. He caught hold of Torman's blade with his bare hands, wrenched it free from him and threw it away. Then he caught him by his throat and lifted him in the air, Torman was helpless. He tried to kick him and landed a few too, but to no effect. Beast curled his fingers in a fist and landed a blow on Torman's stomach. He spurted out blood from his mouth instantly. He was about to land a second when a chain came out of nowhere and wound itself around his neck. Lysandra was holding the other end. He let go of Torman's frail body and turned around. Lysandra gave it pull but Beast didn't even move a little. He caught hold of the chain, took it off his neck and gave it a hard pull. Lysandra lost balance and fell down on the wood of the dock. He started to drag her towards him, she had coiled the chain around her waist and it got stuck.

"You are coming with me, Princess," shouted Beast. Torman grabbed his legs but he kicked him away. Then something happened which Lysandra didn't understand. There was an explosion, and Beast let go of the chain and flew off the ground. There was a huge splash into the water almost twenty or thirty paces away from land. Lysandra looked back and saw the huge cylindrical thing with smoke coming out of its mouth as Kosmas and Agnes stood beside it.

"Now I know what this thing can do," said Kosmas with a smile as he patted the metal body of the thing. Agnes was already with Torman, she helped him up. Lysandra stood up by herself, she was clutching her shoulder.

"Are you all right?" asked Torman as he limped towards her with one hand around Agnes' neck.

"I should be the one asking," she replied with a smile.

"Can anyone see that thing from here? I want to be sure if he is dead or not," said Torman as he went near the edge of the dock with Agnes.

"He is dead for certain, what is there to look," said Kosmas.

"No man could have survived that, General," replied Agnes.

"He is not a man. He is Beast, even literally," said Lysandra with her eyes fixed on the dark water. She dreaded that that thing would creep out from the water any moment. Agnes and Kosmas looked at each other's faces. Torman's knights started to pour in. The captain of the cavalry unit declared with an elated look on his face that Old Theodore and his men had taken the main gate and had entered the city, the enemy was trapped and most of them had been slain. A few that were left had fled through the northern gates to the woods and the others had jumped into the sea. It was a complete victory.

"Princess, Princess," shouted one of Kosmas' men as he waved his hand from the deck of the ship in the middle.

"We have found Sir Damian, he is alive." A broad grin marked her face.

Lysandra looked up at the heavens and thanked her stars.

"It is over," said Torman. "We have won...Victory," he shouted.

"Pride and glory and above all, Leu," shouted the knights of Leu and their roar had carried even to the High towers of Aine.

PRINCE YANI'S PAINTING

Agni entered his room followed by Prince Yani with the scepter in his hand. Agni turned and said, "Where will you put it, we must keep it safe." Yani didn't say a word and simply embraced him with both his hands.

"I will never forget what you have done for me. Now I can look him in the eye. If a brother is like you, Agni, then I wish I had many," he said, his voice cracking. "Father will be so proud."

Agni slowly patted his back, "Its nothing, you deserve it, Yani. You are a good man, maybe a little rough on the edges, but good none the less," said Agni as Sir Drake had said.

Yani started to laugh. He let go of him and held him by the shoulders.

"When we get back, I will tell father of all that you have done for me and Himadri. I know there are a few other reasons too, but that doesn't bother me. I want it to be out of our way and maybe someday we can talk about it when you feel like it, but not now," said Yani smiling.

Agni remained silent for a moment and then simply nodded his head.

"Good," said Yani. "I want you to be by my side always. I will make you a 'Zamindar' (landlord) and then find you a beautiful bride, maybe one of Aadrika's cousins and then your sons will grow up with mine like you did with me."

"Its all too tempting," lied Agni. "But first you must keep this scepter safe, it will be the heirloom of your house in the coming days," said Agni.

"Are we interrupting something?" came Vrish's voice from the door. Sir Drake was also with him.

"Don't be silly, come in," said Yani in a jovial tone. The sun was about to set. Agni saw that Sir Drake was staring at the scepter.

"You need to put it someplace safe," he said to Yani.

"Right, right," said Yani. "Why is everyone so obsessed with this thing? I have already spoken to Agam on my way here. He will take it to my room and guard it alongside Paksha."

"Why Paksha?" asked Agni instantly. Yani smiled in reply and said, "I know you don't like him, Agni, but he is a good sword. He will be of use in future, even to you. And he wanted this little honour when I was speaking to Agam. He said he wanted to be the second guardian of the heirloom of my house. I didn't let him fight but I can give him this much."

Agni had no choice but to agree with him.

"Two guards wont be enough, Prince," said Sir Drake.

"Don't worry, good Sir, dark sorcerer or not, it will be tough for any man to get past two of the best warriors of Himadri. Moreover, we are mere twenty or so paces away from our room and we also have 'the mesmerizing Agni' with us," joked Yani. Agni smiled back. He knew that Agam and Paksha were good fighters but he also knew that Stranger was a different thing altogether.

Agni looked at Yani and said, "Yani, if you don't mind, Vrish and I would like to stay in your room with the two of you, only for tonight."

Yani was a bit taken aback. Then he shook his head and said, "If you are worried about the sceptre, then you already know that I also have Sir Drake with me besides Agam and Paksha. Still if you want to, you are most welcome. We have at least ten beds in there. Don't we, Sir?" Yani asked Sir Drake.

"Yes, we do Prince, and Agni and Vrish are most welcome on my part. We can also have a bit of celebration, but we got to go easy with the sura. Don't want a clouded head if something happens," said Sir Drake.

"You are beginning to worry like Agni, Sir, but I think it holds true for Vrish," said Yani smiling at Vrish after a long time.

"A few things about me have always been exaggerated," said Vrish curtly. All of them laughed at his words.

"I doubt it," replied Yani.

There was a gentle knock on the door. Vrish opened it and Agam walked in. He had something in his hand, a small wooden cylindrical tube enclosed on both sides. He gave a courtly bow to Yani as he stopped in front of him.

"Now it is time to put away this thing that has been causing so much distraction," said Yani. "I see that you have brought it with you Agam, my gratitude," said Yani.

"I am here only to serve my Prince and it was Paksha who had fetched it for me from your room," said the modest Agam as he held the object in front of him.

He took it from Agam's hands and handed him the scepter. "Guard it well, Agam," said Yani.

"With my life, my Prince," replied Agam as he took the scepter from Yani's hand. Agni didn't want it out of his sight but there was little choice.

Yani sensed the anxiousness in Agni. "It will be safe. Your efforts will not go waste," said Yani in a reassuring voice. Agni gave a nod, maybe Yani was right, he thought. It was only the last hour of the Sun and the palace was still bustling with people. Stranger wouldn't risk it at this hour, for sure. The cover of the night would be more preferable.

"Now let me present you with a little gift, a token of my gratitude," said Yani and opened one side of the wooden tube. He took out a large sheet of rolled paper from the encasement.

"What is it?" asked Agni as Yani handed it to him.

"This is my first work of art, my first painting and I want you have it. I hope you like it," he said with a coy smile on his face.

"You were always 'the artist' Yani, this is surely going to be beautiful," said Agni as he started to unroll the sheet with utmost care.

He unrolled it and held it in front of him, "Let me see, too," said Vrish and peeked over his shoulder. Agni saw that it was very high on details. It was a painting of King Adhirath sitting on his throne with four men kneeling in front of him with their hands extended towards the king. One of them looked like Briksha and there was a man who stood in between the kneeling men and the king. The man had his face covered by a hood. The man with the hooded face had four spherical objects in his hand with strange markings on them. He wore no gloves and had nine fingers, the little finger of his right hand was missing. Agni kept looking at it, his eyes wide with shock.

"I must not lie to you, Agni, I made this for my father," said Yani. "But I learnt that," he paused for a moment, "he does not have any interest in these kind of things. But I assure you that you are the first one to see it," said Yani. Agni merely looked at the painting, his face expressionless.

Yani continued, "I drew it because the scene had an artistic value. I knew from that moment that it will be marvelous if I can put it in colours properly, but you be the judge of it."

"When did you see this happen?" asked Agni, the smile on his face was gone.

"Why?" asked Yani, a bit surprised by the odd question instead of praise.

"When did you see this happen?" Agni repeated his question but that time more sternly.

The smile on Yani's face disappeared. Vrish looked at Agni once and then again at Yani, he was at a loss.

"I am not sure, but it was sometime before the festival. My father honored the four merchants including Vrish's father Briksha with four tokens of gratitude for lending a hand in the prosperity of Himadri through their trading activities," said Yani. There was a hint of anger in his voice.

"Why? Don't you like it?" asked Yani.

"Vrish, come with me," said Agni as he put down the painting on the bed with haste. Sir Drake took it up and then his expression changed too.

"Why? What's wrong, Agni?" asked Vrish.

"Now," shouted Agni as he made his way towards the door. Yani was a bit stunned by the sudden change in the air. He was clueless as he kept staring at Agni who was already near the door and had broken into a sprint.

"I am coming, too," said Sir Drake and rushed after them. Yani was dumbstruck by the sudden chain of events.

"Wait for me, Sir," he shouted and ran after him.

ભ

Agni ran as fast as he could through the corridor, Vrish right behind him. He could see the turn around the corner ahead, he went round it and came to a sudden halt. Vrish stopped a little short of where Agni stood.

"What the…" the words got stuck in his throat.

Sir Drake had reached the spot followed by Yani who he was panting hard trying to catch his breath. Then he looked up and his eyes became wide. Agam lay in a pool of blood on the floor right at the doorstep of his room.

"What happened here?" he shouted out of anxiety and ran to Agam. He turned him over and saw that his eyes were open and his throat was slit. "Paksha," said Yani and ran inside the room.

"Wait, Yani," shouted Agni and ran after him followed by the others but Yani was already inside.

Agni entered the room and saw that it had been ransacked. Paksha lay cuddled in the corner clutching the right side of his chest with a few bruises on his face and around his neck, blood dripping from his wound. Yani was kneeling beside him.

"Are you all right, Paksha?" asked Yani as he took his hand in his own.

"I am sorry, Prince Yani, that man from the tournament was waiting for us in your room. He attacked us as soon as we came in. He jumped on Agam and killed him and when I tried to stop him, he wounded me and took the scepter. He ran away Prince, I couldn't stop him. I am so sorry," said Paksha, his face twisted in agony.

"Don't worry about it. I will take you to the practitioner right now. You need help," said Yani and then turned to Sir

Drake. "Sir, please help me with him," he said. But Sir Drake stood there still like a stone, his gaze fixed on Paksha.

"He is not going anywhere," said Agni, his sword was already out in his hand and the tip was pointing at Paksha. The look of agony had instantly disappeared from his face.

"What are you doing, Agni? Have you gone mad?" flared Yani angrily.

"Step back, Yani," said Agni sternly, Yani could feel the rage from his friend.

"What?" asked Yani. He was stunned, Agni had never spoken to him like that before.

"Do as he says, Prince," said Sir Drake. Yani looked at him, he felt as if he was losing his senses. He could not understand a thing. He slowly took a step back. Vrish was also confused, he looked at Yani and then at Agni.

"Take off the gauntlet of your right hand," said Agni. Paksha did not move. "Now," shouted Agni. Yani and Vrish looked on as silent spectators. Paksha slowly took off his gauntlet. Yani and Vrish looked on in awe; there was a wooden finger in place of where his little finger of the right hand was supposed to be. It was attached to a clamp around his wrist with leather straps to hold it in its place.

"I was right then," said Agni and looked Paksha in the eye.

"Are you going to start by yourself or do I have to make you?" asked Agni with malice in his voice.

"You don't scare me," said Paksha and there was a smacking sound. Paksha rolled over to his left and blood oozed out of his right ear. Agni had struck him hard with the flat of his blade.

"I will not ask you again," roared Agni. Paksha started to chuckle and spat out some blood on the ground.

"You won't get anything from me, Agni. I have lost everything for you, you," he shouted. "And I don't have anything more to lose."

"Agni never did anything to you, you maniac," shouted Vrish.

"Oh, he did. He did. I lost my father, my mother and my sister because of him," "Him," shouted Paksha. The smile still persisted on his face.

"I don't know what you are babbling about," said Agni angrily.

"Babbling, am I? I will tell you then," said Paksha with a sneer on his face.

"My father was the landlord of the southern villages of Himadri, one of the four Lords. He was very close to the King. Prince Yani was still in the womb of the queen. King Adhirath decided to choose a ward who will also be the Prince's companion when he grows up. I was the one chosen," his face had turned grim. "Then the King changed his mind after the Prince was born. He told my father that someone else was to be his ward and it was promised. My father protested but the King did not listen. My father started a rebellion as he was humiliated by the king in front of the other lords. The rebellion was put down and my father was taken prisoner. We were stripped of all our belongings and were brought down to the streets. My father took his own life in the prison and my mother passed away soon after that from her illness. Me and my little sister were left to fend for ourselves." Then Agni saw drops of tears trickle down Paksha's cheeks. "We wandered from door to door for a mouthful of rice. My sister died of hunger as I couldn't buy milk for her." He wiped away his tears. "Then you were brought to Himadri by Briksha and King Adhirath made you his ward along with Vrish. I understood that it was promised to the sewer rats like you two," he said pointing at them with disgust. "That day when you were chosen, I took an oath that I will revive the honor of my family and will avenge their death. I joined the army of Himadri and this finger was the price I paid to the King when I grew up to become his most trusted hand. Fate gave me the opportunity. I knew that they planned on burning those ships and Briksha's too," then he smiled and said, "I also knew that you loved that girl. I was there that day when you gave her your token of love and proposed marriage by the sea near the old docks. I knew that she would die and yet I let them do it. Now my oath is fulfilled. I let them take from you what you took from me ages ago Agni." Paksha started to laugh, Agni stood there stunned.

"You have nothing to threaten me with," shouted Paksha as he continued to laugh hysterically. The cackle filled Agni's ears as he stood there shocked and perplexed. Sir Drake looked at Agni and then at Paksha. Agni was staring at him blankly.

"You leave me no choice," said Sir Drake and stepped up. He took out a small vial of liquid from his pocket. A slimy creature with many legs was wriggling inside it. He caught hold of Paksha and forced open his mouth. Paksha resisted but he emptied the contents into his mouth.

"What are you doing?" shouted Yani.

"I am doing what I have to. There isn't much time," he said and took a step back. Paksha almost choked and then he tried to cough it up but soon after, he started to scream. His horrible screams made Yani press his hands over his ears. He screeched and rolled over holding his head in his hands. A moment or so later, he became still. Agni watched the horror unfold in front of his eyes.

"What did you give to him?" screamed Yani at Sir Drake.

"An anarchid," said Sir Drake calmly.

"It has entered his brain. He will soon tell us everything he knows. He may not survive but it's a price he chose to pay."

"What?" shouted Yani. Agni felt his innards twist and the taste of bile at the back of his throat.

"I am sorry Prince that you have to witness such things as this but there is little choice and lesser time. This was the only solution," said Sir Drake looking at Yani. Yani looked on, Sir Drake had changed like a snake changes his skin. He didn't look like the man he knew.

"Who are you?" asked Agni.

Sir Drake smiled. "I knew that you would be the first to ask me this."

He turned to Agni and said, "My true name is Lonan, I am a servant of the Seven."

୧

Paksha lay still as a dead man. Sir Drake continued, "I was sent to the eastern shores by the Abode to look for this man you know as the Stranger. He escaped from the prison of Aine a year back and I have been chasing him since. Then the news came that he had left the western shores and had escaped to Himadri. So I came here as Sir Drake as per the order of the Abode. I came to learn from my sources that he was being helped here by someone but never thought that it would be Paksha. In my eyes he is as much a criminal as Stranger, and I mean all his aides," said the man called Lonan as he gave one quick glance at Yani. The Prince fell short of words and couldn't believe anything that was happening around him. It all seemed like a bad dream. Then his gaze went to Paksha. Paksha slowly sat up, his eyes were wide and his mouth was open.

"Good, it has worked," said Lonan. He walked up to him and knelt down beside him.

"What is your name?" he asked.

"Paksha, son of Pari," replied Paksha in a voice which Agni couldn't recognize.

"Where were you born?" asked Lonan.

"The village of Ruli in the kingdom of Himadri," replied Paksha again.

"Do you know a man by the name of Stranger?"

"Yes," replied Paksha.

"Did you help him in starting the fire at the docks of Himadri?"

"Yes," replied Paksha.

"Did King Adhirath ask you to help him?"

"Yes," he replied again.

"What? He is lying. Why would my father help in killing those men who had helped Himadri prosper?" asked Yani angrily.

"He is incapable of lying, Prince, I assure you that," said Lonan turning to Yani and turned his gaze back to Paksha again without any further explanations.

"Why did King Adhirath ask you to help Stranger?" he asked.

"I do not know," he replied. Lonan was staring at him.

"In spite of the sceptre, what else did he seek?" he asked after some thought.

"A map," replied Paksha.

"A map of what, damn it?" asked Lonan in an irritated voice.

"The catacombs below the city," replied Paksha as he spurted out some blood.

"Was Stranger heading for the catacombs after he left this room?"

"Yes," replied Paksha again, but his voice grew faint.

"Where are the entry points?" asked Lonan quickly.

"To the south of the canal below the statue of Darshana, the door in the back of the throne in the throne room and the last through the store room of the kitchen," said Paksha.

"Which one will he use?" asked Lonan again.

"The one through the kitchen's store room," he replied and his eyes started to close.

Lonan shook him violently, "Why that one?" he asked.

"Because the other two are closed," were Paksha's last words as a thin line of blood started to trickle down from his nose. Lonan looked pleased.

"Good, that's all I need to know," smiled Lonan as he stood up. Paksha sat there still, blood oozing from his eyes and ears as well.

"Agni, you can come with me, and Vrish too, if you two want to find Stranger," said Lonan turning to Agni and Vrish. Agni looked at Vrish and then slowly nodded his head.

"Good, come then," said Lonan and started for the door.

"What will happen to him?" asked Agni staring at Paksha's expressionless face.

"I am sorry Agni, but I don't think he will make it. It is better that we leave him here," said Lonan.

"We should call a practitioner," said Yani.

"He is way beyond that now, Prince," said Lonan with a smile and walked out of the door.

Agni stood there staring at Paksha's gaunt face. He had caused him so much pain, maybe indirectly yet he never knew. He felt a surging hatred for him on the one hand and pity on the other. He knew what loss was.

"I never meant it to be like this," whispered Agni to himself as he tore his gaze away. Agni started for the door followed by Vrish. Lonan had already left. Agni gave one last glance at Yani as he stood there silent, bewildered in the middle of things he only half understood.

THE REVELATION

Lonan, followed by Agni and Vrish found the palace kitchen after some asking around. The door lay ajar as the servants went in and out carrying large dishes filled with different kinds of food towards the royal dining hall. It was the first hour of the moon and the servants were busy preparing the feast to celebrate Prince Yani's engagement to the High Senator's daughter Aadrika. Lonan walked around paying little heed to the servants who turned their heads on seeing three of the guests inside the kitchen hall.

Lonan caught hold of one of the passing maids and asked, "Where is the store room?" She was a bit surprised and then pointed towards her right without saying a word. Then her eyes fell on Agni. He didn't say another word and started towards that direction.

"You are Agni, aren't you?" asked the maid enthusiastically. Agni smiled out of courtesy and then rushed after Lonan.

"This way Agni," he called out as he stood in front of a small door. He had taken out a torch from the wall stand beside the door and disappeared behind it. A few servants turned their heads at the mention of his name and started to murmur. Agni rushed towards the door, followed by Vrish before any one of them could ask him anything. Agni saw that the store room was huge and there was a chill to it. The wall was at least five hands of thick marble to keep the room cold enough for the preservation of food. Vrish closed the door behind them.

"The entrance is somewhere in here," said Lonan. "But how did he make it till here? The kitchen is bustling with servants, someone must have seen him," said Agni.

"He is a dark sorcerer, Agni, and the best as I know it. He has many ways of concealing himself from unwanted gaze," said Lonan.

"Or probably he disguised himself like any other thief," said Vrish as he picked up a servant's clothes from the ground.

Agni looked at Lonan. "And also that," said Lonan quickly.

"We better start looking for the entrance, he is already way ahead of us," said Lonan. Agni and Vrish nodded their heads; there was a smirk on Vrish's face which Lonan ignored.

"Look for anything strange on the walls, it is supposed to be a door," he said. Agni didn't ask how he knew that but somewhere he felt like it.

"We will need more torches," said Lonan.

Agni and Vrish were about to move when their eyes fell on a shadowy figure emerging out of the darkness. Agni's first thought was it being the Stranger. He pulled Lonan by his sleeve and he turned. They took out their swords instantly. Lonan raised the torch high above their heads and shouted.

"Who is there? Show your face."

"Relax! It's me," came a known voice. Droh walked out of the darkness.

"Droh," shouted Vrish as he ran up to him and embraced him. Then he let go of him and held him by his shoulders.

"Where have you been? We thought that something has happened to you," said Vrish with a broad grin on his face.

"I am fine, Vrish," said Droh as he slowly took off his hand from his shoulders. "I found the man called Stranger and have been following him since. I didn't get the chance to send back word but I think Paksha is helping him. I am not sure but I have seen the two of them meet after the end of the tournament today," he told Agni.

"Paksha is dead," said Agni coldly.

"Oh, how?" asked Droh. Agni saw that somehow he wasn't that surprised.

"We don't have time for this, did you find the entrance?" asked Lonan angrily.

"No. I only saw him come inside dressed as a servant but when I came in, he was already gone. I started looking for the entrance from then but still..." he stopped short of completing the sentence. Agni felt confused but he knew that the time for questions was past. He decided to go with the flow for his priority was Stranger.

"Then we better start looking," said Lonan. Vrish and Droh went out to gather three more torches from the kitchen. Agni was with Lonan.

"Sir Drake, sorry Lonan," apologized Agni, Lonan smiled.

"It's all right Agni, you can call me by either of those names. Drake is my other name given to by 'the archmaster'."

"Right," said Agni, although he didn't know what an archmaster was.

"You were asking something?" asked Lonan.

Vrish and Droh had come in by then with two torches in their hand. "Could find only two," said Vrish.

"It's all right, you two take those. Agni will stay by me," said Lonan.

"All right," said Droh and both of them took one torch each and started looking.

"Yes Agni, carry on," said Lonan as both of them walked to two opposite corners of the room.

"Who is this 'Stranger'? And why would he kill those merchants?" asked Agni.

Lonan gave out a deep breath and said, "I can tell you who this man is but I do not know why he caused the fire. It completely escapes me." Lonan continued, "We do not know the birth name of Stranger. But he rose to power almost twenty years back. It was said that he tried to unite the villages of the Acropolis against Aine and the Seven. He was a master sorcerer and a wanted man. The Seven proved to be stronger than him and they put down the rebellion. He was captured and sent to prison. Then he escaped after nineteen years and came here to Himadri. We knew that he had friends in the eastern shores but never expected a king. King Adhirath will be dealt with after I capture Stranger." For some reason, Agni felt a little sad.

"What will happen to Yani?" he asked.

"I will plead to the Seven to show compassion to him as he is not a part of any of this and had no knowledge of it," said Lonan with compassion. "I have come to like the Prince too but I must tell you this Agni, even if he is spared he won't be a Prince any longer." Agni didn't say a word but somehow he felt a little guilty for Yani's sake. He had no part in all this and the way he knew Yani, it was going to destroy his life and his marriage.

"Couldn't you stop them in any way?" asked Agni.

"You mean with respect to Yani?" asked Lonan.

Agni nodded his head. "It all depends on the Seven and their decision. But I promise you that I will do all in my power to persuade them to let him retain his title and kingdom,' he said in a reassuring voice.

Vrish called out. "There is something here," he said. "We will speak of this later," said Lonan and Agni nodded his head.

Lonan rushed to Vrish followed by Agni and Droh from the other side. There was something on the wall. Lonan leaned closer to look. Agni saw that it was a symbol curved out of different pieces of stone. It had four hands and seemed to be broken from the middle. It somehow seemed familiar to Agni.

Lonan touched it, it seemed that there were four pieces and they could be rotated.

"It's a puzzle," he said and moved his hand away. He looked closer, "It's a gate lock. If we do it wrong it will lock itself and if we try to open it by force the gate will collapse. It's an ancient form of protection, the Gianna trap. Only the user with proper knowledge of the trap when it was made can enter. Damned door," he shouted and muttered a few curses out of his frustration.

"Isn't there any other way into the catacombs?" asked Vrish.

"Yes, there are many. The catacombs of Nisarga are spread below the entire city. We can find a way even through the sewers if we search but it will not take us to the right place. Many have tried before to find another way but none have returned. The whole thing was carefully planned ages ago by some of the greatest brains of our time to keep its location a secret," replied Lonan.

"What location?" asked Agni. Lonan looked at him and their eyes met. Agni did not blink. Lonan hesitated for a moment and said, "The tomb of Darshana, it is where his ashes are kept."

"Why does Stranger want to go to Darshana' tomb?" asked Vrish. Agni's eyes became wide.

"The theory of origin," said Agni. Lonan was staring at him, his brows were furrowed.

"How do you know that?" he asked.

"Forget about that. So, what *is* the theory of origin?" he asked him. Lonan seemed hesitant.

"We don't have much time. You need to tell me the truth if you want the both of us to work together," said Agni sternly.

Lonan smiled and said, "You are right, Agni. The credit of finding Stranger goes to you. So, you have the right to know it. Moreover, there is no use hiding it from you as you will learn of it soon." He took in a deep breath and said, "It is more aptly called the secrets of origin in the west. It was called a theory because only a few outside the Abode knew of the whole truth. It is known that Darshana wrote two prophecies when he went to Mount Avatar, beyond the wastelands. But that is not entirely true, actually he wrote three. The third speaks of a power so strong that it could stop the Destroyer from turning this world to ashes. A power greater than the Seven true Guardians of Gaya who watch us from the sky. But if it falls in the wrong hands, it could devastate the whole world even without the Destroyer coming to this plane of existence." Then he looked at Agni in the eye and said, "The Stranger came to know this third prophecy somehow and he came here, the birthplace of Darshana, where it was rumoured to be hidden by his three disciples ages ago after his death. I have been sent by the Abode to stop him."

Then he gave out a deep breath and smiled, "There you go, Agni! I have told you the whole truth. I know this is a lot difficult to understand or believe right now but all I want you to do is keep your faith in me. A few things may happen in there that you may not understand but it will only be your trust in me that will matter in there when we come face to face with Stranger."

Lonan extended his hand, "So can I count on you, Agni?" he asked.

Agni nodded his head and then took his hand and shook it.

"Good," said Lonan smiling. Then he turned to Vrish and Droh, "You two with us?" he asked.

"If Agni trusts you, so do I," said Vrish plainly.

"Me too," replied Droh.

"Very well then, I thank the three of you for keeping your faith in me and now we better find a way to open this bloody door," said Lonan.

Agni looked at the symbol for some more time, intently. After learning the entire truth of the theory of origin, things started becoming clear to him. "I think I know how to solve this," said Agni and put his hand on it. Then he started to rotate two pieces at once.

"Be careful," said Lonan anxiously. His breath seemed to have been caught in his throat.

Agni finished rotating the first two and then the second two. When he completed it formed the same symbol.

The wall started to vibrate as everyone held on to their breath. Then the symbol turned upside down as a whole and the wall lifted by itself and unveiled a hidden tunnel. Lonan was stunned, but quickly gathered himself.

"Bravo, excellent work, Agni," shouted Lonan out of excitement as he gave a pat on his back.

"Come, let us get inside before it closes," he said and walked in before the others. He had his torch held high in his hand. Agni saw that the spider webs were torn and there was enough dust in there to choke a hundred men. They entered one after the other with their torches held high. The door closed behind them. It was very hot in there and Agni saw that the large tunnel had other small tunnels running into it.

"We need to follow the main tunnel and the torn spider webs," said Lonan as he led them deeper inside the tunnel.

The spider webs were torn all through the large tunnel. "We are on the right track," said Lonan. Agni knew that they were, he was a good tracker himself. He looked back and saw Vrish walking alongside Droh, but none of them spoke a single word. They looked around with wary eyes. Agni looked forward and there was only darkness.

"How long is this tunnel?" asked Agni.

Lonan smiled and said, "The catacombs are based on a natural cave system. It is said that some of these caves lead to the Mountain of Kumbha in Viratbhumi." Then he looked at him and said, "I hope you can guess now."

Agni was shocked. No wonder no one had been able to find the secret location for all those years, thought Agni. "The tomb was said to be built by Darshana's three disciples and so was this maze. Their names are not known yet and it is said that one of them was his own son," he said. Then Lonan came to a sudden halt. Agni looked forward and saw that their way was barred by a door made of stone.

"What is this?" said Lonan standing in front of him. "This isn't supposed to be here," he said with a confused look on his face. Lonan looked at it closely, there was no symbol, no lock, no hole, nothing. It was simply a giant piece of rock carved into a door.

"How are we supposed to open it?" asked Agni. "There is nothing on it."

"Maybe it's a dead end," said Droh.

"No, it can't be. There must be a way through it," he said looking at it from side to side.

"Help me," he said and started to push. Agni joined in and so did the others. They kept at it for some time but the door didn't budge a single bit.

Then they gave up. "This is impossible. This tunnel is supposed to lead us straight to the Tomb," said Lonan.

"Maybe we missed a turn or something," said Vrish.

"No," pressed Lonan. "We followed the trail correctly."

"Maybe he is also lost like us," said Droh.

"He has a map, remember," said Agni.

"No, Agni," said Lonan. "No map leads directly to the tomb; they only show the entry points. Even those are hard to find. It was said that only three of them were made by the three disciples. I don't know how Paksha managed to find one of those."

"Then maybe Droh is right," said Agni.

"No he isn't, the main tunnel leads directly to the tomb; there are three of them. Paksha said that two of them were blocked so it leaves only this one. But he has something that we don't, with which he might have opened this door, but I am not sure," said Lonan.

"What?" asked the three of them in unison.

"The key. It is said that the tomb of Darshana can be reached by anyone who has one of the three maps. Only reached, not opened. For that, one requires the key. But there is no mention of a door like this anywhere in the old texts. The key is said to have been broken into two parts, one is said to bear the mark of Darshana and of the other nothing is known. It is only said that the key is made of a strange metal. The actual truth was passed down from generation after generation of the three disciples whom we do not know of," said Lonan with contempt.

Agni's eyes became wide. He immediately thought back on the pendant he had seen around Stranger's neck. It bore the mark of Darshana, his sigil and it was made of a strange metal.

"What of the other part of the key? Is it also made of the same strange metal as the first?" asked Agni. Lonan was eyeing him suspiciously.

"Not that I know of. But it is supposed to be something ancient, of great value I suppose," he replied. "But I have a theory," he continued. "The other part of the key is required to open the tomb and Stranger knew that very well. So he came to Nisarga. But then comes the part of Akakios and the tournament."

"The scepter," said Agni. "It is the second part of the key. That is why he entered the tournament in the first place."

"Excellent," said Lonan. "My thoughts precisely. He must have known about the scepter beforehand. But the question is how?"

Then he started to pace, "I am sure that Kubha knew nothing of it or else he wouldn't have given it away so easily." It all started to become clear to Agni but he still couldn't understand the relation between all this and the burning of the ships.

"This thing goes deeper everytime we reach some surface. I swear that I will uncover the whole truth, but first we need to stop Stranger. And for that, we need to go through this door," said Lonan angrily as beads of sweat dotted his forehead and started to trickle down into his eyes. Agni's eyes were burning from his sweat too.

"He will have to come out this way. We can wait for him here," said Vrish.

"No Vrish, the tomb was made in such a way that getting in is tough, not going out. There are several ways out of here," said Lonan.

"But didn't Paksha say the other two were blocked?" asked Vrish.

"From the outside, not from the inside; that is the very essence of the Gianna trap. He can choose any of the three tunnels from the inside," said Lonan.

"Then there is little choice. We need to find a way to unlock this bloody door," said Droh.

"Maybe if we ram it with something heavy, it will open," said Vrish.

"This door is almost three hands of solid rock or more, I presume. We will need a battering ram to break it," said Lonan in an irritated voice.

"Then Trinetra help us," said Vrish and sat down on the floor with his back resting on it. The three of them stood there thinking, they were in a predicament. There was complete silence. Agni was trying hard to concentrate so that he could find a way out. He couldn't let Stranger escape again. Then he heard something. It was like a faint whisper, he tried to listen more carefully. There he heard it again, it was coming from Vrish's direction. He turned to Vrish and said, "Did you say something to me right now?"

Vrish was a bit taken aback. "No Agni, I didn't say anything." Agni turned to the others and they shook their heads. Agni was staring at the door and then he started to walk towards it. There it was again, very faint but clear. Agni stood in front of it and pressed his ears on the solid rock, the others looked on.

The noise was coming from the bare rock. It was a strange hum, a melody of sorts.

"Lonan," called out Agni. "Come here quick." Lonan came and stood by him. "Press your ear against the door," said Agni. Lonan looked atAgni with a strange expression and then he did what Agni said. Vrish and Droh looked at each other. A broad grin spread across Lonan's face.

"It's the rhyming language or ancient Chhanda, whatever you may call it. I know this language a little," said Lonan.

"What does it say?" asked Vrish. Lonan pressed his ears harder against the door. "It's a riddle," he said. Then he stood up straight and spoke in the language of 'Dialect' so that the others could understand.

"A man may sow and till the land with lust,

And he may ask the one to be quick and just.

But then and there all he shall receive is .... It ends there," said Lonan.

"He may sow and till the land with lust, but the crops won't grow faster even if he asks Trinetra to be quick and just. Justice will be done only if he waits for the time when the seeds grow into plants and then bear fruit. So if he wants the result then and there then all he shall receive is..."

"Dust," said the two of them together.

"Dust," spoke Lonan aloud in ancient chhanda. The door started to open.

"Well done again, Agni," shouted Lonan, he seemed very pleased.

"You did the most of it, I only helped," said Agni with a smile.

"Sometimes you should leave your sense of modesty back at home. The riddle was easy if one knew the language. But your ears did the most important part," said Lonan with another pat on his back.

"He is right, you know," said Droh. Agni smiled at him too. Vrish gave him a thumb's up.

The door opened into a decorated hall. It was made of marble and wood. Several tapestries hung from the wall and the ceiling was glowing with the same strange white metal.

"Finally, the tomb of Darshana," exhilarated Lonan as he stepped inside first.

Agni could see a dim light flickering at the end of the hall. His goal, his answers and his revenge was within his grasp. His quest was finally at its end.

ca

The corridor was long and unusually damp. There was a persistent sound and the light still flickered at the end of the hall. Lonan led them from the front. "We must be right under the canal," he said as they slowly made their way towards the main chamber so as to be able to catch Stranger unawares.

"Put out the torches," he whispered to the others.

"There are four of us against him alone, and we also have Agni with us," said Vrish.

"But," Lonan hesitated. Agni understood that he didn't want to show his doubt about Agni's credibility as a fighter.

"No Vrish, Lonan is right. Stranger must not be taken lightly, it was by mere luck that I won the fight against him," said Agni but this time not out of his sense of modesty.

"And besides," said Droh, "prevention is better than cure." Vrish was surprised and so was Agni.

"Have you been reading books again?" japed Vrish but Droh ignored him completely. Something had changed about Droh for sure, thought Agni. But the way things were happening right now, he knew that it was not the time to pay heed to it. They put out their torches and walked behind Lonan with soft feet.

The main chamber was huge. The ceiling was shaped like a dome and ornately designed, most of which Agni couldn't see due to the lack of light. Stranger's torch was the only one afire. He himself stood in front of a sarcophagus with the scepter in his hand. The symbol made of the strange metal was glowing at one end of the scepter. Agni darted for him but was stopped midway by Lonan' outstretched hand.

"Let me go," said Agni.

"No Agni, let me. We need to plan our steps carefully. Haste will only ruin things. I will go first and then when I give the signal, you three will come out and jump on him," said Lonan.

Agni controlled his burning desire to go out and kill the man who was the reason of it all. But first, he wanted a few answers. Agni nodded his head controlling his rage.

"Let him first open the sarcophagus," said Lonan.

Agni saw Stranger walking around the sarcophagus with the key in his hand. He knelt down in front of something and put the key somewhere and turned it. There was a clicking sound and he took out the key. He took back a few steps and stood there. The effect of unlocking could be seen first in the torches on the wall. Each of them caught fire, one by one, and lit up the whole place.

"Shit," said Lonan and pushed the others behind the corner as he jumped for cover. Stranger looked from one side to the other.

"So much for our plan to take cover of darkness. These damned torches have ruined everything," he hissed angrily. Agni peeked out and saw that the thick iron slab of the sarcophagus had started to move and there began a chant in ancient chhanda. Lonan translated it for them,

"The sky shall fall and the earth shall shake,
And thus a new dawn shall break;
I give the knowledge to change man's own destiny,
With Darshana' prophecy."

The chant stopped as the lid moved completely revealing the inside of the sarcophagus. Stranger put a hand inside it and took out a scroll. Lonan quickly jumped out and rushed towards him with an unsheathed sword in his hand. It happened in a single moment: he made a mad dash to kill Stranger with one stroke. "Repel," shouted Stranger without even looking, Lonan flew off the ground and crashed on the marble floor.

"You can hide yourself but never your shadow," said Stranger in his deep voice. Agni was about to rush out but Stranger turned to Lonan and said, "Up to your old childhood tricks again, Lonan? It seems that you have not learnt your lesson yet." Agni stopped.

"What's wrong, Agni?" asked Vrish.

"Wait," he replied. He wanted to listen. Lonan had never mentioned that he knew Stranger from before.

Lonan stood up. "I don't know what you are saying," he said as he gave a sideway glance towards the door.

"You think that you can crop off your beard and cut your hair short and I won't recognize you?" said stranger with a visible smile on his face.

Lonan looked at the door to the main chamber and said, "One is never alone in the path of justice."

"That's our cue," said Droh.

"Wait, nobody goes out until I say so," said Agni sternly.

"Stop patronizing yourself, Lonan. Do you honestly think that I will believe that you know nothing of the Seven and their deeds," said Stranger angrily.

Lonan pointed his sword towards the Stranger, "You will not utter another word," he retorted.

"That's more like it," said Stranger with the smile returning on his face. "When out of words use the sword, only if you were any good with it," he finished and took out his own sword, the searing black blade.

Droh ran out from behind them. "Droh," whispered Agni angrily but it was too late. He was already out there.

"So you have brought a friend, it will be easy enough yet," said Stranger confidently. Then Agni and Vrish rushed out too.

"What?" shouted Stranger.

"This won't be easy," said Lonan with a contemptuous sneer on his face.

Stranger was staring at Agni. "You shouldn't have come," he spoke calmly.

Agni stepped up. "I will kill you, that I promise. But first, I want a few answers."

"The time for talk is over," roared Lonan and pounced on him even before he could utter another word. Lonan made a furious swing but Stranger blocked it with ease. Droh moved in from behind and made a jab but Stranger turned quickly and kicked him in the guts.

"Come on, Agni, this ends here today," shouted Vrish and charged in. Agni was right behind him. They needed to put him down before he could get anything out of him. Stranger dodged all their attacks, even the four of them were no match to him. Stranger leapt in the air and shouted 'fury'. He came down with an amazing speed and knocked over all the four of them together. He went after Lonan first. Agni quickly leapt up and followed him in his steps. Lonan tried to stand up but he knocked him over and went for the kill. Lonan rolled over and went behind Agni. Stranger stayed his blade for some reason, which Agni couldn't understand. His blade should have cut through him easily.

"You are done for," shouted Lonan and rushed out of Agni's shadow. He made a furious swing but Stranger dodged it, though not completely. He jumped back a few paces, a little blood oozing out of the scratch on his left arm. Lonan' blade had torn through the tunic and scraped his skin a little. Lonan went after him and rendered blow after blow. Stranger blocked them but Agni saw that his pace had reduced considerably. Stranger tried to push back but then it seemed that Lonan blocked them easily, the tide had turned.

"Repel," shouted Lonan and Stranger flew back a few paces and fell on the ground. Agni was stunned. He did not understand how Lonan could have known such magic. He stood there still and confused, his sword bare in his hand.

Lonan started to laugh. "Isn't it miraculous, how fast it works? Serpent's kiss. How it spreads all over the body and drags a man to his death. It is done then, and thus falls the mighty Stranger," he said and continued to laugh.

Stranger tried to get up but fell back on the ground.

"Droh, finish him," said Lonan to Droh who was standing close to Stranger's limp body.

"No, wait," shouted Agni but Droh paid him no heed. His sword was already lifted in the air for the final blow. Then there was a scream. It was not Stranger; it was Droh. Stranger had used the last ounce of his energy to make a quick turn as Droh's sword came down on him, pushing the dagger hidden in his sleeves into Droh's belly as he had leaned forwards for the blow. Droh fell down on the floor, clutching his belly as the blade got stuck inside the flesh.

"Repel," shouted Lonan in rage. Stranger flew for the second time and crashed on the sarcophagus and the heavy lid fell on him.

"No," shouted Vrish and ran up to the spot where Droh had collapsed. Agni felt deranged; he couldn't understand anything that was going on. He followed Vrish in slow steps.

"No, no, no. Not here, my friend. What will I tell Bani?" sobbed Vrish as he held on to Droh's soulless body. Droh had died instantly, the blood had clotted around the wound and his face had turned blue. It had something on it like Lonan's blade. Agni looked over Vrish's shoulders who was down on his knees. So much death, it sickened him. Lonan picked up the scroll from the ground and came and stood beside Agni. Vrish continued to lament over Droh's dead body.

"Droh was a good man," said Lonan in a solemn voice as he put a hand on Agni's shoulder. "If only all the inn-keepers are as talented as he was," he said more to himself and turned around.

"Come, Agni, take you friend and then let us get out of this cursed place. There is no use of shedding tears for the one who has already left us," said Lonan as he made his way towards the door.

"How do you know Droh was an inn-keep?" asked Agni. Lonan stopped dead in his tracks. He turned around slowly and licked his lips. Vrish had stopped his sobbing and was staring at him too.

"I, I…" Lonan fumbled for words as he looked at Agni and then at Vrish.

"I had told you Droh was a tracker, and that his name was Brahma. Yet when Vrish said his real name aloud in front of you, you weren't surprised at all and you also knew Stranger from before," said Agni and took out his sword. "What is your true purpose here, Lonan, or whatever your real name is," said Agni pointing the tip of the blade at him, Vrish stood up. Lonan dropped his gaze and smiled.

"You are truly very smart, Agni. I should have been more careful around you," he said as he looked up at him. "Well, anyway, now that it has come to this, there is no sense in hiding the facts anymore. The Dark Guardians shall be here any moment, so now I can tell you everything," said Lonan as his smile changed into a sneer.

"It is true that my name is Lonan and I was sent to the Eastern shores to search for the scroll and also Solon, the one you know as Stranger, after he escaped from the prison of Aine. But the actual truth is that he was set free because the Seven believed that he might be the only one who could find the scroll for them. I was sent to make sure that he doesn't get away with it. I was amused to know that the great Solon came to Himadri instead of going to Nisarga, which was presumed to be the location of the scroll. That created some doubt in my heart. I was starting to doubt the myths about Nisarga being the actual location of the scroll. Then there was the fire at the docks and Solon disappeared soon after. Then Vrish came looking for Droh with a vital piece of information which opened new avenues. Droh had been working for me even before the fire; he had been after Solon even before Vrish came to him. I had offered him so much gold that he couldn't have refused," said Lonan. Agni looked back at Droh with a bit of hatred in his eyes.

"I didn't want the two of you to be engaged in all this but it was Droh's decision that made everything clear to me after some time. And I will always be thankful to him for that. But let us not get out of track. We lost the trail of your 'Stranger'.

I knew that he was heading for Nisarga but I wanted to be sure. One false move would have ruined everything, but as it turns out, I made the right choice," he said with an air full of pride.

"It is true that I would not have been any match for Solon; even with Droh by my side, it would have proved difficult. I needed allies and protection after reaching the city and what more security could I have had other than being by the side of a Prince. The news was in the air that High Senator Kubha was looking for a match for her wayward daughter. The King was hesitant at first as he knew that Yani wouldn't have had a chance against the other suitors. So I played a little trick on the King. I told him to keep the whole affair a secret between him, Yani and me and on the other hand, send the Prince to Nisarga to try his luck. As I suspected, he took the bait. But I wanted you two to come with us also. The appearance of Solon in a small city like Himadri, the fire at the docks and you, Agni, not being the real son of Briksha raised too many questions. I had started to guess but what happened soon after that made everything as clear as water," said Lonan looking straight into his eyes.

"What event?" asked Agni calmly. Lonan started to pace. Agni followed him with his eyes.

"The Destroyer was already said to have been born in the western shores sometime back, a truth known to only a few, including me. He was said to have been siphoned off by a ship to the eastern shores right after his birth and from then on, his whereabouts had remained unknown. The Abode had searched for him through a long span of nineteen years but all of it proved fruitless. The Abode has been on the lookout for him ever since. Then you summoned the dark fire in the forest of Seshnag, which is known as the symbol of the Destroyer and burned Bali's brother. Droh came to me and told me everything. It started to trouble me, so I sent back word to the Abode to Lord Snake," said Lonan. Agni eyes were wide with fear. He felt the same dread rising in his heart again.

"I was ordered not to lose you at any cost and that the dark guardians were being sent to take you back to Aine. I was asked to be on the look out of the ship named Dut which I later learned had already been burnt down by the fire at the docks. I became sure then. Then Droh came and told me about the captain of Ryau and I got the opportunity to be sure that Stranger was headed for Nisarga," he said.

Then he smiled, "And you have seen what my little pets can do and I got every little detail out of him and much more easily than in the case of Paksha. He was not much of a fighter like him. Then everything started to fall in place so easily. We came to Nisarga with you by my side. Then came the tournament. It surprised me to see Solon entering the tournament under King Akakios's banner. Then you jumped in out of nowhere. I was repeatedly told to keep you safe. It caused me so much anxiety, you have no idea. You won the first fight and then I decided to make it sure that you went all the way so that you could come out of it alive as you couldn't be swayed from your decision. But then, when I thought of it, it dawned to me that your participation in the tournament would work in my favour. If I could make you win the damn thing as a whole, that is. That way I would know why Solon entered the tournament. My guess was that he wanted the scepter but I wanted to be sure. So I brought in the practitioner. It is an old saying that there is never a problem big enough which cannot be solved with gold. He gave you the herb and you proved yourself to be stronger than I expected. It all worked so well. I was proved right again when Agam brought in that performer posing as Akakios. I wanted to keep the scepter safe because I knew Solon would come looking for it. But he proved to be smarter than I presumed. I knew someone was helping him in all this but never thought it to be King Adhirath and his little pet. But then you came in and our little naïve Prince."

He had a broad grin on his face, "You solved the final piece of the riddle with a little help from our Prince. I cannot deny him the credit."

Then he chuckled and said, "If the fool would have painted something else then Solon would have gotten away with the scroll even before we could have started our search for him. It is true that Droh had followed him but even if he had come back to us with the news we couldn't have chased Solon down in time. All my meticulous planning would have been in vain and the scroll would have gone out of my reach forever."

Lonan took in a deep breath and said, "So this is my part in all this, my little tale. I hope you liked it. I told you all this because I wanted you to know the truth before you were taken away and then I couldn't have let you know of the great deeds of the great Lonan." He gave a courtly bow to Agni as he finished.

"Bastard," shouted Vrish and then his eyes fell on Droh. He tore them away with a grimaced look on his face.

Lonan scratched his chin and said, "Now as I come to think of it, I can add one final chapter to my tale."

Then he smiled and said, "Lord Snake had asked me to keep you safe so that you can be sent back to Aine without a scratch on your skin. As I think of it, I can do that by myself. I can always knock you unconscious and take out your friend and then take you back with me instead of handing my prize over to those blood suckers." Then he looked Agni in the eye and said, "You are thinking that if the great Solon couldn't beat you, then how can I. But do you know the truth? If Solon would have fought you seriously, you wouldn't have had a chance. But frankly, I don't know why he didn't? This is what I noticed at the tournament. Back then, I feared that you would come face to face with Solon sometime in the tournament and then, the herb wouldn't have been enough for you to defeat Solon by yourself. So I hired Sir Justim to take care of him and force Solon out of the tournament. But that bloke proved to be bloody useless. He was no match to Solon. The final match came and I feared that you would lose . So I went to Lord Kubha and also to the Prince. I talked then into cancelling the fight and also that you would be declared the victor. But you were more arrogant than I thought. You insisted on fighting and went ahead with it. I was ready to coax the Prince into calling it off if it turned bad but then I noticed something strange. I saw that Solon wasn't fighting you seriously. In fact, he wasn't even trying to harm you in any way. I knew I could use that to my advantage, and that is the exact reason why I brought you along." He was smiling. "Maybe there are a few secrets that I don't know of yet, but frankly, I don't want to."

Lonan took out his sword. "Agni, I know you won't come with me on your own; you are just not that type. So let us make this easier for you," he said and broke into a sudden sprint.

"Repel," he shouted pointing at Vrish who flew and crashed on the ground.

"Now, it's your turn," he shouted at Agni and rushed towards him. Agni simply moved to his left and used Lonan's speed against him as he pushed his unsheathed sword deep into his chest. Lonan couldn't stop himself and ended up forcing the blade as it went in deeper right through his heart. Agni wrenched his sword free and Lonan stepped back clutching his chest as his sword fell on the ground, his eyes wide with shock.

"How is this possible?" he said as he gulped for air.

"The final chapter of your tale is that you should never underestimate your opponent," said Agni with a cruel smile on his face. Lonan collapsed on the ground, his eyes still wide as he still couldn't believe what had happened. Agni saw him take his last breath.

"Bastard," cursed Agni as he wiped the blade of his sword. That was the first time he had cursed a dead man.

"Vrish," called out Agni and turned around. Vrish lay on the floor as Agni ran up to him.

"Are you all right?" he asked as he helped him sit.

"My head," complained Vrish and Agni smiled. His friend was all right.

Vrish stood up by himself as he rubbed the back of his head. Then his eyes fell on Lonan who lay there dead, in a pool of blood. "You killed him?" asked Vrish blankly. Agni dropped his gaze and nodded his head. "Good job, that scumbag deserved it," he said and Agni looked up. He was mildly surprised. He had thought his friend wouldn't understand.

"Finally it's over," said Vrish with a deep breath.

Then he looked at Droh. "I don't know what I will say to Bani, she will never believe the truth," he said his eyes were fixed on Droh.

"Then she doesn't have to know the entire truth," said Agni and started towards the sarcophagus.

"Where are you going, Agni?" asked Vrish but Agni didn't reply. He must be dead, Agni, no man could have survived that," said Vrish with a tired look on his face.

Agni wanted to be sure. He still had many questions which had remained unanswered.

To Agni's surprise, Vrish was wrong. The man was alive, barely. His chest heaved and his hood had fallen over his face.

Agni slowly removed the hood with the tip of his blade as he stood over him. His face was scarred completely and his right eye was white. His lips were red with his own blood. Vrish had walked up behind Agni.

"So your name is Solon," said Agni with contempt. "Why didn't you kill me when you had the chance?" he asked.

The man tried to laugh but only spurted out some blood.

"How can I kill the one whom I had sworn to protect?" he said.

"Don't play with me," said Agni angrily. Agni saw that the man who lay in front of him was not the Stranger he knew and imagined. He seemed more like a normal being, only tormented by fate.

"You look a lot like your father, you have his eyes," said Solon smiling.

"My father?" repeated Agni.

"Yes and you talk like him too," said Solon, the smile was persistent on his face. Agni knelt down and grasped him by his hood.

"You knew my father. What's his name? Tell me now," he shouted. Vrish was standing behind him.

"Easy Agni, he doesn't have much time left," said Vrish and Agni calmed down a bit. But the questions began swirling inside his head.

"Your father's name is Arkansas, King Arkansas of Athena. He was a great man, Agni, and he gave his life for you," said Solon looking into his eyes. Agni could not utter a single word to that revelation. He had never imagined he'd see this day.

"How?" was the only question he managed to ask.

"I think it is the time for you to know, for now I have no choice but to break my promise. Your safety comes first, and now, without knowledge, it is impossible," he replied.

He took in a deep breath and started, "The land of the Setting Sun has no Prince. They are taken at birth by the dark guardians because of the two prophecies of Darshana. Your father wanted to change that. The whole concept of the Abode stood on the concept of those two prophecies. So he started looking for a fallacy, a way to rule them out before you were born. Then one night your mother's bed caught fire with you in her belly, but she came out unscathed. The fire was black.

"He was deeply troubled. So he came to Nisarga, the birthplace of Darshana and also the birthplace of your mother to know more about the prophecies. Here he learned from some great guru that there is also a third prophecy which outrules the first two. He never told me his name as he did not want me to get engaged in all that. He had made me your guardian before he came here. He said that my lack of knowledge would be my edge in protecting you. Then he went to King Crixus of Leu, his old friend for help and he had agreed as he also had lost many sons to the guardians like the other kings of the west. He then went to Aine and came back to Athena a few days later. He said to me that he wanted your mother to be moved to safety immediately and you must be protected at all costs. Then he went back to the eastern shores again. But right after he was gone, the army of the Seven had come looking for him. I hid your mother with you in her belly in the old villa as he had asked of me. Your mother's water broke and I felt helpless. The same night, King Arkansas came back like a thief. The Abode had declared him a heretic by then and turned his own people against him. But the Seven never told the people the entire truth. They only said that your father was working with dark sorcerers, who were the worshippers of the destroyer. I told him that you will be born by the fourth hour of the moon and he asked me in turn to go to the docks and look for a man called Briksha. I was to pay him the gold and ask him to wait for you at Sonata till the fifth hour of the moon. You were to leave with him to the city of Himadri and to be brought up under the care of King Adhirath. All of that had been arranged, he had said to me. He also gave me the key, the use of which I came to know of later. He said that I must keep it safe at all costs and I was to go with you to Himadri. When I protested he only said that the prophecies were not the exact truth and the Seven were not what they seemed. You should be protected at all costs, and also the sons of your sons. You are the only hope. He said I will understand everything once I reach Himadri with you. He said that King Adhirath will tell me the truth, which he did when I went back nineteen years later," smiled Solon.

"Then you were born, the son he always wanted. But then something went wrong. The dark guardians came unexpectedly," said Solon with dread in his voice.

"How did he die?" asked Agni, his voice shaking and his eyes were moist.

"He took you from your mother that fateful night. The dark guardians were already at the gates. We fled through the hidden door and they chased us. I fell back to hinder them despite your father's wishes. I tried my best but I was taken prisoner. Then the gravest of news reached my ears that your father had been killed in his attempt to save you. But I also learnt that you had escaped your fate and that brought me hope. Your father gave his life to save you." Tears streamed out of Agni's eyes.

"I knew that your father was betrayed. If it wasn't for King Crixus, the word wouldn't have reached us and you wouldn't have escaped. The dark guardians knew where we were hiding, and yet they failed. They tortured me and tormented me to know of your whereabouts, but they failed at that too," he laughed and coughed up some blood.

"Then when they had given up, the word reached my ears that Dut had been spotted in some northern port. They knew of the ship and as they had seen you leave on it that cursed night. They had been searching for it for a long time, but their hands could have never reached the eastern shores, ever. Briksha made the very mistake which he had avoided for nineteen years. He might have thought that the guardians have forgotten. But he did not know that the guardians *never* forget; they always remember, and they wait.

"Briksha knew nothing about you, or the significance of your existence. He did not know the truth. The Abode then became sure that you were in the Land of the Rising Sun. And then abruptly, I escaped, or was set free. The Seven sent Lonan after me. I found that out when I came to Himadri. But as usual, the Seven didn't tell him the entire truth; they sent him only to follow me. I came at Himadri sometime before the festival and I knew that once Lonan ran into Briksha or Dut, the truth would come tumbling out. I wanted to remove every proof of your existence. Briksha was the last after me, even King Adhirath didn't know the full truth and he was bound to keep whatever he knew a secret," said Solon. Agni saw Vrish clench his fist.

"Why?" asked Agni.

"Because your father had left a letter for me with King Adhirath which was only to be opened by me. The letter had the unbroken seal of Old Gianna which is the heirloom of your house. The King was also bound by a blood oath that he was not to open it at any cost. Your father had left me the leverage to get things started. The letter said that King Adhirath did not have any true blooded heir. Yani was not his real son. He was brought to Himadri by your father when he was an infant and that too after the queen gave birth to a stillborn and passed away. A true blooded heir can be one to follow the line ascension. If there was none, a new King would be chosen by the people, that is the law of the east. King Adhirath had no sons ever, not even from the three queens he had married one after the other and you are grown enough to understand what I mean. I learnt all of this from your father's letter. Your father used that to his advantage and made the pact with him that he was to take care of you and keep you. In turn, your father would bring him a son and the secret would be kept from his own people. King Adhirath had agreed. That is why he was bound to help me in any possible way," replied Solon. Agni was stunned, the shocks came one after the other.

"Your father wrote in his letter the details of the location of the scroll. He said that once I find it, I will know what to do next but he had insisted that you should be kept safe whatever maybe the circumstances."

"What happened to my mother?" asked Agni in anticipation.

"I don't know, Agni. I went looking for her after I escaped from Aine. But it was as if she had disappeared into thin air," replied Solon. It became much difficult for him to draw breath but he gulped in some air to keep going.

"Why Malini?" asked Agni at last. "Why did you kill her?" Solon started to bleed from his nose by then and his breathing became heavier.

"I didn't mean to harm that girl, Agni, I swear it in the name of your father. But she heard everything I said to Briksha when I went abroad Dut to activate the device. I wasn't left with a choice," repented Solon. "Later I came to know everything from Paksha. I didn't mean to destroy everything, Agni. I just didn't know," there was remorse in his voice. Agni saw that Vrish's eyes were red with tears and rage alike, but he restrained himself, the man was already at the doorstep of the next world.

"I was not left with a choice but that very choice brought you here, the thing which I didn't want to happen at all costs. I have failed your father and you, too. I did my best but it seems that fate has other designs."

Agni stood up but Solon grabbed his hand gathering all his strength and said, "Take the prophecy and run, Agni. Run as far away as you can and start anew. Somewhere no one will know who you are. That is the gift your father wanted you to have, the gift of life and freedom."

Agni took his hand out of his clutches; there was a little pity in his eyes for him as hatred overwhelmed his every emotion.

"You have taken my future away to save me from my past. I know you wanted to protect me, but you took the wrong way. There is always a choice. I cannot forgive you," said Agni.

"Then do what you must, but be sure to remember that your father gave his life for you. So I ask of you to do it for him," said Solon looking at him in the eye.

"You slit her throat and then left her to burn. All I can do for you is to ease your passing, that is my gift and my curse for you," said Agni with hatred in his heart as he placed the tip of his sword on his chest right where his heart was supposed to be.

Solon only smiled. "Use this," he said and held up his own blade in front of him. "This was given to me by your father and as I see it, you will need it more than I do from now on. After all, you are your father's son." Agni took the sword from his hand and unsheathed it. It gave out heat as if something was burning inside. He placed the tip of the blade on his chest.

"Farewell, Agni," were Solon's final words to the one he had given up everything for. Agni pushed the blade into his flesh with force. Solon only groaned as his eyes became still.

"Rest in peace, my father's friend," said Agni and took the sword out gently.

Agni looked on at the man for some more time, letting all the words sink in. Solon's serene face was scarred to the core. He had gone through so much for his sake and had now even given up his life for his quest. He didn't know whether to hate him or love him, but there was pity somewhere in his heart and there was remorse, which he didn't understand. There is a thin line between right and wrong and sometimes it is blurred. That leaves the one in a predicament. The vengeance he had nurtured for this man for so long had not turned out to be as sweet as he had thought it would be. Instead, there was a void; a void so large which he thought could never be filled. He only wished that things were different. Agni went and picked up the scroll but didn't open it.

"Let's go, Vrish. It's done," he said and started to walk towards the same door without another word. Vrish quietly followed him, his soul wearier than his body and he spared one last glance at Solon, 'the wise'. The way leading them out appeared to be darker than the way by which they had come. All had changed.

EPILOGUE

The rain was lashing hard across their faces; it was the first shower of the monsoon. The sky was overcast and the moon had gone into a deep slumber hiding her face behind the veil. Agni and Vrish, along with two other men raced through the forest on their horses to get far away from Nisarga, as quickly as possible. The two others were Mahaguru Sidak and Param. Agni and Vrish had come out of the same door in the store room. It seemed what Lonan had said earlier was true, getting out was much simpler than getting in. When they had reached the kitchen, it was completely deserted and the horn was blasting relentlessly. Agni had seen an elderly servant rush out of the kitchen and when he had called out to him asking of what was wrong, in turn the only answer he received was, "Get out of the Palace, intruders on black wings inside the city. The palace is under attack."

Agni had understood them to be the Dark Guardians. They had rushed out of the kitchen like the servant and had seen some serious fighting near the palace gates from the pavement of the guests' quarters. They were about to head towards Yani's room when someone had caught Agni by his shoulders. He was surprised to see Param's smiling face, with Mahaguru Sidak beside him. Agni was dumbstruck and when he had asked Mahaguru Sidak of why he was there, the Mahaguru had refused to explain and had said that getting out of Nisarga was to be their only priority. The dark guardians had come looking for him. The Mahaguru had led them outside through the back gate of the palace towards the great canal. There was a boat waiting for them there. The boat reached the base of the wall from where the canal had passed beneath it. They had left their boats there and had swam deep down below and had snuck out of the city from underneath the wall. Agni had seen that one of the small sewer holes beneath the wall had its iron bars removed. When they had come out on the other side, three horses had been waiting for them. Agni had been certain then that his escape had been planned beforehand. But what surprised him the most was that the Mahaguru possessed such detailed knowledge of the city itself. Vrish and Agni had been on the same horse and the four of them had started their race towards a destination not known to Agni. The rain had started by then.

"Where are we going, Guruji?" asked Vrish.

"Someplace safe, where we can hide for the moment. Then we will head back to my home in Himadri. You two will be safe there," said Mahaguru Sidak as the horses slowed down a bit.

Agni was staring at the old man. He seemed different; his radiance from their first meet had turned into exhaustion.

"How did you know?" asked Agni finally, he had refrained himself from asking that question until they were a fair distance away.

"There, we have reached the hut," said Param before Mahaguru Sidak could answer.

"We will stay here for the night," he said to Vrish and Agni.

"Here?" asked Vrish. "But what about the dark guardians?"

"We will be safe here, I assure you. I have taken all the necessary precautions," said Mahaguru Sidak. Agni calculated that they were almost half a day's journey from Nisarga near the outskirts of the forest of Jambu.

Mahaguru Sidak came down from his horse followed by Param. He seemed to be much agile for a man of his age. The rain had stopped by then.

"You didn't answer my question," said Agni as he came down from his horse.

"First let us go inside," he replied calmly.

"No," said Agni flatly. It had become much difficult for him to trust anyone so easily after what had happened that night.

Mahaguru Sidak took in a deep breath. "I presume you have learned everything about your father from Solon by now?" he asked.

"Yes," replied Agni hesitantly. "Did he mention some 'guru' who was helping your father back then?" he asked again. Agni nodded his head.

"It was me, Agni. I was helping King Arkansas to uncover the prophecy," said Sidak looking straight into his eyes. Agni couldn't believe what he had heard; he was not expecting more revelations than he had already heard.

"Your father sent you to Himadri because of me. I was the one who told him the truth about King Adhirath as I knew his wife would give birth to a still born. I made the plan to keep you safe. But King Adhirath's ill fate was not my doing. I never felt a soul inside the womb of the queen. We were to go looking for the scroll after you were brought here to safety but that did not happen, and I think you know why," said Sidak.

Agni stood there staring, he felt dizzy, his head hurt. "Why didn't you tell me before?" he asked.

"Your father's wish was that you shouldn't be dragged into all this," replied Sidak.

"How can I trust you?" asked Agni.

"That is for you to decide, Agni, as I cannot force you to trust me. That scroll in your hand is the only proof of the Abode's wrong-doings. There is a fallacy in the first two prophecies, as we were taught from our childhood. The legend of the Destroyer is not what has always been portrayed by the Abode. There is a choice," replied Sidak.

"Who are you?" asked Agni.

Sidak smiled. "I am the successor of one of the three disciples. I am the seventh successor of the line of Darshana. I am the one who told your father about the scroll and I would have told you, too, but only for my oath to your father. But as you had passed the two tests and the three questions I was bound to tell you the truth against my honour. So I decided not to lie and also not to tell you the exact truth," he said. Agni still had doubts in his heart and the Mahaguru sensed that, he smiled and started to recite the very words in the tongue of 'Dialect',

"The sky shall fall and the earth shall shake,
    And thus a new dawn shall break.
  I give the knowledge to change man's own destiny,
    With Darshana' prophecy."

"I gave the map to Paksha, Agni, when he came to the library looking for it," finished the Mahaguru. Agni was staring at him blankly.

"Now, if you trust me, then let me open the scroll. Let me see that our efforts have not been in vain," said Mahaguru

Sidak and extended his open hand towards Agni. Agni looked at him and slowly handed him the scroll. He took a deep breath and twisted the mouth of the encasement. Then he took out the scroll with gentle hands and unrolled it. As he read it, his brows became furrowed as against the smile that Agni had expected.

"What's wrong?" asked Agni.

"I do not understand. This is not supposed to be it. It's a poem written by Darshana in his last days in Chhanda,"

Then he translated it for the other three.

"As I turned the most shadowy corner,
    I came by the river, the river of Musket Horner.
    A beautiful sight of flowing cascades of water,
    But the stillness of my road ahead gave me a jitter.
    Lonely as I was still hadn't yet paved a desert so green,
    The coldness of the beauty gave me goose bumps on my
skin.
    But with no road ahead I walked by the flowing river,
    Even the warmth of the Sun gave me a shiver.
    As I walked and walked I could feel my feet no more,
    My heart so heavy with the weight of all the grief it bore.
    Then suddenly, amidst the coldness of nature I was
surprised,
    A lifeless rock came to life through some magic or device.
    Then stood there in front of me a beauty so divine,
    Her expressions were like pages to be read, her gaze to
confine.
    Her beautiful locks dangled on the floor and her skin
shone like silver,
    Her body seemed to be carved by a God with a chisel
and a cleaver.

I knelt down in front of her and said aloud my name,
Her smile warmed my frozen heart, with a sparkling, golden flame.
She started to walk by my side and I could see the darkness dissolve,
In my heart I knew it was a start that I didn't deserve.
Soon our words took a tune, the tune a melody which became a song,
Our friendship turned to something else, our bond of togetherness strong.
From humans and gods, I wished for her protection,
But never realised, it was turning into an obsession.
Slowly and steadily it grew inside me like a weed,
And in the darkest corner of my heart new thoughts began to breed.
I tried to guide her every step and all her emotions,
Soon I saw her expressions turning into vague prepositions.
The more I tried, the harder it became,
And soon I found a folly in her and she was the one to blame.
The dent deepened into her perfection,
Anguish and anger grew in my heart and it all turned to vexation.
In my heart grew a new boldness that seemed to make me brave,
I leashed her to my very will and turned her into my slave.
But soon I saw her beauty fading like a moon behind a veil of cloud,
But it reduced her follies, I thought, and that made me feel proud.
Alas! Came the final blow when I saw a drop of tear trickle down her cheek,

The dazzling stream of nature beside turned into a lifeless creek.

I wanted the road to end, the one I once loved so much,
But there wasn't a finish line and an ending as such.

In my anguish and my guilt my frustration turned to full bloom,
There was nothing left in my heart and love had no room.

As I succumbed in my own shell, I cried out aloud,
'Make her perfect Maker,' and she was turned to stone again without a second doubt.

I was stunned and slowly those thoughts came back to me,
'What have I done?' I thought as I stood alone under the tree.

Greif and sadness crept up on me and tears came to my aid,
It was a dark morning as even the sky had turned red.

In my grief I dashed my head on the rock,
Darnkness engulfed my vision, as I thought of her dangling locks.

How many days and nights had passed I did not know,
The first thing I heard was the noise of the river's flow.

I woke up and found myself again at the start of the river,
I stared at the dreaded path which seemed to have lasted forever.

I did not walk that path again for the reasons I do not know,
For there were new places to go."

The Mahaguru turned to the other side of the scroll and saw a small note in the Dialect language:
"I hide the secret where my soul is at peace."

ABOUT THE FICTIONAL LAND OF GAYA

The Land of Gaya

The land of Gaya was separated into two large continents –
The Land of the Rising Sun and The Land of the Setting Sun.
There were eight seas and two oceans which surrounded the
two continents. The seas were named after the explorers of
the first era.

The Ages and Eras of Gaya

Gaya had gone through seven ages and the eighth one had
started. The eighth age was then divided by the scholars of
the third era into three eras. The first era started from the rise
of Gianna and ended five hundred years after its downfall,
the reasons of which were still not known. It was said that
the men of the west had travelled east at the end of the first
era led by a savior called Vayu who belonged to the lower
caste of the Great Empire of Gianna. The second era started
after that, when the men of the west settled down again in
form of small kingdoms and tribes and the people of the east
flourished as the first city of Chakragarhwas founded; while
the men of the west went south and settled down at the base
of the great mountains. From there, mankind spread over the
entire lands of the east and the west alike. The second era

ended with the founding of great empires in both the shores of Gaya. The third era began with the founding of the Abode of the Seven in the west and the religion of Trinetra in the east. The third era ended with the prophecy of Darshana and, thus, began the fourth era. Gaya was in the five hundred and twentieth year of the fourth era during the time of Agni.

Languages

The ancient language of Chhanda in the east, also known as the 'Rhyming language' in the west was used during the period of the first era for writing. But there was said to be a general language of which nothing was known by the great gurus or the scholars of the fourth era. The predominant languages which were used in the east were Vakya and Kal; in the west, the language of Dialect was predominant. Other regional languages like Bani, Katha and Akkhar were used in the east; language of the leaf, the murmur of the wind and Bosporas were also predominant in some parts. overall in all, twenty-seven types of languages were used in total by the people of Gaya.

Currency

In the east, Mudra represented gold coins, Gini represented silver coins, and Tama represented copper coins.
1 Mudra = 24 Ginis; 1 Gini = 24 Tamas.

In the west, Bar represented gold, Nuggets represented silver, and Marbles represented copper.
1 Bar = 30 nuggets; 1 nugget = 30 marbles.

Weights and measurements

Weights were measured by iron pellets.

One hand was the length of a standard wooden beam used in every part of Gaya for official measurements.

Sea distances were measured by flights. 1 Flight = 10000 hands.

Land distances were measured by paces. 1 Pace = 10 hands.

But it must be noted that long distances were immeasurable and were counted as per the days generally required to complete the journey.

Time

Time was measured by bell hours by the time keepers: 24 bell hours for one day, 12 for the hours of the Sun and 12 for the hours of the moon, varying with seasons. The sundial was used by the general people to note time and also the bells tolled to inform the coming of a new hour during day time while the time was announced by the time keepers at night.

LIST OF CHARACTERS

The Land of the Rising Sun
1. Agni: Son of King Arkansas and Queen Serene. Born at Athena in the five hundred and fourth year of the fifth era of the eighth age and grew up at Himadri under the care of King Adhirath. House : Old Gianna.
2. Vrish: Son of the merchant Briksha and Kali. Born at Himadri in the five hundred and fifth year of the fifth era of the eighth age, he grew up under the care of King Adhirath of Himadri. Malini's brother and Agni's best friend.
3. Malini: Daughter of Briksha and Kali, born at Himadri in the five hundred and fourth year of the fifth era of the eighth age. Vrish's sister and Agni's fiancée.
4. Prince Yama: Crown Prince of Himadri, son of King Adhirath who grew up with Agni and Vrish. House: Yashodhara.
5. King Adhirath: King of Himadri, son of King Yash and Queen Dhara. House: Yashodhara. Sigil: The great mountain and the river.
6. King Yash: Founder of the house of Yashodhara and the one king who was said to have brought everlasting peace and prosperity to Himadri. Father of King Adhirath.

House: Yashodhara. Sigil: The great mountain and the river.

7. Sir Lonan: The famed knight of Erythrea and said to be the right arm of King Hermes (Sigil: Preying Vulture), was sent to the eastern lands as an ambassador of peace to Himadri.

8. Paksha: Son of the landlord of the southern villages of Himadri, Zaminder Pari. The second Captain of the Royal Guards of Himadri and was said to be King Adhirath's most trusted servant.

9. Guru Bhas: Royal tutor of Himadri.

10. Mahaguru Sidak: One of the three great gurus of the east, respected guest of King Adhirath who lived with three disciples Param, Pushya and Dhir.

11. Kirti: Vrish's friend and 'the master of the port' of Himadri.

12. Droh: The most infamous inn keeper of Himadri, known to be the perfect spy for the rich as well as the poor alike. Vrish's old friend, Bani's brother.

13. Bali: Eldest son of the old witch, Krumi. Infamous for being the hired muscle around the docks.

14. Agam: The head captain of the Royal guards of Himadri, the famed warrior who had served the royal family for forty years. Master of Arms of Himadri.

15. Lord Kubha: The High Senator of Nisarga, the direct descendant of the house of Cabhan, the mighty. House: House of Cabhan. Sigil: The scepter.

16. Aadrika: The daughter of the high Senator, Lord Kubha.

17. Cabhan: The General of Hala who conquered Nisarga and then his son Cabasa liberated it from Hala's rule.

18. Guru Satadru: One of the five sages of Jambu, a learned scholar.

19. Dobra: The head librarian of the Library of Darshana at Nisarga.
20. King Akakios: The king of Euphrasia. House: Mountain Hermit. Sigil: Iron Knight.
21. Lord Augus: Lord and ruler of Helios, the second city of Athena.
22. Sir Justim: Famed young knight of Athena, most trusted hand of Lord Augus.
23. Prince Sudrak: Rajkumar of Durg, brother of Princess Abharana. Son of King Bibhuti.
24. Aadi: Son of High Senator of Hala.
25. Lord Zama Of Khara: Ruler of the desert tribes of Khara.

The Land of the Setting Sun

1. Darshana: The great sage of the east born, the noble overseer of the villages of Sandhya, Nisarga and Kutir, Vasudev. His quest of ultimate knowledge led him to brave the wastelands of the Land of the Setting Sun to Mount Avatar, known as the birthplace of humanity, where he wrote the two prophecies prophesying the advent and life of the destroyer of man. House: Devgan. Sigil: Soaring eagle.
2. King Ixus: The first King of Gaya of the eighth age to unite man under one banner and claim the title of The Emperor.
3. King Arkansas: Son of Lord Xavier, 'the master of coins' of Athena. King Arkansas was chosen by the Council of the Seven for his bravery and valour in the battle of Bosporas. Agni's father.
   House: Old Gianna. Sigil: The city on the mountain.
4. Queen Serene: Born at Nisarga, wife of King Arkansas and Agni's mother.

5. Priest Solon: Former servant of the Council of the Seven. Went to Athena with King Arkansas at the age of twenty and gave up his title of 'the servant of the seven' to become the royal priest of Athena.
6. King Crixus: The fourteenth king of Leu, father of Lysandra. Wife: Alicia. House: Sentinels. Sigil: Lone Warrior.
7. Lysandra: Daughter of King Crixus and Queen Alicia. Charged with the duty of being the protector of citizens, dubbed as the warrior maiden with the golden heart. House: Sentinels. Sigil: Lone warrior.
8. Damian: Younger son of the deceased Lord Dacian, the elder brother of King Crixus. Damian was chosen as the King's ward at a very tender age of three years and had a brother called Demetrius. House: Sentinels. Sigil: Lone Warrior.
9. Demetrius: Son of the deceased Lord Dacian and elder brother of Damian. Chosen to take his father's seat at a tender age of sixteen by the Senate for wit and intelligence was the next favorite of the Senate in the line of ascension. House: High Sentinels (Founder: Lord Demetrius himself). Sigil: the fanged serpent.
10. General Torman: The general of Leu and the trusted friend of King Crixus, he was also Lysandra's teacher in the practice field.
11. Lord Agapito: The oldest member of the council of the members of the Senate of Leu and a dear friend of King Crixus.
12. Melissa: The only survivor of the massacre at the village of Old Gate, found by Princess Lysandra.
13. Old Andre and his son: The gatekeepers of the Royal palace of Leu, Old Andre had served the royal family for more than forty years. He had a son who was also appointed in the same service to help his father.

14. Agnes, Kosmas and Old Theodore: The three captains under General Torman, where Agnes was the youngest and Old Theodore was the oldest.

15. Irene: Damian's childhood love whom he wanted to marry but Demetrius had forced her father to give her hand in his. Damian had stepped aside for his elder brother but soon the marriage had culminated with an undefined, accidental dealth of his lady love.

16. Lord Light: The high lord of the Council of the Seven and the ruler of Aine.

17. Lord Dark: The second in power and brother of Lord Light and the ruler of Basporas.

18. Aqua: The fourth in power in the Council of the Seven and the most trusted servant of the Lord Light.

19. The Beast: The third of the seven, bearing the symbol of the Chimera.

20. Snake: The lowest of the Seven after the Raven.

21. The Raven: The sixth of the seven.

22. Rock: The giant of the west, the fifth of the Seven.

Srishti's all time bestsellers ₹ 100 each

- A Dilli-Mumbai Love Story
- A Feeling Beyond Words
- A half baked love story
- A Life that you knew..
- A Little Bit of Love...
- A Little Love Incident
- And then it rained....
- Anyone Else but you
- A Roller Coaster Ride!
- As Long as I Love you...
- A thing beyond forever
- A Walk Down the Lane...
- Because you Loved me..
- Beep you! you BeepHole
- Belong
- Boundless Saga of Love
- By the River Pampa I...
- Careful what u Wish for
- Coming up on the show..
- Can't Cook a Love Story
- Corporate Atyaachaar
- Crazy Bloody Thing LOV
- Dancing with Maharaja
- Everything you Desire

- Few things left unsaid
- Forever in these pages
- From Cubicles 2 Cabins
- Heartbreaks & Dreams!
- Here Sat A Key Maker
- I am Broke....! Love me
- I am Still Committed..
- If God Had A Desk Job..
- If God went to B-School
- If I Pretend I am Sorry!
- It Happened that Night
- In Course of True Love
- I too had a love story..
- It's all About Love...
- It Should Be u!! My Love
- It wasn't Love at First
- I will Love Once Again!
- Jab se you have loved me
- Journey of two Hearts
- Just Like in the Movies
- Life is What you Make it
- Love Happens Like that
- Love, Life & A Beer Can!
- Love, Life and Dream on

- Love, Life and Lust...
- Love Life & all the Dots
- Love, me and Bullshit!
- Love Power Politics!!
- Love a Rather Bad Idea
- Love & Urban Melodrama
- LUV is a Dirty Business
- My Love Never Faked...
- Nothing for you my Dear
- Nothing Lasts Forever
- Of Tattoos and Taboos!
- Oops! 'I' fell in Love!
- Ouch! that 'Hearts'..
- Patyala Down De Throat
- Plz.. Kiss me or Kill me
- Reality Bytes 'Bites'
- She is Single I'm Taken
- Simple Things Make LUV
- Something in your Eyes
- Sumthing of a Mocktale
- 34 Bubblegums and Candies

- That Kiss in the Rain..
- The Dev-D Syndrome...
- The Equation of my Love
- The Funda of Mix-ology
- The Idiot-Dudes.....
- The India I Dream of
- The Journey of Rock...
- The Journey to Nowhere
- The Lost Scraps of Love
- The Off-Site Tamasha
- The Other way Round
- The Quest for Nothing!
- The Thing Between U & Me
- Those Small Lil Things
- Three Times Loser....
- To Whom it May Concern:
- When Life Tricked me..
- What... if not I.I.T.?
- Will you Marry Me Cupid
- Your Place or Mine?

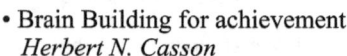

- Brain Building for achievement
  Herbert N. Casson

- Cheiro's : Language of the Hand

- Winning Personality:
  The Magic key to success
  F. Oss